D1440829

Of
Lessons
Lost

By Fred Snyder

Copyright © 2016, 2022 by Alfred Arthur Snyder

Registration number. TXu-2-033-192

All Rights Reserved

ISBN 979-8-21-803952-3

No part of this book may be used or reproduced in any form or by electronic or mechanical means, including information storage and retrieval systems, without permission in writing from the author.

This book is a work of fiction. Names, characters, places and events in this book are either the product of the author's imagination or used fictitiously, and any resemblance to actual persons living or dead, business establishments, events or locales is entirely coincidental.

Dedication

For Fay, Jonathan, Yael, Louis, Benjamin, Ari, Adar, Baby

"Who created the Liberal movement in Austria? . . . the Jews. By whom have the Jews been betrayed and deserted? By the Liberals. Who created the National-German movement in Austria? the Jews. By whom were the Jews left in the lurch? . . . what—left in the lurch! . . . Spat upon like dogs! . . . By the National-Germans, and precisely the same thing will happen in the case of Socialism and Communism. As soon as you've drawn the chestnuts out of the fire, they'll start driving you away from the table. It always has been so and always will be so."

—Excerpt from The Road to the Open by Arthur Schnitzler, Austrian Jewish playwright, author, physician 1862–1931

Contents

Part Three: *A Most Unkindest Cut*

Part One

Leaving Europe

Chapter 1

Sarny, Poland, October 12, 1942

Yaakov looked up to an empty, bleached sky and cursed his failings, his reckless optimism. He could have run. Why hadn't he? His parents, sisters, his brother—didn't they need him?

He looked to his right. The German soldier, expressionless, motioned with his rifle toward the open back of the truck, thereby communicating to Yaakov Bikel his intended command. Yaakov guessed this soldier was about twenty-five, yet he had the bearing of a seasoned warrior who had performed such duty many times. Two more soldiers twenty meters away were approaching, pointing their rifles at Yaakov, and restraining growling shepherds on taut leashes. The truck was parked by the edge of the familiar packed-dirt road that was used to transport trees to the lumber factory just north of Sarny. The air was heavy with dust and scented with lumber from harvested trees.

In Yaakov's dreams, over and over, the Germans had come for him. Now, on a chilly, joyless day, it was real. He felt himself oddly accepting, as if the dreams had been a rehearsal. He had been here before.

Yaakov obeyed and approached the truck. His brother, Lazer, was already in the open back. Yaakov reached to take his brother's extended hand and climbed up. He looked into his brother's blue eyes and could see fear.

Yaakov knew the other ten skinny men standing there, shaking, shivering, frightened beyond their limit. A few of them already had the absent look of dead men. One of the thin faces, a religious, bearded neighbor, pointed his index finger at Yaakov. "You convinced us we could fight back, damn you! Now they're going to make an example of us."

Yaakov turned away. He did feel responsible for this man and the others, and his failure to orchestrate any uprising shamed him.

"How could they have possibly uncovered us?" he whispered to his brother.

Lazer shrugged. "Don't know."

Fischer, their red-haired, red-bearded cousin, overheard the question. "It's our Council," he shouted angrily. "That new boss gave our names to the Germans."

Yaakov couldn't believe it. Fischer had to be wrong.

"You know this? He would do that?" asked Lazer.

"Of course," Fischer retorted. "Easier to be a Nazi collaborator than fight them. Chomelstien sold us out. No doubt."

Maybe it's true, Yaakov thought. Only Chomelstien, the Council head, knew of his plan to resist. And only Chomelstien knew who had joined his group. Yaakov's humiliation and ever-present hunger were now replaced by revulsion. He had trusted the appointed leader of Sarny's Jewish Council. He had gone to him for help and had asked Chomelstien for money to buy more guns. He had never imagined Chomelstien would undermine him. Did Chomelstien think he was winning favors? Was he so gullible to think he'd save himself?

The truck started with a jerk and a few of the men fell backward. Yaakov gripped the splintered side rails. The tires kicked up dirt that blurred his view of the Germans in the other truck following behind. Yaakov spotted a flash of yellow—a small plant between the road and the unkempt wilderness. This cheery blossom intruded on his despair and failure. In a moment, as quickly as it appeared, the color dissolved into the blandness of the tired, beaten trail.

Ahead, the road was empty of traffic. No chance they'd be going to work in the factory. The Nazis had other plans for them.

The wind intensified as the truck picked up speed, and Yaakov was chilled. He rubbed his shoulders to get warm, pulled his brother to his side, and whispered, "See the truck with the soldiers behind us? They will take us to the forest or the open fields by the forest. They'll make us dig our own graves. Then shoot us."

Lazer listened, as still as a statue. On the other side of Yaakov, Fischer leaned in to hear.

"We know this road well," Yaakov continued. "Ahead there will be a turn, yes? Just as we make the turn, there's a drop to the right—yes? If we jump at the right moment, we can roll into the hill. Maybe they won't see us. We can hide in the drop until the truck behind passes."

Lazer looked away and was quiet.

"Don't think about it. We've nothing to lose," Yaakov whispered.

His brother didn't answer, and Yaakov felt a familiar resentment. *Damn it, Lazer, you never get the obvious. A tiny chance is better than no chance.*

"Do what you want," Lazer finally said, his voice flat. "I'll take my chances."

"I've already lost the rest of our family." Yaakov's voice was low and frustrated. "I can't lose you, too." For a wild moment, he thought about pushing his brother off the truck, but he couldn't do that; it had to be Lazer's choice.

They approached the turn and Yaakov positioned himself to jump. "Lazer, if you're interested, the curve in the road will give us about five seconds when the Germans will lose sight of us."

Yaakov listened to the engine, the wind, and the chugging over the packed road of dirt, tree bark, and horse feces. His friends stood beside him, attempting to hold back tears.

The turn in the road came and Yaakov jumped and rolled into the side of the drop. He hugged the ground and held his breath.

Lazer jumped. And Fischer jumped.

Yaakov couldn't see the road above them, but he knew they'd been spotted. Shouting and screeching brakes came from the second truck.

"Too damn long. The bastards know," Yaakov whispered. He called out to his brother, "Run to the trees!" while launching himself away from the slope. He heard Lazer following off to his left and guessed Fischer was also running.

Gunfire! He ran as fast as he could for as long as he could. His lungs hurt. His legs hurt. He ran through the mist generated by his own hard breathing. More gunshots. The shots pushed him to run even faster.

He tripped, and his nose hit the hard ground, suddenly numb. His eyes watered. *Yaakov, you idiot, you've killed yourself.* But at the same instant, bullets whistled overhead and punched into the packed soil just a few meters beyond. Maybe the fall wasn't so unlucky.

He jumped to his feet and began to run in a zigzag pattern. Now the forest was in sight. The forest would bring safety. The Germans couldn't shoot them if they were in the forest. *God, help me make it to the forest.*

The trees were drawing closer, the gunshots less frequent. Yaakov dared hope he'd make it. Just a little bit more.

Before the trees were the trenches that Yaakov had helped build in early 1939 in anticipation of the Russian invasion. Yaakov jumped into a trench, ran through it, and climbed out the rear without looking back.

He sped into the forest and stopped behind a thick oak, a charitable, beautiful, forgiving, protective, tall creation. He fell to his knees and elbows on the rocky ground. He couldn't catch his breath. He reached to touch the tree, which was colored green with moss at the base of one side, and rubbed his hand appreciatively against the thick, coarse, grooved bark. He began to breathe normally again.

Lazer found him, stopped beside him, and bent forward from his waist. He was also trying to catch his breath.

"Fischer—see him?"

Lazer shook his head. "He'll be all right. He was in our Polish army. If anyone can make it, Fischer can." Lazer managed a confident smile.

"Hope he makes—"

"What's that sound, Yaakov?" Lazer straightened.

Yaakov stayed on the ground, listening.

"Dogs—the *schaferhunds!*" Lazer shouted.

"The bastards released those damn shepherds?" Yaakov stood up. He was too tired to run again. And the barking was getting louder every second.

Chapter 2

The Forest of the Sarny Region, Eastern Poland
October 12, 1942

Yaakov resumed running. Lazer followed. After twenty minutes, Yaakov stopped, exhausted. He was prepared to surrender.

The dogs were closer, and their barks had reached a crescendo that could only mean their attack was imminent. Fear consumed him, a reflexive and all-consuming panic that rekindled his will to escape. Unable to sprint or jump anymore, Yaakov managed to limp over dead branches and fallen logs, sidestepping tall brush and loose rock. He didn't know where he was going, just that he was moving away from the dogs as fast as he could. Lazer was keeping up on his right.

But the gap between the brothers and the dogs was quickly contracting.

They came to a rustic stream. Yaakov had to stop, though he expected the barking beasts were right behind him, ready to spring any moment and clamp their fangs onto him. He walked into the stream.

"Is it cold?" Lazer asked.

"What do you think? It's colder than ice," answered Yaakov.

Lazer hesitated.

"Come on!" Yaakov yelled. "You can't wait here. They'll make you into brisket."

Lazer ran in. "Kosher brisket," he shouted with a trace of his old humor.

Yaakov was in up to his waist when the current knocked him down. He felt himself being pulled downstream on his back, but he managed to use his feet to push off boulders and dead tree limbs. Finally, he came to a shallow section that allowed him to stand. He had swallowed a good deal of water.

Yaakov looked back and saw Lazer still floating in the deep water with his arms flailing against the current. He ran back and caught Lazer's arm. He pulled his brother into the shallow water and released him. Shivering and shaking, Yaakov crossed to the far bank, climbed out, and maneuvered through the woods. He heard Lazer following a few steps behind. He no longer heard dogs. He was soaked, freezing, hungry, exhausted—but he was alive.

He slumped down against a tree. Lazer caught up to him and stood by the tree; he began to chant a prayer of thanksgiving. Yaakov wasn't tempted to pray. He believed that God had once again confirmed his abandonment of the Jews. He didn't want to pray to an indifferent God.

When he finished, Lazer turned back to his brother with a wry smile. He was shivering. "Now we'll just die from the elements, maybe freeze."

Yaakov didn't laugh or smile. "Let's keep moving."

———

Another hour into the woods, and they noticed birds hovering over a clearing two hundred meters ahead. A noxious smell hit them. "Must be a dead animal," guessed Lazer.

"Smells like a garbage dump, like the Sarny ghetto."

"No. It's a different stink."

After a few more steps, the brothers came across six bodies lying in a row in a small field that had been cleared of trees. It appeared they had been shot and left to rot. "They're Christians," Yaakov said, pointing to two small crosses on the ground beside the bodies. "See? I'll bet this one, maybe that one, too, were holding those crucifixes before they were shot."

"The Germans will be killing all the Poles after they're done with us," Lazer predicted.

"They won't wait that long," Yaakov said.

"They don't look like resistors."

"You think they look too soft? Maybe they are resistors. Maybe they helped Jews. Maybe they were in the Polish army but dressed as civilians. Maybe they just pissed off the wrong German or something."

Lazer nodded. "Maybe they were just in the wrong place at the wrong time . . . Hey, do any of them resemble that guy who sold you the revolver, with the three bullets?"

Yaakov shook his head. "Wish I had that revolver now."

"What happened to it?"

"I hid it pretty good."

"I'll say a prayer for them," Lazer announced.

"What, Lazer? You know the Christian prayer for the dead?"

"I know how to pray to God, Yaakov." Lazer lowered his head and softly recited a prayer for departed souls.

As soon as Lazer finished, Yaakov started walking again, then changed his mind and headed back to the corpses.

"What're you doing?" Lazer shouted.

Yaakov didn't answer. He searched through the pockets of the dead and examined their clothes, which were dry and relatively free of maggots and other insects. He soon returned to Lazer with two pairs of pants, shirts, shoes, socks, and coats.

"Here, these will warm you up." Yaakov tossed half the clothes to his brother, then changed his own clothes.

"What's that extra coat for?"

"It's your towel," Yaakov said, rubbing his head and clothing with the third coat. "Here, try it. Pretty dry. Almost. Better than nothing."

Lazer took the coat to dry himself as well.

After they were dressed in the dead men's clothes, Yaakov shared his finds. He opened his right hand to reveal bread and a piece of potato. In his left hand was a gold coin.

Lazer's eyes opened wide. "You're so damn lucky."

"Don't ask where I found the coin."

———

That day and the next, Yaakov looked for berries and forced himself to swallow a few insects without chewing or tasting them. Lazer declined the insects. Yaakov caught a wounded bird, which he ate raw, though it took a while to chew the little bones and gulp them down.

They came to an old, deserted farm with the remnants of a barn. Lazer went inside while Yaakov searched the surroundings. To the side of the structure, Lazer found a piece of potato buried in the shallow soil. He couldn't find anything else. He entered the barn. "What do you think?"

"It'll keep us out of the wind."

Later that night, Yaakov heard the howl of a wolf. He imagined being surrounded by a hungry wolf pack and fighting them off with a stick. But he didn't have a stick. No damn weapons at all. He had to get a weapon. *Think, Yaakov, think. You won't survive in the woods without one.*

Yaakov was awakened by a voice. It was Lazer. Was Lazer talking to him? No, he wasn't talking. He was crying. *Should I try to comfort him? No, there's nothing I can do. Let him cry.* But even if he cried all night, it wouldn't help. The memories would always be there. They would never escape them, especially at night.

Yaakov wanted to live for the future. He had to try. But was he fooling himself? Would they last even one more day? Would they make it to the Land? He pictured himself and his brother working on their own farm. It was a comforting image, but he knew it could never happen.

———

Early the next morning, Yaakov attempted to catch a mouse with a broken, rusted pitchfork, but it got away.

"They're going to get us sooner or later," Lazer said.

"Why think the worst?" Yaakov responded, though he'd had the same thought just moments before.

"We have good reason to think the worst. The worst always happens, especially to. Jews."

"We beat them, yes?" Yaakov managed a weak smile. "We escaped certain death. We showed them. That felt pretty good. The rest of our lives, however long, is a gift." *Am I trying to convince Lazer or myself?*

"We were just lucky," Lazer said, his voice flat. "That's us all right, the lucky Bikels."

"We have to *make* our luck."

Lazer looked at him, his expression earnest. "What do you think, Yaakov? Will we ever make it to the Land of Israel?"

Yaakov didn't answer. The odds were against them. He didn't even want to know what a miniscule chance they had of actually surviving this war. Still, he wasn't about to give up on his dream. He remembered committing to the Zionists back in 1932 after attending a meeting in Kiev. Yes, he and his brother would survive and reach the Land. It was all he now thought about.

Yaakov knew that Lazer had other passions. He remembered how well Lazer had played his violin. Music had always made his brother happy. "I miss your violin playing, Lazer."

"I miss my violin, too."

"Lazer, play something for me? Yes?"

"With my imaginary violin or my imaginary weapon?"

Yaakov laughed. And Lazer began to hum.

"That's pretty good, Lazer. Beautiful."

"Chopin."

"Ahhh."

"How about this?"

Lazer hummed another classical melody while both of his arms accompanied, as if conducting an orchestra.

"Who's this one?"

"Mendelssohn."

"Oh, I don't need to listen to ex-Jews. Go back to the Chopin."

"Okay. Here's another Chopin piece set to full orchestra."

When Lazer stopped, Yaakov said, "Even your humming sounds good. What talent you have. I never had the patience to learn to play."

"You've other talents, I think. Though I don't know what."

Yaakov laughed and it felt good. Then they both laughed.

"I wish I could still play the violin," Lazer said. "I wish I could teach children again to play and to enjoy music. It was such a wonderful way to make a living."

"I'm sure that day will come again."

"Yaakov, I don't think we'll make it to the Land."

"Maybe not," Yaakov admitted. "But it's good we have that dream. Something to push for, something to keep us going."

"Is that all it is? A dream?"

"Not anymore, at least for those who are there."

"I'm scared."

"Me too," Yaakov said, his voice soft.

"You're never afraid. You're a conniver—a conniver and an ass."

Yaakov grinned. "Probably. The truth is, I've had nightmares since the Germans invaded from the West. And the Russians invaded from the East. What a year—my worst."

"I doubt you've had nightmares."

"Lazer, listen to me. You're not the only one who's scared. I know about fear and what it does, how it can lock you up so you can barely move."

Lazer looked skeptical. "I've never seen you like that. You don't show it. Hell, you organized a resistance group."

"I do feel it. I just . . . push through it." Yaakov shrugged awkwardly. "Maybe it pushes me."

After a while, Lazer resumed his humming.

———

The next morning, Yaakov saw smoke rising above the trees. He and Lazer walked toward a chimney, figuring that smoke meant a fireplace and a home and food. Yaakov hoped someone would be home and walked right up to the old wood door and knocked.

"They could be anti-Semites," Lazer warned.

Yaakov shrugged.

A short, old woman wearing a wrinkled scarf and a black sweater with holes opened the door and regarded them suspiciously.

"Good day," Yaakov greeted her. He removed his cap. "I'm sorry to bother you, but we are very hungry. Can you spare some bread?"

"I barely have enough for myself and my husband, who will be home soon. He's coming in a few minutes." She started to close the door.

Lazer put his hand against it, holding it open. "I can see from your face you have enough to eat. To look so healthy, you must have a wheat grinder. You know, the Germans might find out."

Yaakov was surprised by his brother's boldness. And even more surprised when the woman stopped trying to push the door shut. She stood there for a long moment, staring at Lazer, before retreating into the house. A few minutes later, she returned with half a loaf of dark bread. "That's all I can do," she said.

"Thank you," Lazer said quickly, smiling wide. "We'll keep your secret."

Yaakov and Lazer went back to find a comfortable place in the woods to enjoy their feast. The bread was soft and warm and tasted better than any food they'd ever eaten. It was quickly gone.

"Lazer, how did you know she had a wheat grinder?"

"I didn't know," Lazer said.

———

That night, Yaakov decided he'd make himself more comfortable in the barn by using leaves and branches as cushioning. The effort made his bed marginally better, but he still couldn't sleep. Lazer was lying beside him snoring away. Yaakov stared up through the branches to the scattered stars across a clear, black sky and tried to focus on something besides the pain his poor family had endured. But as hard as he tried to put recent events out of his mind, they flooded through him with the fury of the North winds.

So much loss. He could see his sisters as if they were still alive and standing a few feet away. His eyes were wet now. He missed them. All three so pretty. Beautiful and nice. They would have made wonderful wives and mothers. Now he pictured his mother and father. He missed them. He imagined them all with him now, standing by the big pine.

Tears rolled down the rough stubble on his cheeks. How could he go on? What was the point of struggling? He was as good as dead. He was naive, wasn't he? Now many tears were rolling down. He was sure it was just a matter of time before he'd join his dead family. Might as well accept it. What made him think he had a chance? *Lazer is probably right—but we have to try, don't we?*

He rubbed away the new tears. He imagined himself with a gun, killing Germans and winning. It felt good, but it would never happen. He was so tired. Couldn't sleep, but he closed his eyes anyway.

The next thing he knew, he was awake, and the sun was bright and high. Lazer was standing over him with an impatient frown. It was morning.

"Yaakov, you getting up?"

"Yes . . . yes."

Lazer reached for his hand and helped pull him up.

"It's all clear to me now," Lazer announced.

"What are you talking about?"

"What happened to the Jewish Council—I never stopped thinking about it. Yaakov, you remember why the chair of the Council, Rosenberg, killed himself?"

"He really had no options, yes? He wasn't a man to follow the Germans' orders."

"Right. He had no way out. I respect him more than someone who would go along with the Nazis. And I believe the rest of the Council wouldn't go along either. What was Chomelstien's first name? I can't remember."

"I remember. You're talking about Wilus Chomelstien."

"That's it," said Lazer. "Wilus. Of course. It could only be Wilus who cooperated with the Germans and told them what we were planning."

13

"Oh, there's no doubt," Yaakov said slowly. "Giving us up, our friends, our hopeless plot, that wasn't a big deal for him. That's why the Germans appointed him. They knew how he'd see it—give us up and get a little favor."

"He's the worst of the worst. You remember when he asked parents to round up their children and hand them over to the Nazis?"

Yaakov shook his head. "I cried that day. I was too hungry to move, but I did cry that day."

"We don't have children. What about those that did? How would any of them react to a Jew that says that . . . does that?"

"I can't even conceive of it. But it did happen. No one will ever believe it."

"That was worse than giving us up," whispered Lazer. "But he did give our plot up, didn't he?"

"The Germans didn't know about our group, our plans. No one did. Chomelstien loves the power he got. He cares about his ego. He's power hungry. If I get out of this alive, I'll—."

"You'll what, Yaakov?"

"Kill the bastard," he vowed. "With my bare hands if I have to. I don't care."

Lazer responded calmly. "Okay, no problem, I'll help you kill him. Why not?" Both brothers started to laugh. "You and your crazy schemes," Lazer joked.

"Yeah, we'll be lucky if we last a week here," Yaakov admitted. "You're a few inches shorter than me, so you don't need as much food. You might last a few extra days."

"I might be shorter, but I'm better looking."

"Says who?"

"Everyone." Lazer laughed.

"We look alike. Except your eyes are blue, like our mother's eyes."

"You're the ugly, tall brother. I'm the cute brother."

They both laughed.

"Right now, I'm so hungry," said Lazer, "I don't have the energy to kill a fly."

They began walking and went until they came to a stream, where they drank water that tasted metallic and tried to catch fish. "We're terrible at this fishing," Lazer concluded. Neither brother caught a single one.

"Okay," Yaakov agreed. "But let's camp here. We'll try to catch fish again tomorrow."

"We will either starve or freeze out here. It's only October. We won't last one day in the winter."

"Do we have a choice, brother?"

Lazer cleared his throat and spit. "A bullet might be better than freezing and starving."

"Don't give up yet."

"Be realistic, Yaakov, for a change."

"I know some folks who might take us in."

"Who would risk their lives for us? You're a dreamer."

———

At first light, Yaakov was kicked awake. "Hey," he protested, "let me sleep, Lazer."

Yaakov opened his eyes to find an old rifle pointed right between his eyes. And there were more rifles to the left and right.

What now? He swallowed hard. They had been caught.

Chapter 3

The Polish-Russian Frontier, October 16, 1942

"Who are you?" demanded a shrill voice in Polish. The rising sun blinded Yaakov, and he felt the rifle's cold, hard barrel pressing against his forehead. The man who held the rifle was speaking with a Warsaw accent. They weren't Germans.

"Jews" was all Yaakov said, slowly pulling his head away from the rifle. He was afraid.

He listened to them debate. "What should we do with these Jews? These Jews are dirty. They're disgusting. They can't be trusted . . . The Germans are after them, so we need to be rid of them. . . .. We have to move out now."

"There is no one after us," Yaakov said quickly. "We fought the Germans," he lied. "We were known as fighters. That's why we're in the forest, and we want to fight again."

The Poles continued their debate.

Yaakov interrupted, "If you fight the Germans, let us fight with you."

The group's leader, older than most of them, perhaps forty, was a tall, rugged man with dirty blond hair. He was wearing a wool cap and had a bushy mustache. He stepped forward, and as he did, the others stepped back and lowered their rifles.

"Okay, Jews, get up," he said, obviously accustomed to being obeyed.

Yaakov and Lazer rose quickly.

"I see you are tall Jews. Your names?"

"Yaakov."

"Lazer."

"I'm Cas," said the leader, and he smiled.

Relieved, the brothers extended their hands, and Cas shook them. "Have you been rolling in mud?"

Before the brothers could answer, Cas touched their rags, pulling his finger through one of the holes in Yaakov's shirt. "We have clothes for you. You're welcome to join us, to kill Germans. But if you make a problem, you are dead men. I'll kill you myself."

Yaakov nodded nervously.

Cas slapped him on the shoulder. "Come on, join us. We have food at our camp. Follow us." Cas pointed to one of his men, who appeared to be waiting for the brothers to accompany him.

The group pushed deeper into the woods and up a mountain. It was a hard march, and the brothers struggled to keep pace. Finally, they reached camp. There were tents and barricades, trees with wooden lookouts, and boxes of supplies kept in dugouts below ground.

Cas came over and patted Yaakov's shoulder. "Go, eat, eat. We have food left."

Yaakov felt happy disbelief as someone brought him and his brother bowls of broth with little pieces of fat and potato. It was tasteless but hot and wonderful. They finished the soup quickly. Then someone handed them blankets and suggested a spot on the ground where they could sleep.

Another guerrilla fighter, Lachowitz, approached Yaakov. "I have no use for kikes. If it were up to me, you'd be dead. I'd have killed you right out. Just give me a reason, kike, any reason at all, and I'll finish what should've happened today."

Yaakov walked within an inch of Lachowitz and stared into his eyes. That seemed to subdue the man's bravado a bit. "Remember, we are on the same side now," Yaakov whispered. "You can take me on, if you wish, *after* we win this war. We need every man right now on Poland's side." He turned and walked away.

Yaakov knew where he stood in the group. He put the threat out of his mind. He had to. Cas seemed like a good man. Yaakov had to escape the Germans, and Cas could be a leader with tolerance who might help him do just that.

They slept on the ground between blankets that night by a wood fire. It felt almost civilized. Yaakov remembered digging trenches to help Poles fight the Russian invasion. Now he was with Poles who were armed and supplied by the Russians. He lived in a turbulent land at a confusing and dangerous time. But he was grateful to be alive, to be fed, and he was excited by the anticipation of striking back at a powerful enemy.

———

Three days later, the Bikel brothers helped six of the partisans set explosives on the east side of the bridge that provided a river crossing for the trains, while other partisans moved into flanking positions on both sides of the river. There were no weapons yet available for Yaakov or Lazer. But to protect them from appearing defenseless, Cas provided wooden cutouts soaked in dye that resembled rifles.

"Great, we can point this at them and say bang bang," Lazer joked to Yaakov.

"And throw your paper grenade, yes?"

Lazer began to hum a happy tune.

"Well, we have food and blankets," Yaakov said.

"We are rich! What more could we want?" added Lazer, laughing.

The brothers marched at the rear of the partisan group until they reached a hill. Cas pointed to each man and then to their assigned tree or rock. He turned to the Bikel brothers. "Stay back at first. When a rifle's available, move up, take the rifle, follow my commands."

Yaakov hid behind a gnarled oak and pressed low to the ground. He reviewed the location of everyone in his group.

The train's whistle sounded, and Yaakov's heart hammered. The train had stopped before the bridge, and German soldiers jumped off and ran single file across its wooden expanse. Apparently, they had learned to expect sabotage at key points.

"They know we're here," Lazer whispered.

Yaakov put his finger across his lips.

A few minutes later, up ahead from the right—gunfire! Yaakov couldn't pinpoint where exactly it was coming from. Both sides were shooting. Yaakov knew the Poles were outgunned, and if the battle lasted much longer, the Germans would destroy them.

Now the volleys of gunfire sounded closer. He poked out from behind the tree. He hesitated. What to do? He was scared and anxious, afraid he'd do something stupid. He carefully moved into the tall grass and crawled forward toward a dead Pole. "May you rest in peace," he whispered to this partisan, who bequeathed to him a real rifle and real bullets.

Yaakov examined the rifle and affectionately ran his fingers along its wood frame. He searched for targets, thought he spied a German, and fired. *What the hell? Missed by at least ten meters.* He had held the weapon too loose. *Try again.* This time, he strayed a little too far to the left. Still no return fire. He accidentally touched the trigger and the gun fired into the air, scaring the birds. *Goddamn it. Are the Germans still here?*

The answer soon came as three Germans suddenly appeared. They advanced toward him quickly, firing head-on in the open, arrogantly showing contempt for his inability to shoot straight.

One of the nearby Poles cried out and fell dead to the ground. Two more partisans immediately retreated.

Yaakov didn't move. *God help me. Can't run, no matter what. I might die but I'll send one to hell.*

The three Germans were firing as they ran from tree to tree, still moving toward him. Yaakov squeezed the trigger. A German went down, and the others reflexively dropped behind rocks. A grateful Yaakov instinctively sprang to his feet and ran to find cover on a hill behind a wide old tree. He crawled forward a bit to see better. He didn't expect to spot them, but there they were. He whispered a quick prayer while twice squeezing his trigger. *Did I get them? I think I did.*

Boom! A loud explosion shook the ground. The blast ricocheted through the woods, startling a family of deer that bolted southward. Cas had blown the bridge. Yaakov saw flames and smoke even from his distant vantage point. He thought he also heard human cries. Minutes later, someone nearby yelled, "Back to the rendezvous point, now!"

Yaakov looked around for Lazer, finally spotting him in full retreat with six other partisans. Soon they were out of sight, blocked from view by the dense woods.

As Yaakov approached camp, he heard his fellow partisans cheering and laughing. He looked around for his brother. Most of the men were guzzling vodka. Yaakov found Lazer on a log drinking a cup of water. He sat beside him. Laser looked at him and smiled wide. Yaakov smiled as well but said nothing. He was still reliving the events of the day.

Cas came by and patted his shoulder. "I see you have a gun now, Yaakov. I'm told you used it well."

Yaakov nodded, then noticed Cas was wearing a gold chain with two Hebrew letters around his neck. He pointed to it.

"Oh, this," Cas said, touching it. "One of my men gave me this. He was a good soldier, a good man, a Jew fighter like you. He was shot and I went to him. He knew he was dying. He asked me to take his chain to his family. I said I would. He didn't know his family was no more. I wear it because it reminds me, you know, reminds me what we did together. Is it lucky? I escaped death more times than you can imagine."

Yaakov slowly nodded.

"So, I wear it. Why do you people wear it?"

"Some believe it brings protection."

Cas nodded and smiled wide. "Well, Yaakov, now you have a good rifle. Use it well."

Yaakov nodded. Cas laughed and continued his patrol.

"A great day, yes? Isn't this a great day?" Yaakov was feeling euphoric for the first time in a long time.

"I got my rifle, too," Lazer said, showing Yaakov the rifle he'd set behind him.

"It's beautiful." Yaakov picked up Lazer's weapon and took aim, as if he were suddenly an expert. He smiled and returned it to his brother.

"No enemy killed though," Lazer said.

"Next time." Yaakov rubbed the barrel of his own new weapon and continued thinking of the day's success. He was energized now and a bit less anxious and afraid. Better to be the hunter than the hunted. They were far from equal to the German war machine, but it felt good to fight back.

Suddenly a sadness came over Yaakov, like a dark cloud blotting out the light. He could see his parents and his sisters as if they were directly in front of him. They looked exactly as they had the day he had been assigned to work the lumber, a few days before the liquidations that destroyed his family.

One of the older Poles, they called him Bru, the one who had given them blankets on the first day in camp, sat down beside Yaakov. He nodded to the brothers. "So, Cas thinks you do well, that's . . ." He didn't finish. He used a rusty old hunting knife to slice an apple. He had no teeth but managed to eat the apple by cutting it into little bites and gumming the fruit.

"Cas said we did well?" asked Lazer.

"That's saying a lot," said Bru. "Cas doesn't give praise. He's total soldier."

"What's his background?" asked Yaakov.

"No one told you? Polish military. From Warsaw. An officer. Captain, I think. Fought Russians. Now Germans. Germans caught him but he escaped. Smart man. Tough, too. Too tough, I think. No one can say he doesn't know his business. Was captured a few times they say. He escaped. Smart. The Nazis would've worked him dead for sure if he hadn't escaped." Bru threw his apple core into the brush. "We're near a slave camp, you know. The Russians want us to free the prisoners. Cas said we're not strong enough yet. But one of the Russian officers, a Jew I think, said the prisoners don't have time. That's how it is sometimes."

"Where's this camp?" Yaakov asked.

"By the Shuch River."

"We know the area."

"We've had Jews fight with us before," Bru said, spitting out a seed. "Germans hate Jew fighters."

Lazer spoke up. "They hate us even if we don't resist, so what difference does it make?"

"Ah, there is a difference. And you have the right to know. Germans think Jews who've escaped and fight are the strongest of their race. They must be dealt with hard. You know, special treatment."

"Treatment?"

Bru cleared his throat and spit again. "Special treatment," he repeated. "Yes, you should know this because you are Jews. I saw the Germans tie one of our Jew fighters to a post and set him on fire." He shook his head. "Terrible, terrible. I saw them hang another by his balls. Pulled him up the beam and let him scream. Even one of the Germans couldn't take it. He pulled out his revolver and shot the bastard." Bru looked at the brothers with something like pity. "You should know this. You should not be captured." His apple finished, Bru stood up and walked away.

"Well, that was cheerful," Yaakov said dryly. His mind drifted off to another time. He was back in the open truck, en route to his own execution. He thought about his parents, his sisters, and all that had been lost.

Lazer just shook his head and began to hum. He seemed to go somewhere far away.

Their fellow partisans were drinking and singing anti-Semitic songs.

Chapter 4

The Forests of Rivne Oblast, Poland, September 15, 1943

A loud boom and Yaakov woke up. What was it? Then another explosion, louder and closer than the last one, followed by a cascade of enemy missiles. The sun had yet to rise over their encampment, adding to the confusion. Yaakov instinctively scooped up his weapon and signaled his brother to follow, unintentionally knocking over their lean-to, and ran for cover behind trees. *What the hell is happening? Who are they?* The intensity of the attack made the tree cover inadequate. He retreated about eighty meters to position himself behind a big rock formation. He called to Lazer, "Where are you? I'm in these rocks!"

Lazer slid down beside him and took aim. The brothers managed to hear Cas over the blasts. He was twenty meters to the East, and shouting, "The Germans are supporting their partisans. Hold this line—you hear me? We will hold this line!"

Yaakov saw some men run back immediately. Others stood up to fire and slowly stepped backward. Yaakov and Lazer stayed on the line. It seemed like they might actually be able to hold the advance.

"We can beat them back. Keep firing," Cas shouted.

For an hour, the intensity of fire was high, and then seemed more sporadic. Yaakov began to search for targets. Perhaps they were pulling back? Were they retreating? Or assembling for a new assault?

Out of the corner of his eye, he saw Cas on the ground, and he cautiously approached.

"Cas?"

Cas didn't move. Yaakov bent down to examine him. His eyes were wide open, and blood oozed from the corner of his mouth. He was gasping for air and trying to say something.

Yaakov leaned forward so that his ear was positioned over Cas's mouth, but he couldn't make out any words.

"Cas?"

His captain stayed quiet. "Cas!" he repeated, giving him a little shake. Now blood was welling up from Cas's chest, soaking through his shirt. Yaakov didn't move. It felt wrong to leave the man that had rescued him from the elements.

Lazer grabbed Yaakov's shoulder. "Let's go!" he shouted. "No time for that. They're all falling back!"

Yaakov nodded and pulled the gold chain hard, breaking it free from Cas's neck. He jumped up and retreated with his brother.

"Ow," Yaakov yelled. "I'm hit . . . I think."

Rock and earth rained down on the brothers.

"Where?" Lazer asked, barely loud enough to be heard.

Yaakov examined his chest and realized he was just bruised by a rock fragment. "I'm okay. Sure hurt, though."

"Fall back!" one of the partisans shouted, racing past them to the rear.

Lazer turned to run, but Yaakov grabbed his shoulder and spoke softly. "Don't follow them. I don't trust them without Cas."

"Then where in the hell—"

"We'll figure it out."

More rock fragments fell on them.

"Really?" Lazer asked sarcastically. "You still think there's time to figure it out?"

"Can't go forward, can't go back. East or west? You decide."

"That way," Lazer said, pointing west.

They ran, ducking behind cover wherever they found it. They scrambled down a ravine and maneuvered through thick brush and a dense stand of pines. They followed another more accessible path to a clearing where, exhausted, they settled down to catch their breath.

"I think we got away," Lazer said, managing a slight smile. He thanked God for deliverance and recited a prayer.

Yaakov's breathing slowed and he was able to hear distant shooting. "Listen!"

"Yes, Yaakov. The battle continues some distance away."

"No, it's still too close. Let's keep moving."

They stood up and resumed heading west. "We're on our own in the forest once again," Lazer said.

"Only now we have rifles and bullets, matches, blankets, food."

"We'll need those blankets. It's getting cold again. And when it snows—"

"I see something," Yaakov said, dropping to his knee and positioning his weapon.

Lazer dropped down as well. "What?"

"Looks like a barn and old farmhouse in the clearing. Let's be sure before we get close."

They enjoyed the vantage from inside a tall thicket. They stayed still and watched the barn, settling down deep in the grass. After what seemed like hours of watching, they slowly approached, rifles ready. The house and barn still had traces of faded red paint. All the doors and windows were gone. A few shutters hung at an angle from a second-floor window. Outside were remnants of wire fencing for two or three animal pens. The brothers found the abandoned farmhouse empty except for rusty pots and broken plates on the dirt floor, and a rotted table and chair in one corner. The barn had a straw floor. There was some rope, parts of an old plow, a stool for milking. There was a wire cutter beside the stool. Yaakov picked up the cutter, opened and closed it. "It still works," he said.

"Want to stay here tonight?" Lazer asked.

Yaakov nodded and sat down on the stool, still holding the wire cutter. "I have an idea," he announced.

"Oh?"

"We can go to the slave labor camp and cut the barbed wire."

"What camp?"

"Remember the one the Russians wanted Cas to take?"

"That was a while ago. Who knows if it's still there?" Lazer laughed.

Yaakov didn't respond. He picked up a flat rock and rubbed it over the blades of the wire cutter. He was confident he could sharpen the edges.

———

That night, Yaakov and Lazer, totally exhausted by their retreat, wrapped themselves in their blankets and fell asleep almost instantly on small piles of tousled hay in the barn. When Yaakov woke up nearly twelve hours later, he felt as if he had come out of a coma.

Later that morning, he and Lazer ate a small piece of bread they had pocketed two days prior to their retreat. It now seemed like long ago, back when Cas and his little army were still intact and giving hell to the Germans and their allies. He remembered the rations had come in a Russian airdrop from a cargo plane donated by Americans.

After they ate, Yaakov reached for the wire cutter and snapped it open and closed a few times. "There's a reason this came into our hands," he said slowly while rotating and examining it as if it were a customized surgical instrument.

"Don't start that nonsense again," said Lazer. "I'll tell you the reason it came into our hands: There's no one else anywhere near here. We're in an abandoned farm in the middle of the woods in the middle of nowhere. That's the damn reason." Then he relaxed and smiled. "Well, we both could use a good haircut, I suppose."

"But there are Jews and Poles from our town in the camp," Yaakov pressed.

"It's sad. But there's nothing we can do about it. Wish there was, but we're powerless. We can't save anyone. Still not sure we'll save ourselves."

"Maybe there really is something we can do, dear brother," said Yaakov with a hint of a smile.

"Oh no. Now I'm getting scared. My big brother has an idea. That scares me more than the Germans. What's with you today?"

Yaakov laughed. "We can approach the camp and figure it out. Maybe we can cut the fence so a few slaves can escape. Yes? Why not?"

"Why not? Aren't the fence or fences electrified? We'll become slaves if they catch us. Remember how they treat their prisoners? They work them hard day and night and don't feed them."

Lazer was always logical, always averse to unnecessary risk. The smart thing to do was to just survive. That had always been their focus—just live long enough to make it to the Land. Someone had to continue the Bikel line. Still, something inside Yaakov was shouting that he must help these people. *Better to die trying than to walk away.* But another voice told him to play it safe.

"I'll go alone," Yaakov said at last.

"Go. Don't expect me to follow you."

"I can put myself at risk, but I can't do that to you. I'll go tomorrow."

The next day, Yaakov stuck the wire cutter in his backpack and started walking.

"Do you have any idea where you're going, Yaakov?"

"To the Sloch River. Bru said the slave camp is by the river, not far from the tree line."

"Idiot," Lazer said, but reluctantly followed his brother.

———

A day's walk later, just as the sun was rising and they had reached the top of a hill in the forest, they saw the camp. Four wooden barracks stood in the distance, enclosed by barbed-wire fencing. More barracks were beyond the four. The fence was supported by tall beams that were placed every twenty or thirty meters. Yaakov saw lights mounted on the fence posts and searchlights on the interior beams. He didn't see any fixed gun positions. There was, however, a rough terrain vehicle with a mounted machine gun parked in the rear of the first barrack.

Keeping his voice low, Yaakov pointed out the camp's security features.

"So, genius, what do you think you can do?" Lazer asked, squinting.

"I don't know. We'll watch for a while. We'll figure it out, yes?"

"Do you know how insane this is? The prisoners have guards. Their guards have guns that will make our weapons look like slingshots. We don't stand a chance against them."

"Germans have automatic guns, but the Ukrainians only have single-shot bolt-action guns."

"How do you know? And what makes you think the guards are Ukrainians?"

Yaakov shrugged and smiled. "I know some things."

"You mean you've learned how to hide in the forest?"

Yaakov laughed. "I was thinking more about how we might plan and prepare better. Maybe next time—"

"So, shall we leave?" Lazer asked hopefully.

"I'd like to watch for a while—see what happens."

———

After two days and nights of watching, Yaakov learned that at 3:00 a.m., there were no guards on one side of the camp. And he noticed the rotating searchlights consistently missed the North edge of the camp for five minutes or so. He figured he could make it to the North corner, cut the wire fence, and run back to the forest. It'd be up to the inmates to make a run for it, their only chance to escape.

He explained his plan to Lazer.

"That's a terrible plan, Yaakov. We survived so much. Why push our luck? Why get shot when we don't have to?"

"How can we not do this? Our friends, people we know and care about, are in that camp. What if you were in their place?"

Lazer thought about that. "How do you know it's our friends who are the prisoners? Maybe Chomelstien is in there. Is he worth risking your life?"

"Don't be ridiculous," Yaakov said, though he knew the risks were real. Still, that didn't change his mind. "For me, there's no choice."

"This is a suicide plan."

"There's no light for the first hundred meters beyond the trees, yes? We can make it there for sure. You stay here and fire back if they shoot at me. Or just run away from this place. I'll go with the wire cutter and do the job as fast as I can. Simple, yes?"

"You can be so damn stubborn. You've been a partisan beginner for a short time and now you think you're a military planner."

Just before 3:00 a.m., the two brothers slowly stepped beyond the protection of the forest into the pitch darkness to a barren rise overlooking the camp's outer fencing. Yaakov used his rifle as a probe into the emptiness ahead. He tripped over a branch but managed to catch his fall. He cursed softly.

He heard Lazer behind him and smiled. Lazer always complained—but his brother always had his back. They hesitated at the edge of the hill before slowly maneuvering down an incline to the valley, stopping just before they reached the range of the searchlights. Lazer assumed a sniper's prone position and nodded. "If you still insist on your plan, Yaakov, do it now. Quick. I'll be right here."

"Don't worry," Yaakov said while looking at his brother on the ground. "This will be quick. I'm not going to hang around. If I get in trouble, save yourself and don't look back."

Yaakov waited for the searchlights to pass. Then, just to be sure, he waited for a second pass. His rifle strapped over one shoulder and the wire cutter in his clenched fist, he ran with a deliberate stride to minimize noise. He kept his body low, focusing on where to step. *So far so good.* He knew the fence could be electrified, but this camp was small, so he had minimized that risk when planning the operation. Now he was here, and the risk was very real. He'd figured he'd just pad his hands with some scrap wool he'd found at the old farmhouse. Would it work? He wasn't as confident now as he had been when plotting the action.

When he reached the north edge of the fencing, he dropped down. He was breathing hard. *Where to start cutting? Quick. Quick. Not much time.*

He rested the wire cutter on the camp's prison wiring. *Good. No sparks.*

His finger touched the wire for a second. Nothing happened. He started cutting the rusted wire on the side adjacent to the wood post. *Good. Not electrified.*

He heard footsteps and flattened himself against the earth and waited. *Is it a guard?* He held his breath as long as he could. The steps were getting louder. He slowly reached for his weapon and moved it forward until his finger touched the trigger.

He heard two voices. Now they were laughing. *Hope that means they're distracted.* He took a deep breath and held it. *Will they notice me?*

The footsteps passed and continued into the blackness. He took another slow and quiet breath, then raised his head and peeked into the camp. All seemed clear.

It took three long minutes to cut three strands of rusted wire on one side of the wood post. Yaakov told himself it wasn't enough to be noticed. He crawled over to the next post and cut a larger hole, more likely to be noticed. *Hold on, Lazer, it'll just take a little longer than planned.* He cut this wire and strategically placed the cutter on the ground inside the fence. It was a risk. If one of the prisoners found it, as he hoped, it could mean freedom. But if the wire cutter was found by one of the guards . . . well, he had no control over that.

Then he heard voices. German voices. They were coming his way. *Should I make a run for it now?*

He wasn't sure what to do. He lay as flat as he could on top of the rocky soil. Too late now to run. The voices were loud and getting louder. *Damn! Keep walking.*

He could see them walking slowly. He waited until the two figures passed by and blended into the darkness. Then he hopped to his feet and retreated back to where his brother was crouched. He bent low as he ran, trying to avoid any movement that might call attention.

"Done," he managed, sliding to the ground beside Lazer. He was trying to catch his breath.

"Thank God, Yaakov. You were gone so long. I thought you were dead. Let's go."

The brothers ran back into the forest and kept running west until they couldn't run any longer. The deep woods made them feel safe. But were they really safe?

"Well, did you have fun today, dear brother?" Lazer asked. "Hey, now I have an idea. Really. It's a great idea. Let's go to Berlin and get Hitler. Are you ready?"

Yaakov smiled. "This is your idea. So, *you* go after Hitler. I'll wait in the car for you. Okay?" The two brothers exchanged grins. Then they ate more of their rations and went to sleep.

———

A few hours later, Yaakov felt Lazer shaking him. "Yaakov, get up. I hear something."

Yaakov jumped to his feet, automatically grabbing his rifle. Now he heard it, too: the sound of gunfire, single shots, ripping through the night. "I think my cuts in the wires got noticed."

"Maybe they're punishing the prisoners," Lazer speculated.

"Too intermittent. Sounds like they're taking aim."

Now automatic gunfire joined the single shots.

"I think you're right, Yaakov."

"Some of them will make it, yes?" Yaakov asked his brother, sounding almost desperate. *Could I have made things worse for the prisoners? For us?*

"We can hope. But we better move, too," Lazer said as he turned to run.

They retreated farther into the dense woods. Yaakov remembered how the Germans dealt with fighting Jews.

Chapter 5

The Polesia Forest, Poland, June 15, 1945

"Let's rest by that big old oak there," Lazer said. "I can't walk anymore."

"Okay. For a little while. We still need to keep going."

"Give me a damn break, Yaakov."

They sat down and drank water from their full canteens.

"It's so hot out," Lazer complained.

"It's June, I think? Anyway, it's some time in spring or summer."

A noise startled the brothers and they reached for their rifles. Someone was walking in the woods. Yaakov hadn't seen a human in the woods for a long time. He relaxed when he realized it was a short, hunched-over old woman. She was wearing a black scarf as a head cover. She appeared to be alone. She was mumbling prayers but stopped instantly when she saw the Bikel brothers. Yaakov could see the fear in her face.

"Don't worry, we won't harm you," Yaakov assured her in a calm, friendly voice.

"Please, I'm looking for my dog," she said. "God bless you." She crossed herself and turned around. But suddenly she stopped and turned back to face the brothers. "Have you heard?" she asked.

"Heard? What?"

"You have been long in the forest, I see that. You don't know, do you?" She paused a moment. "The war is over, thank you Jesus. I see you don't know this."

The brothers looked at each other. Yaakov wanted to believe he had heard right. "This is true?" *Can I believe this old woman?*

"Yes. It's over. Germans give up—it's true."

Yaakov couldn't hold back a big smile.

Lazer yelled out, "Wahoo!"

Yaakov thanked the woman. She nodded, turned around, and began calling for her dog.

Stunned, the brothers turned to each other again. "I'd like to believe her," Yaakov said.

"But you're afraid it isn't true," said Lazer. "Or it is true but not recognized by all the combatants, and someone will blow our heads off as soon as we come out."

"Yeah. Even if it's true, does everyone know? Hell, *we* didn't know."

"Yaakov, we only talk to the deer. We've been hiding from the world. Not the best way to keep up on news. Anyway, the deer make for better conversations."

"You believe her?"

"Only one way to find out," Lazer said, smiling, then patted Yaakov's shoulder.

———

Later that day, Yaakov and Lazer dared to venture out of the forest and approach a farmer and his sons and daughter.

"Where have you been?" the farmer called out as he examined the two men approaching him from the woods.

"Killing Germans," Yaakov answered.

"Good for you," the farmer said. He spit on the ground in a way that clearly expressed his loathing of the German occupation.

"Look at these two," said one of the farmer's sons, likely the oldest.

"Yeah, those boys have been at it for a while," agreed the younger son. "Show them your mirror."

The farmer's daughter handed Yaakov a small hand mirror.

Only now did Yaakov consider how others would assess his appearance. His beard was long and straggly, and like his hair, was stuck together in clumps, crawling with lice, and trailing in curls down his upper back. His face was gaunt and hard looking. His teeth were chipped and stained brown like his brother's. He had sores and skin infections. His clothes were little better than rags, ripped and soiled.

"We fought with Cas," Lazer said. "We fought by his side when he went down."

"A great Pole," the farmer said.

"He was a great leader, a great soldier," Yaakov agreed.

"You are heroes," the farmer said. He told one of his sons to escort Yaakov and Lazer to the house. "They are a mess. Show them where to wash up first, then feed them."

"Tell me, did the Germans . . . did they surrender?" Lazer asked after being seated at the kitchen table.

The farmer laughed, looked to his sons and daughter, and in a new, louder voice, bellowed, "They've been in the woods so long, they don't know the biggest news, the best news in a hundred years. The best news in history, damn it! Yes, my poor guests, the Germans surrendered on seven May and effective the next day. In case you don't know, the year is 1945. I will drink well on that date the rest of my life. And the Germans, and those who helped them, will suffer in hell forever."

Everyone clicked their vodka glasses and promptly emptied them. The drink was a welcome return to a forgotten treat, Yaakov's first alcoholic beverage in years. It went down quickly, warmed him, and made him cough. He suppressed the cough as best he could and leaned back again to quickly empty the refill someone had just poured into his glass.

The farmer cheered and laughed and poured everyone another full glass. He laughed again. Then, in a softer, somber tone, he mumbled, "Now we just have to accept the damn Russkies. For a little while."

Yaakov embraced Lazer and felt a few tears streaming down his cheeks. He couldn't speak.

"Thank you, God. Thank you, God," Lazer said over and over.

The brothers wiped their eyes and embraced the farmer and his children.

"We made it," Yaakov managed to say.

The next morning, after a full breakfast, the farmer drove the Bikel brothers to the train station. He assured them, "You won't need money. Heroes can go wherever they want."

Chapter 6
Return to Sarny, June 16, 1945

The train station was teeming with an emaciated population, including survivors of the camps. There were also many soldiers, some in Red Army uniforms and some in tattered Polish uniforms. Yaakov recognized a few fellow partisans but didn't make the effort to connect. Everyone was in a hurry to get somewhere else. Yaakov inched forward until he made his way to the train. There was standing room only. He didn't mind being packed tight and he tried to ignore the harsh and varied smells from his fellow humanity, intimate and powerful and unavoidably shared.

They disembarked in Byalystok to transfer to another train. Yaakov wanted to get to a big city where he might find a way to Palestine, the logical destination for a surviving Zionist. As they walked through the terminal they heard someone shouting, "Lazer! Yaakov!"

There was cousin Fischer. He was wearing a clean, brown Red Army uniform. He looked fresh and well-fed and strong.

"Well, can I believe my eyes? Is that you? You're alive!" Lazer smiled ear to ear. He hugged and kissed his cousin, although Fischer wasn't eager to get close to these rough-looking men, cousins or not.

Yaakov laughed. "Amazing, yes?" He also hugged and kissed his cousin. "I was sure you were shot. So good to see you, Fischer, so good."

"You made it!" Fischer cheered. "Wonderful! I thought I was the only one to survive."

"You fought for the Communists, yes?"

"Strange. Never thought I'd fight alongside them ...even become one of them. We had only fought against them. But we had to fight the Nazis if only to survive. I wasn't alone. There were many, many of us in the Red Army."

Fischer's eyes welled up, and Lazer's smile disappeared. This had been the worst of times, the bleakest possible years of their lives. Yaakov, too, felt a terrible pain that could never heal or be forgotten, and he was still unsure of his next steps.

"Any ideas what to do now?" Fischer asked.

"Go to Palestine," Yaakov answered automatically.

"I'm going back to Sarny to look for family. I'm going to find Wilus Chomelstien. I hear he's in Sarny, working for the new Poland."

"Huh? Where did you hear that?" Lazer asked, his tone challenging.

"My Russian friends know everything and tell me everything. You wouldn't believe what they control already, or what they're planning. Only when I finish my business with Wilus will I decide where to go. Maybe Palestine, maybe Russia. I'm not going to stay here in the new Poland."

"What is the new Poland?"

"They're trying to start a new government, something better, stronger. I hear some Jews are in it—that won't be good. The Jews will be blamed for Russian mistakes and behaviors. The new government needs Russian approval for everything. It's too new to know what it'll be. Hope it's better. I hope it won't be anti-Semitic. Don't know."

"It was Chomelstien that gave us up, yes?" said Yaakov.

"No doubt about it. It's not a rumor. My cousin witnessed him telling the Nazis what we were planning. He wanted to win favors. Save himself. Everyone knows he's a snake. Now he's claiming hero status because he escaped the slave camp."

"Escaped?" asked Lazer.

"They say he cut the fence and ran to the woods and helped others escape. He was one of the lucky bastards that made it to the forest."

Lazer and Yaakov looked at each other but said nothing.

"Fischer, we will go with you back to Sarny," Yaakov said, stroking the barrel of his rifle. "Like you, I have some business with that Wilus."

Sarny, Poland, June 29, 1945

They got off the train at the imposing gray concrete structure that was the Sarny station, near Centralnia Street. There were three large windows at the front of the station, arched by decorative stone, and the light poured through these windows as if promising a better future.

Yaakov was intimately familiar with this section of his old town, and there was comfort in that, but there was now an unmistakable difference. The people and the town were broken by the 1939 Russian occupation and the 1941 German occupation. Now the Russians were back, and no one seemed to be smiling. As he continued walking, passing mound after mound of rubble and ubiquitous dust, he sensed the residual traces of struggle and despair. The town seemed stifling, as if everything was weighed down by collective pain and horrible secrets.

Yaakov recalled a few pleasant memories, like laughing with his friends, and singing at the holidays. He passed the conical water tower, which he had once called the "dunce cap". He walked by the little white wooden building by the clock tower where he used to teach Hebrew to the young Zionists. The clock on the tower still pointed to 12:32, just as it had the last time he had been there, a lifetime ago.

As they walked, Yaakov became aware that people were staring at them. He knew he and Lazer were a sight, like wild and threatening wolves on the prowl.

Fischer had pictures of his brothers and sisters, and he showed them to everyone they passed. But few bothered to really look at the pictures. There were so many victims, and no one seemed to have the energy or interest to get involved with someone else's tragedy.

Fischer approached everyone anyway. "Please, madam, maybe you've seen this girl or this other girl or this boy, maybe this boy?"

He ran to the next person he saw on the other side of the street. "Please, mister, my sisters, maybe you've seen them, my brothers, maybe you've seen them?"

The old town hall was no more, but a nearby single-story wooden structure had a sign indicating it was the new temporary town hall. Three Russian soldiers were standing outside smoking cigarettes. Fischer said something in Russian and the soldiers laughed. One of them patted Fischer on the shoulder. Fischer invited them to follow him into the building.

Yaakov was the first to enter. Lazer, Fischer, and the Russians followed. Two women and a man sat at a table, stamping, and sorting thick piles of papers.

"Where's Wilus Chomelstien?" Yaakov spoke with a curt, sharp edge.

The man glanced up and pointed to a smaller room in the back of the building.

Yaakov led the way, followed by Fischer and Lazer, and behind them the Russians.

"There he is," Lazer said, inclining his head toward the very back of the room. Yaakov entered the room and soon recognized Chomelstien. He looked older, bony, but that face was unmistakable.

"Hello, Wilus," Yaakov said, striding toward him. "Glad to see us?"

Chomelstien turned around. "Who are you?"

"He doesn't recognize us," Lazer said. "I'm insulted."

Fischer was in no mood to joke. He walked up to Chomelstien, grabbed his collar, and placed the barrel of his pistol against Chomelstien's forehead. "You son of a bitch, recognize this?"

Chomelstien froze.

Fischer tightened his grip on the collar and pressed the pistol harder between Chomelstien's eyes. "Try," he said in a low voice. "Try to remember who we are. Surely you know our names. You had no trouble giving them to the Nazis."

"You're Fischer . . . you're Bikels," Chomelstien nervously confessed.

Yaakov raised his rifle and pointed it toward Chomelstien. "So, you recognize us after all."

"Please," Chomelstien said. His voice trembled. "Please, I didn't do anything."

"You turned us in, you bastard," said Yaakov.

"No, please, I didn't. Someone else did. It was . . . Yankel. I'm sure. It was Yankel."

"You're sure it was Yankel? Blaming a dead old man who could hardly see or hear and wasn't even on the Council when the Germans came?" shouted Fischer.

"Now I hear you're telling everyone you liberated the slave labor camp," Yaakov said. "You must be very strong, really special, to liberate the camp."

"I—I cut the fence," Chomelstien insisted.

"You are a liar, yes?" Yaakov shouted. "Truth means nothing to you. You don't know what's true, what's a lie. You care about no one but yourself. *I* was the one who cut the fence. I risked my life to cut through that barbed wire. You just found the wire cutter I left there. Now you say you did it? Do you ever tell the truth? Do you even know what the word 'truth' means?"

"I—"

Lazer interrupted, "We lost a dozen men—friends, neighbors, family men, brave men. What should we do with this lying—"

"Simple," said Fischer. "I'm going to blow his brains out."

"And I'll fire through his gut," Yaakov said. "Just to make sure the job gets done." He punched Chomelstien's stomach. Chomelstien doubled over and fell to the floor, and Yaakov kicked his face.

"No!" Chomelstien wailed. "Please, I'll do anything. You want money? I can get. I had to do it to save my sister. She would die if she didn't get her medicine. I had to trade with the Germans. No choice."

"I don't believe you," Yaakov shouted back. "Do you even have a sister? You betrayed us, your own people. Get up—now!"

Chomelstien's face communicated his pain as he got up off the floor. "Every one of you would have done exactly what I did if you were in my shoes." His voice was garbled.

Lazer yelled, "Shut up, or we'll—"

Chomelstien coughed while rising, then shouted, "You would absolutely do the same in my place. Oh, you are so high and mighty now that the Germans are gone. You have no idea what you really would have done. I'll tell you what you'd have done... exactly what I did. You bastards—you deny the truth. You were not in my place. You don't know what you'd do until it's real." Chomelstien cleared his throat and continued speaking faster and louder. "Don't do this. You'll be just like the Germans if you do this. I saved as many people as I could. And I really did cut the fence wider to allow—to save more. Please. I'm begging you."

Yaakov had been dreaming about this moment for years. Revenge was a motivator that had long kept him going. He heard his own voice saying, "Just shoot the sniveling, miserable snake. He doesn't deserve mercy."

Fischer said, "I'll do it, no problem. I've learned a few things from the Russians." He raised his pistol and pressed the barrel squarely against Chomelstien's temple.

Chomelstien was shaking hard now. "Don't . . . please." He continued pleading quietly, over, and over.

Yaakov instinctively brushed his hand along Fischer's gun-bearing arm. "Wait," he commanded, without giving any consideration to what he was saying.

Fischer relaxed his pistol grip. He looked back at Yaakov, confused. "Yaakov? You're changing your mind?"

"I don't know."

"He's a nothing. Do you remember what he did to us? To our friends?"

"I'll never, ever forget." Yaakov turned toward his brother. "Lazer, what do you think?"

"Yaakov, I don't know. He doesn't deserve any . . . I don't know."

At last, Yaakov said, "He's not worth the bullets," his voice filled with disgust.

Fischer said something to the Russians and lowered his pistol. He ordered Chomelstien to leave Sarny. "In fact, I want you out of Poland. I told my Russian friends to shoot you on sight if they ever see you set foot here again. And they said they'll be happy to do it."

Chomelstien tried to get up but tripped and fell back to the floor. "Can't do it," he mumbled to himself. He squealed and tried again and awkwardly managed to stand up.

Then one of the Russians punched Chomelstien hard in the back, unleashing a loud cracking sound. Chomelstien cried out while dropping like a game animal to the floor. The Russians laughed.

"Get up and get out of my sight," Fischer yelled. "If the Bikels don't want to kill you, I'll do it." Fischer aimed his gun at Chomelstien's head.

Chomelstien didn't move. He made no sound.

"He's dead, I think," said Yaakov. "That was some punch."

"All right, then. Let's go," said Lazer as he stepped back.

"Yeah, he got what he deserved," agreed Fischer. "No one will mourn for him. We better move. Come on. Go, go."

"No, wait!" shouted Yaakov. "He's breathing."

There was moaning coming from the floor. Chomelstien was still alive. All eyes were focused on his token movements. He was drooling, moaning, gasping for air. Finally, after several failed efforts, he slowly rose to his knees. He held his stomach and continued to whimper for a while. Finally, he managed to stand. Then he stepped gingerly away from Fischer, the Bikels, and the Russians. He groaned as he inched toward the exit. They watched as he slowly maneuvered his way out.

One of the Russians laughed. Another Russian spoke up, and Fischer translated. "He says we are weak for not killing him. Our weakness is why Jews are persecuted."

Yaakov nodded, then wiped his forehead. "Tell them they are right, Fischer. I don't know why I stopped you. I don't know."

Chapter 7

From Poland to Italy, September 9, 1945

"No more questions," the tall Palestinian Jew instructed Yaakov. "I don't have time for *questions*."

"You're sending us to a store?" Yaakov asked.

The Palestinian laughed. "We call it a store. It's code. Don't you know? We have to hide you. Or else . . ."

"Or else what?"

The tall man handed Yaakov the Red Cross documents he'd need to identify himself as a Greek refugee.

"We aren't Greek," Yaakov whispered. "Can't speak Greek."

The Palestinian Jew ignored Yaakov's question and handed him a paper document with Hebrew scribbles.

"What's this?"

"Another code . . . so the Brichah at the border can know you are Jews. When you get to Czechoslovakia, someone there will get you on the train. Jews can travel free on the train courtesy of the Czech government. At the last stop, you will find drivers waiting for all you refugees. They are good men, good truck drivers. We pay them well. They will take you to Austria."

Three days later, Yaakov and Lazer crossed into the Italian Alps and connected with other Brichah agents. The Bikel brothers received coats and backpacks and followed a Brichah guide over the mountains to a waiting truck. Yaakov looked to Lazer and saw that he, too, found a ride in an open truck reminiscent of a ride years ago back in Sarny. This time they didn't have to jump off the truck.

They arrived at a Displaced Persons camp somewhere in Italy surrounded by barbed wire. "The camp is supported by international charities, the Jewish agencies, others," a woman in a light gray uniform informed them.

There were lines of men and women waiting for a turn at the open-air toilets that were positioned in a row over shoveled holes. The toilets were separated by blankets hanging over wire and the blankets would frequently lift in the wind. A meeting hall had been converted into a synagogue. Outside this hall were four bulletin boards full of names and pictures of missing loved ones.

A social worker handed him a meal card. "Food is rationed but it's better than where you've been."

Yaakov later noticed hand-painted Yiddish signs that read "Infirmary," "Office," and "Dining". He was soon routed to the infirmary to be treated for skin infections and fever. The doctor asked questions and the young woman, maybe a nurse, translated the doctor's Italian into Yiddish. She asked, "Did you know a section of this DP camp used to be a prison?"

"I didn't know. For me it's the opposite. It's freedom."

"Yes, you are free now," the woman said. "And safe."

"That's all I need."

"The doctor says that with freedom will come more needs. You will see." The doctor was standing nearby and smiling wide.

"Yaakov, the doctor says you must eat modestly until your body can adapt to regular meals at regular intervals."

"I know. Been told a dozen times."

"Your brother is Lazer?" the translator asked.

"Yes."

"Does he seem depressed to you?"

"Of course. We're all depressed. And with good reason."

"Want a cigarette?" the doctor said in English as he handed a full pack to Yaakov. "American. Very good."

Yaakov took a cigarette and handed the pack back to the doctor.

"Keep it," the doctor said, smiling again.

Yaakov turned around and left the tent. He sat on a log and lit a cigarette. The doctor was right about one thing: American cigarettes were very good.

Chapter 8

Displaced Persons Camp, Italy, October 2, 1946

Time passed slowly. Yaakov awoke alone, lying on his cot in the same old surplus US Army tent. He lit up an Italian cigarette. The camp had grown to include many more tents.

The mornings were the worst. The tent smelled of mold and unrelenting dampness that penetrated his bones and smothered any remnant of a positive spirit. Even under the khaki blanket, he was chilled. Sure, it was nothing like the Polish winters he had endured. Perhaps it was simply being plain worn out. The long days and weeks of inactivity drained him. He was now sick of the place and found it hard to get involved in the social and artistic activities that others happily immersed themselves. Those activities were a waste of time. They were kidding themselves about resuming a normal life anytime soon.

He lit a cigarette and slowly blew out the smoke. He watched the smoke meander lazily to the roof of the mud-stained army tent. He reminded himself that he had the luxury of sleeping on a cot instead of a hole in the ground. He had food and medical care, and he no longer slept with one eye open. *So why complain?*

But everyone complained. Their expectations were higher now, and the promise of seeing the Land was becoming an intolerable tease. He had recently read that a survey of Jews in DP camps reported that 98 percent would only accept Palestine and nowhere else. But he figured people would soon be settling for anywhere, if only to resume a normal life. Marriages took place every day and births were as frequent as the media visitors. Pregnant women proudly paraded their enlarged bellies like trophies.

Today he smelled something different, and he peered through the flap at the front of the tent to find a familiar and wonderful scent: fresh bread baking. It brought memories of another time—of the Sabbath with his family, bright flickering candles, sweet red wine, his father with his nose in the prayer book, his mother preparing the meals, always smiling, always eager to enable happiness and eating. The scent of the braided bread evoked memories of her bright blue eyes, her warmth, her overprotective caring, and the wonderful feeling from a full belly. Yaakov went back in the tent, put on a pair of pants, and left to eat. He was pleased that his body weight gain made him look almost normal again.

When his turn in line came, he held out his plate, and the volunteers loaded chicken stew and boiled potatoes and that wonderful bread on his plate. The rations had become more generous.

While eating, he overheard the buzz at the tables. There was bad news from Poland. In the town of Kielce, a boy had told the police that Jews had taken him to the basement of a building where he was to be killed and his blood used to make matzah. The Jews tried to explain that there was no truth to the old blood libel, and furthermore there was no basement in the building. Shots rang out, and in the end, a pogrom led to forty-two dead Jews.

A newspaper reported that at least 353 Jews had been killed in Poland since the war ended. Desperation to get out of Europe was mounting. But there was still nowhere to go.

Lazer

Lazer couldn't believe he was hearing music. *Where is it coming from? Yes, it was a violin and well played.* Lazer followed the sound across an open field, which brought him to a tent where one of the local Italian workers, probably a driver or a groundskeeper, was playing a beautiful classical piece. When the Italian stopped playing, Lazer applauded. "A Beriot piece?" he managed to ask in Italian.

The Italian shouted, "*Si.*" Then he asked in English, "You play?"

Lazer nodded.

"*Suoni uno strumento musicale?* You want . . . play?"

It had been so long since he'd touched a violin. He wanted to, but could he?

"You play," the Italian repeated as he extended the precious instrument toward him.

Lazer received the violin and bow and played a few notes. It was good. He began to play a piece that was once routine. It was written by Vivaldi, a great Italian composer. Surely this Italian violinist must know it. What was the title? Yes, of course, it was called "The Four Seasons." *Okay, let's see how it goes.*

Lazer's finger slipped off the string. *Very bad start—and you call yourself a musician.* Start again. This time he started perfectly. He smiled wide. The music was coming back to him, and he felt more confident and began to relax. His arms and fingers seemed somehow to remember what to do. He played for about three minutes, stopped, and smiled. He looked over the violin and rubbed it with admiration and love. It felt so good in his hands. He walked back to the Italian. "*Molto grazie,*" he said as he returned the instrument. "That felt great," he said under his breath. Playing reminded him how much the music still meant to him. He shouldn't feel surprised by that.

And then he heard applause from behind. He turned around. It was a tall, very thin woman with long black hair. He thought she was Italian until he heard her speak Yiddish. "I like your playing," she said. "Were you a musician?"

"Yes. I performed sometimes, but mostly I taught children to play."

"Wonderful. I would love to hear more. Maybe?"

"Well, that would be nice. It would be nice to have my old violin once more. It would be nice to still have my family listening, too."

They started to walk back toward the cafeteria. "I'm Lazer. Lazer Bikel."

"I'm Malka."

"Hello Malka."

"Everyone asks me where I'm from. I'm from Warsaw, from a big and happy family. I was in Majdeneck, Dachau, others, and yes, I was their slave. For men's needs. Which camp were you in?"

"I was fortunate. No camps."

"The Russians saved us. But the rest of my family, I don't know. I'm still looking, still hoping."

"I understand. So many . . ."

"Are you looking for family, too?"

"No. I'm afraid my brother and I are the only survivors. So far. Maybe some distant relatives survived. Don't know. ...I... want to eat some lunch with me?"

August 17, 1947

Yaakov

At the lunch table, someone said, "I don't understand why some Jews still want to remain in Poland. Why, after all that's happened?"

Yaakov responded, "Is it better for us here? The Italians just gave in to the British and stopped two ships from embarking to Palestine. Now those passengers are hunger striking. What good do they think that will do?" Yaakov wiped his mouth and scooped up another spoonful of potatoes. "The food is very good here. There's so much food. Even meat."

"We have plenty of food," said an older man sitting across from him.

"Why?"

"Don't you know? The Irish shipped one million pounds of meat to refugees all over Europe. Not just here. And all the meat is kosher. Can you believe this?"

Yaakov shook his head. "That can't be right. One million pounds of kosher meat?"

"It's fact. The Irish did a study to satisfy their issues on the ethical slaughter of animals for food. And, of course, they found kosher slaughtering was the most humane. Then they hired many rabbis, twenty, maybe even more, to manage it all. Food for refugees."

Yaakov nodded. He wanted to believe the story, but there were so many stories, he didn't know what to believe.

As Yaakov headed back to his tent, Lazer called his name. He turned to see his brother coming toward him, holding a woman's hand.

"This is my brother," Lazer told the woman.

Yaakov greeted her with a nod.

"Yaakov, this is Malka," Lazer said, smiling at the woman. "She is from Warsaw." Lazer spoke with his old energetic voice, not his recent voice of a man resigned to his miserable lot.

Yaakov nodded again and said, "Hello."

"Hello, how are you? Pleased to meet you," she replied in Yiddish, touching her mouth as she spoke, her arm exposing the dark blue numbers tattooed on the top of her right forearm. She was thin, so much so that Yaakov, now very accustomed to seeing concentration-camp survivors, couldn't help being taken aback by this woman's inability to regain normal weight after liberation. He guessed she had learned, like many camp survivors, to live with little food. He was sure she'd fill out over time.

Lazer was clearly taken with her, though Yaakov noticed her expression sometimes seemed so molded by fear that, even in a casual social situation, she could project a look of terror. But he knew Lazer didn't see her that way. He was happy with her.

Malka held a paper bag. "What's in there?" Yaakov asked.

She opened the bag to show bits of bread and food scraps. "The aid workers leave food on their plates," Malka explained proudly, as if anyone would take advantage of these foreigners who were no more astute than children.

Lazer put his arm around Malka and asked Yaakov if he cared to join them for the newsreels and the movie.

Yaakov declined. "I've already learned too much news."

A few days later, Yaakov did attend the newsreels. They were in English with Yiddish subtitles.

The British fired on a boatload of death-camp refugees. These refugees had survived the camps, climbed the Balkan Mountains, and made it to a ship that was to take them to the Land. Everyone was lost.

Yaakov stood up and walked back to his tent. He saw others walk out as well. He sat on his cot and tried to put the news out of his mind. He was determined to stay focused on his goal to reach Palestine. He couldn't let the news destroy him.

But Yaakov couldn't isolate himself. The news surrounded him. Everyone was hungry for news of relatives, news of their birth country, news of Palestine. It was on the boards, in the papers and newsreels, and debated at each meal. He learned only a few days later of more bad news. The newsreel reported:

A ship named Exodus was intentionally rammed by the British. An American volunteer named Bill Bernstein and two others were clubbed to death and twenty-eight were injured. The Exodus was towed to Haifa where the refugees boarded another ship for France. When the ship arrived at a French port, however, the French did not allow the British to force passengers to disembark. The British brought them to a British-run facility in Germany.

Yaakov knew that the refugees in his DP camp didn't have the will to protest or go on a hunger strike. Protest over injustice was beyond their reach.

In early September, the newsreel and movie were canceled because of a power outage. Yaakov headed back to his tent in the dark to find his brother on his cot, apparently lost in thought.

"Feeling okay?" he asked, worried that Lazer might be ill.

Lazer nodded. "I'm okay. Malka and I want to get married."

Yaakov laughed. "Is that all? Wonderful." He laughed again. "I thought you might be coming down with something. Hey, you're in love, a most wonderful fever, yes?"

"We're happy together. We talk and talk about everything that's happened. We talk about the future. It helps. Very much. We want to start something together. There is one thing—" Lazer stopped suddenly.

"Yes? One thing?"

"Malka has papers for America."

"Oh, I see," Yaakov responded slowly.

"She also wants to go to Palestine. But after camps like Dachau and this place, she can't wait. She wants to have a real life. And she wants peace."

"We all want a normal life."

"I don't know what to tell her," Lazer admitted. "Can I ask her to wait longer? We may never leave here. Is that fair? I don't think I can ask her. Not when she has the ticket out of here. She is very excited by the idea of becoming an American citizen. I don't want to lose her."

"You won't lose her."

"I don't know what to do," Lazer said anxiously, looking down at the ground, rubbing his chin. Yaakov saw how torn he was and felt a terrible ache in his own heart. He would miss Lazer if he went to America. They had been through so much together. Sometimes he thought it was Lazer's humor that had maintained their sanity. It was hard to imagine a future without his brother.

"Yaakov?" Lazer's voice was quiet. "You must tell me the truth. What do you think I should do?"

Yaakov now understood that Lazer wanted his approval to go to America. "Listen," he said with an authoritative voice "Go with her to America. We've been wandering, starving, fighting, living in this stinking camp. It's enough, yes? Who knows how long before we can get to Palestine? Go with her to America and wait there. When the time is right, you can still go to Palestine."

"You and I, we've dreamt so long about—"

"That dream kept us alive. This is another time. We survived because we took chances and adjusted to every new situation.

You've got a chance to get out of this place, so go. Marry her and have many children. You need to continue the Bikel line. Marry Malka, make babies, be happy. No one will judge you. Certainly not me."

Lazer shut his eyes, as if forcing back tears. "It's an impossible decision."

Yaakov took a deep breath, willing his voice to sound calm and strong. He couldn't let Lazer know how hard this was for him. "Life presents forks in the road. We all have to make choices, yes?"

"Yes."

"No one can tell you what to do. You must make the decision. What does your heart say?"

"My heart has two passions that are incompatible. My heart isn't good at this."

Yaakov tried to smile. "Give it more thought. Perhaps the answer will come."

Lazer shook his head. "Okay, big brother, what about you? How would you feel if I left?"

"I'm not important. I'm your brother no matter what. That's unshakable. Though if you left, I'd be freed from your silly jokes."

Lazer rubbed his chin. "It's my decision," he said, as if he needed to remind himself.

"Of course."

Lazer shrugged. "If I'm lucky enough to have a son, I'll name him Jonathan, for our gift of a new life."

"Very nice," Yaakov said, nodding.

———

The following day, Yaakov smoked a cigarette after lunch while ignoring the chatter at the communal table. It was a comfortable sunny day, but, unlike the refugees beside him, Yaakov was focused on the situation in Palestine.

Two men approached the table. They were both tanned and clean shaven, and they wore khaki pants and white short-sleeved shirts opened at the throat. One was tall and blondish; the other was short and had a dark complexion and black, curly hair.

"Shalom," the tall one greeted everyone at the table.

The short one walked directly over to Yaakov. "You're Bikel, the partisan?" he asked in Yiddish.

Yaakov nodded and turned to the side to blow a long puff of smoke away from the visitors. "Who are you?"

"We're from Palestine," the taller man said in Hebrew. "We've heard about you and your brother. My name is Mordi. This is Benny." He pointed to the shorter man.

"Is there somewhere we can talk?" Benny asked.

Yaakov nodded and got up to lead them to his tent.

"You a Palestinian?" Yaakov asked Mordi in Hebrew.

"Yes."

"A native born?"

"Yes."

"When did your parents come to the Land?"

"When they were born."

They reached the tent. Yaakov sat on his cot. Benny and Mordi sat on Lazer's cot.

"You have a brother. Is he here?"

"Yes, you know of Lazer. He was also a partisan."

"We know," Benny said. "That's why we're here. We will soon need your skills desperately. We'll be in the fight of our lives, and we have too many immigrants without military training."

Mordi winced. "We are training the immigrants, but real combat experience is something different. We need the veterans who can lead."

Benny shook his head. "I've seen many die during the training—"

"Where have you been?" Yaakov interrupted. "I've wasted so much time in this damn camp. Get me out of here and I'll teach the newcomers how to shoot. I speak their language and yours, too."

"We've been busy," Mordi said.

"Don't get us wrong, we know that's not an excuse," Benny added quickly. "But we're getting better. We got along fine with our local Arabs. But in recent times . . ."

"Some American and British veterans are volunteering to join us," Mordi added. "Jews and Christians, too. We still get along well with most of the Arabs. They are good people and wonderful hosts. Many did very well by selling us land. But for a few . . . they think they know what God wants, and it doesn't include us. They stir the pot."

"Just as in Europe," Yaakov said quietly, a painful acceptance in his voice.

"In Europe we didn't have the will or organization to fight back. Yaakov, isn't it time to change that? How would you like to join the Palmach, the best-organized Jewish fighting force in nineteen hundred years?"

Yaakov nodded. "I think you know how I feel."

Mordi lit up a cigarette and offered one to Yaakov. "American," Mordi said while extending the pack.

Yaakov accepted one, lit it, and took a deep, slow drag. "Yes, American." He stretched and smiled.

"Good, now it's time to get down to business," Benny said. "Your Hebrew, Yiddish, Polish, and your military experience are precisely what we need. All our neighboring countries want to take Palestine for themselves. The British already gave away most of Palestine. They now call it Transjordan."

"Of course, your brother is also invited to the party," Mordi said.

Yaakov studied the men sitting across from him, calmly smoking cigarettes while speaking of going to a war they couldn't logically win. He had never seen men like them. They were so confident without justification, so enterprising without resources. They reminded Yaakov of Cas. They seemed relaxed yet impatient. Mordi spoke in a throaty, slow voice, with a touch of arrogance, as if life held no surprises. Benny spoke fast, as if he might run out of time to get his points across. Yaakov finally came around to liking them—and someday he might even trust them. "I've been here too long," he said. "I'm ready. And . . . I'll be coming by myself." With that comment, Yaakov realized he had just decided for his brother.

Benny nodded, and Mordi said, "Be ready. You'll be on a boat very soon."

Yaakov nodded. "I'm ready now."

The Palestinian Jews smiled and nodded, then stood up and were soon gone. Yaakov remained seated. What should he tell his brother? What could he tell him? He dreaded saying good-bye. He was sure they would still get together, still talk as they always did—except it might soon feel very different.

He found his brother and his fiancée in the crowded social hall. He nodded to his future sister-in-law and sat down next to Lazer.

"Hey, Yaakov. What's new?"

"The usual. Nothing special. Met with some Palestinians. They say they can get me to the Land."

"Yeah, well, don't believe them."

"You're right to be suspicious of them, but I do think these folks might be legitimate. Time will tell."

Lazer said nothing. He nodded and looked away. His soon-to-be wife whispered something that made him laugh.

"You two look very happy together."

"Yes," answered Lazer. "We both like to laugh."

"That's good. Very good."

They said nothing for a while. Then Yaakov stood up. "I need to get going. Have to get ready in case they . . . you know."

Lazer stood up as well and didn't ask any questions. That surprised Yaakov, and he was relieved. They hugged each other. Then Yaakov turned and walked away.

———

In the moonless, stark night, Yaakov and a dozen men and women he didn't know quietly took their seats in a long rowboat. Two men with oars powered the boat to an old fishing ship. The passengers quickly pulled themselves up with the help of a seaweed-infested rope and boarded the port access.

The rowboat shuttled back and forth with full loads of illegal immigrants until there were no more impatient, anxious immigrants on shore.

This was it. After so many years, he might soon be in Palestine. Or captured and interned. And he was well aware he just might be shot.

Chapter 9
On a Fishing Boat—The Sylvia Starita, September 30, 1947

Yaakov walked to the stern and observed Benny in the darkness giving a hand signal to the American captain, the volunteer everyone calls Murray. Then someone pulled up the anchor and Murray started the engine, and now the boat was moving slowly, quietly, escaping to the open sea. Soon the boat was rocking from side to side in the blackness. Yaakov had never experienced anything like this. He felt anxious and a bit nauseous.

Another passenger pointed to the first mate. "He's a volunteer from Ireland—everyone calls him Patty. Us passengers love him. Yeah, sure, there's a language barrier, but we manage. He hates the British."

Mordi told Yaakov that the "special" passengers comprised nineteen men and three women, all in their teens, twenties, a few over thirty. "That's only about fifteen percent of the passenger list. Like you, they're eager and experienced partisans or Red Army. A few escaped from camps, others were captured and sent to the camps."

Yaakov already knew most of the survivors' stories, as they all needed to share how they stayed alive. Yaakov, however, had no interest in talking about his past. He was focused on getting to the Land. And yet he knew that everyone on this boat had a past they couldn't escape. Their past was in the air they breathed.

"They call me Natan," one of the survivors told Yaakov while shaking his hand. "I'm from Krakow. I'm so grateful to be on this boat." The man smiled wide. "Grateful and scared. Couldn't sleep."

"I sleep fine," Yaakov said.

"I envy you. Your name?"

"I'm Yaakov. From Sarny."

"Sarny? I remember some news about Sarny. That's near Kiev, isn't it? It was in the paper. I remember someone went back there to see his old house, maybe look for family. He was shot and killed. Terrible. So sad. He survives the wars and everything, only to go home—Well, maybe the killers figured he'd want his house back."

Is that why we lost contact with Fischer? God, I hope not. Yaakov cleared his throat. "Was anyone arrested?"

"It didn't say. I doubt it."

Yaakov leaned against a railing. "That's why I don't want to hear any news. It's never good."

"Let me tell you, Yaakov, how I survived. It's a much better story. Before I joined a partisan group, I was helped by a Polish farming family. This family hid me and my brothers in their barn under a stack of hay. They brought us food every day, rain or snow. And they did all this for three years. Twice the Germans searched the family's home and barn, but they never found the trapdoor under the hay."

"They risked their own family to save yours?"

"Isn't that amazing?"

Yaakov nodded and noticed tears flowing freely down the man's cheeks. "You speak of remarkable people," Yaakov said, more to himself than to Natan.

Yaakov decided he was still proud of being a Pole, of building defenses against the Russians, proud that his father was a Polish veteran. Recent events made it easy to forget that Poland had been the best refuge for Jews for centuries.

He looked back at Natan, who was wiping away his tears. "Tell me, Natan, did you read the name of the man that was killed in Sarny?"

"Yes, but I don't remember."

"Could it have been 'Fischer'?"

Natan's eyes widened. "That's it. I think that is the name. Did you know him?"

The boat struggled through the churning of the ocean, wheezing, and coughing up thick black smoke that could expose their location from a distance. Yaakov thought it smelled like rat poison and caused his nausea. The boat rocked from side to side, and he had to hold on to a rusty old post to keep his balance. By the third day at sea, there was no more chatting for Yaakov, and no more incredulous stories from anyone. Most passengers were now quietly reflective, trying to keep down food or nurse a headache. More than a few vomited over the railings. The boat's toilet was clogged and no longer functional, so passengers resorted to attaching a rope to the bucket and lowering it in the sea. But Yaakov couldn't help thinking about the British blockade. It felt like he was swimming in a sea of sharks that were sure to strike at any moment.

Suddenly the engine stopped. The abrupt quiet was unnerving, although the dissipation of the black exhaust was welcome. Breathing was easier, but Yaakov's emotions ran wild. He watched Captain Murray and Patty trying to restart the engine, but it didn't go. Patty left to retrieve some tools and came back and tried again. Yaakov heard Patty curse and add some words Yaakov didn't know, then, minutes later, Patty tried to start the engine again. Nothing. They were stuck somewhere in the Mediterranean. Yaakov said nothing but listened to opinions on every possible option.

"We'll probably wind up in Cyprus or Germany," a young woman concluded. She wasn't one of the experienced combatants.

"I'll fight the British with whatever I have left before I go back to Germany," one of the German-Jewish partisans vowed.

"Do not resist if the British come," Benny shouted. "We now need them to rescue us. And you will one day get to the Land. Remember, you are needed alive in the Land."

"We're used to resisting," another passenger rejoined.

Yaakov knew Patty didn't understand the languages spoken by the passengers, but he was sure Patty understood their despair. Patty was tall and thin with long, curly black hair. He was clean-shaven, and he almost always smiled when trying to communicate to the passengers. Sometimes he did a little song and dance on the upper deck. "Irish music," he explained. The passengers encircled him and began to clap to his beat. For a little while, there were smiles on the deck again.

———

At first light the next morning, Yaakov was awoken by a loud commotion on deck. He got up and joined a cluster of passengers at the rail just to the right of the bow. There was a ship in the distance coming hard at them. Soon its flag came into view, and it was definitely British.

Yaakov retrieved his rifle. Another passenger pulled out a hunting knife. Others held rocks, tin cans, or broken handles from old hoses. Patty had a big, shiny pistol.

Yaakov pulled his rifle off his shoulder and checked it over. He crouched down and aimed at the looming ship, peripherally aware that immediately to his left and right, others had done the same, only most had no weapon.

Leaning against the bow, he looked beyond the approaching ship to the blue horizon. Birds squealed just off to his side. Yaakov saw Benny, Mordi, and Murray running around to restore calm. But he didn't care, and from what he could tell, no one seemed to be listening.

"You hate the British?" a short man at his side asked in Yiddish.

"What do you think," grunted Yaakov.

"The British aren't our enemy. They liberated me from Bergen-Belsen."

Now Yaakov turned to his right and studied the short man. He was clean-shaven and had a look of affluence, except that he was wearing clothing fit for a street beggar.

"I remember when the British liberated the camp. I didn't expect anything, didn't know we would be freed. I saw how the British soldiers reacted to a barrel of dog food. That reminded me what a normal human reaction should be to such a sight."

"What are you saying? A barrel of dog food is an issue?"

"The barrel was full of bloody penises, you know, cut from the dead. That's what the Germans fed their dogs. They thought it was funny—feedings dogs that way. The Germans— they were once supposed to be a cultured people. After a while I got numb to such sights. I was surprised by the Brits' reaction. Some vomited. That's how I knew some people still had their humanity. The Brits saved us. They were the first and once the only ones that stood up to Hitler. The world owes them. Especially us."

Yaakov shook his head. "That's a horrible story."

The stranger continued, "None of this would be happening if Churchill was still in power. I know this. He was a real leader. He stood up to Hitler. He was a Zionist, too. And he rallied his people. He rallied Canada and, in some ways, America, too, I would say."

Yaakov lowered his rifle and walked away. He paced back and forth for a while, then went below to the boat's interior and sat down.

———

The British ship was now just off their bow and Yaakov returned to the deck. He could see their cannons and many sailors lined up with rifles.

Had he done something wrong in his life, something so bad that he could come so close and not reach the Land? If his brother were with him now, he'd be praying for sure. But he wasn't there, and Yaakov missed him. Yaakov saw other men swaying back and forth and side to side in prayer, and he closed his eyes and, for the first time in many years, silently appealed for help.

He now expected he'd be forced back to Europe to be interned in some prison camp. He'd just have to accept it. He spit into the sea.

An English officer shouted something loud enough to be clearly heard. Murray immediately responded.

"What did they say?" someone shouted.

Mordi translated. "They want to know if we are having trouble. They called us 'lads,' which is not a bad thing to be called in English. It's friendly. Murray told them our engine is dead."

There was more dialogue between the English and Captain Murray. Murray said, "Okay," and the British threw ropes to the disabled fishing vessel. Patty tied the ropes to the bow while whispering to himself, "Bloody Brits."

"Are they taking us to Cyprus?" one of the men asked angrily in Yiddish.

Mordi answered in Hebrew, and Yaakov translated. "Mordi says we are the luckiest bastards." Yaakov stopped to laugh. "He says they're towing us to Palestine. For some reason, they're helping us."

Yaakov didn't trust the news. Others also found it too good to be true.

There was a long silence before the shouting started. Then came the laughing and cheering and slapping of shoulders and backs.

"Maybe, after all, there are some people out there that care," someone said.

The British asked for and received permission to board. Their sailors smiled as they transferred containers of water and food and one bottle of whiskey. There were celebrations throughout the boat, but Yaakov suspected it could be a trap. He said nothing, figuring the others needed a break to feel human and happy again. Passengers began to sing Yiddish songs, but not Yaakov, who held on to his rifle, prepared for the worst.

The British towed them for a day. The next morning, Yaakov could see land at first light. He pressed against the rail on the starboard side and stared. He saw ships tied up in the harbor and many small boats as well. Beyond the port were tall buildings and a big hill in the distance. Others joined him at the rail. Each of them seemed to be lost in private thoughts. Yaakov thought of his parents and siblings and remembered those he had taught Hebrew, all of them hoping to one day make new lives for themselves in this Land.

The British towed them in closer and they passed a cluster of small fishing boats. They sailed down the coast until they came to an empty beach. Captain Murray untied the ropes and threw them back toward the British ship. He let their boat float toward the shore.

Yaakov watched the British boat, his benefactors, sail away and recede into the distant fog. He was one of the last in line and he watched Patty and Captain Murray at the stern helping passengers disembark. Captain Murray looked him in the eye. "Off," he commanded in English. Then in Yiddish, without the bark, "Stay safe, Yaakov."

And with that command, Yaakov looked back to the open ocean. Europe was somewhere beyond the horizon, the only world he had ever known. Now he turned to face the shoreline where he would live out the next stage of his life, the place he had always wanted. He thought of kissing the sand as soon as he stepped ashore. At the same time, he realized he was afraid.

Chapter 10
Haifa, April 24, 1948

Yaakov was relaxing by himself, smoking a cigarette in the shade provided by an old tree. It felt strange to be fighting in a congested city. *So different from European forests. Where will I go next?*

A voice called out, "Are you Bikel?"

Yaakov turned to find a two-seat jeep, probably American army surplus, pulling up beside him.

"Hop in," the driver said in Hebrew, with a heavy, unfamiliar accent. Yaakov guessed French.

Yaakov hesitated for a moment, as if frozen to the tree.

"Hey, buddy, I don't give a crap," the driver shouted, "but they want to see you in the command tent. You coming or not?"

Yaakov got into the jeep.

"I heard you had it tough." This time the driver spoke with a softer tone as he turned the vehicle around.

"My unit is new to this kind of fight," Yaakov explained with a sigh. He was tired of explaining why he was ignorant of their protocol.

They reached the tent forty minutes later. Yaakov saw Mordi and approached him. Mordi greeted Yaakov with a few taps on his shoulder. "Yaakov, listen now, this is what's happening. We've been able to reverse the Haifa attack and get control. Local Arab leadership asked the British to help arrange a truce. We're going to meet Stockwell—the English general. I want you with me as a translator in case someone talks in Yiddish. You need to tell me what they are really saying, you know what I mean? Don't whitewash. The Brits set up their command post in an old stucco building at the port, you know, at the edge of Haifa's old city."

Twenty minutes later, Yaakov and Mordi were the last to enter the large room, where men sat shoulder-to-shoulder around a long, rectangular table—Arabs on one side, Jews on the other. At the head of the table sat a pale-skinned man with a light brown mustache who Yaakov assumed was Major General Hugh Stockwell, commander of the British forces in northern Palestine. Yaakov and Mordi remained standing until someone brought chairs from an adjacent room. Most of the conversation was in English, but once in a while, they called on Mordi to translate to Arabic.

One woman, petite and dark, also sat at the table. She was taking notes on the meeting, and Yaakov soon realized she spoke Arabic, Hebrew, and English. Her name was Liza, and when they first entered the room, she turned around to say a warm hello to Mordi. When she did, Yaakov locked eyes with her. He liked her dark, exotic look, and he wondered if she was Mordi's lover.

Haifa's Jewish mayor, a thin old man named Levy—wearing a suit that made him look like a kid wearing his big brother's clothing—pleaded with the Arabs, "Let us make peace." He went through every statement in the truce agreement, point by point. Whenever there was an objection, Levy changed the language to accommodate the Arabs' concerns.

The Arabs were passionate and argued intensely. Yaakov thought it strange that the Jews controlled the city but were pushing hard, perhaps too hard, for their reluctant neighbors to accept a very generous truce. Certainly, this wasn't the way the Germans, Russians, or partisans would have handled a situation in which they held the upper hand on the field.

The Arabs were led by the elder in their group, a big-boned but short man with skin that revealed years of exposure to harsh wind and sun. He wore a red keffiyeh and sported a thick, white handlebar mustache.

The meeting took another hour to reach an agreement. "You will have equal rights and control of what you have asked for," old Levy assured the Arabs.

During a recess, the papers were drawn up for signatures. Yaakov noticed that Liza came back to chat with Mordi. They both went outside. Yaakov stayed in the conference room and lit a cigarette. He went over to the window, where he could catch a partial view of Mount Carmel. The sun was setting over the city, casting a shadow over Carmel's western slope.

An hour later, the Arabs returned, but their expressions telegraphed something was very wrong. They looked tired and lacked the passion they had demonstrated earlier. "We can't sign the agreement," a tall man said as he waited for his leader to seat himself.

"*Voos?*" asked one of the Jews.

"What?" shouted Major General Stockwell, clearly confused.

Mordi asked the tall man to repeat what he had said. The Arab repeated his new position and Mordi translated into English and Hebrew. Yaakov translated into Yiddish.

"Why? We only agreed a little while ago," said Levy.

"We have been instructed not to sign," the short leader with the handlebar mustache answered quietly. As he spoke, he looked away from the Jews and nervously rubbed his chin. "We would be grateful to the British for their assistance for those of us who wish to evacuate the town."

"Who instructed you not to sign?" Stockwell demanded. His face had turned red.

"Our brothers in other countries. But it doesn't matter. We do not control the military elements in town. So, we really couldn't fulfill our end of the truce even if we were to sign it."

"Why should your brothers, as you call them, make the decision for you?" asked Levy, pointing at the Arab leader, his finger shaking. "You and I have lived in Haifa all our adult lives, side by side. We shop at your markets. We've made this a beautiful city with gardens and wonderful views. I don't understand. Why would you leave your home?"

The Arab leader didn't answer. He wouldn't look at the old man.

Mordi leaned over to Yaakov and whispered that he had overheard the other Arabs say something about instructions from Beirut. "They must have been told to get out of the way for their own safety," Mordi explained.

"Don't listen to the others up north," old Levy pleaded. "Didn't your father come from there? Didn't he leave there for a good reason, a very good reason? You certainly have no responsibility to those in Lebanon or Syria now."

There was no response.

Levy continued, "Why abandon your homes and live like refugees? Do you think they'll take care of you in Lebanon or Syria? You're better off here. You can stay out of the conflict. We've been neighbors all our lives. You know us. We know you. I don't understand this."

"You're making a foolish decision," the Major General said, swiveling his chair to face the Arab side of the table. "Let's talk frankly here. You attacked them and they responded and won. That's a fact. Normally, they would evacuate combatants. Most armies would. But they *want* you to stay. And they're offering equal treatment. Seems like a generous truce. Better than other truce agreements I've seen. I know other countries are telling you to get out of their way—- make it easier for them to destroy the Jews. You should not listen to them."

The Arab leader turned to the Englishman and said in a polite, soft-spoken voice, "Major General, will you guarantee our safety to the harbor? Yes, we will need assistance and food for the people."

———

Yaakov left the building with other Jews, but he stopped in the courtyard to the left of the entrance. He looked down at the wildflowers and dandelion weeds growing between cobblestones. Then he looked up to see Liza dangling an unlit cigarette in her fingers. "Come, give me a light," she said.

"Sure." He lit her cigarette and tried to light one for himself. He had trouble on the first few attempts. His fingers were shaking.

She was thin and wiry, but compared to the women in the DP camp, she was voluptuous. Her hair was as black as tar and reached below her shoulder blades. Yaakov decided she was pretty, especially when she smiled.

"You're a new immigrant?" she asked.

"I guess so, but I don't feel new anymore. And I'm not new to fighting."

"So, you found another war," she said sarcastically.

He nodded. "I know how to fight," he assured her.

"What's your name?" she asked, but from her tone Yaakov imagined she really was asking *Aren't you just another desperate refugee who knows nothing about this Land, this war, and will likely soon be dead like so many I've seen?*

"My name? It's Yaakov."

"Ah, a very old name, a Hebrew name. Your Hebrew's good for a newcomer."

"I once taught Hebrew before the war."

"A noble profession. We'll need teachers if we survive all this. We'll need every profession for that matter. Except rabbis. We've already got plenty of rabbis."

"And your name?"

"Liza Ahuva. That means I have a lot of love to give."

He couldn't tell if she was teasing him.

Liza turned to blow cigarette smoke behind her. "But you speak Hebrew, so you know that. Or some of it."

He nodded, sure now that she was teasing him and uncertain how to respond. He decided to ask the question he'd been wondering about ever since he first saw her. "You are with Mordi?"

"With?"

"His girlfriend."

"Once, for a very short while—not now. We're friends."

"It's good to have friends, yes?"

"Yes, indeed."

Yaakov took a long drag and watched the smoke as he blew it out. It came out as if from a steam kettle and it relaxed him.

"You were a partisan?" she asked in a different, kinder voice. He noticed her studying his face perhaps for the first time.

"Yes." Her stare flattered him but also made him uncomfortable. "You can tell I was a partisan?"

"You just told me you were. So, Mr. Partisan, are you interested in me?"

Yaakov laughed. "You are different from the other women. Yes, I am interested. You're beautiful. I wish I had time to get to know you. But in war . . . . there's . . . no time." He shrugged.

Liza smiled, took a long drag on her cigarette, and looked him up and down as if examining a prized racehorse. "This isn't Poland, Mr. Bikel. We have a way of making time despite everything."

Galilee, November 28, 1948

Yaakov had been ordered to return to the command tent northwest of the Jezreel Valley. He cautiously pushed back the canvas flap that served as a doorway for the senior officers' tent. He walked in and stood at attention by the entrance. The three officers ignored him—two of them were shouting at the same time. One bellowed, "We must move now." The others apparently didn't agree. The shouting grew louder and faster.

After a while, one of them finally acknowledged Yaakov's presence. "Yaakov, come in, yes, over here," a tall, sandy-haired man greeted him. "I'm Aron. This is Moshe and Ari."

The three men now appeared comfortable with one another despite their combative debate moments ago. At the same time, they looked exhausted. They stood around a small table that had a map with black markings and arrows written all over it.

"Mordi thought highly of you," Aron said.

At the mention of Mordi's name, Yaakov felt as if an electric spark had shot through his body. He looked down and nodded. "I thought highly—very highly of him."

"Of course. We all did," Aron said, but with those few words his voice cracked. He quickly recovered, and there were no more hints of bottled-up mourning.

"Were you with him... when he died?" Moshe asked. "It was two days ago, right?"

"Yes. I was standing right next to him. We were about to take the compound that had been attacking our supply line. There were four or five women showing white flags, or so we thought, and we directed them to a safe place away from the action. You understand what I describe? One of the women turned out to be a man holding a gun under her— I mean, *his* robe." Yaakov was overwhelmed with emotion while describing the death of his friend and benefactor. He struggled to regain his composure.

"Come to the table, Yaakov," said Aron.

Yaakov slowly walked over and joined the three officers.

"Yaakov, show us where their compound is, the one you just took."

Yaakov pointed on the map. "Here."

"Okay, fine. We're discussing this village over here." Ari pointed to another location. "I think we can bypass the village so we can move faster and stop the Syrian advance farther north."

"That's not a problem. I know this village and they are staying out of the fighting. Mordi was planning to go around it. He made it very clear to everyone there would be no offensive against any Arab village in the Galilee unless they initiate the fight."

"This is still the situation?" asked Aron.

"Yes, they don't want any part of it."

"That's what we needed to know," said Aron. Then he turned and directed his attention to Moshe. "You heard it. Direct your command to join the effort. And block the damn Syrian advance."

Moshe mumbled that he understood and left the tent.

"Come here, Yaakov," said Aron. "Let me explain the plan to push the Syrians out of the Galilee and back to Syria. We need to protect the kibbutzim and settlements there, too. You will need to understand the subtleties of this." Aron pointed to a spot near the top center of the map. "You will bring your men here."

Yaakov wondered if this meant he was now the leader of the forty to sixty men that had served under Mordi. He wasn't sure what to think.

"Do you know this point?"

"I'm afraid I don't," said Yaakov.

Aron laughed. "Of course. But you will, Yaakov. You will soon know it very well."

It took two hours for Yaakov to understand the plan and his role in the counter-offensive in the upper Galilee. It felt good to have been brought into the circle of leaders, but he knew he lacked the experience and stature of his mentor. Mordi had been respected by everyone. Could he really take his place?

"Yaakov, I've got a dozen or so new arrivals on the way here, fresh from Europe, a mix of languages. You want them to join your mission?"

Yaakov nodded.

"They're on the way, a few hours away. Their truck will stop at the bend by the orange groves, they'll get supplies, refuel. I'll let them know to pick you up there. And I'll let them know you are their leader."

Yaakov nodded, awkwardly saluted, and stepped outside the command tent.

He saw Liza about thirty meters away addressing a small cluster of soldiers. He hadn't seen her since that first meeting. She left the soldiers as soon as her eyes caught Yaakov's stare. As she approached, Yaakov realized she had been crying. She, too, was mourning Mordi.

"Yaakov, it's so horrible," she said, her voice trembling. "I hate this war." She embraced Yaakov, seeming to take comfort in his arms.

It had been many years since he'd held a woman. She was just seeking comfort after hearing the terrible news, but her touch made him wish there was another reason. Everything about her felt wonderful—her perfect frame, her delicate, smooth skin, her smell, her hair against his cheek. He wanted to comfort her, but suddenly he wanted to be more than just a shoulder to cry on. And he, too, was mourning the loss of his friend, his leader, the man who had smuggled him out of Europe.

They began to walk. Clearly, Liza also needed to walk and to talk.

"They want me to accompany you on your mission," she said in a new voice, a voice without mourning. "They think I can help you. I know the terrain, I speak Arabic, I can shoot. I'm a very good shooter. I'll be very useful. They told me to help you. Is that okay with you?"

"I welcome your help."

She sighed. "Mordi was so capable, a good friend, a good human being."

"The best," Yaakov agreed. He waited a moment before asking, "Liza, were you born here, in the Land?"

"Iraq. Came here in 1940. Actually, I should say we escaped in 1940."

"Escaped?"

"The Iraqis decided to kill Jews. My uncle was one of the early victims. He was hung and his corpse displayed for days in the town center. My family, the survivors, left everything behind and walked to Palestine. Yes, we really walked all that way. But we were the lucky ones—we got out."

"That doesn't sound very lucky. Sounds like what happened in Europe."

She nodded. "When war broke out between Britain and Germany, many of the Iraqis in power thought it smarter to side with the Germans. One way to gain favor with Germany was to persecute their own Jews, their own citizens, a people who'd lived there since long before Islam. It made no sense then and still makes no sense, but that's what they said. That's what they did. Does this surprise you?"

"No."

"We were once very well-established in Iraq. We had a good life there."

Yaakov could hear the pain in her voice.

"The Iraqis in power grabbed all the wealth of their Jews. Very substantial wealth. We arrived here with nothing. Now I worry about the Arabs in Yafo, Jerusalem, other cities. I don't wish on them what happened to my family in Iraq."

"There's no comparison. They aren't being forced to leave Haifa. They are encouraged to stay."

"Yes. Some have decided to leave. But majority will stay. They have a good life in Haifa and we get along well. Other cities...I don't know."

Avi shrugged. "What do you mean?"

Liza took a deep breath. "There are Arabs who will maintain peace and some who will fight us, who don't remember how much we paid for land, our initiatives for their benefit, all our peace agreements, how we improved the land. Some only listen to foreign propaganda and... can we talk about something else?"

"What should we do when surrounded by militants as well as innocent neighbors?"

Liza shook her head. "Please. Enough. I don't have the answers."

"Sorry. I don't wish to upset you. And I had no idea what your family went through."

Yaakov enjoyed talking with Liza, and he didn't want to offend or alienate her. Before he knew it, they had reached the dirt path between two orange groves. He was so engrossed in their conversation that he stepped into a deep pothole. His foot turned and he fell to the right, landing on a large *sabra* cactus along the roadside. As the plant's needle-like thorns penetrated his pants, he cried out, and when his full weight came down on the prickly pear, he yelled again. He rolled away from the cactus as quickly as he could, swearing repeatedly in Polish.

"Are you alright?" asked Liza. Her voice changed. It was now soft and concerned.

While pulling out thorns, Yaakov sat up.

Liza sat down beside him on the edge of the road. "Twist your ankle?"

"It's fine," Yaakov said, now somewhat composed. He managed a slight smile. "I just feel foolish. You see, I do need a lot of help."

Liza laughed. "You're not the first one to do this, or to feel foolish. The Land has a way of making us all feel foolish at one time or another."

They both laughed, then silently looked at each other. She looked different now that she was smiling. She looked very appealing. Beautiful. Yaakov pulled her close and kissed her quickly. He pulled back to look in her eyes, and decided they were very striking brown eyes. And they were not upset by his kiss.

She moved forward to kiss him. Her lips felt delicate, warm, nurturing, gifting him with a sensation long forgotten. Yaakov wanted more of her. He rolled on top of her. Her body against his was electric, and every inch of him responded to her touch.

Yaakov realized Liza was as aggressive as he was. His hands were all over her and her hands moved quickly to feel every part of him. Somehow, he had managed to roll with her out of the *sabra* and into rows of orange trees. The trees stood like protective soldiers in precise rows, motionless despite a strong breeze. His arms and legs wrapped around Liza desperately. Yaakov and Liza rolled deeper into the privacy of the groves. They made love on the soft moist earth to the scent of sweet oranges.

———

Nine months later, in an abandoned building converted to a hospital near Tel Aviv's Rothschild Boulevard, the midwife handed Yaakov a baby wrapped in a blue-and-white towel. "He's beautiful," the midwife said.

"He is," Yaakov agreed. He walked over to Liza's bed. Her face was wet with sweat, but she managed a smile.

"Our son," he said proudly.

"The nurse said he's a healthy one—and she predicts he will be good-natured," Liza whispered, her head supported by three pillows.

"He's perfect," Yaakov said, smiling wide. He was happier than at any time in his life.

The war for Israel's independence had ended for now. Yaakov envisioned Avi, his new son, growing up in peace and never needing to know about war or hiding in a forest. He couldn't help smiling.

———

As time passed, Yaakov often recalled that day in the orange groves with Liza. He remembered he was mourning a friend, and he remembered Liza's story and the pain she had suffered and continued to carry. He guessed they were two people from families that had suffered from the worst of human-inflicted tragedies, but somehow had managed to suppress their anguish, their fears, their personal and emotional needs. Yaakov had learned that he and his wife must adjust and live for the moment, to take whatever relief or pleasure might be available. They knew well the lesson that there might be no tomorrow.

Part Two

The Next Generation

Chapter 11
The Bronx, NY, July 3, 1961

Neal Chomelstien

Neal unlocked the front door to his family's third-floor apartment. Debbie, his annoying elder sister, was standing in the foyer as he entered. He rolled his eyes, stepped past her, and said nothing.

"What about 'hello'?" she said, as if being the elder sister entitled her to some respect.

"What about leave me alone, Debbie."

"Oh, just stop with your attitude. It's so stupid." She shook her head. "We've had an awful tough day. Dad's upset again—we can't even get him to talk about it."

"He never talks. Where's Mom?"

"Stop being a jerk. Wilus usually responds to you on the rare occasion you make an effort. Mom is shopping. She wants to feed an ungrateful bastard like you for some reason."

"Give me a break. I just got home and need to pee."

"Go pee. Then talk to Dad."

While relieving himself, Neal cursed his sister. *Such an annoying bitch. Who does she think she is? She ain't no boss of me.*

Wilus Chomelstien was sitting on a plastic-covered stuffed armchair. His eyes were wide open, and his disheveled white-gray hair made him look more distant than usual. Was the old man afraid of something? The thirteen-inch TV, crowned with a doily, was broadcasting some soap opera, but Pop's attention was clearly elsewhere.

"So, Pops, how's things in the union business?" Neal asked cheerfully, trying to restore some of his father's old energy. "Hey, you know what would be really cool? You and your buddies striking against your union. Yeah, that'd be a cool move, union employees striking their unfair management that organizes strikes against other companies. What do ya think?" He was sure he'd get some reaction, but his old man didn't flinch. He just sat in the chair, staring straight ahead.

"Hey, anything bothering you, old man?" Neal persisted.

His father remained quiet for a moment, then looked up at Neal and softly said in Yiddish, "Met someone I knew in the old country."

Neal hated Yiddish. "Yeah, so?" he asked in English.

"He threatened me," the old man said in a monotone, as if threats were normal conversation.

"Did you say he threatened you? A German?"

"A Jew."

"Where did this happen? Why?"

"Gimbels Department Store," his father answered, this time in accented English. "In shoes."

Neal sat down on the plastic-covered green couch that was separated from his father's chair by a small, scratched-up, antique table. "What did this ass from the old country say to you?"

The old man was quiet awhile before continuing. "He said he regretted not killing me."

That was not the answer Neal had expected. Perhaps his father had misunderstood the man. "Are you really saying he wanted to kill you? What are you telling me?"

His father returned to speaking Yiddish. "You know I was head of the Jewish Council in the city, in the old country. This man and his brother were problems. Then they turned me in to the Germans. They said I had guns to shoot Germans. I didn't have guns."

Neal tried to put the pieces together. His father had never before shared much of his past. "Why did they do that? Did you plan a revolt?"

He shrugged. "I can't talk more about it . . ."

Why hasn't Pop ever mentioned this before? Maybe it's too painful for him, or maybe he wants to protect us. Maybe he's reluctant to burden us. "So, what happened when he turned you over to the Nazis?"

"Because of this man, Germans put me in the *arbeit lager*."

"The what? Lager? You mean a concentration camp?"

The old man nodded and looked up to the ceiling as if something was written there. "You know my back is no good. I have pain just from walking or standing all the time. You ask why my back is so bad. This man, or maybe his brother, I don't know because I was hit from behind, but one of them nearly broke my back. The doctors can't do anything for it. Just pain pills."

"I knew you had a bad back, but you never told us the reason. Not until now."

"You are older now. You can understand now. I am always in pain. Now you know."

"Yes. I can understand."

"The camp was terrible, just terrible. Americans call it a concentration camp, but that doesn't tell the whole story. It was really hell, a living hell. They treated us worse than slaves. No one would believe what I went through. They worked us all day. If you couldn't work, you would be killed. Our lives meant nothing to them. I was so weak, so sick. So, one day I found a cutting thing. Did I tell you this?"

"You found what?"

"A tool. How to say—to cut the, uhh . . . fence wire." He shook his head. "A miracle, there was a cutting thing, a giant steel scissors. On the ground. Couldn't believe it."

The old man's voice suddenly changed to an upbeat tone. The memory of finding a wire cutter seemed to bring him back to life. He even managed a slight smile.

"I cut the fence and ran free. It was very hard to cut, very hard. But I did it and I did it alone. Others followed, but most . . . I don't know, I think most didn't . . ." He shook his head, and suddenly his face revealed a sadness that Neal had never seen before. He continued, "It was a miracle. And today, again, someone tells me he wants to kill me."

"I don't get why he's threatening you. It's all backwards. You should be the one to threaten him. He's lucky you don't hire someone to settle the score."

The old man shook his head slowly. "Don't know. Maybe he doesn't want other people to know. Maybe he doesn't want his friends to think less of him. Maybe that is it, but I couldn't know this." The old man reached for his handkerchief and wiped his mouth. He coughed a few times and cleared his throat. "Your mother also made it to the woods. And she knew a nice Ukrainian family that took us in and hid us. That was another miracle. That's how we survived."

"Pops, I don't know what to say." Neal's voice cracked, surprising himself. He had only known his parents had met in the woods. Neither of them had ever shared details.

"I recognized the bastard as soon as I saw him," the old man continued. "He was trouble many years ago. I never forgot. Some people are like that. You know, my son, I will never forget what happened. And I tell you this, he is still trouble. His whole family, all the Bikels, they were troublemakers. They were all—"

"Pops, what's the name of this asshole?"

"Lazer. He and his brother—what was his brother's name . . . . Yaakov. They were trouble, always trying to convince others of their view of the world. Crazy family. Yeah."

"Convince them of what?"

"Crazy people. The whole family. The lot of them."

Neal was fascinated. "Dad, you never told us you were in a slave labor camp. Why?"

The old man didn't answer. "I have tremors when I think about it. Look at my hand now." He extended his shaking hand briefly, then returned it to rest by his side. "*Ikh ton nit visn vos tsu zogn,*" he mumbled, then switched back to English with a clear voice. "I don't know what to say. I can't talk about it or think about it. I won't sleep. I don't want to remember."

Neal nodded. "What happened to the other brother? Is he in New York, too?"

"I don't know. I don't want to know anything about him or think about him. Someone said . . . maybe Israel. I don't know.

Listen, your two sisters know nothing. Don't tell them. They will be upset. I don't want to upset the girls."

"I won't say anything. Don't worry, old man. We can talk about something else if you want."

His father's face relaxed a bit. "How did you do at school? What is your ranking?"

"I'm in the top three, of course. Should know my official standing this month."

"Wonderful," said the old man. He smiled slightly.

Chapter 12

Kibbutz Ma'ayan Baruch, Upper Galilee, Israel, July 5, 1961

Avi

A vi Bikel loved swimming in the nearby pond that was fed by the Hatzbani River and underground streams. Even when the water level dropped, as it did by early autumn, it continued to reflect the murk of surrounding vegetation and trees. Avi recalled many foreign visitors assuming the pond was impure, but the locals knew the crystal waters were pristine and therapeutic. Some locals claimed the waters had a mystical quality, and others were quick to point out that the setting had inspired landscape artists.

Avi had observed the water level rising with the advent of spring, nourished by melting snowcaps from the Golan and distant heights. He was excited when summer finally arrived and, although he had exchanged schooling for harvesting crops, there was adequate time for sports and swimming. He recalled many happy experiences by the pond: showing off with his friends, splashing the girls, everyone chiding one another. He smiled as he approached the pond with his American cousin, Jonathan, who had just arrived for his first visit to Israel.

Today was especially hot. Avi launched himself from his favorite boulder, broke the water with his outstretched hands, and remained underwater nearly the entire length of the pond. It was like diving into a magical solution with powers to restore, cool, and nourish. It was the best remedy after his long morning under an unrelenting sun. He had been helping the men toss bales of hay, "cow food" as he called it, onto the flatbed behind the John Deere tractor.

"So, Jonathan, later you want to toss more bales?"

"No way. Never again."

Avi laughed. "You don't do like this in New York?"

"No way. My arm is still bleeding from those damn—"

Avi dove down for twenty seconds, then popped up again to exhale and take a big bite of fresh air. He looked for his cousin.

Jonathan wore a long yellow bathing suit that reached below his knees, very different from the skimpy all-black Israeli version. Jonathan placed his eyeglasses delicately on a flat rock and, instead of jumping in, chose to advance slowly into the pond. He stopped periodically to adapt to the water's rising chill. The mist over the pond probably made it difficult for Jonathan to navigate, especially without his thick glasses.

"Come, Jon. The water great," said Avi with a wide smile.

"I'm coming." The water was almost up to Jonathan's nipples. Avi laughed and submerged himself again, then swam toward his cousin. He came up to the surface and Jonathan pointed to the gold chain around his neck. "Nice."

"My father give to me. He got it from man that saved him in war. Said it was, how you say, lucky."

"Is it?"

Avi shrugged. "Who know this?"

Suddenly, Avi heard voices in a language he didn't understand. *Arabic? Infiltrators? What am I supposed to do?*

Avi instinctively dropped under the water. Thirty-seconds later he popped up to breathe.

Are they gone?

Jonathan said, "It's pretty muddy, isn't it, and the rocks—"

Avi put his hand over Jonathan's mouth and whispered in his ear, "Syrian Fedayeen, I think. Shh."

Jonathan's awkward expression instantly changed to shock. "Really? I–"

Avi put a finger over his own mouth. *This idiot will get us both killed.*

Avi ran out of the water and slid between a boulder and a big bush. Jonathan followed. They both squatted down. Avi dared not move a muscle. Jonathan crouched, hugging his knees, looking terrified and confused.

Avi was scarcely aware of a whistling sound far away. He was very aware how frightened he and his cousin were. The whistling turned into a louder hissing-spitting sound, and as that noise grew louder, Avi looked north through the branches, but could see nothing.

Then came the crashing boom, a thunderous ripping and crunching sound. Earth and trees and stone were instantly wrenched from the earth and became projectiles. Birds screeched and flapped.

What should we do? Dive back in the water? Hide in the brush? Run? Where should we run?

It was the only time Avi had been at the pond during an infiltration. And the only time he had been away from the shelters during shelling.

"Avi!" a voice shouted. It was his father. "Avi . . . Avi," the voice repeated.

Avi stepped out from behind the bushes.

More hissing and spitting in the air, then another explosion.

His father saw him, and his face clearly telegraphed frustration.

"Sorry," Avi said sheepishly.

"Avi, Jon, I worried about you boys." Yaakov's voice was calmer now. "Quick. Come out of there." Yaakov had an Uzi strapped over his shoulder. Trailing behind him were four soldiers from the Nahal unit that had been assigned to Ma'ayan Baruch. All were carrying Uzis. "Avi, get on the tractor with the others. Ilan will drive you to the perimeter shelter. Remember what to do?"

"Hop into the trench. Lie flat. Cover the back of my head." Avi looked at the ground as he spoke.

Yaakov nodded. "Hurry up now. Move it." He turned to Jonathan and managed to say in English, "Jonathan, go now quick, yes?"

Avi sheepishly said, "Dad, I heard voices—"

"I know. They've moved. We know where they are. Now, go."

Avi and Jonathan ran to the tractor, stepped onto the coupling bar, and held on. Two other boys were already there. Avi looked back and saw his father counseling the soldiers. His father seemed indifferent to the shells landing a little north of their position.

How does Dad do this? How does he always know what to do? Why is he never afraid?

"My dad isn't like anyone else," Avi told his cousin. "I wish I was like him, but I don't think I have or will ever have..." He stopped talking to Jonathan when he heard his name called. There were four teenagers already standing in the trench just ahead. Avi was greeted as he approached. The cousins jumped into the trench and sat down, conforming more to their peers' positions than to Yaakov's instructions. Avi introduced Jonathan to the others. Most of them were giggling and gossiping. One boy even told a joke. Avi translated the joke for his cousin, but Jonathan didn't laugh or react.

Did Jonathan get the joke? Maybe he didn't understand my English.

"We just saw something like what happened . . . our fathers," said Avi.

"What?"

"What our fathers did in Europa."

"What happened to our fathers?" Jonathan asked again, this time louder and slower. "I don't know what they did in Europe."

"Lazer didn't tell you?"

"Tell what?"

"How they survive the war."

"My father told me he lived in the woods. Was there something more?"

"Better your father tells. My English—"

"Your mother speaks English, doesn't she? I heard your mother speaking English with the South Africans in the nursery."

Avi nodded.

"Good, I'll ask her what the hell you're talking about."

Avi nodded again. "Many South Africans here. They come to Israel to leave—how you say—apar . . ."

"Apartheid."

Avi nodded. "They no like zee aparth—"

Jonathan looked down the length of the trench where a few of the girls were speaking loudly and laughing, as if they were at a party. Jonathan snapped, "What's wrong with you? Hiding in trenches isn't funny."

"What's wrong with *you?*" one of the girls responded immediately in perfect English. She whispered something in Hebrew and the other girls laughed.

Twenty minutes later, a jeep with two soldiers came to the edge of the trench. One of the soldiers yelled, "All clear," and the jeep continued down the dirt road.

Avi stood up and peeked over the edge of the trench. Others began climbing out.

"Is it over? Is it safe now?" asked Jonathan.

Avi shrugged. "Who knows?" He climbed out of the trench and dusted himself off. "Hungry?"

Jonathan followed and caught up to Avi. "I shouldn't have yelled at that girl," he said.

"So, go tell her. Say sorry."

"Can you do it for me?"

"I think you have to do."

"Please."

Avi wasn't proud of his own behavior this day. "Sure, I'll do it," he said as he turned to look at his much-relieved cousin.

Occasional shelling continued far off in the distance. Avi stopped, turned around, and looked north to the source of the attack. He stood there watching like a statue for a while. Then he turned back to Jonathan. "Come," he said while beckoning his cousin. "Let's get some dry clothes."

The next morning was the sabbath, so breakfast was served late in the community dining room. Avi noticed Jonathan shoveling in his scrambled eggs while staring at one of the girls.

"You like her, Jon?" Avi asked. "Her name Sarah. A good one. Want to meet?"

"N-n-no. And I wasn't looking at her."

"Yes, I saw. Is true. Is okay. Is normal."

"No, I wasn't."

"You were."

"No."

Avi suspected Jonathan was afraid of girls. He was getting tired of trying with Jonathan, yet something about his cousin was endearing. Jon didn't play soccer or basketball and couldn't swim or ride a bicycle. He spoke no Hebrew and complained about everything. Yet, underneath it all, Avi could see Jon's efforts to learn everything about kibbutzim, the people, and Israel. Avi wondered if Jonathan's behavior was typical of Americans. There were a few Americans who had settled in the kibbutz, and they weren't like Jonathan, but Avi wondered if most Americans were.

"After breakfast, I am playing soccer," Avi informed his cousin. "You don't want to come?"

"N-no, Avi, I don't want to play."

"What do you want to do?"

Without hesitation, Jonathan announced, "Play chess."

"Chess? I also play chess. We play after soccer?"

Only now did Jonathan smile. He had the look of a predator waiting in the weeds for prey.

After his soccer game Avi found an old chess set and brought it back to the cottage. The set was missing a black rook, so he substituted a half lira coin.

Jonathan looked animated for the first time since he had arrived. "You can take white and go first," he said, smiling.

"Okay." Avi moved a pawn.

Jonathan moved a knight.

Avi played three more moves and announced, "Check mate."

Jonathan laughed before studying the board. His smile soon faded into a pained grimace as if Avi had just stabbed him.

Avi smiled wide. "They call it, how you say—fool's mate. See?"

Jonathan studied the board for another minute. Then he got up and ran out of the room.

Avi laughed quietly, but soon decided he should reassure Jonathan. He went to find his American cousin and maybe play another match. *But Jon should know what happened to his family in Europe. Yes, I'll bring him to Mother. She'll tell him. He needs to know.*

Chapter 13

Kibbutz Ma'ayan Baruch Upper Galilee, Israel, August 12, 1964

Avi

A loud knock at the door woke Avi up from his nightmare. He managed to sit up, rub his eyes. "What . . ."

"It's me."

Avi recognized his father's deep voice, got up, and approached the door his father had just opened. The clock on the dresser pointed to four o'clock. His roommate was fast asleep.

His father seemed edgy and impatient as he stood in the threshold. The moonlight exposed many sunspots on his dad's receding hairline. Dad never liked to bother with hats.

"You awake, Avi? Want to join me today?" Yaakov asked loudly. He was much too energetic, given the hour.

Avi didn't hesitate. "Sure. I'll get dressed."

"Quick then. Can't be late."

Avi knew the harvest needed to be finished and only the apples on the upper branches of the tallest trees remained. He was grateful to be excused this day from moving ladders around and picking apples that others would turn into brandy.

"You can go work in the orchards tomorrow. I told them yesterday you would be with me today. It's all okay." Yaakov was smiling, he had anticipated his son's concern. "Get dressed. I'll wait a few minutes in the truck. Then I'm off."

Avi looked again at his roommate, who somehow remained fast asleep. Then he rushed to get dressed. He was excited. He had always wanted to observe his father working with the new immigrants, but he had no idea what his dad did for them. Dad was one of the few kibbutz members that worked elsewhere a few days or more per week and had his government salary directly deposited into the kibbutz treasury.

But why today, just before the harvest completion, did Yaakov invite him? Dad had never asked or hinted for him to come to the immigrant settlements. Could Mother have said something? Maybe this was her idea.

Avi closed the spring-loaded screen door slowly and ran to his father's gray Peugeot half-truck, engine idling, with two folded benches in the back. He opened the door to the cab and hopped in.

They didn't speak for a while. Avi thought about the approach of another school year, but he was in no hurry for that. He loved everything summer provided, but by August he was tired of the heat and mosquitoes. Life in the upper Galilee would be unbearable without the bats that appeared at sundown to feast on the insects. He had worked all week in the boring apple orchards and would likely work there a few more weeks. He couldn't see himself making a career of farming and gave no thought to any other vocation.

Yaakov drove up and down the hills of the upper Galilee on a narrow serpentine road bordered by sand-filled barrels that provided some minimal protection against skidding into the valley below. Avi noticed his father gave no consideration to the sharp curves, probably because Dad knew there'd be no other vehicles heading north at this early hour. But what if a car did come in that lane? Dad was afraid of nothing.

"You are old enough to know."

"Know what?"

"That's what I want to tell you today. You should know about your family. I want you to know how I survived Europe."

That's why dad asked me to come today? Avi smiled. "Okay. I'm old enough."

"Yes, you are now old enough to understand. There's a lot I want to share with you."

"I'll understand."

"Good. I'm glad you say this." Yaakov smiled. "Okay, now, other fathers don't want to talk about the past. But I think it's important each generation learn from one another, yes?"

"Yes," Avi agreed, still unsure what his father intended. "Dad, why did it have to be today?"

"A few days ago, I was chatting with a friend about the old days. Then it just came to me that I should be talking to you. It's our family's story and it belongs to you as well. Better now than after school starts."

A slice of rising sun crested over the hills on the eastern horizon. It would be another hot, dry day.

"It's all good. So, let's start?"

"Why not," Avi responded while still looking out the side window.

"Well, your uncle Lazer and I had three sisters. The oldest, Shana, was married and moved to Tarnapol, then returned to Sarny, our little town in eastern Poland, after her husband got sick and died. Then there was me and my younger brother, Lazer. You spent much time with his son, yes? And we had younger sisters, beautiful girls."

"They were all killed. I know."

Yaakov was quiet for a while. Avi knew that silence was Dad's way of managing his emotions. When Yaakov resumed speaking, his voice had a different tone, softer and slower. "Anyway, your grandfather served in the Polish army in the First World War. The fighting continued in our district after that war ended. Sometimes the Russians took over Sarny, sometimes the Germans, sometimes the Poles. The senior officer of each army often stayed in our house when they controlled the area. We had a nice house. In the old days, it was the Germans that treated us the best. Hard to believe now. Their officers were more civilized. The Russians were uncivilized, and they treated us the worst. All that changed a few decades later. Strange how things turned out."

Avi nodded. "It does seem . . . strange."

"Your uncle and I were forced to work in the lumber yard and other factories after the Germans took over and turned part of our nice little town into a regional ghetto. We'd never worked in a mill, and we were not good at it. During that time, they took away our parents and sisters."

Yaakov stopped speaking again. A minute passed before he continued. "Lazer and I wanted to fight back—even if it meant we'd be killed. We just didn't know how to do it."

"So, what happened?"

"Exactly, Avi. We never implemented our plans. Things just happened. We just did what we had to do to survive. We were like animals in the wild." He stopped at an intersection to allow an army transport vehicle to cross the intersection. Then Yaakov slowly turned his vehicle into the government immigration center. "You will soon see how lucky you are, Avi."

Yaakov parked his truck beside the administration building in Be'er Ya'akov, not far from kibbutz Netzer Sereni. Avi knew that his father had many survivor friends residing in that kibbutz.

"I've heard of the transition centers," Avi mumbled

"Seeing one is different from hearing about it."

"I guess."

As soon as Yaakov stepped out of his parked Peugeot, he was rushed by over a dozen people from every direction, all declaring at the same time their desperate and immediate need for his help. Their faces revealed their anxiety and confusion, which was consistent with Avi's image of refugees. A few were missing limbs, one was missing an eye, and several had visible skin infections. Most were dressed in clothes either too big or too small. Avi guessed they had helped themselves to whatever clothing was distributed by the Jewish Agency.

Yaakov remained calm. "Okay, everyone, follow me to the administration building."

Avi stayed behind and leaned against the truck. A man wearing a religious head cover asked him, "You're Yaakov's boy?" He was short, stocky, and hadn't shaved for a week or so.

Avi nodded.

The man smiled and patted his belly and then Avi's shoulder. "I'm Yair. Welcome to our tent city, one of the best in the Land. They call it a transition center now. Did you know that? I met your dad back in the forties. We work together now in the Department of Absorption. Your dad's very respected here. They love him. I love him. Hey, they loved him in the army, too. He listens to these immigrants. That's why they like him. He respects them, never looks down on them. And they know the difference. You should be very proud of your father."

"I am."

"You see those tin huts? They're left over from the First World War. You must have heard of Allenby in school, you know, the British General? His men put these huts up. They serve the purpose. Maybe a little better than tents. Maybe not. Did you know about them?"

"No."

"They all like your father here. He knows the art of getting things done in spite of . . . you know what I'm saying?"

There were tents and tin hovels as far as Avi could see, spaced out as if they occupied every square on a giant chessboard. Nursing mothers were overseeing toddlers and other children. Ten men were praying outside, and most had long side curls and beards. Little girls held hands and sang songs in French and Arabic and other languages Avi didn't recognize. Long lines of laundry hung from pole to pole. A horse-drawn cart was delivering milk to the huts and tents. A blind man was squatting and holding up his open right hand. No one was giving him charity, but Avi guessed it was all the man knew how to do. Another man was using his arms to walk. He had no legs, and his arms were long and strong enough to carry his arched torso just above the ground.

Avi didn't like the prevailing smell. Then he realized it was just the residents' meal preparations that merged together and lingered. It was as pungent as it was exotic. But after a while, he got used to it and decided it might not be so bad after all.

Between the tents were sandy pathways beaten down by foot traffic and accented by an occasional patch of prickly pear. To the West three boys were kicking around an old soccer ball and using sticks to mark off goals on two ends of a makeshift field. Their game ended when two young soldiers approached. The boys stopped playing to greet the soldiers. A few girls came over from the sidelines to greet the soldiers as well. The girls were tanned, energetic, and beautiful, so different looking from their parents, who looked impoverished and drained. Avi had never seen such a contrast between those of enlistment age and their parents.

Yaakov returned and put his hand on Avi's shoulder. "See, Avi? Look at all this. They are the future of Israel. I'm sure I didn't look like much when I stepped off the boat. But they are the future." He smiled. "They are so proud of their soldiers because their soldiers can defend them. Most of these immigrants come from the Middle East, North Africa, and a few from Europe. They suffered very much before they could get here, and what happened to them was horrible. And they all have stories of friends and family that didn't make it. But they will be an important part, a crucial part, of Israel."

Avi nodded. "How long have they been here?"

"Most have been here less than two years. We try to get them into better housing in the development towns as soon as we can. Some stay much longer. Some we can't get to move. They're used to living here and it's free."

"Why would anyone choose to live in a tent or a metal house?"

Yaakov laughed. "It's hard to live this way even for a short time. That's why I want to get these people into real homes as soon as I can. I didn't like living in a tent. Did you know that I lived in one?"

"No. You never said anything."

"You should know that story, too. I hated it and was grateful for it at the same time. We'll get into that soon enough." He laughed again. "I want you to know everything."

Chapter 14
Kibbutz Ma'ayan Baruch, October 7, 1966

Avi

It was Avi's first leave from basic training in the southern desert. He hitchhiked most of the way and took a bus for the last five miles. Wearing his bright new khaki uniform and black beret, he strutted into his kibbutz grounds like a peacock alpha male.

"Well, Avi, you make it? Pilot training?" asked a boy about ten years old.

Avi shook his head. "No. That didn't work out for me."

The boy looked disappointed.

"It's okay," said Avi, smiling. "I'm going to be a tanker. And I'm fine with that. Really. I'm happy."

More teenagers soon surrounded Avi and followed him. "Avi, how tough was it?" one of them asked.

"Did you like it?" came a girl's voice from behind.

"Nice uniform," another boy said while rubbing Avi's sleeve.

"The paratroopers have better colors," the girl said.

"I think pilots have the best," argued another teen.

"Screw what they say, Avi, I think you look cool," said an older kid.

Now that's a smart kid. Avi liked the attention but tried to conceal just how much he liked it. Shouldering his duffle bag, he entered the communal dining room. His mother and his sister, Rena, were at their preferred table by the big window. They stared at Avi as if they had never seen him before. He figured they were no longer seeing a boy, they were seeing a soldier, and that might be unsettling them.

His mother got over it first, rushed over to him, and wrapped him in a tight hug. "Oh, Avi, we've missed you," she said, pulling him toward a chair. "Come, sit down, talk to us."

"Tell us all about it," said Rena. She seemed genuinely friendly and interested. Perhaps she now suddenly saw her annoying older brother as no longer an irritant to be ignored.

"It's fun," he managed with a hint of sarcasm. Their faces wore expressions of pride with a mix of worry and concern. "These new tanks are invincible," he reassured them. "I'm in the safest branch of the army."

Rena rolled her eyes, clearly not buying his story. "I'm sorry, I should've introduced you." She pointed to the girl on her left. "This is my friend Gila. She's from Kibbutz Dan. Gila, meet my big brother, Avi."

"Shalom, Gila."

"Shalom and welcome home," she said. "I really like the tankers' berets."

Avi smiled and nodded.

"I'm seventeen now, so starting army training isn't far away. Can't wait," Gila announced. "So, tell us. Everyone experiences it differently. What's it really like for you?"

"You really want to know? Okay, I'll tell you." Avi sat down. "Well, we had to get used to military discipline quickly. There were more tests in the first month than in a year at school, and a million things to memorize, from emergency procedures to every nut and bolt on a tank."

"Really?"

"No." Avi smiled wide. "I haven't really memorized much. I don't know the terminology yet. Maybe I know a little, like the basics of being a tanker—how to steer and accelerate and fire. Oh, and I looked at some topographic maps. Don't ask what they all mean."

His mother smiled and appeared impressed, but Avi suspected she was just happy to see him. He couldn't help looking over at Gila. She was very pretty. She had long, curly, black hair and blue eyes and a copper tan. Her nose and mouth were a bit larger than average but perfectly chiseled. She had high, prominent cheekbones. He turned away quickly when her eyes caught his gaze. She must have known he'd been staring at her. He noticed she allowed herself a slight smile.

———

The next day, Avi worked in the kibbutz fields at his least favorite assignment, catching bales of hay from someone tossing them to him as he stood on the flatbed. He caught the hay-stock bales and positioned them like bricks. Soon both forearms were dripping blood. *I hate this job.*

That night, he began to think about Gila again. He didn't know anything about her and certainly wasn't going to pump Rena for information. *Hell, just call her.* What's the worst that could happen? Rejection? Who cared? He was a soldier now and fearing rejection seemed juvenile.

He called Gila's kibbutz and left messages, but never heard from her. *Screw it.* But he really didn't want to give up.

———

On his next leave, he hitchhiked directly to Kibbutz Dan. He had been to the kibbutz before to play soccer. He recalled that he had played a good game and his team had won. Someone walking by the main gate directed him to Gila's cottage. He waited on her door stoop about an hour until she came home.

She approached her front door with another young woman and came to an abrupt stop when she saw him. "Shalom," she said. "You are . . ."

"Avi. Rena's brother."

"What are you doing here?" She twirled the edges of her long, dark hair.

"Well, actually, I came to talk to you."

"He came to talk to you," her friend repeated, her tone mischievous. "I'll leave you two alone." She waved to Gila and left with a wide smile.

Gila rolled her eyes but didn't try to stop her friend. She turned to Avi, waiting.

"I left you phone messages," he began.

She shrugged, as if she didn't know anything about phone messages.

"Can we talk?"

"Sure." She opened the door, and they went in and sat on chairs in her bungalow's tight sitting area, even smaller than his room. "Want tea?"

"Please."

She went into the kitchenette, which was separated from the sitting room by a half wall. "So, what do you want to talk about? Is Rena okay? Everything all right?"

"Yes, everyone is fine, thank you. I . . . I just wanted to get to know you better."

"Why?"

"Why? . . . Can I be honest?"

"No, please lie to me," she responded, giggling.

"You're very pretty. You know that already. I'd like to know what kind of person you are."

"Did Rena tell you I just broke up with my boyfriend?"

"I didn't ask Rena anything about you. She doesn't know I'm here. If you had a boyfriend, this is the first I heard of it. I guess that was a risk I was willing to take. But I'm not disappointed to hear you are between boyfriends."

She walked back into the sitting area and handed Avi the cup of tea and a plate of cookies. She sat down. She looked so damn beautiful, more beautiful than before. She had cute little freckles on her nose and prettier eyes than he remembered, and a perfect body that he certainly did remember. And she wasn't seeing anyone else, so he couldn't stop smiling.

"To be honest, I don't think I'm ready to meet anyone or date anyone," she said.

He abruptly lost his smile.

"My boyfriend and I were together for almost a year," she went on. "Thanks for coming out here. But I'm just not ready to date."

Suddenly he was deflated and didn't know what to say. They were uncomfortably silent.

"I like Rena," she said. "We always have a good time together."

She was likely trying to break the quiet by changing the subject. Avi didn't want to talk about his sister. "Listen, we don't have to date until you're ready. How about if we just talk? You know, just to get to know one another. Just talk. Just in case."

"Just in case what?"

"In case one day you'll want to date me. Call it pre-dating preparation."

He thought she might laugh, but all she said was, "I don't think so."

"You're a friend of my sister's. So, you can be a friend to both of us."

"I'm so lucky," she said sarcastically.

"No pressure. Just talk. For instance, umm." He cast around for something to say. "Are you upset about the breakup?"

"Yes, but I'm not comfortable talking about it with anyone, even my friends."

"So, what are you comfortable talking about?"

"You're persistent."

"Thank you."

"That wasn't a compliment. Anyway, I really don't have time now. I must go back to work. Kitchen duty. You know what that's like."

"I do. So . . . when can we talk?"

This time she smiled, and, from that slight involuntary signal, Avi felt his heart thump. After five or six very long seconds, she said, "Tomorrow morning."

"Tomorrow it is. Meet you here?"

"I'll meet you in Kiryat Shmone. At the central bus station. It's close for both of us."

"When?" asked Avi.

"I don't know. When's good for you?"

"Anytime you want."

"Okay, eleven," she said. "The bus pulls in about eleven. Bye now."

Surprised by her abruptness, Avi stood up and turned toward the door. "See you," he said. He left her bungalow and walked quickly down the stone path with the painted white rocks marking the perimeter. Plants bearing beautiful flowers—reds, oranges, blues, and whites—adorned the edgework and complemented the veins of color in the stones. But there were many weeds running between the stones and contrasting with the palette of brightly colored flowers. At that moment, he chose to dwell only on the positives, so he focused on the flowers and ignored the weeds. Things had gone far from perfectly with Gila, but he was optimistic.

On the bus back to kibbutz Ma'ayan Baruch, he stared out the window and thought about Gila. She was reserved, and yet, she'd been willing to see him again. That meant there was hope for him, he thought, while practicing his technique of eating sunflower seeds and spitting out the shells without using his hands.

Avi didn't sleep much that night. He kept thinking about what might develop with Gila.

———

The next day, Avi was up early. He got a ride with Reuven, an older kibbutz friend who managed apple production. Avi arrived in Kiryat Shmone nearly two hours early.

At 11:15, he began to worry. Gila hadn't shown and he wondered if she had changed her mind. Or worse. Perhaps she was playing a sick joke on him, saying she would meet only to leave him hanging for the whole morning. He remembered girls that had bragged about doing that and, for some reason, considered it humorous.

At 11:30, a bus pulled into the stall in front of him. Avi watched the passengers disembarking, and the sixth one to descend was Gila, vibrant and sexy, just as she always was in his pastel fantasies. She was wearing beige shorts and sandals and a tight red shirt that read *Maccabi Beer*. She saw him and allowed herself a big, wonderful smile.

She came over. "Shalom, how's things?"

"Okay, how's things with you?"

"Fine." She offered him a stick of gum and he declined. "Sorry I'm late. I forgot they changed the bus schedule, and the bus doesn't arrive at eleven anymore. Have you been waiting long?"

"No, not long," he lied.

"That's good. I've got some shopping to do, so why don't we just walk awhile? Then I'll have to leave to get the shopping done."

Avi wished he wasn't just an appendage to her shopping trip. "What're you shopping for?"

"A Beatles record and shoes."

"That's the English group?"

"Of course," she said, cringing, as if he had just asked the stupidest question on the planet.

"How about an ice cream?" he suggested.

"Maybe later."

Avi escorted Gila up and down the main street of Kiryat Shmone. She looked into the shops, and he looked at her. When he stood beside her, he felt electricity, an invisible force that was pulling him toward her. He didn't just want to embrace her. He felt an overwhelming and compelling need to take her in his arms and press her body tight against his. He had never experienced such magnetism before. His desire was so strong, he wasn't sure he could suppress it.

"Don't you just love Bob Dylan?" she asked. "I like songwriters that make you think."

"Yeah, he's pretty good." Avi decided he was already in love with Gila.

"Someday I'll travel," said Gila. "Portugal for sure, Spain, Turkey, Africa, and of course America."

"Yeah, I'd like to travel one day. Not now. I've got my life planned for the next three years."

"You seem to really like the army."

"So far, I do. I don't like farming much, so I might like to stay in the army as a career."

"Really?" she asked. "We're both kibbutzniks. Our parents signed up for the Zionist ideal—for Jews to return to the Land and equitably share the fruits of their labor. But you don't like it?"

"There are things I like and things I don't like. I'll see how it goes."

"You've got a lot to figure out, don't you, Private Avi?" She smiled at him. Now he believed he had a chance with her. At least he hoped so.

"Yes, I have a lot to learn about tanks. Have you given any thought to a branch of service?"

"I might like to go into the paratroopers because I like their red berets. Besides, folding parachutes is very important work."

"It is," he agreed. He was tempted to tell her that deciding her branch of service for the red beret was dumb. *She must be joking.*

"But I've no desire to jump out of planes," Gila went on. "I do know a few girls who've jumped. They're really something."

"Want me to join you while you shop?" he asked.

"No, no, I prefer to shop by myself."

Avi felt he was being brushed off and it hurt. *Should I keep trying, or just get back on the bus?*

"Well, Avi, I do want to hear how the rest of your basic training goes."

Did I hear her right? Is it a positive sign or does she just feel a need to fill the silence?

"I know a number of boys in the tanks," she told him. "Maybe you'll run into them. Next time I'll give you their names."

"Yeah. Sure."

She said there'd be a next time as if there's no question! Don't let her see how much you want her.

"I guess I'll go now. When can I see you again?" Avi asked, perhaps a little too anxiously.

She thought for a moment. "How long are you on leave?"

"A few days. But I'll be back in three weeks for Shabbat. Maybe—"

"Shabbat? Why don't you come to my kibbutz for the Sabbath?"

"See you in three weeks, Friday evening." He smiled, waved, and headed back to the bus stop. A moment later, he turned around to catch her entering the record store.

He was no longer afraid she'd reject him. *She was clear she wants to see me at my next visit!* "Yes," he shouted out loud as he clapped his hands. *Could she have been as nervous as me?* Damn, he wanted her so badly, but he had no idea how she felt about him. She was impossible to read. He wasn't the best conversationalist either. He needed to get to know her better. It was the only way to learn what she was all about.

Chapter 15
October 8, 1966

Neal

Neal answered his phone. It was his older sister. "Hi, sis."
"Hello Neal. I . . . I . . ." She was quiet for a moment, then broke down in tears.

"What's going on? You okay?"

No response. Just tears. After a while she said, "I can't talk." More crying.

Neal waited patiently. Then, as her whimpering quieted, he whispered, "It's okay, Deb. When you are ready."

She resumed crying for a short while, then managed, "He died."

"What?"

"Our dad passed away." There were more sniffles. She spoke again but her words were unintelligible. Finally, she said, loud and clear, "Neal, listen, please. Dad is dead. He's gone."

Neal said nothing. He couldn't speak or move, but his mind, his emotions, his memories were ablaze.

His sister broke the quiet. "Sorry, Neal. This is so hard. I just wanted you to know."

"What happened? When did this happen?"

"His heart gave out overnight. You know how bad he's been for a very long time. He was in constant pain. I can't remember when he was healthy. His back was so bad, you know, from what happened in Europe, he couldn't sit up or walk straight or even walk very far. His back was destroyed in the war, probably in the concentration camp. He was a smoker and certainly didn't have a healthy diet. He ate the fattiest junk. He survived the death

103

camps, and that had to take something . . . whatever. And he was overweight. Remember how he hid underground for years in someone's dump? He's gone now. No more pain. No more struggle to survive. He cut the barbed wire and escaped. Now he escaped again. And for the last time."

"How's Mom?"

"You know how she reacts. Every little thing is the end of the world, and this is a big thing. She's in shock. Depressed. I'm serious. We might have to put her in one of those special nursing homes."

"She's taking it bad?"

"Why do you even ask? Of course, she's mortified. Damn it, Neal."

"So, what's next?"

"She can't take care of herself. I'd put her on the phone, but she's not ready. Let me know if you know a good shrink. No, a shrink can't help. We need you here now to help. You hear me? Now! She always responds to you. And we've got to figure out if Mom can stay at home, take care of herself, get outside help, or—I don't know—maybe move her to a good facility."

"Okay, okay. I'll leave tomorrow."

"Fine."

"Anything you need?"

"I can't talk anymore."

Mount Olive Cemetery, Newark, New Jersey, October 12, 1966

"I am Rabbi Gould, the senior rabbi here for Temple Hashalom. Today we will mark the truly inspirational story and the incredible life of one of our congregants, a man who lived and forged an exceptional story in the most terrible time. Yes, his accomplishments, his remarkable heroic life will serve as an inspiration for all of us. I feel honored today to share with you the story of Wilus Chomelstien that his wife and all his children have shared with me. He served the Jewish people and Polish people well, and I am proud to have known him. He volunteered to manage his Polish town during the Nazi occupation. This was an enormous and dangerous responsibility. No one wanted this job. He put his life on the line to save others. And this is only a piece of his story. That's why I feel honored to speak about his life and the examples he set. His family has spent generous amounts of time to help convey for me the extent of what their father did in his lifetime and how he saved lives. He stood up to the Nazis despite their threats to kill him. After their town was emptied, he was put in a concentration camp where he managed somehow to find something that could cut fence wire, and he used it to open the fencing, enabling hundreds of people to escape. Yes, that's what made him a celebrated hero. And that's how he met his lovely wife.

"Escaping from these camps was unheard of. What he accomplished was also unheard of. That makes it remarkable. He came to our country with nothing and couldn't speak a word of English. But he overcame all that. And he became a respected member of our community, a respected union employee, and, eventually, he held an important position in the union. And, of course, he was a loving family man. This is the man we are putting to rest today."

The rabbi stopped for a moment and nodded to the row where the immediate family was sitting. Everyone could hear crying and the rabbi waited a moment for the tears to subside.

Then he continued. "While in the concentration camp, he figured out how to acquire one of the Germans' wire cutters. Then, day by day, little by little, so it wasn't noticed, he cut away at the barbed wire until he could make an escape. And many people made that escape successfully with him because of the action he took. Yes, he saved lives. Some who were saved I think are here today with us. He had a friend that hid him and his lovely wife and others for years. Yes, these very brave and daring friends were extraordinary people, too, real heroes who put their own family, their own lives in danger. Why? Because it was the right thing to do."

Neal's mother and sisters were crying. There seemed to be tears everywhere. Tears ran down Neal's cheeks, too. He managed to remain silent while wiping his cheeks with his handkerchief.

Yes, he was a rock, albeit an angry rock. And he missed his old man. He wanted to get even. He was angry with himself. He never gave his father the respect the man deserved. Now, finally, he appreciated him, but it was too late to share his appreciation. He had been an ass to his father. He understood that now. But it was too late.

He wanted to hurt the Bikel brothers. He wanted to hurt them the way he was hurting. No—even more than he was hurting.

Chapter 16

Negev Junction, Israel, November 14, 1966

Avi

A vi went back to the army, and everything felt different. He couldn't help thinking about Gila. He imagined she was with him everywhere, enabling him to silently share his feelings with her, including opinions on everyone and everything.

He received a letter from his cousin Jonathan who requested Avi write about every detail of army training. Avi couldn't do that, but he was still happy to get Jonathan's letters. He enjoyed hearing about Jonathan's college experiences, which seemed like life on another planet, and they helped him improve his English. He was getting less and less dependent on the dictionary.

Avi's training included the requisite maneuvers in the desert of Revivim, under what might be the harshest sun and in the driest heat in the world. He gingerly climbed onboard a tank that felt like a frying pan and lowered himself inside. The heat by the entrance hit like an invisible wall, requiring him to take deep, slow breaths as he adjusted.

Yoam, his bearded, burly commander, routinely barked, "I order you to become the best damn tank crew in the company or I'll break your asses."

Avi and his fellow tankers practiced daily maneuvers, each of them performing their roles so the tank became a powerful and coordinated weapon. The entire company of tanks moved like a choreographed dance company.

Avi was assigned to water down and rake the tent area at night. He had to carry water and gasoline in large jugs, which he held under his arms. Finally, exhausted, it was time to sleep. But first he pictured a certain woman in north Galilee. He couldn't wait for his next leave.

Upper Galilee, December 7, 1966

Avi anxiously packed up for the short visit. But on the long ride to the north, he had doubts. Gila had sent mixed signals on their date. Was it all wishful thinking on his part? Was he setting himself up to be hurt?

When he arrived at her kibbutz, Gila was waiting for him at the bus stop. That was a positive sign. She greeted him with a quick kiss on his cheek. "How was the ride?"

"It seemed like it took forever," he said.

Gila laughed. "Well, I'm glad you're here. I was beginning to forget what you looked like."

"I'm here. How do I look?"

She pretended to examine his face. "Oh yes, I remember you now."

"Good, because I forgot what I looked like."

"Oh, I told my parents we'd come by. I need to borrow their iron. It'll only take a few minutes."

"Fine." Did she want her parents to meet him? That was another good sign. "Wait. I brought you something. A little gift." He reached into his backpack.

"For me?"

"For you. Hope you like it." He handed her the thin rectangular paper-wrapped package.

"What could . . ." She tore back the paper wrapping. "A Beatles record. Thank you. I love them."

"I'm told it is new—just came out."

"How sweet. Thank you so much. What a nice gesture."

Avi smiled wide.

"Really, so thoughtful," Gila said. "We'll listen to it later. Let's go borrow the iron."

"Let's do that."

They walked for fifteen minutes to the other side of the kibbutz where the older generations were housed.

Her father stood up and shook Avi's hand, said "Shabat shalom," and offered him a glass of wine. Avi declined the wine, and Gila's father quickly returned to the couch so as not to miss the soccer action on an Arabic channel.

"Nice to meet you," Gila's gray-haired mother said while extending a tray of little pastries and cookies. Avi could see that Gila's good looks clearly came from her mother. He wondered where her parents had come from; he didn't recognize their accents.

Twenty minutes later, Gila thanked her mother for the iron, and Avi thanked her parents for the pastries. Then they headed back to Gila's bungalow. Avi hoped she might be ready to move beyond "just talking".

Gila put on the Beatles album and sat on the couch while Avi remained standing by the door.

"There's an American movie at the cinema," said Avi. "I've heard it's good. Want to go tomorrow?"

"Tomorrow?"

"I don't know when I'll get my next leave—so tomorrow is all I have for a while."

"Then tomorrow it'll have to be," Gila said, smiling and turning her head in such a way that made him laugh. He wanted to hold her and kiss her all over.

He sat beside her on the couch. He attempted to put an arm around her shoulder, but she carefully guided it downward and took his hand. "Not so fast, private," she teased.

Being close to her and holding her hand excited Avi. So, he changed the subject, trying to act as cool as she was. "Your parents have a slight accent. Where are they from?"

"Portugal. Where are your parents from?"

"My father from Poland, my mother from Iraq."

"Of course, Rena told me. Nice combination. When did they make *aliyah*?"

"My mother came to Israel around 1940, my father after the war and some time in Italy."

"Your mother was in Iraq until 1940? And your father was in Europe during the Second World War? They went through a lot."

109

"My mother told me details of what her family had to endure in Iraq. My father told me some of what he and his brother went through in Poland. He was one of the few that sometimes worked away from the kibbutz with new immigrants. And the immigrants loved him. And he respected them. They liked that he had once lived in a tent, like the way they were living."

"And you could see the pride in their faces despite how they were living," added Gila. "Am I right?"

Avi nodded. "So now I realize why those people were so kind to me. They were not happy with the way most government workers managed them, but I was the son of Yaakov. I felt proud, welcomed, even honored. It was a special feeling."

"I understand, Avi. Very nice."

"When did your parents come?"

She tilted her head. Then her eyes scanned the ceiling while she twisted the ends of her hair. "I think '37. Yes, 1937."

"From where?

"Portugal. A major port city called Porto. Heard of it? It's supposed to have a beautiful river front."

Avi shook his head. "No, never heard of it."

"A very interesting story. Do you know Jewish history?"

Avi shrugged. "What my father taught me, and what I learned in school."

She laughed. "I bet you know more about sports."

"Tel Aviv won yesterday's match, three to one."

She laughed again. "It's okay. Boys love sports. But I love history . . . our history."

"So, what happened in Porl—"

"Porto," she corrected with a grin. "Well, in the middle of the Depression, with anti-Semitism growing all over the world, Captain Barros Basto—a famous guy, you know him?"

"No."

"He was a decorated veteran, well known in Portugal. His mother was Catholic, his father was descended from secret Jews. Anyway, he was able to get the secret Marranos to come forward and openly celebrate their Judaism. He founded a synagogue for Marranos in Porto. I believe he converted to Judaism."

"Marranos. They were still around in the 1930s?"

"Believe it or not, there are Marrano communities even today."

"I thought they disappeared a long time ago during the Inquisition, or something."

"Most did disappear for one reason or another. But some real stubborn ones held out. Like my family. We were secret Jews in Portugal. It was the captain—Captain Basto—who encouraged the Marranos to come out and publicly practice Judaism."

"Your family survived as secret Jews for generations?"

She laughed. "We weren't the only ones. Anyway, the first synagogue the captain built was on the second floor above a store. But as more and more Jews came forward, Captain Basto was able to raise money from around the world to build a beautiful, large synagogue. At the time the Nazis were burning synagogues, one was being built for a forgotten community of secret Jews."

"How many Jews were there in Porto?"

"I don't know. No one really knows because they're secret. But I read an estimate that there were about ten thousand across Portugal and in the mountain region closer to the border with Spain."

"Then what happened?"

"Certain authorities set out to undermine his efforts. The secret Jews went back to being secret again. But not all. That's when my family came to Palestine. We made it." She smiled and looked up at Avi.

"You certainly made it. Stiff-necked and stubborn—like the Biblical description."

"Funny thing is, we don't light the candles or go to synagogue now. We held on to those rituals for hundreds of years under the most difficult of circumstances, but not in the Land." She paused and looked in his eyes. "Strange, don't you think?"

"Living here makes it all right," Avi said, gently touching her shoulder. "You're living the freedom that your ancestors could only dream of. And that includes living any way you see fit. All those stiff-necked people that came before you only had religion to connect them to their history. They're all looking to you now."

"Ah, not a problem, I can handle it. Doesn't everybody in Israel have a story? Your parents have a story, my parents have a story. Who knows, maybe one day you'll have a story to tell your children."

Avi shrugged. That seemed very unlikely. But he did know for sure that he wanted Gila very much.

Then, unexpectedly, Gila leaned over and kissed him lightly on the lips. He quickly responded to her kiss by pressing his lips to hers and putting his arms around her back and pulling her body tight against him. This time it wasn't a dream. She was kissing him back! Now he knew she really did want him.

New Jersey, December 15, 1966

Jonathan

Jonathan studied the chess board before him. He reached to rub his cheek and then his nose, then scratched his scalp. He moved his knight, smiled, and announced, "Your turn, Mr. Sayyid."

"I know your convention, Mr. Jonathan. I know this trap." Mahmud moved a bishop.

Jonathan ignored his chess opponent's attempt to engage him. *He wants me to abort my strategy. Should I? No way.* Jonathan moved his queen and looked up from the chess board. "You do know your chess, Mahmud. I see that. By the way, I'm new to this chess club. You like it?"

Mahmud nodded.

"You have an accent, Mr. Sayyid. Lebanese?"

"Jordan. Where are you from?"

"New Jersey. Heard of it?"

Mahmud laughed and moved his rook. "No. Never heard of it."

"Yes, Mr. Sayyid. That's a good move. And yes, I am a local." *Sure, I have many acquaintances here from high school, but they're all so quirky.*

Jonathan noticed that Mahmud was slightly shorter and maybe a bit heavier than he was, but otherwise Mahmud could easily have been taken as his brother.

This Mahmud is a smart and strategic player. I must take him seriously. Jonathan recalled their first match when Mahmud had opened with a strategy he had never seen before. It was an opening with more use of pawns than any other convention he

113

had seen. He recalled how he had assumed the strategy was a weakness and had expected an easy win. Instead, he had played right into Mahmud's trap. *Can't let that happen again.*

"By the way, where did you get this opening, you used now?" asked Jonathan.

"I developed it."

At the end of the game, hyper-focused and afraid he might lose, Jonathan managed to come back and gain the upper hand. But Mahmud deprived him of victory by eking out a stalemate.

———

On a rainy Tuesday afternoon after most classes were finished for the day, Jonathan was meeting Susan Stone in the student union. She was a psych major having trouble with her requirement in statistics. "Simple stuff, really," Jonathan mumbled quietly to himself as he pushed open the doors. *And she ain't bad looking either.*

Susan was sitting in a lounge chair and appeared restless. Perhaps she had been waiting a long time?

"Sorry I'm late," Jonathan explained as he approached. "Had a meeting that went overtime." He didn't want to admit he was so engrossed in a math problem that he had lost track of time. He dragged a chair over and sat down next to her and looked at the problem she was trying to solve. She didn't make him nervous. She was with him only for help in math. Nothing to get nervous about.

"Are you Jewish, Jonathan?"

"Yes."

"Thought so. Me, too. But my family and I don't observe, you know, the religious stuff."

"I don't go to synagogue much either, but my parents are observant and keep kosher. I do Friday night dinner with them."

"Interesting." She sighed and held out her textbook, pointing to a problem that was stumping her. He scanned the text quickly. "Listen, Susan, the unknown, or X, is the number of samples you need in order to be assured of the result to a degree of ninety-five percent certain."

"Jon, can you go a little slower—I mean a lot slower. I mean baby steps."

"Sure." He started again. "It's all about how many samples are needed before you can draw reasonable conclusions that are likely to be correct, that is, within an acceptable margin of error. In that table, they're saying a margin of error of five percent is acceptable. So, if you wanted to win in a poker game, a hand that'd win ninety-five percent of the time might be good enough, right? However, if it was a protocol for a serious medical condition, you'd likely need more, like ninety-nine percent or higher."

Susan smiled wide. It was as if he had turned on a light bulb over her head. "Is that what it means? Okay, let's do this next problem. No, let me do it. I think I can do it now. For true." For some reason she preferred "for true" over "for sure."

"Go ahead. Give it a try, and I'll watch."

Susan got the next two problems right without assistance. She stumbled on the third, but Jonathan steered her in the right direction.

"Got it," she cheered. She smiled wide. "Hey, maybe I'm going to survive this class after all, at least enough to get by." She frowned suddenly. "Or maybe not. Hey, all I need is for you to sit by me while I take the exam. What do you think?"

"You'll do fine. When is the big test?"

"Wednesday. Oh, my God, that's so soon. Maybe I should ask for an extension?"

"Oh, you've plenty of time to study," Jonathan said as he stood up.

Susan looked up at Jonathan, and something in her expression changed. She was smiling but also gazing into his eyes, as if trying to understand who he was. This flattered him and made him uncomfortable at the same time. He stood there, not knowing what to say. He kept shifting his weight from one foot to the other and crossed his arms tightly against his chest.

"Well, I guess I should be going now," he managed while looking at his wrist where his watch would have been had he not forgotten to wear his watch. He realized he didn't really want to go.

"Jonathan, thank-you sooo much. I could never have gotten this stuff without your help. For true."

"Well, I'm just glad I could help. You're really a good student. You're open to learning and open to the material. You've got the ability to handle it. You'll do fine for sure. Or for true . . . whatever."

"I don't get how anyone can major in math. It's so hard. I think you're a genius. Normal people can't do this. Really. I'm not kidding."

Jonathan chuckled shyly and didn't say anything. Susan had lost the look of desperation. She was relaxed and happy and now looked very pretty.

Jonathan removed his black-framed glasses. He folded them and put them in his shirt pocket.

"Can I do another problem?" asked Susan. "Do you have time?"

"Sure," Jonathan said, sitting down beside her again.

She chose problems similar to the ones she had just solved. Jonathan couldn't help watching her while she worked. She looked up at him, caught his gaze and smiled, and returned to her textbook. Jonathan felt foolish when she caught his obvious stare. But she didn't seem to mind. He relaxed.

She finished the problems and checked the answers at the end of the chapter. "I got them right," she said, sounding amazed, and raised both arms in the shape of a V.

"Congratulations. And you did it without my help. Good for you." He stood up again and looked automatically at his naked wrist. "Well, I've really got to go now. Good luck on the test."

"Thank you. You are a great tutor. You should think about becoming a professor someday. Really."

"See you."

"Bye." While glancing at her watch, she muttered, "Oh no," and quickly grabbed her books.

"Where are you off to?" Jonathan asked.

"I'm late for a meeting," she said. "Got to go."

"What kind of meeting?"

"It's the SDS."

Jonathan had never heard of the group and couldn't resist one more question. "What do they do?"

She flashed him that luminous and now-familiar smile. "Today we're making plans to take over the Administration Building."

She rushed out of the Student Center before he could say another word.

———

"Pass the salt," he requested after his mother lit the candles and Lazer concluded the ritual blessings. His father promptly handed over the salt while asking, "Anything interesting today?"

"No," Jonathan said, very much aware he was thwarting his father's attempt to engage him.

His mother could talk with or without a conversational partner.

"They say you forget as you get older," Malka mumbled. "They say getting old . . . the survivors, they . . . everything is coming back, but they don't have much to live with—"

"Malka, not the Holocaust again," Lazer interrupted.

"I don't mind," Jonathan said. "Say whatever you need to say."

"Sometimes I am eating, and I remember everything," Malka said, leaning back and away from the table. "I remember I got through this. And now the only thing I am asking, one question: why, why all my friends, why they disappeared? And what did I do, something good, or maybe something bad because I was pretty then, and they let me live as a slave to the soldiers' needs. I'm not going to get into this because you are young. I don't want to disturb you. The young generation doesn't want to listen. I'm not going to talk about Holocaust no more. Your father doesn't like it."

"Mom, it's okay."

The three continued eating their dinner silently.

Malka started again. "Hitler said the Jewish people must be exterminated. You hear Nasser say the same now. It's happening all over again. Now Jewish people are still shrinking."

"You mean the population of Jews is shrinking?" asked Jonathan.

"Malka, please, we've heard it all before," Lazer said.

"Mom, I heard it before, but your talking about it doesn't upset me. I figure, if you need to talk about it, then talk. I really don't mind. I learned a lot in Israel from Yaakov and Liza. Dad, I learned from you, too. I want to know more about Mom's life."

"Okay," Lazer said, shrugging, and scooped up a spoonful of applesauce. "Welcome to the famous Bikel learning center. Yes, that's us, the learned Bikels."

Malka resumed her telling. "They put in Auschwitz, children. I saw that they chased the Jews, you know, and they put them on the wagon, you know, and the people didn't know there was an Auschwitz."

"Mom, we're lucky to be in the United States. No one is making up stories about Jews being subhuman, no racial laws. No one is accusing Jews of bad things, of using Christian blood for matzah or killing Christ. We have religious freedom. No group parades with anti-Semitic signs, chanting bad things about Jews. You now live in the United States, land of the free. All that can't ever, ever happen again."

But Malka continued as if she hadn't heard her son. "They came to the house, they killed, and nobody wanted to kill me. Many times they caught me. They had their fun with me. One Gestapo caught me, it was snowing, and I said, 'If you are going to kill me, do it now. I don't want to go in the cemetery and take off my clothes. You should kill me here.' He said, all right, he'd find me tomorrow. Because in the cemetery there are a few hundred people in one grave. They sometimes shot them, and they were still alive on the second day. I feel faint when I hear the bad aggravations from Israel. There are so many survivors there in Israel, your father's brother's family. Thank God, I have a son. Some survivors couldn't have children. I think God didn't want the Jewish people. If he would want it, he would not do it like this. Ohhh. Jewish people, they treated them worse than animals."

Malka stood up and retrieved the dishes and silverware and quietly, with care, washed them in the sink.

Jonathan followed Lazer to the living room and watched him pick up his violin.

"Jon, tell me, how does one get music out of this violin thing?" Lazer asked as he lifted his violin up in the air with his left hand.

"Just blow on the handle?" answered Jonathan as he and Lazer laughed together.

Lazer played Shubert's Concerto in D Major, one of his favorite pieces. Jonathan's favorite was his father's interpretation of Shubert's Fantasy in C. His father played with the technical agility of a gymnast and the soul of a poet. Lazer was also a supportive and patient teacher, but Jonathan was sure his dad was much more demanding of him than his other students. Jonathan had accepted long ago that he didn't have the requisite talent to play the instrument beyond a mediocre level. He could never expect to play like his father. Yet, when he heard the sweet hypnotic strains of the instrument in the hands of a capable master like his dad, he couldn't help feeling a tug of regret. But he knew he had other talents.

Chapter 18

The Revivim Desert, Israel, May 19, 1967

Avi

The desert night was oddly windy and quiet and tar black but for the unobstructed speckling from countless stars. It was deceptively innocent at a time Avi knew his first tank battle was imminent. He wanted to sleep. He might not have the luxury of sleep for quite a while. Lying wide-eyed in the tent, he couldn't help recalling Egypt's President Nasser successfully maneuvering to evict the UN "peacekeeping" force from the Sinai border and at the same time pledging to drive the Jews into the sea. Avi was infuriated by the blockade of the port city of Eilat, and by the newspaper photos of hate-filled crowds celebrating with shouts of, "Death to the Jews."

He fell asleep.

He opened his eyes at dawn, grateful for a few hours of sleep. Later, as the temperature peaked for the day, Avi was standing and sweating in desert sand, and at attention in full battle gear. The entire battalion stood in rows for inspection as Prime Minister Eshkol and his entourage paraded before them. The Prime Minister stopped in front of Avi and asked something in Yiddish. Avi didn't understand, but an aide quickly translated into Hebrew, "Are you prepared, young man? Do you know what needs to be done?"

"All of us are very confident and know we will win. We've trained hard and know our jobs." Avi spoke with authority, belying his own nervous anticipation.

At day's end, as Avi and his fellow tankers sat beside their tank, his friend, Eli, announced, "Minister Eshkol is telling

Dayan, right now, not to worry—Bikel knows that everything will be fine. Just a walk in the park."

"Go fuck a camel," said Avi, now embarrassed by his earlier pretense.

"Eshkol is so relieved after hearing from Bikel, he decided to take his vacation now," said Yoam.

"The papers are calling Bikel the new military expert. He knows everything there is to know about tank strategy," added another voice from behind the tank.

Avi knew it was all good-natured bluster, but he had to respond. "Have you guys had enough fun yet? What else could I tell him? That we don't know what we're doing, so please put me with another crew?"

Everyone laughed, including Avi. A part of him felt embarrassment over his reassurances; another part was confident he had delivered what Eshkol had needed to hear.

As the crew ate dinner alongside their tank, a truck pulled up. "Hey, wake up. Got something," shouted the driver. "Egyptians used gas in Yemen. You might need these gas masks," the truck driver explained impatiently. "Let's go, ladies, I have to deliver them to every tank on the line."

Twenty minutes later someone passed around a champagne bottle. The entire tank crew signed the bottle label after taking a healthy swig. Avi looked at the signatures randomly scribbled in all directions over the label and imagined he'd arrange for his crew to rendezvous for better vintage after the war.

Time advanced quickly, and now everyone was settling into their chosen sleeping spot under the stars. It was still warm for midnight, but a chill was imminent. If he were with Gila, Avi would've loved being in the desert, enjoying nature's display of countless brilliant stars without a hint of cloud or obstruction. She'd call it romantic and smile at him. He missed her.

Someone started to sing an old peace song. Avi remembered most of the lyrics. *What's the title? Who is singing? Eli is. Not a bad voice.* Eli sang quietly into an empty night, into nature's perfect setting, with lyrics of yearning and finding an elusive peace. His voice filled the star-studded void as if in a dream. Another tanker began to accompany Eli. A few minutes later, everyone was singing, even Avi, though he could hardly carry a tune.

June 5, 1967

Avi's tank was positioned at the edge of the eucalyptus groves. He looked up to the bluest of skies, cloudless but for one lonely white puff that seemed to float by especially fast, as if the heavens were impatient. Avi rested on top of his tank, hoping to steal a quick break. It could be quite some time before the next one.

An hour later, the siren went off, jolting everyone to action. Five Israeli jets flew over, breaking the sound barrier. Avi took his position as the tank driver on the lower level to the left of the cannon. He looked through the narrow view port, steered the tank out of the groves, and headed west, leading a column of Sherman and Patton tanks. He liked the fact that they were the only tank in the column permitted, for safety reasons, to drive with a "ready round" positioned in the canon. With the tanks behind him, Avi steered past an infantry battalion that split ranks to create an opening for the tankers. The infantry cheered as the tanks passed by.

"This is like a parade," shouted Eli cheerfully from his position as machine gunner on Avi's right. Avi laughed, as did the gunner seated above him who was responsible for the big cannon. It was a nervous laugh.

"Stop it," bellowed Yoam from just below the main hatch. "This is no joke. We're leading a dozen tanks. Keep focused or some ace Egyptian will incinerate all of us."

"Yes, sir." Avi steered across irrigated farmland that belonged to a border kibbutz and continued west toward Gaza, which he knew was the most densely populated part of Egypt bordering Israel.

Ten minutes into Egyptian territory, Avi saw chips of paint flying off his tank. He couldn't hear well over the tank engine and tread grinding. His tankers returned the fire while Avi kept the tank moving forward.

Avi was energized. Adrenaline was flowing.

Now Avi slowed his tank. Directly blocking them was a thick stand of prickly pear cactus that towered over them. The only opening was carpeted with piles of branches and metal debris. He drove over it anyway, confident the tank tread would be unaffected.

Avi heard a big blast, and the controls shook in his hands. He swallowed hard. "One of our tanks hit a mine," Yoam yelled. "Keep it rolling, Avi. Don't slow down."

Two little Arab kids jumped out from behind the cactus. They were right in Avi's path. It was clear they were innocents who'd made a big mistake. Their mother, wearing a full black niqab with two tiny slits for her eyes, came out screaming after them. Avi couldn't stop the tank or slow it down, but he pulled to the side as much as possible. The mother waved her arms and shrieked as she ran to the children. She picked up the younger one first, then grabbed the other by the neck of his shirt and dragged them behind the prickly pear.

After he passed the children, Avi spotted a few Egyptian infantrymen. Eli opened fire. A *tat-tat-tat* reverberated throughout the interior, and Avi kept the tank advancing. A few kilometers farther, Avi rode by a row of small shanty homes. An Egyptian soldier stepped out from one of the homes and began walking toward Avi's tank. As soon as he saw the Star of David, the soldier turned fast, dropped his rifle, and ran back behind the houses. No one fired at him.

Now Avi was in an urban area and enemy fire came at them from all directions. Avi's tank came alongside a deep trench, presumably full of enemy troops, and his crew opened their hatches and tossed grenades into the trench. He could smell the fire and smoke. He saw one Egyptian manage to toss a grenade at Avi's tank. Someone closed the hatch. There was a loud explosion as the grenade fell far forward of their path. Avi drove through the residual smoke.

Soon Avi's tank reached a dirt road, and he could accelerate faster. Most of the shanties were flying white flags.

Avi's crew came upon another trench. This time the enemy jumped out and ran. Eli fired at them.

"Enemy T-34 to the right," yelled Yoam. "Fast! Hit it, damn it!" The Russian-made T-34 was already in position to fire.

The T-34 exploded, and metal and shrapnel rained against Avi's right side, forcing his tank to tilt for a few seconds. His heart was in his throat. Another Israeli tank behind him had taken out the enemy T-34.

At the next trench position, Yoam instructed the gunner to fire the cannon. The tank rocked as the cannon extended and discharged its projectile. The blast destroyed the anti-aircraft guns and equipment behind the trench. Avi felt a surge of relief.

The tankers opened the hatch and looked south. There were hundreds of Egyptian infantry on foot fleeing into the Sinai sand. They had taken off their boots and thrown away their rifles. They were heading to the high sand dunes where it would be difficult for tanks to follow them. Others were surrendering, apparently aware that captivity was better than exposure in the desert. Many silos of black smoke funneled skyward.

Yoam yelled out, "We're changing course. The paratroopers need armored help."

Avi's tank now headed southwest toward the coast. They approached a burned-out Israeli personnel carrier on the road. Just behind it, Israeli soldiers were pinned down in the brush. One of them yelled out, "Enemy tanks!" while pointing straight ahead. Avi's tank moved ahead but at a slower speed.

Soon there were explosions all around. Avi stopped as Yoam ordered the gunners to fire the cannon. Eli was using the machine gun. Their projectile took out an enemy tank. Avi could see it and hear it explode. A flash of flames engulfed the entire enemy tank.

"Keep at it. Keep firing. No letup!" screamed Yoam at the top of his lungs. The team kept firing and destroyed another one. And the gunners kept loading and firing like a machine.

"Avi, move it up twenty, thirty meters on the right shoulder," Yoam yelled.

An earsplitting blast shook the whole tank. Avi fell to the floor. His chest hurt like hell. His tank had been hit by something.

Smoke everywhere. He couldn't breathe. He couldn't hear. He was coughing and rubbing his aching chest.

Avi saw Eli lying on the floor beside his seat. He wasn't moving. Avi looked up toward the main hatch, but the whole area was smoking. *God, —the poor gunners. Poor Yoam. Are they okay? Not likely.*

Shit! The left side was quickly filling with smoke. *Got to get out or . . . can't breathe.* Everything he touched was flaming hot. He gasped for air but only breathed in more smoke.

He tried to make his way to his hatch, but it didn't open. He was trapped. He fell back to the floor. *Can't breathe.* He touched the gold chain around his neck. It was supposed to be good luck.

He gave up. It was hopeless. He was bleeding from the fall. He thought of his parents, his sister. He found a rag on the floor and wrapped it over his head and secured it with his helmet. It reduced the smoke, and he could breathe better. He remembered his father and his tenacity. Could he be like Yaakov? He pictured Gila. He could sense her presence inside the tank with him. "Fight hard," she told him. "Fight for me. You have more in you. Push harder."

And then his father's voice commanded, "Now's the time to show what you're made of. Take the flames. Don't fear them. Take the fire or die." Avi crawled up toward the main hatch, pushed through the flames to the hatch, and opened it. He screamed as he was being burned. He couldn't take the flame any longer and fell to the floor. He coughed hard. He tried to suck in air, but mostly inhaled smoke. He choked. *Can't breathe. It's . . . it's impossible.*

But the hatch was now open, and smoke was escaping. He knew the reprieve wouldn't last as the flames were beginning to consume everything combustible, including the dead. He heard escalating cannon fire, blast overlapping blast, and he realized the rest of the battalion was in a firefight and weren't concerned with him or his tank.

"One more try," his imaginary Gila told him. "Remember, I'm waiting for you and I love you."

The pain in his chest was still sharp. He was burned badly, making it harder to move. He rewrapped the rag around his head and went through the flames again. He screamed as his flesh burned. He was sure he was about to die, but somehow his hands managed to hold on and lift him up. It occurred to him that an

Egyptian sniper could be waiting for him, ready to shoot as soon as he emerged from the hatch. But there was no other option. He pushed himself out as fast as he could.

Chapter 19

Beersheba Hospital, Beersheba, Israel, June 12, 1967

Avi

Avi woke up in a hospital bed, bandaged from his neck down. "Where am—"

"Don't worry. You're in Beersheba. You're in good hands." It was a woman's voice, or so he thought. *From where?*

"How long?" he asked.

"You came in this morning. They scrubbed this place thoroughly." He could see her now. She said, "Without doubt, it's now the cleanest floor of the hospital."

Sometime later, he woke up again from a deep, drug-induced sleep. He tried to remember what had happened. He guessed he had lost consciousness after coming out of the hatch. He remembered seeing men lying on stretchers; some had giant Xs on their foreheads, and there were many medics. He remembered hearing doctors discuss how they should handle the next wave of wounded. He recalled seeing an IV bag hanging on a tree branch above him. He looked around the ward and there were no trees. *Must have happened before I got to this place.* He remembered a doctor struggling to find a spot where his flesh wasn't burned to insert the needle. He remembered being in a helicopter. He tried unsuccessfully to remember more. He remembered thinking he had died and was surrounded by angels.

He realized his gold chain was missing. *Did I lose it? Oh, no.*

He now realized he had tubes attached, and he quickly became aware of the antiseptic smell and the groans coming from other beds in a large ward, which was painted green and blue and white. A nurse, or maybe she was an aide, said, "I see you are awake now. Welcome to the Burn Unit, which until yesterday was the Maternity Unit."

Two days later, a doctor came by and spoke in a soft, friendly tone while reviewing papers on a clipboard. "Welcome back, Avi. You've been sleeping for a long time. I'm Svi." The doctor took off his wire-rimmed glasses. "This hospital wing is very clean," he explained. "You see, burn victims are the most vulnerable to infection. We'll take good care of you here. We've brought in staff that has lots of experience with burns."

Avi tried to nod, but the motion hurt.

"You'll be going for skin grafts when you're stronger. We will take little healthy pieces of skin from your bottom and legs and place them where you're missing the most skin. It'll take time, I'm afraid."

"What's happening in the war?" Avi's throat felt raw, and his voice came out as a rasp.

"It just ended. Only six days. Can you imagine? We will not be pushed into the sea. We owe so much to you young boys. The whole nation is proud of you—and very grateful. So, we'll take good care of you."

"Thank . . ."

"You'll be here awhile. These things take time. After the surgeries—"

"Surgeries?"

"Then we'll also give you what they call a *jobe*. It presses on the skin, so it heals flat. That way it'll look almost normal."

"Almost? My face, is it . . ."

"You were lucky. Just little scars. No worries there. Most of them will heal perfectly without needing medical intervention. You'll still drive the girls crazy."

Avi pressed a finger against his left cheek and felt a bandage just below and in front of his ear. *Will I look like a freak? Will I still have a chance with Gila?* "My chain that my father gave me, the gold chain I had around my neck, it's—"

"Don't worry. We have it. We had to remove it."

"You have it?"

"That happens all the time. You have more important things to worry about—like surgery."

"Doctor, I wonder if you can do something for me."

"Of course. What is it?"

"Take the damn tube out of my penis."

Uri smiled. "Soon."

"Please. I don't need it. It's very annoying."

"Okay, after all you've been through, if that's your only complaint, well, maybe we can give it a try. I'll tell the nurse."

The next morning, a pretty nurse, a few years older than Avi, came by his bed. "I have heard that you made a request?"

"I did."

"Are you ready?"

"Please."

She gently removed the catheter.

At night, when the ward was filled with cries and moans, Avi's pain was the worst. His pain medication was running low, and the hospital staff was small. He felt as if his skin was still on fire. He was ready to give up. *My God, please help. I feel like I'm still in the flames. Someone, please.*

"Help me," he finally shouted out loud. Someone heard him and gave him something to swallow. He was grateful as he fell into a deep, benevolent sleep.

At dawn, a voice in the bed to his right asked, "What happened to you?"

"Tanker. Got hit in Gaza. You?"

"Golani Brigade. I was a gunner in a half-truck that charged the Syrians on their hill. We got creamed, but our infantry flanked them, got into their bunkers. The Syrians had to fight to the death. They were chained to their posts."

"Your unit took direct fire just to support the flanking movement? You were the diversion?"

"It worked. We took the Golan. They call it the battle of Tel Fakher."

Avi turned on his right side to better see who he was talking to, but the poor bastard had white bandages all over his body and face.

The doctor had been right about the catheter: it was too soon to remove it. It wasn't long before he felt like his bladder was about to burst. "Please put the damn thing back. You were right. I can't stand the pressure."

Vered was the name of the nurse that was assigned to insert a new catheter, and she wasn't as gentle as the other nurse. "Why did you take it out?" she scolded.

"It hurt. But not as much as you're hurting me now."

"Stop moving. You're making it difficult."

The next day, two senior officers from Avi's division showed up. Avi had never met them, but he had heard them once speak to the brigade. The bald one said, "Avi, you are going to be awarded the Distinguished Service Medal, the third-highest medal. You and your battalion performed very well."

"What did I do? I just got burned up when my tank got hit."

"You were in the lead tank of your column. You led a successful advance and eliminated the enemy in your way. You deserve this. Your nation wants to tell you they appreciate what you did."

"My fellow tankers are dead."

"They also will get the medal. Perhaps it will help their families. We can't bring them back."

Avi wondered if he was getting this medal just to help the families of those who had died. Would these chunks of brass really matter to Eli's parents? To Yoam's wife?

It took a few more days before Avi no longer felt like he was on fire. Then Nurse Vered was assigned to remove his face bandage. "Can I touch the skin now?" he asked.

"Touch all you want," she said.

He felt a slight rise from a scar in his cheek but was relieved it was small. That was good. "Can I see it? Do you have a mirror?"

"Look, soldier, this isn't a beauty parlor," said Vered. "You're fine. You're worried about a little scar? I've got patients with serious wounds, life and death wounds." She left his bedside.

Avi ran his fingers over his new beard. The hair felt strange, as did his facial scar. He touched the bandages covering his chest and thighs. These were not small bandages, and it was sinking in just how disfigured his body would appear for the rest of his life. He wondered if Gila, or any woman, could love a man with this hideous scarring.

———

Two days later, he had four visitors: his parents, sister, and Gila. The hospital dressed them in white sanitized covers and made them wear hospital masks. Yaakov and Liza approached his hospital bed slowly. Rena and Gila stayed back.

He heard his mother gasp in horror as she approached. "Oh, Avi," she murmured, and then tried to steady herself. "Avi, I'm so proud of you. You're a hero."

"Why? All I did was get blown up in my tank."

"Your commander told me all about it," Yaakov said. "It's in the papers, too. I knew they were talking about your battalion. You did so much. You were in the leading tank, were you not? That is something . . . yes? I am very proud of you. We, everyone, we are proud of you."

"We were covered in the paper?"

"Definitely," said Liza. There's so much news—Jerusalem, Hebron, Sinai, the Golan . . ."

"We have the Old City?" Avi asked.

"Yes." Yaakov and Liza were smiling very wide.

"My God," he said. He considered they could be teasing him. "What are you saying? We got back Jerusalem, the part we lost in the '48 war? We have the Sinai, the Golan?"

"Yes."

"We got back Hebron?"

"Yes."

Rena and Gila came forward. They looked like surgeons in their whites.

"You are so lazy," Rena said. "You'll do anything to get out of work. Just like when we were kids."

"Well, Rena, nice to see you, too."

Yaakov approached Avi's bedside and gently patted his arm. "They told me everything," his father said. "I know you were in the lead tank of the first armor unit into Gaza's active battle. They tell me it was a big, horrific firefight. A long and tough battle. And you were the only one in that tank to survive. Very lucky. Very, very lucky."

"Tell us everything about you, what you did," Rena said.

"I was driving. The tank blew up. Doc says I'll need some surgeries. I'll be all right. Just routine stuff."

"They told us to be careful," said Rena. "High risk for infection."

"Well, they like to be extra cautious I suppose," Avi said.

"We were so worried about you," added Liza. "We watched the news. We had no idea what you were doing, where you were . . ." Tears rolled down her cheeks. She put her hand over her mouth and shook her head.

"I figured you were in Sinai somewhere. That's all," added Yaakov. "I'd like to hear more details when you're feeling better."

"Dad, there's not much to tell," Avi said.

Yaakov laughed. "Sure."

Nurse Vered charged over and whispered something to the visitors.

His mother said, "They want us to leave now, dear. We'll be back soon." She wiped away her tears. "We love you."

"Love you, too." He didn't want them to leave.

"We are so very proud of you," added Yaakov. "You will recover from your physical wounds. For sure. Don't worry about that. Don't let anything get you down. You are going to be fine. We can talk on the phone if you need. Yes?"

On the third visit, Gila stayed long after Yaakov, Liza, and Rena left. "Okay, *habibi* sweetie, now I'll read the paper for you," she offered, her voice muffled a bit by her face mask.

"Thank you. There's a letter from America on the table next to my bed. It's from my cousin Jonathan. Can you read that first?"

She opened the letter and easily read the English. "Dear Avi, everyone in America is so proud of what you and Israel have accomplished in six days. There have been parades. And talk shows and news people discussing everything in detail. We were afraid for you. Now we're all so relieved. Some are calling it a miracle."

Gila stopped reading and her face turned very sad. "My kibbutz lost a good one, Asher Ben Tzvi," she whispered. "I grew up with him. A paratrooper. He was the best of the best in every way. You've heard how hard it was on Ammunition Hill in Jerusalem?"

"Yes, Gila. I'm sorry for you, his family, and the kibbutz."

She took a moment and resumed reading the rest of Jonathan's letter. "Avi, my chess playing has improved, so I'm looking forward to another match. Take care of yourself—Jon."

"Thank you, Gila," he said.

"Thank you," said two other wounded soldiers in adjacent beds.

Gila gave Avi a long, hard look. "I know your body is healing. But how are you really doing? How are you managing your pain—and the memories of what happened?"

"I'm managing," Avi said. "Because of you. You're my strength, Gila. I think about you all the time."

Gila shook her head. "Me? I haven't done anything."

"You were there in the burning tank with me. I heard your voice. You told me I had to survive."

"Was I bossy?"

"Very."

"Oh, good, I want to take credit for your survival."

"Even now," Avi said, "I have my invisible Gila to talk to when I'm feeling all alone."

"And what does your invisible Gila say to you?"

"You mean besides how wonderful I am?"

"Yes, besides that."

"You tell me to cooperate with the doctors and nurses, and I better heal quick, or else."

"I'm still bossy?" Gila sounded amused. "Don't I ever say anything nice—or sexy?"

"I don't care if you're nice. I just enjoy you. You make me happy."

"Oh, Avi . . ."

"Gila, I love you."

"And I love you, too, *habibi*. Really, I do."

When she said that, the pain went away. It was the best anesthetic ever.

The pain returned after she left.

———

One week later, Avi realized that his skin smelled bad. He was embarrassed for Gila and his mother, sister, and father when they visited, though they never mentioned the smell.

Gila read the newspaper to him, "Moshe Dayan says all the land gained in the war was negotiable for peace, and that he would welcome a phone call."

"That sounds promising."

"Let's hope," Gila said.

A few days later, she read the paper to him again. "Eight Arab countries convened in Khartoum, Sudan. Their unanimous resolution was no peace with Israel. No recognition. No negotiations."

Avi sighed and looked up at the ceiling. "I was hoping this time it'd be different."

"Really? Did you really think it would?"

Chapter 20

Beersheva Hospital Burn Unit, January 13, 1968

Avi

Avi glanced up from his book as Gila approached his hospital bed. She looked especially sexy in her smart-looking, tight-fitting uniform, with her red paratroopers' cap tipped just over her forehead and her hair pressed tight by a dozen hair clips. He noticed there were other eyes in the ward following her as she approached.

Her presence seemed to ignite some dormant energy within him and, whenever she was near him, he was able to forget about his wounds.

"Hello soldier, you look better," she said, smiling.

"Now that you're here."

"Aww, thank you, my *habibi* sweetie." She tilted her head and looked as if she were examining him.

"What is it?"

"Trying to decide if I like your beard or not."

"Well, should I keep it?"

"Mmm. I don't know. I like it for now. It's different."

"And?"

"But I think you should shave it when you get home."

"Oh. Really? Well, . . . okay."

"Am I too bossy? I don't want to tell you what to do. I don't want to be bossy." She came over to give him a quick kiss on his lips, and an extremely gentle quick hug, the kind of hug she had probably learned when he only had a little bit of safe skin to touch.

"You don't have to be so careful touching me now," Avi said.

"Really?" She gave him a worried look. "I think as long as you're in a hospital bed, I'll be careful. But I'm glad you're healing." She pulled a chair over. "I have magazines and more books for you, including a novel and one more book on Jewish history. This one's about the Dreyfus Affair."

"Thank you. The novel and this French book will have to wait until I finish the book on the inquisitors from Spain and Portugal."

She laughed. "It's more about what happened during the plague. Am I too much for you?"

"Never."

"Well, do you find the history interesting?"

Avi was about to give a sarcastic response but thought better of it. "Honestly, I never read that much history before you took over my book selection. Now, strangely enough, I actually enjoy it. Not that there's anything pleasant or entertaining. It's horrible history. So much persecution and pain. But I like learning."

"Really?"

"Yeah," he responded. "Makes me feel smarter." Every book from Gila interested him. Everything she did interested him.

"Did you know the city of Netanya was named after a generous American benefactor? His name was Nathan."

"No, Gila. Who was he?"

"He and a brother owned some store in New York City named Mashee Store, or Masy's, something like that. Ever hear of it?"

"No," Avi said. "He couldn't have been very rich from owning just one store."

"Okay, my historian," Gila said. "Now to completely change the subject. Guess what? I made my first jump!"

"You jumped? Out of a plane?"

"Of course, out of a plane. What did you think I meant?"

"I thought maybe over a rope."

"Come on. No, I jumped out of a real plane. I'm a paratrooper. I have wings now. See?" She pointed to the wing pendant on her uniform.

"I thought you said you'd never do a jump. You just wanted to fold parachutes."

"Well, *habibi*, I guess I got tired of folding. It's important work, but . . . when did I say I'd never jump?"

"When we first started dating."

"Oh, well, I was just a kid then. Forget all that. The army ages you, don't you think?"

Rena walked in, and Gila greeted her with a hug.

"Tell me about the paratroopers," Rena said.

Gila shrugged. "It's like any other combat unit."

"The men are different." Rena's voice was teasing.

"I didn't notice," Gila answered matter-of-factly. "I only think about your brother."

"Right answer," Avi said as Rena walked over and carefully hugged his shoulders and gently kissed his cheek. "Just wanted to check on you, dear brother. You doing all right?"

"Everything is in order."

"Have you given any thought to life after the hospital? I should tell you that Mom already knows with absolute certainty that you'll take a job on the kibbutz."

"I'm glad at least someone in the family has figured out my next move. I thought my next move was deciding on bedpans, surgeries, or pain medication. How is Mom?"

"Oh, she's fine. She's still running the laundry with her finger on the gossip pulse. Anyway, I've got to get back. I'll leave you love birds alone. Gila, please call me when you get to the north. Got to go. Shalom-shalom."

After Rena left, Gila closed the curtains surrounding Avi's hospital bed and came to sit beside him on the edge of the bed. "Is it safe to touch you now?"

"Yes. See?" Avi poked his chest. "No pain."

"Is it safe to kiss you now?" She leaned toward him and gave him the most delicate and delicious of kisses. "Did you like?"

He nodded.

She lifted his shirt and ran her fingers over his chest.

Now she sees how ugly my body looks. Will it turn her off? "Ugly scars," Avi said. "But they don't hurt anymore, and it's okay to touch them."

"They're not ugly. They're the mark of a hero that I love."

"They really don't bother you?"

"Of course not. You have no scars on your beautiful face."

"Luck," he said, wondering if she really hadn't noticed the scars on his cheek and neck.

Gila touched his cheeks, forehead, nose, and thigh. "Let me see if you have more scars," she said, opening his hospital gown. She held his penis and moved it as if she were performing a medical exam, and they both watched as his cock instantly hardened. "You're perfect here, no scars at all. You were lucky. Someone looked out for you."

"My God, Gila . . ."

"Do you like my touch? Do you like this motion?"

"Mmm-mmm." But Avi was distracted by Nurse Vered's unmistakable hoarse bark directed at some poor bastard down the hall.

Gila rolled over closer to Avi on the bed, rubbed him some more, and asked again if he liked it.

Avi groaned. "Very, very much, but that nurse—damn it."

Gila stopped rubbing and looked as if she had forgotten something. Quickly, she unbuttoned her uniform and removed her top, then her bra, and dropped both to the floor. She didn't appear concerned about anything except pleasuring him. She resumed the rubbing as if they were all alone in his bedroom. "Yes, yes," she moaned in harmony with his own muffled groans.

Avi tried to warn her one more time. "The nurse—"

"Forget her," Gila said. "All that matters now is you and me. We're not going to hurry, and we're not going to stop."

Gila finished taking care of him with her sweet, tender, slow, most perfect way of lovemaking. And just at that moment, Nurse Vered opened their curtain.

Kibbutz Ma'ayan Baruch, April 22, 1968

Avi was released from the hospital and returned to his kibbutz. A week later, he was assigned to the office a few hours a day. He didn't mind it. It was better than piling bales of straw or working in the chicken coops or orchards. And the odd thing was that his status on the kibbutz seemed to have changed. It was as if the entire community was now his extended family.

Everyone knew of his brigade's accomplishments and his medal—he didn't say anything, but word had spread—and things were a little different. He was no longer just the young Bikel kid who was pretty good at soccer. He suddenly had status. Perhaps it was nothing more than sympathy over his wounds. It came with the way he was addressed, and the way people looked at him. Whatever it was, it was only a slight change, but it was definitely there and definitely different.

Yaakov and Liza came to see Avi nearly every night. Their conversations focused on Avi's recovery, the recent war, Israel's 1948 war of independence, and the 1956 Sinai War. Avi appreciated their visits and looked forward to them. They knew what he had been through, and Avi learned they had made sure everyone else on the kibbutz understood his contribution to the war, his suffering, and his prognosis.

One night, Yaakov came over very late. Avi was surprised but guessed Yaakov wanted to talk.

"Dad, I can tell you have something on your mind. Why don't you just tell me?"

"Oh, it's nothing about you. You're doing fine."

"What is it?"

"My brother. He's been hospitalized for a few days. It has something to do with his heart. I don't know more than that. My mind keeps me up. I worry. We're not kids anymore."

"Dad, it could be nothing."

Yaakov laughed. "You're right. I'm getting like my father used to be. And he didn't have modern medical care. I'm sure they'll let me know if there's anything serious." He stood up to leave. "Forget about this, okay?"

"Sure."

Avi went to bed after his father left. He thought about Gila. He knew her brigade was called to another part of the country. About three weeks had passed without a Gila visit. He missed her. He was impatient to see her.

Chapter 21
Kibbutz Ma'ayan Baruch, May 30, 1968

"Feeling okay?" Gila asked. It was a drizzly, damp day. Avi sat beside Gila on his couch.

"The best," he assured her. He was well enough and confident enough to initiate a real kiss and a real hug. He took off his shirt. "Is it ugly?"

Her fingertips gently caressed his back. She slowly ran the palm of her right hand along the sections where the skin had been the most raised. "It's good, it's fine. They did a wonderful job." Her sincere tone convinced him she was genuine and not just trying to make him feel better.

His skin felt normal and there was no pain when she touched him. In fact, her touch excited him and made him want to grab her and make love to her. He turned around and looked into her eyes. Her hands were still around his naked back and her touch was wonderful, the most perfect and purest of medicines. He looked into her bright blue eyes, into her mind and soul, and recalled all the days he had ached for her touch and her presence. His body had been in pain for a long time, insulated due to fear of infection. Now he was free to experience her warmth, her touch, and to respond with full intensity. Now he was free to kiss her and feel her embrace.

Avi pulled her T-shirt over her head and dropped it to the floor. He unhooked her bra and tossed it toward a chair. He kissed her lips hard and long, then slowly pulled back and looked into her eyes.

Gila smiled and said, "It's so nice to touch you everywhere without a worry I'd hurt you, or maybe infect you."

"It's so nice to be touched everywhere. Please continue to touch me everywhere."

He pulled down her jeans and panties.

"I want you inside me," she whispered.

He undressed quickly and kissed her breasts.

"Please. Come inside," she pleaded.

He smiled and complied.

———

Two hours later, Avi accompanied Gila to the communal dining hall. They ate chicken schnitzel, a kibbutz staple, and talked about his scheduled return to the army.

"I've enrolled in the tank commander program," he told her. "If I'm fit enough, I begin next month. But there's another program in September if I'm not ready."

Gila was quiet a moment. Then she said, "Sounds like you're still thinking of a military career."

"I guess I just like the life, the challenges, the feeling I get by contributing. Yes, I know the danger. I've lost friends sitting right next to me. But . . . lots of jobs have risks."

"But most of them don't put you in a burning tank, Avi. I'm surprised—in fact, very surprised—you want to do this after all you've been through."

Avi studied her bright eyes. "Are you upset by this decision?"

"No." Gila took his hand. "Not at all, Avi, this is your decision, and I respect it. I'm just surprised, that's all."

Avi smiled. "Would it also surprise you that I want to become an officer, maybe a company commander? Maybe one day lead a major operation? I think I have what it takes. We need more trained officers, so why not me? If I don't step up, why should anyone else?"

"If that's what you want, sweetie. I'll support any decision you make about your career."

Avi smiled wide. They put away the dirty dishes and silverware in the kibbutz-designated station. He took Gila's hand and escorted her back to his cottage. It was a quiet night but for the usual bats and the distant machine-gun blasts coming from the north.

"I love you, Gila."

"I love you, Avi."

She was wonderful and he knew he always wanted to be with her. He decided at that moment that he wanted to marry her, to never again be without her. When should he ask her? Should he talk to her parents first? Should he talk to his parents? Did he need a ring? He would soon be enrolled in Armor Commander School. And immediately after that he'd be enrolled in officer training. So how could he manage this? When was a good time? Would she accept his proposal right away?

"Where are you, Avi?" she asked, apparently sensing his stress.

"I'm here in my bed with you."

"What were you thinking?" she pressed.

"Nothing."

"I don't believe you. Don't you trust me?"

"I was thinking, well, I was thinking about you, us, our future together. If you really must know."

"I really must. In fact, I want to know everything you're thinking, everything you're doing and planning."

"I'm not so interesting."

"You are to me. Aren't I interesting to you?"

"More than you could know."

"Better believe it." She laughed. "That's just what I wanted to hear—what I needed to hear."

"Yeah? Why is that?"

"Because I've been thinking we should get married."

Avi turned and looked at her. "What?" was all he managed to say. He was so happy. Did he hear correctly?

She laughed again. "Don't look so scared."

"Scared? I was thinking just now about asking you to marry me. That's what I was thinking when you asked me what I was thinking."

"So go ahead and ask. You can ask me now, *habibi*, if you want. I won't bite."

"Gila, I love you. Will you marry me?"

"Yes, I'll marry you tomorrow or any day," she said. She smiled wide.

Avi rolled over on top of her and made love to her again, and soon drifted off into a deep and satisfying sleep.

July 17, 1968

Avi panicked when he looked at the time. The wall clock had to be wrong. He was late for his own wedding. Damn it all to hell. Gila would kill him. *First she'll marry me and then she'll kill me.* He put down the book on tank strategy and dressed as quickly as he could. *Why do I do this?*

Much of kibbutz Dan and Ma'ayan Baruch's membership, including Avi's parents and sister, were waiting in the kibbutz dining hall, as were thirty-two uniformed soldiers who had trained or served with Avi or Gila. A collective sigh arose as he entered the dining hall.

Avi followed Gila around the great hall to greet their friends and family members and made their way through the crowd to stand under the ceremonial *chuppah*. Four friends from Avi's brigade were holding up the *chuppah*, and a frail-looking elderly rabbi began to chant the traditional prayers. Avi smiled wide. Gila was so beautiful. The rabbi carefully covered a glass cup with a white fabric and placed it on the floor.

Avi recited the traditional promise to never forget Jerusalem and lifted his foot to crush the glass.

"Mazel tov," everyone cheered in unison.

Avi kissed his fresh new wife. "How are you, Mrs. Bikel?"

"Just fine, thank you. And how are you, Mr. Bikel?"

"I'm very happy, in fact happier than I have ever been."

Someone tapped Avi on his shoulder from behind. He turned around to find a grinning Jonathan standing beside his parents. Jonathan enthusiastically shook Avi's hand while shouting, "Congratulations!"

Lazer and Avi embraced one another, then each embraced Yaakov and Liza and Malka.

"Good to see you, Avi, so good," said Lazer. "It's been too long."

"We have much to catch up on, uncle. You're coming to our home after the ceremony?"

"Of course. We'll be in Israel for three weeks. We can catch up. Just like old times."

Yaakov swallowed a generous shot of whiskey and turned towards his brother, "So good to see you and Malka."

"We miss you, too," said Lazer. "I could really have used your talent when I cut down and replaced my old wire fence around our vegetable garden. I heard you're an expert when it comes to wire fences?"

Yaakov laughed with his brother and patted his shoulder. "Call me whenever you need to cut a fence."

———

Avi and Gila honeymooned the rest of the week at the Palace Hotel in Netanya near the beach. It was the absolute best of weeks for Avi, and he was certain he'd always remember their getaway there with a smile.

He wished he could forget being late to his own wedding.

Chapter 22

Princeton, New Jersey, November 4, 1972

Neal

Neal's mailbox was stuffed with advertising inserts, mostly from local pizza joints. There was one letter. He quickly tore it open, read it, then, to be sure, he read it all again. "All right now. Yes, baby!" He raised one fist triumphantly into the air and reread the key sentence: "We do hope your schedule permits you to participate in our lecture series." He was on his way to bigger things, at least as far as speaking to a fringe group would take him. It was a start.

The next four weeks passed slowly, and he used the time to tweak his lecture until he reached the point where none of the changes he contemplated would make meaningful differences. When the big day arrived, he spent the morning debating what to wear. He finally put on a brown tweed sports jacket and tie. That seemed to be the right look. It had been a long time since he'd worn a tie, but he figured it'd make him appear more sophisticated. *Isn't this the way invited speakers are supposed to dress?*

He drove to Bloomfield, New Jersey, where a local college rented space to this group. When he arrived and looked for a parking space, he observed the parade of factory employees exiting in march-step from the Westinghouse and General Electric plants. He thought the tired-looking factory workers resembled prisoners in the Gulag. *Poor bastards. They work hard and make others rich. None of the politicians think of them except at voting time. All they have is their union to help them. Maybe Pop's longtime employment in his union did deserve more respect.*

He found a parking spot. The sidewalks were slick with ice. The event was scheduled in a stone building with a tall steeple crowned by an inverted cone. A middle-aged man approached him moments after he entered the vestibule. He wore a sweater over a gray button-down shirt and no tie. "Mr. Chomelstien, I'm Arthur Cummings. We're glad you could make it."

Neal shook his hand. "A pleasure," he said, smiling, grateful that he managed to respond somewhat appropriately. He tried not to reveal how nervous he really was. "Just call me Neal," he managed.

"Come now, Neal, follow me. I'll show you to the stage."

"Nice building," said Neal, following a half step behind Mr. Cummings while looking up at the underside of the steeple.

"It's very nice. We're fortunate it was available. Everyone here will welcome you. You'll find us to be a small, friendly group."

Neal took the chair next to three other speakers behind the podium.

There was polite applause after the first and second speakers. Arthur approached the microphone and leaned forward. "Our next speaker is Neal Chomelstien, a recent doctoral graduate of Princeton who will shortly be assuming a teaching position at MIT. By the way, Neal, what is your focus?"

"English. I have a Doctorate in English."

"Excellent. When you hear him speak, you'll understand why we've invited him to this forum."

Neal nearly ran to the lectern. He adjusted the mike and cleared his throat. "Thank you, Arthur. I'm here today to deliver a message. It is clear now, unquestionable that we have been subjected to waves of falsehoods and propaganda. Who is lying to us? It's our very own U.S. government. Why? Because those with political power cater to special interests. These special interests make millions while factory workers, like those workers in the plants here in Bloomfield, barely get by. The special interest groups see themselves as above the rest of us.

"Let me give you one example. You've heard of Mao Zedong of China. But what have you heard? You've heard that the Chinese are starving under his rule. You've heard he's a dictator who

146

has killed millions of people and sent millions into forced labor farms. I've seen numbers as high as seventy-million dead. But who provides this data? It's our government, not independent research. Have you ever seen scholarly corroboration?

"They want you to believe that Mao's approach to a modern society isn't working. The fact is the Chinese people revere Mao. There's really no evidence to support that anyone was murdered. Aristocrats were sent to farms to experience the value of real labor. The people revere Mao because he's modernized China. He's made women equal. Young girls no longer have to bind their feet. Life expectancy has increased dramatically. The population of China has doubled.

"So, whom do you believe? Do you believe what the U.S. government wants you to believe? Or do you believe what my Chinese researchers say? And by the way, these researchers are very diligent."

Neal loved the enthusiastic applause.

"Now let me talk about another lie. All we hear about is the miracle of the Six-Day War. The facts are that it was nothing more than another Israeli land grab, like the ones in 1948 and 1956. The Arabs didn't attack first. Israel attacked Syria, Jordan, and Egypt. And they increased the size of Israel dramatically. The Arabs did talk about retaking some land, but they clearly were unprepared. It was just talk, but, unfortunately, it gave Israel an excuse to invade and occupy more Arab land. Government and media outlets have advanced this lie. Why does the media go along with such lies? It's about increasing their advertising revenues."

There was more applause. Neal's smile widened, and he continued his thesis for another fifteen minutes. He thanked the audience and returned to his chair.

After the last speaker finished, Neal stepped down from the stage and headed in the direction of the exit. But with every step, someone stopped him to congratulate him. A young, attractive woman approached him. "I loved your lecture," she said. "May I ask you a question? Do you believe that there weren't any atrocities committed by Mao's government? Or do you dismiss them as necessary for the long-term good?"

"Good question, Miss . . . what's your name?"

"Oh, I'm sorry." She extended her hand. "I'm Susan. Welcome to my Jersey town. I think it takes courage to speak up against what most people assume to be the truth." They shook hands.

At that moment, a heavyset man—Neal guessed he was about fifty—handed Neal his card. "My name is Russo. Jack Russo." The man had a loud, raspy voice, was dressed in a stylish charcoal suit with a blue tie and had combed his thick white hair straight back. "I own a small publishing company. We cater to a segment a bit out of the mainstream, like the people here, but we're better and more honest than a lot of the mainstream publishers. Just like you are. Ever think of doing a book?"

"N-no. But I'd like to," said Neal. *A book? That's something cool to consider—if this fat guy is for real.*

"Send me a sample," Russo said. "No guarantees but send a sample to my personal attention."

Neal hesitated.

"I think you got some powerful stuff in you," the man went on. "Think about it. I can help you make it big-time. This isn't bull. There are lots of experienced writers out there begging me to read their stuff."

"Okay, I'll think about it," Neal cautiously agreed, trying not to telegraph his excitement.

"We like controversial and unconventional. New ways of looking at old things is good. But you'll need data to support your thesis, like endorsement from branded names. Remember that. It's critical."

Neal nodded automatically.

"You might gain a real niche, you know," said Russo as he turned to leave. "Call me. We can talk. You got my card."

"Mr. Russo?"

"Yes?"

"Which topic do you prefer? I have a lot of sources and ideas on China and Vietnam, yes and—"

"No, that's been pretty well covered. Stick to the Middle East. I have an investor—a Jew that doesn't like Jews. You want to know what I mean by that? Well, he doesn't practice the religion and he really just doesn't like Israel, if you can believe it. Some say he helped the Nazis discover hidden Jewish wealth by forging or stealing identity cards that said he wasn't a Jew. I don't care about all that. He's got big money and he's willing to partner with my company. I plan to work with him. But I need to find books that are strong, well-written, with the right slant. You get it? His slant. His angle. Got it?"

Neal nodded.

"Your name's Chomelstien? That a German name? Dutch?"

"Y-yes," said Neal. "Dutch."

Russo smiled, turned, and abruptly left.

Neal asked himself why he claimed to have Dutch ancestry. He could have told him the truth. *After all, Russo's backer is some crazy Wall Street lunatic looking to finance a hate book.* Then again, why should he risk telling the truth and possibly lose the assignment? His dad was recently threatened by a local Jewish guy that had beat him up in Poland. Hell, they broke his back. And his dad struggled and suffered the rest of his life in pain because of what they did to him. Neal laughed and proceeded to look for that woman he was chatting with earlier. She might have moved on when Russo burst on the scene. *Hope I wasn't rude. Maybe she's still here somewhere.* He returned to the crowd lingering inside.

Chapter 23

Cambridge, Massachusetts, September 10, 1973

Jonathan

Jonathan considered late August to mid-October to be the best weather of the year. The summer heat dropped some, signaling the transition to new color in the leaves. And Jonathan's allergies were no more. The river that separated Boston and Cambridge flowed slower, almost like a long, narrow pond, while the wind danced unpredictably in all directions at the water's surface. Nevertheless, many rowers took to their sculls with unhampered enthusiasm.

The city also boasted the most moving vans and overstuffed cars in the country as the students moved in and took control. They were everywhere, moving in and out, up and down, like colonies of ants marching illogically in all directions, making sense and bringing order only with the arrival of the first seasonal chill.

Jonathan took a basement apartment in a gray six-family building that was badly in need of paint and replacements for the rotted window framing. It was near Porter Square, about a thirty-minute walk to the university campus. He bought a used mattress and box spring and set them on the floor. He also bought a small television and used the TV carton for his dining table. That would be fine. It was all he'd need.

He attended MIT's orientation for new assistant professors. At the close of the meeting, he received his assigned class schedule. He was nervous but also excited at the prospect of teaching accomplished undergraduates.

The next day, he realized how much these exceptionally smart students didn't know. He looked them over. They were so young—anxious freshmen that wrote down everything he said and asked him many questions, as if he were a sage down from the mountain to share the answers to life's mysteries. He liked the feeling. It was easy to get used to and now he understood the danger of doing just that. He vowed he would never get too full of himself.

He had just finished teaching his last class for the week and was on his way home from the supermarket when he saw a reasonably attractive woman carrying a chair by herself up the steps that led to the main entrance of his apartment building.

"Want me to hold the door?" Jonathan asked.

"Great," she said.

Jonathan sized up her physical measurements quickly, as if her physical features could be quantitatively measured to reveal her attractiveness quotient: maybe a little overweight, like five pounds or so, not bad, a C cup; round face, nice, long brown hair; very good overall. On a scale of one to ten, she might be a seven or even an eight.

He held the door for her. She brought in a few pieces—a chair, a little table, a box with contents that would be assembled into a desk. He didn't speak to her while holding the door. He just watched her. *Should I help her with the bags? Maybe she's the type who'd resent help.*

"I just have one more thing and I'm done," she said apologetically.

"No rush. My groceries will keep."

He watched her bring another box up and into her apartment on the first landing. She came back to tell him, "Thanks, I'm done now. Want a drink or anything?" She rubbed back a lock of hair that had fallen over her forehead. Her hand continued downward until her fingers pressed against her lips.

Jonathan let go of the door. "I'm not thirsty. Holding a door's no big deal. Don't worry about it."

"Okay," she said. "Where's your apartment?"

"One level down."

"Cool." She gave a wide smile.

"Good night," he said.

"Oh, what's your name?"

"Jonathan Bikel."

"I'm Emily Cohen."

"Good night, Emily Cohen."

"Thank you, and good night, Jonathan."

She smiled again and went to the first floor while he carried his one bag of groceries downstairs to his basement apartment.

Later, in the wee hours of the night, Jonathan lay in bed and thought about Emily. No woman had ever invited him to her apartment before. That little invitation to her apartment meant something, didn't it? Or was he making too much of the invite? After all, she just wanted to show a little gratitude. Maybe she just would have offered him a glass of water and sent him home.

He rolled over and tried to sleep. He tossed and turned. Eventually, he remembered Susan Stone. He hadn't thought of her in years. He had never pursued her. Was she a lost opportunity? Would he let Emily become another missed possibility?

Chapter 24
Cambridge, Massachusetts, September 15, 1973

Neal

Neal turned once again toward the freshman standing beside his office desk. "Look Murphy, you might be a wiz at math or physics, that science stuff, but your use and understanding of the English language needs to substantially improve if you want to pass my course. You need to grow. Did your high school make you read at all?"

"Professor . . ."

"What is it, Murphy?"

"What books do you suggest I study . . . I mean, what can I read that'll help me pass?"

"I marked up your essay pretty thoroughly. And I suggest you consider hiring a tutor. And read books. If you follow my program, I'll teach you geniuses how to read and write. Good day, Mr. Murphy."

An hour later, Neal finished grading papers and looked at his watch. *Time to eat.* He got up slowly and walked toward the cafeteria. He recalled people asking what he did for a living—as if it were their business. He often replied that he taught geniuses how to read. He laughed. A jerk professor once pointed out that the title of "assistant professor" meant very little, that it was light-years from winning a tenured slot and the odds of making it weren't good.

The "publish or perish" mantra had also been drilled into him. Good thing old Russo was in his corner. His book, after so many rewrites, was finally ready—at least according to Russo's latest communication. But Russo's promises no longer had credibility.

Neal walked past the giant white columns on his way to the cafeteria. Now waves of students swarmed around him like schools of piranha, or maybe more like shrimp—except now he was a teacher, the one in command, the one with authority, and grateful his student days were history.

Neal recognized only one person, another new assistant professor, in the cafeteria, sitting alone. He was reading a book while sipping soup. His hair was long, curly, and unkempt. He reminded Neal of a young Harpo Marx.

"May I join you?" asked Neal.

The man looked up from his book and adjusted his black-framed eyeglasses. "Sure." The man nodded while putting down his book. "I answer to Jon or Jonathan." He extended his hand.

"I'm Neal," said Chomelstien as he shook Jon's hand. "I'm teaching English, graduated from Princeton, hail from the Bronx. That answers the usual questions, so I thought I'd get it out of the way." Neal smiled and sat down at the rectangular table.

Jonathan laughed. "Why wait for formalities? I'm from Jersey City. Went to Rutgers—math. So, tell me, Neal, why is it always called 'the Bronx' —- not just 'Bronx' like every normal borough or city?"

"I'll tell you what I read and heard, but I can't guarantee its authenticity."

"Ah, I see you are a professor that wants to be sure of his facts. That's not a problem in math. If you make a mistake, someone, someday, will find it."

"I think that's true in many fields of study. Anyway, legend has it that there was no name for the area when the land was bought from Westchester County. The map at the time only showed the Bronx River, no reference to a name for the land. People referred to it as the Bronx River land area, and over time it became the Bronx. That's how it happened, or so the legend goes."

"Never knew that. I'm new here, too, but I think it's a great school with capable students that I suspect will keep me on my toes. And I think I'm going to like Cambridge and Boston. Lots to do."

"Agreed. What courses do you teach, Jon?"

"Calculus for Engineers, and Advanced Algebra."

"You're at the right school for that." Neal finished his sandwich and stood up to leave. "Take care, Jon."

"Yeah, sure, you too. Hey, what's your last name?"

"Chomelstien. And yours?"

"Bikel."

Neal was stunned. *Did I hear right? He can't be one of those Bikels that threatened my old man. Must be another Bikel.* "You're not related to Lazer Bikel?"

"I think I am. He's my dad." Jonathan smiled wide. "You know him?"

Neal turned to leave without saying another word. How ironic that the one professor he joined for lunch turned out to be the spawn of the bastard that had landed his dad in a concentration camp. And even threatened his dad in this country. Unbelievable.

Neal wanted to spit or punch something. He banged his fist against the wall. He wanted to get even. Somewhere, sometime, somehow, he'd find a way.

Chapter 25

Boston, September 17, 1973

Jonathan

Jonathan was lying in bed, working on one of the classic unsolved math problems that carried a one-million-dollar reward for the solution. The proposition was beginning to appear to be truly unsolvable when his phone rang. It startled him because his phone almost never rang. It was Mahmud.

"How are you, oh favorite chess partner from college?" Jonathan asked.

"Wonderful. Listen, good news. I'm coming up, you see, Boston. I have interview there. They have opening for assistant profess—"

"Which school?"

"Your school, of course. MIT. For second semester. I'm told could work out for few years, maybe more."

"What program?"

"Business finance. I'm interviewing with Dr. Machowsky. Know him?"

"Not well, but I do know him, sort of. Certainly enough to put in a good word."

"I appreciate good word. The word from you, very . . . very. . ."

"Well, it can't hurt. Call me when you come up. We'll get together. I'll bring my chess board."

"Have not played since you left."

"Don't make excuses, Mahmud. Truth is, I also haven't played anyone since I left."

"No excuses. See you, and soon, my friend."

After Mahmud's call, Jonathan didn't feel up to continuing the battle with the unsolvable math proposition, so he got dressed and went out to buy a few things at the supermarket. On the way out, he passed Emily. She waved. He smiled, waved back, and hurried down the stairs to the street as if he had something important to rush to.

He thought more about Emily as he pushed a shopping cart in the food market. He didn't want to miss another opportunity with a woman who might actually like him. He considered just calling Emily to ask her to go to a movie, but that seemed juvenile.

A few days later, he learned there was an event at the university for new instructors. It was a cocktail and hors d'oeuvres reception in some swanky room, and the university president would be speaking. Maybe he could invite Emily?

He decided to call her. He even got her number from information. But he kept finding reasons not to call. He couldn't call during dinner, or too late, or too early. And then he bumped into her again in the hallway.

"Hi, Jonathan," she said without breaking her stride toward the building's front door.

"Oh, wait," he said.

She stopped and looked at him, her expression curious. "What's up?"

"Are you available a week from Sunday?"

"I think so. I'll have to check."

"There's this event at the university. A wine and food thing. Our president will be there. Thought maybe you'd like to—"

"I'd love to go," she said without hesitation.

Jonathan was relieved. *That was easy.*

Emily looked like she wanted to stay and chat, but Jonathan told her he'd firm up the time and details and retreated to his apartment. It was enough stress for the day. He went home and reread a few of his chess books to prepare for his match with Mahmud.

September 30, 1973

It was a Sunday evening affair. At 4:00 pm, Jonathan walked Emily to his car. He observed how different Emily looked in a tight black dress accented by the earth tones of her silk top. She had subtle lipstick, mascara, and looked remarkably different. Her curly hair was the same but somehow better. She was the consummate young professional woman. She was beautiful. *What a transformation.*

"I'm an easy date for you," she said. "I mean you don't exactly have far to go to pick me up."

"You're right," he said. "And it'll only take us five minutes to get to the hall. I should plan all my dates so well."

"What do you mean?"

"Nothing, just a bad joke," he said.

"I heard you. All your dates. How many dates a week do you have?"

"None."

"Oh, I don't believe that either. You're teasing me."

"Sorry," he said. He was pleased she didn't believe him.

Jonathan managed to make his way to the lavish hall with its intricate Oriental carpet in the center. The polished wood floor encircled the carpeting. A crystal chandelier hung in the center of the great room. A string quartet was playing classical music while the waiters and waitresses in tuxedos offered fine wine and gourmet appetizers on silver trays.

"I'm told this event is unusually lavish this year. I think it's because a big donor is here or something. There's a lot of new people like me, too," Jonathan said. "The poor people."

"You're telling me everyone is feeling equally awkward," Emily said.

"Exactly."

She laughed. "At least they know how to do things first class."

"They like to treat themselves very well. I think this event is exceptional. I don't really know. But don't worry, I'm sure the fundraisers for the university are sending out compelling mailers."

"Very different from my world."

"What do you do?"

"I'm in the city planning office."

"For Cambridge?"

"Boston."

"And what do they plan in the Boston planning office?"

"The future. I mean, you know, we figure out needs, trends, try to get developers to buy in, that kind of thing."

"Is it interesting?"

"Sometimes. I chose to study it, so I guess I do find it interesting. It's real stuff that affects the lives of real people. Cities can grow well or ugly. Planning for future growth makes a world of difference in how people live."

"And that makes it important."

"You got it," she said.

After a while they'd had enough of Alumni Hall and decided to drive down to Haymarket.

"So, Jonathan," Emily said, sliding closer to him as he drove, "now that we got work stuff out of the way, what do you like to do for fun?"

"I like chess," Jonathan said, eyes on the road. "I like solving math problems. Sometimes I get calls to consult for local tech companies. You know, R & D."

"What?"

"Research and Development."

"All that sounds pretty intellectual. I mean, it's not like going bowling."

He let out a sigh at the thought of himself with a bowling ball. His angst quickly dissolved into a laugh. "What do you like to do for fun?"

"I like to dance. And I'm into yoga. Well, I'm not a real yogi or anything like that. Yoga has a religious element, too, and I don't go for that. But I do think the exercising and stretching, and relaxing are very beneficial. Gets rid of stress. Know what I mean? It's good to get rid of stress. Something like a massage—you might call it a mental massage. I had a girlfriend that really got hooked into it. Started wearing pendants with portraits of famous yogis around her neck. Unreal."

They drove around the block a few times until they found a parking space only two blocks from Haymarket. He opened the car door for her and took her hand. "You know, you're right," he said as they walked on the cobblestones. "It is pretty convenient to date someone in the same building."

"But it might be awkward if we run into each other with other dates."

"Never thought of that. Was I wrong to ask you out?"

"No, no, I don't mean that. I'm so glad you asked me. It's been fun."

He thought she was just being polite. *Can anyone really have fun at a university cocktail party?*

They walked around Haymarket, chatted with a few of the fruit and vegetable vendors, accidentally stepped on dead fish, then returned to the car and headed home. Jonathan luckily found a parking space right across from their building.

"Want a drink or something?" Emily asked as they walked up the stairs.

"Coke?"

"Amazingly enough, I actually have some," she offered. She smiled, and after she smiled, he noticed she sucked in her lips.

They went into her apartment, which comprised one small bedroom with a queen bed high off the floor, and one other room, a combo dining-living room. Her apartment had nearly the same layout as his. She brought him the Coke, and they quietly watched television. She invited him to sit next to her on the couch, and he readily complied.

She put her hand on his leg above his knee and lightly rubbed the leg.

He rested his arm loosely behind her neck.

She took his hand and pulled it closer to her body and snuggled into him. She continued to rub his leg and he liked it very much despite feeling a little uncomfortable. Soon he lost all feeling in his arms and had to move, if only to get his blood flowing. He slid down and positioned himself to kiss her. She turned to face him and closed her eyes. He moved forward without thinking and pressed his lips against her lips. It felt wonderful to kiss her like that, and he continued kissing her and holding her tight. He expected a protest but it never came. She clearly wanted to kiss as much as he did.

She didn't speak. She only uttered soft, quick moans of pleasure, and he found himself on top of her. He made love to her on the couch for an hour before they retreated to her queen bed where they enjoyed more comfortable lovemaking.

Jonathan woke early the next morning, and, for a while, he just watched Emily sleeping next to him. She looked different now, beautiful and innocent. He admired her prominent cheekbones and thick hair. He enjoyed every minute with her. She was smart, too, and a good conversationalist. And he felt different, more confident, happier, and he couldn't help smiling. He wasn't a virgin anymore.

Chapter 26

Golan Heights, October 6, 1973

Avi

The reverberation from jet engines came suddenly out of nowhere. Jets were flying fast and low and continued unabated southward, disappearing into a smoky gray horizon. Someone shouted, "They're not ours."

They're not our jets? No, can't be. Avi stepped up to a higher elevation with binoculars in hand and looked up as more jets in formation soared southward over them. *Syrian MIGs.*

He returned to the bunker, and someone handed him a radiophone. It was Colonel Mazer. "Major Bikel, get your battalion ready. We're estimating the Syrians have eight hundred tanks north of the line . . . plus one hundred fifty artillery batteries and Sagger missiles. You're going to have to hold your sector. The Egyptians have moved into Sinai so we're being squeezed. But we'll get reserves to you as soon as we can. You know what to do."

The connection clicked off.

Damn! Those idiots. Why didn't we call more reserves sooner? Avi put down the phone, then picked it up again. He called Gila. "I won't be home. Something is going down. Something big."

"What? This baby's due any day. Any minute."

"Can't leave. Watch the news. We're moving north right now. Yes, right now. Damn. I love you."

"Got it. Oh, why does it have to be now? Okay, okay. Please be safe. Please. I love you too."

"My parents are planning to fly to America for my cousin's wedding. Let them know. No, never mind, let them fly out—if they still can."

"Okay. What terrible, terrible timing. I sound like a brat, don't I? I love you. Come back to me. Please."

Avi ran out of the bunker to a waiting jeep. "Let's go," he said to the driver as calmly as he could. He reached for his radiophone. "Remove the camouflage nets."

Upon reaching his battalion, he hopped out of the jeep before it completely stopped, returned the driver's salute, and ran to the command cupola on the lead tank. He waved his right arm forward, and the battalion began its roll in close formation through the farmland, heading north to Syria. *This is what we trained for.*

At sunset, the first enemy artillery shells began falling all around and behind him. Five minutes hadn't passed before the shells fell closer to his position and more MIGs appeared, sweeping the skies unfettered like supernatural predators.

A shell landed just to his left, driving rock and metal projectiles hard against his tank. He instantly ducked down into the turret. He felt a tinge of fear that put him momentarily back in a burning tank. He suppressed that image as best he could. He took two deep breaths. There was a job he had to do. A job he had chosen and trained for. No time to dwell on the past. He was on the front line, and his men, his country, his friends, and family, they were all depending on him.

By nightfall, he had arrived at the Syrian frontier, confronting Syrian tanks intent on storming into Israel. The Syrians had new Russian tanks, better than Israel's older American tanks. He couldn't see the Syrians without turning on headlights or using a small handheld night scope. Shining the lights could be dangerous, and the scope wasn't effective. Enemy shells exploded and momentarily lit up the night. There were panicked calls over the radio. "Who's been hit?" one tanker shouted. Another cried out, "We have. Our second hit in minutes, but we're still mobile." Another voice said, "We cannot see in the dark."

Avi's battalion was already taking losses. The familiar smells of raining missiles and burning tanks permeated the air. *We need to stop their advance. Right now. Somehow.* He panned the terrain. The Syrians had the advantage of surprise, numbers, equipment.

"Should we put on our high beams?" a gunner asked.

"You crazy?" Yonni, his sergeant, responded. "You want to make it easier for them to find us?"

"Get ready to fire," Avi said, "but shoot a flare first."

As soon as the flare burned out, they were back in the dark and sitting ducks.

"Avi, we've got to retreat," shouted Uri over the radio. His tank was one hundred meters west of Avi. He screamed so fast he was hard to understand. "If we do, we can fight another day. If we stay, we'll be chopped to pieces by tomorrow morning."

Avi was in no mood for talk of retreat. He hesitated only for a second. "We move forward," Avi shouted into the radio. *No wonder Uri didn't get my job.*

"But Avi—"

"No, Uri," Avi yelled, even louder this time, "if we pull back, their tanks will flood the Galilee before daybreak. You have your orders."

"What good are we going to be when we're all dead?"

"Don't question my orders!" Avi wiped his spit off the radiophone. "Do your job!"

The Syrians clearly knew their advantages and charged aggressively. Now Avi could make out their forms in the moonlight and shouted into his radiophone, "Baruch, take out their lead, you see him? We'll take the next one, the one on the left!"

Avi's old tank shook as the shells were launched. The amassed cannon fire from both armies was deafening, and flashes of light from the shelling and burning filled the night sky.

"We're hit," cried a voice over the radio.

"To your left," screamed another voice.

More voices: "Our cannon's out."

"I'm hit! Medic! Need a medic!"

Avi wanted to help the wounded, but there was no time. He had to be a commander. His men were fighting for their lives; their fear came across in their radio voices. But they were still advancing. *They are well-trained and motivated. They know what's at stake.*

"We're hit. We're on fire," a voice shouted over the radio. For a moment, Avi saw himself years ago in a burning tank.

Two Syrian tanks went up in flames. They were so close that Avi could smell the smoke. The residual light exposed more Syrian targets.

Avi led the battalion toward a hill on the left flank. "Kohane, take your six tanks up the forward hill. Cover our flank."

"Will do, Avi. Damn, my tank's not—never mind, we're moving now."

The Syrians appeared to be hesitating before pursuing Kohane. Avi figured they must have assumed he had more tanks. Maybe they thought they were being led into a trap. "We're in position," Kohane reported over the radio.

"Now! Give it to them!"

Avi opened the hatch, leaned out of the tank, and spied the Syrians. They were pulling back from Kohane's fire. Syrian planes strafed Avi's battalion from the rear. Avi closed the hatch and ducked back into the tank. *Where are our damn planes?* The Syrian planes passed Avi's battalion, presumably to a better target. He phoned Northern Command. "I need air cover now, damn it. I need ammo, medics, reinforcements. Where the hell are the reserves?"

"Hold your position," ordered Mazer. "The ammo is coming. Reinforcements will come as fast as we can get them to you. It could take a few days for all of them to get to you."

"Days? I don't have fucking days."

"You need medics?"

"Yes, now! I'll lose more good men if they aren't evacuated now."

"I can get medics to you."

Avi turned the radio back to his battalion channel. "Follow me to the level ground, the plain before the valley; when you get there, turn off your engines. Medics are coming for your wounded and your dead. And a team is coming, and they have more ammunition for you. Watch for movement."

There was no smooth path going forward, and Avi's tank twisted left and right over boulders, potholes, and spent projectiles.

No one could sleep. It was the longest, darkest, most anxious night. Avi looked up to the moon. Would the light expose them? No, the skies were darkened from all the smoke. He decided they'd just wait for dawn. It was like waiting with a knife at the throat.

And with first light, the Syrians opened up again. "They found us," Avi shouted into the radio. "Get out fast."

"Avi, this is Amir at Northern Command. The Syrians have taken control of Mount Hermon, the eyes of Israel. You won't be able to hide like you did. They're directing more battalions to your location."

"Understood." Avi addressed his tank commanders. "Call out your name, condition of your tanks, crews, ammo. I need to know how many we lost during the night."

One by one, the tank commanders reported back. Then there was silence.

"I haven't heard from Boaz and Amichai. Please report. Anyone in Boaz's tank hear me? Amichai's tank?"

Silence.

Avi stepped up to the cupola and searched through binoculars for the missing tankers. He couldn't find them. Now he saw that medical teams had arrived and were evacuating the casualties. He panned to the north and guessed about a hundred enemy tanks were over two kilometers away and moving toward him. "They'll be here soon." *God help us.*

Avi reached for the radiophone. "Let's move out of this low ground. Kohane, you take the left flank. I'll stay in the center. Shmuel, to the right."

Avi's lead tank climbed cautiously up from the dell and advanced toward the Syrians. There was a big blast in front of Avi's tank. He couldn't see a thing for a while. When the smoke cleared, he realized a MIG had taken out his cannon. He estimated that a cluster of at least forty Syrian tanks was advancing in the center, firing right at his tankers. The gray sky was filling with smoke-made clouds, and his unserviceable tank was filling with smoke as well. "Find yourselves another tank. I'll join that one," said Avi, while pointing to the closest tank. He lifted the phone he had been holding tight in his hand. "Benny. I'm joining you. Stop a moment. I'll be right there."

He climbed out of the tank and ran over to Benny's functional tank.

Syrian helicopters flew commandos somewhere behind Avi's tanks. He figured they were trying to cut off his resupply of munitions.

As he turned behind a rocky hill, he spotted an enemy T-62 tank, the celebrated Russian tank known for its heavy machine gun, low recoil, and high muzzle velocity. He dropped down into the turret.

"Fire fast," Avi yelled.

"The gun doesn't work," Motti shouted back.

The T-62 was turning and aiming right at them. *We're dead.*

Avi heard an explosion, and it was from his cannon. Motti had gotten it working. The enemy T-62 was engulfed in flames. Avi took a deep breath. "Motti—good shooting."

"The gun is fickle," said Motti.

"There's another one," shouted Benny. "Fire again."

"Where?" Motti asked.

"God damn it, just fire as you're positioned," Benny shouted while slapping Motti's helmet repeatedly.

"Fire!" Avi yelled. "Do it now!"

Another explosion as the second T-62 burst into flames.

Avi climbed back into the cupola, took a deep breath. "Let's move forward," he shouted as clearly as he could muster into the radio. The Syrians were closing in without hesitation. They were competent and tenacious, and they knew they had the advantage.

There were earsplitting explosions in all directions. The field was littered with burning tanks and smoldering depressions. As dusk approached, it was hard to make out who was ahead in the shadows or looming above on the hills.

Avi opened the hatch and stood up. He searched all directions with binoculars, but the darkness and irregular terrain, enemy aircraft, and enemy commandos had a way of blurring the best course of action. Avi's battalion was weaving between enemy tanks, some abandoned or gutted, others deadly active. The men in Avi's battalion showed their stress in the form of aggressive bickering. His battalion now needed to use their training, to work as a team and focus on the tasks at hand.

"Listen to me, and shut up," Avi yelled into the phone as loud as he could. "You will listen to my orders, and we will prevail." There was quiet on the radiophone now. He took a deep breath and pushed himself to continue. "We will advance as we have trained. I will advise you soon on when to advance. We can stop them. And we will."

It was another bitter sleepless night of cat and mouse. This time, Avi applied the strategy of moving all the time, of crisscrossing and weaving through the terrain. He tried to plan the next day's strategies, but ideas weren't coming easy. He imagined his father encouraging him to be creative. "Figure it out, Avi," Yaakov would say. And he imaged Gila. "Focus on the job, sweetie. It'll come to you. You always figure it out." But he had no ideas.

It was another night with death all around. And fighting sleep was like fighting another battle. He was outnumbered and his equipment inferior. Would his battalion survive? He feared for his men, his friends, his country.

———

The long night gave way to a cloudy, smoke-filled dawn. His team had survived another night and the Syrians hadn't advanced any farther, but he knew he couldn't hold them another day. *How can we stall them until the reserves reach us?*

His tank climbed up a hill so that he could see the other side of the valley that had been taken by the Syrians. In the valley were the still-smoking remnants of Syrian and Israeli tanks.

"My God," he mumbled while changing the focus on his binoculars to see the Syrian T-62s coming into focus. Another cluster of a dozen-plus tanks was farther to the right. They were all on their way up to the highest hill.

Avi radioed Colonel Mazer. "Syrian tanks ahead. I need reinforcements, air support, need help now. We slowed them, but hear me now, I can't stop what's coming at me with what I have."

"How many more tanks are you requesting?" asked Mazer.

"Send me twenty-five tanks. And night-vision equipment."

"I'll send eight. No night equipment. I can't do more. We're outnumbered eight-to-one across the northern frontier." The commander clicked off.

Avi looked back through his binoculars and couldn't find most of the Syrians. Had they vanished? Somehow that was just as unnerving as counting their tanks. They had to be advancing across the gully.

"Let's move!" he commanded. His tank went down the small rise, across a valley, and started up the rocky terrain of the big hill. Avi was sure that his brigade, if it could move quickly, would gain the advantage overlooking the Syrians before they emerged from the gully.

The Syrians came into view. All his tankers could see them.

The Syrians didn't slow down at all. They fired their cannons and charged through the gully.

"Move forward up the hill!" Avi barked into the radio, knowing that everyone understood they'd be exposed for some time to the Syrians' fire.

All his tank commanders, including the eight approaching reinforcements, were on the same channel. Avi shouted, "We need to move—need to get to the big rise, while the Syrians are in the gully. Follow me. Quick now!" He commenced the unprotected climb to gain the strategic high ground.

No one was following.

Enemy fire was landing all around, his tank was firing back, but his brigade wasn't following. They weren't behaving like themselves. Sure, they were sleep-deprived, exhausted, hungry, beyond their limits. So what? They had been trained for this and they weren't doing their job. For just a moment, he wondered if they were right, and he was wrong to charge forward. But he knew the truth. They were afraid.

Avi yelled into the radio, "Where are you? We have to take advantage of this moment. And do it now! No time to waste! What are you made of? Show me. Move now!"

One tank began to move forward. The tank commander, Tzachi, was an immigrant from Ethiopia, just seven years in Israel. *Good for you, Tzachi. But what's wrong with everyone else?*

"Sons of bitches," Avi muttered. He shouted impatiently into the radio, "Are you all chickens? Failing here is not happening, you damn chickens. Let's go. I mean it. We go right now. We can beat them, but we have to move."

One more tank started to follow.

A shell blew right in front of Avi's tank, raining rocks and shrapnel against the turret. His tank would have been blown to pieces if he hadn't stopped to berate the brigade.

"Are the Syrians braver than you are?" He was spitting into the radio. "Do you have balls? Have you forgotten what's at stake, what your jobs are, how your families back home are counting on you?"

That worked. They were all moving and firing now.

Avi relaxed a bit as if he had somehow already won. But they still had to charge through enemy fire.

The battalion raced to a higher elevation, losing one tank, and formed a position facing down at the enemy.

Avi took a deep breath. He now held the high ground during daylight. All the Syrian division was exposed, and he knew his tankers could hold them.

"Aim and fire as fast as you can!" he yelled.

The battalion worked like a precision machine. Smoke filled the air and blackened the heavens. Avi's tankers unloaded nearly all of their ammunition. They decimated the enemy.

Avi climbed down from the cupola to the ground and stepped forward for a better vantage point on a small ledge. He lifted his binoculars and panned the valley. Scattered pockets of flames and smoke funneled to a charcoal cloud hanging just above, filling the view all the way to a dark horizon with a foreboding uncertainty.

It was a sad scene, this valley of death. So much loss on both sides.

Avi considered again the poor bastards burned by the flames. He understood only too well the pain and suffering, and that many families would never be the same.

For a moment he imagined being with his pregnant wife. He loved her, missed her. He ached for her. She must have given birth by now. He couldn't dwell on it. *Is it a girl or a boy? Hope Gila is okay. The baby, too.*

He walked farther away from the tanks. He lifted the binoculars again to take in the entire geography in all directions, just to confirm once more there was no more enemy activity in this part of the Golan. The war wasn't over, but they had held them at this northern strategic point. They had done their job. They had held on long enough, but he wondered if the Syrians had penetrated the line elsewhere.

Tzachi approached him. "As you requested, Avi. I counted them all." Then Tzachi handed a summary of Avi's battalion. There were now only three fully functional tanks left in his battalion.

Avi could hear reinforcements approaching. He knew he'd soon be sharing the status of his tankers with the approaching commanders. They should maintain the momentum. Perhaps he'll be advancing with them into Syria.

Someone handed Avi a radiophone. The call was from Colonel Yosef Goldberg, the commander of a large reserve brigade. Avi advised where they could rendezvous. After hanging up and stepping away from the tank, his mind filled with images of friends who were no more. He began to shake. He pulled off his helmet and sat on the ground. He just stared off into space and drifted back to that moment when Gila had held him and informed him, she was pregnant. He wished for his child to live in a time without war.

A moment later he was back on his feet. His attention returned to the Golan and Syria, unable to consider anything else. He tried to reveal no emotion—no wincing, no choking up—always the warrior. But his heart ached, and a tear rolled down his cheek, wetting his freshly grown beard.

Avi panned once more the valley before him. It was still burning and gushing flames, smoke extending to the heavens— the saddest place in the world—a valley of tears.

Chapter 27
Cambridge, Massachusetts, April 27, 1974

Jonathan

"Thank you for invite," Mahmud said upon entering Jon and Emily's little apartment. He took off his coat and handed it to Jonathan, who promptly carried it to his master bedroom closet.

"We're glad you could join us," Emily said while handing him a soft drink.

"You have nice home," Mahmud offered as he looked around the apartment.

"I had to force your friend to help pick out new furniture with me," Emily told him.

"Hey, a chair is a chair, a bed is a bed," Jonathan said, defending his lack of interest in a pastime as mundane as furniture selection.

"A nice home is important; don't you think Mahmud? And isn't furniture for our baby very important, Mahmud?"

"Most assuredly," said Mahmud quietly, reluctantly.

Jonathan patted Mahmud's shoulder and said, "Come, let's sit in the living room." He was eager to show off his new record player that, at the moment, was sharing Debussy's artistry in stereo.

He handed Mahmud a wineglass filled with grape juice and poured a glass of California merlot for himself. They clinked glasses and began to talk about the institute and New England. After those topics were exhausted, they sat quietly listening to someone perform a Mozart inspiration.

After a while, Mahmud asked, "How's the algebra solution coming?"

"I think I'm making progress. It intrigues me. It's not as difficult as the Fermat problem."

"The what?"

"The Fermat problem is a math proposition made about three hundred and fifty years ago that no one has figured out. I'm going after a more contemporary proposition, so I think I have a chance of solving it and making some serious cash. Haven't I told you about Fermat's Last Theorem?"

"Yes, I remember now. You told me."

"I don't think it can be solved. I could be wrong, but I'm beginning to think the proposition was a sadistic hoax."

At that moment, Emily excused herself. "Got to check the oven now," she said.

Mahmud asked, "How close are you to solving . . . the challenge . . . the project you are working on?"

"So close to solving it, I can taste it. But I'll soon see if I'm on the right track."

"If anyone can solve it, you can, my friend Mr. Bikel."

"If I do solve it, there are more mathematical problems with big dollar bounties. I'd just move on to the next one."

"Solutions are found today that were not found in the past. Businesses keep...moving. Technology keeps moving."

"True, Mahmud, for most fields," said Jonathan as he poured himself another glass of wine. "It might be different for mathematics with cash reward potential. I'd grant you that business and technical applications do evolve. Solving an insolvable problem in mathematics is different. Complex solutions, if there are any, can be well camouflaged."

"Until solution is uncovered?" added Mahmud quickly.

Jonathan thought for a moment and didn't respond. He smiled and took a long drink.

Emily walked back into the room. "Dinner's ready, boys," she said, waving them toward the kitchen table.

They slowly rose from their cushioned chairs, still holding their glasses. Mindful of Mahmud's preferences, Emily served the lamb she had bought from a halal market. At the conclusion of the meal, Emily looked to both men. "Well, guys, what do you think of the lamb?"

"Is wonderful," Mahmud said. "Thank you. You make best lamb."

"Excellent, dear. You've outdone yourself this time," Jonathan added. He was pleased to see Mahmud and Emily getting along.

After dinner, Jonathan and Mahmud retreated to the living room and sat by the coffee table to play chess. Emily cleaned up the kitchen.

After Mahmud left, Jonathan joined Emily to wash the few remaining dishes. "You made a wonderful meal. It was a lot of work for you. Thank you, Emily. It went very well."

"I'm glad. But next time don't leave me to clean up all your messes. You guys are the messiest, sloppiest eaters I've ever seen. Really."

"I like Mahmud."

"I know. He's easy, very friendly," she agreed.

"And smart, possibly the smartest man I know. He really taxes me when we play chess."

"You won, right?"

"Barely. Last time he won."

They continued washing dishes without speaking. Jonathan sensed a sudden cooling from his wife. She had been so warm with Mahmud. Did he do something or say something wrong? No way. He was just imagining it.

Chapter 28
September 24, 1975

Neal

Neal checked the address he had written on his notepad and looked for the street sign. *Yes, this is the right address.* He steered his Oldsmobile sedan to the curb in front of the apartment building. He picked up his binoculars. "Okay, Bikel, now I know where you live. And you live in the basement with the trash." He recalled his father crying out in pain many times. It was the Bikel family that was responsible for his dad's suffering for so many years. Dad had died young.

A beat-up old Chevrolet pulled over and parked in the space in front of him. It was none other than Jonathan Bikel, the bastard himself, toting what appeared to be a bag of groceries and a young woman.

Jonathan has a girlfriend? Maybe a wife? Interesting. She's pretty. Yeah, I'd do her.

September 26, 1975

After a long day scoring student tests, his publisher called. Neal was sure he was in for another long pontification on the do's and don'ts of writing, or the secret keys to a successful book launch.

"How you doin' kid? Hey, look, you know your book's doing okay." This time his voice was animated. "It's no best seller, but it'll make money. You like that, right? That Wall Street guy knew what he was talking about after all. There's a real audience for it."

Neal had thought this small publisher was nuts. But it seems he might reap some benefits for himself. "I'm glad it's off to a good start," said Neal. "You were tough on me, and it took much longer than predicted. Are you saying it's selling well?"

"Neal, it'll pay off big-time. Of course, I had to be tough with you—this is tough stuff. But now you discovered a niche and you're building a following. There's a market out there. And I'll finance the next book myself."

"We don't need the Wall Street—"

"No. He's an ass to work with. And he's happy he got his message out. Most people would be happy with that. He'll make good money on our book, our message. Anyways, the money is peanuts in his world." He laughed. "The anti-Israel sentiment is out there. And who knows where it'll take us? Neal, why don't you get deeper on the topic with the next book? You can establish your own audience."

Neal smiled. "I do have some other ideas on other parts of the world, especially Vietnam and China. Lot of material there. I could do a lot in Africa, too, and not just South Africa, but—"

"No, no, not now anyway. We've got a whale on the line and you're thinking of cut bait? Forget it. This is a cyclical business. When it's hot, it's hot. And when it's not, well, it can get cold as ice in a heartbeat. I've been in this business, kid, for a long time. Understand what I'm saying?"

Neal sighed. "I guess. I mean, I do. I'll get you the best book ever written on the subject you want. Until you tell me otherwise."

"Fine. That's the spirit. Let's get to work and make some real money."

April 7, 1976

Neal quick-stepped to his car parked on Massachusetts Avenue. But before reaching the street, someone called out from behind. "Professor Chomelstien. One moment please."

Neal stopped and turned around. Standing before him was a short but solidly built man with a big head and large frame. He had a thin scar running from his forehead, through his eyebrow, to his cheek, reminiscent of a character in a 1950s gangster movie. "Yeah, what? I'm already late for my appointment."

"I won't be long," said this bearded man with an unusual accent. He spoke with an authority that made Neal feel as if he were the annoying, intrusive one. Now Neal was curious as to what this daunting figure wanted.

"My name Khalid. I was given the honor to read your book. Without any question, no question, you should have good—"

"I'm in a hurry, Khalid . . . Did I say your name right?"

"I want to talk to you about our cause, *mon ami*. You can help us even more. I think what I say will be of much interest to you."

"Are you just looking for a donation?"

"No. Of course, we'd be grateful for that, and I know how busy you are. But I just want to invite you to speak at my mosque in Boston, and, if you are willing, at another mosque in Cambridge at another time. I've heard you speak about your book. You're an impressive speaker and will move many people. I would like—"

"Sure, I'll do it." Neal smiled wide.

"You will?" asked Khalid, his voice happily energized. "*Bien.* So very good. Very good."

"When?"

"Whenever it is convenient. Is next Friday evening too soon?"

"I can do it Friday. I'll have to check my calendar, but I think that day is clear."

"Professor, you will enjoy this experience. Have you been to a mosque before?"

"No."

"It is beautiful. I will introduce you to everyone. You will be my personal honored guest."

"Thank you."

"Your publisher speaks highly of you. And you're a professor at MIT, your book, your knowledge, they are most important. The worshipers will learn much from you."

"I'll do what I can."

"Thank you, professor. I will look forward to Friday."

Chapter 29
Cambridge, MA, April 1, 1980

Neal

Khalid was sipping a cup of tea at the Kabob Restaurant in Kendall Square. He took a bite of the lamb and leaned to the right as he spoke. "Yes, Professor Neal, I'm teaching French this semester at the Community College in Charlestown. Not sure what next year brings."

"You like it?"

"*C'est bien*, all good, but I will be glad when semester is over," said Khalid.

"I will be glad, too, for the semester to end," said Neal. He scooped hummus off his plate with a pie-shaped piece of pita bread.

"I like your summer." Kahlid looked up to the heavens, as if doing so would somehow enhance the experience of an American spring. "I like the warmth of your sun. Why do Americans complain about heat? Your winters are terrible, and life is too short to live indoors. In your winter . . . I want to leave your city. Then the spring comes and . . . somehow, I forget all my complaints."

Neal laughed. "That's New England for you."

Khalid nodded several times with his mouth full and straightened up in the wire-back chair. "Shall I get to the reason I asked to meet you today? And I know it is busy time. You must be preparing the finals?"

Neal nodded. "Haven't I helped your cause?"

"Very generous with your time and donations. Your books and speeches have been very influential. They help us. *Merci*."

Khalid appeared to look past Neal as if there were a ghost behind him.

Neal turned his head but saw nothing of note. "I know you invited me to lunch for, as you put it, something very important. Why don't we get to that now? What is it you want, Khalid?"

"Yes. Of course. I have a few things to discuss. First, we are prepared to donate considerable funds to your university. And we would like you to be the agent to arrange the transfer. I mean you will be our representative to receive the funds and interact with the financial department at your university. By the way, this isn't unusual. We've already been doing this for some time at other universities including Harvard and Yale. We are grooming some strong future leaders there that will support our . . . well, you know, support our interests. And we are successfully undermining Israel's interests."

"If I can do this successfully, and I'm not sure I can, what's in it for me?"

"You will get a commission of sorts. A very nice sum. It depends on how things work out."

"'Things'? What are you talking about? Get to the point."

"We have books with our point of view that should be read by everyone, especially the intellectual elite. The future leaders of your country go to the elite universities. We are willing to pay . . . so our point of view grows an audience. Well, not a general audience, I mean a world view to change the thinking of students that are likely to assume tomorrow's leadership positions in politics and even business."

"How much for me?"

"You will be well taken care of. I assure you. It depends on how well you do. And if you raise money for the university, they will take care of you as well. You will be swimming in George Washingtons."

"I will think about this."

"Of course. Just imagine your position if you are the one to funnel millions. Do you see how important you will be? Yes, you think about this, about how to change your life to a higher level, a very nice future. There are many others that are begging us.

Really. No falsehood. I'm coming to you first. You already have books circulated. Your book's message is same as our message. That's why I am coming to you now."

Neal was excited yet determined not to show how excited he was.

Now Khalid's voice changed. He looked Neal in the eye and said, "Now I have a simple request, my friend. I have a friend who needs a place to stay for one week, no more."

"Are you asking me to recommend a hotel?"

Khalid's confused look dissolved into laughter. "*Monsieur*, you are a funny man. No, professor, I am not looking for hotel. This man cannot go to hotel or to my . . . associates. His tourist visa has expired. And FBI is already watching everyone, including me. I need to deposit him somewhere they would never look, some place beyond suspicion."

"And I suppose I can't ask what he has done to earn such recognition?"

Khalid shrugged.

"Didn't think so. You're evasive," said Neal. "A week, you say?"

"Absolutely. Probably less, but I don't want to . . . mislead you."

"When?"

"Tonight."

"What? Tonight? You kidding?"

"I wouldn't ask if it were not important. And I didn't want to discuss this on the phone with you."

Neal thought for a moment. "None of this makes sense to me. You could hide him in a million places. What will happen in a week that'll make a difference?"

"We need to get him out of the country before he is arrested and interrogated. Yes, we can put him in a cabin in New Hampshire or a basement in some town in the mountains. But why do that to someone if we can make his stay more comfortable with someone we trust, like you? Can we trust you, my friend?"

"That's for you to answer, isn't it?"

"In a week we will have all the documents we need to get him out of the country as well as . . . other arrangements."

"It doesn't make sense to me, but I don't really care. Putting him up is not a big imposition. All right then."

"That means . . . what?"

"Bring him over." Neal scratched out his address on a napkin and handed it to Khalid. "I live alone in Lincoln. I have a lot of space."

"Very good."

"You're welcome," said Neal. "But I don't want any trouble coming my way. Is this man being followed?"

"No, nothing like that, I'd never ask of you anything that will be a problem for you."

"Well, why not drop him in a hotel?"

"His face is well known to some people even here in America. If a hotel worker or guest knows him, there will be a problem."

"And there won't be any problem for me? You're sure?"

Khalid nodded. "Very sure. I'd never create a problem for you. I'd put my life down to save you."

"You don't need to do that. At least I hope not. Okay, sure, bring him over."

"You'll do it? Thank you. He will not be a burden. He will just sleep and eat."

"Just like a pet?" Neal laughed and wiped his mouth, and then placed his napkin over his near-empty plate.

Khalid also laughed. "*Exacte.*"

"I'm full," Neal announced. He was trying to be nonchalant but couldn't deny feelings of excitement mixed with a strong dose of anxiety.

"Thank you, let me get lunch," said Khalid as he reached for his wallet.

"It's okay, Khalid, I'll take care of the lunch."

"Thank you." Khalid stood up. "Sorry my friend. I must go. Will drop the package at your house at six pm. Do you have an extra key for our guest?"

Neal nodded.

Soon after Khalid left, the waitress came by. "Everything okay?" she asked in the sweetest voice.'

"Perfect."

"Anything else I can get for you?" she asked.

Neal studied her. She was a very cute young coed. "Just the check. Tell me, which school do you go to?" And before she could answer, he asked, "What's your name?"

"I'm a junior at Emerson. I'm Joy," she said.

"You certainly are," said Neal.

April 8, 1980

While shopping at Stop & Shop, Neal saw a familiar woman. He was sure he had met her somewhere. Could she be the woman he saw with Bikel? She was entering the coffee aisle. He pulled his shopping cart beside hers and asked, "Are you Mrs. Bikel? Mrs. Jonathan Bikel?"

"Why yes, I am." She smiled widely. "And you are?"

He watched her eyes move down and up. This woman was definitely checking him out. Did he pass her test? "I'm Neal. I teach at the same university as your husband. We must have met at some event there. You look very familiar to me."

"Maybe. You also look familiar." She seemed to be buying his bull. Or maybe she was pretending to buy it. That could even be better.

She extended her hand, and he shook it.

"I teach English mostly to engineering students . . . and they don't really give a hoot about proper English."

She laughed.

"I'd like to hear your opinion of the school events," said Neal. "Do you have a few minutes for a cup of coffee?"

She thought for just a moment, then smiled. "I'd love to."

Neal also smiled. He was almost sure she wasn't joining him to give an opinion on school crap.

April 9, 1980

At precisely six o'clock, Neal's bell rang. It was Khalid and someone else, the "package," who was wearing a knapsack and a baseball cap, and wheeling an oversized black suitcase.

"Evening, Neal. Meet Mohammed. He doesn't speak much English."

"Hello, Mohammed. *Alayhi as-Salem*," said Neal.

Mohammed was thin and had a gentleness about him, and, despite his scraggly black beard, he looked very innocent, not at all like a fugitive in hiding.

"How . . . are . . . you?" Mohammed said in accented English and added some Arabic that Neal didn't understand.

Neal shook his guest's hand and turned to Khalid. "You just heard all the Arabic I know, so you better stay to translate my house tour before you leave, or he won't know where to eat or piss."

"Yeah, yeah, I'll stay for a little while. It's a big house. Nice." Khalid scanned the expansive open living room beyond the entranceway. "A beautiful house."

"It works for me now. It's small for the neighborhood. One day I'll expand it. Let's start in the kitchen. By the way, he looks like he brought enough luggage to stay a few years."

Khalid didn't laugh. He mumbled, "Don't worry."

———

Mohammed kept mostly to the spare bedroom on the first floor. He only said "hello" or "bye-bye" when he occasionally passed by Neal on his way to the bathroom or refrigerator. Neal wouldn't have known he was in the house had he not heard a cell phone ring or Arabic spoken.

Two nights after Mohammed arrived, Neal came home from the university to find no sign of Mohammed or his bags.

Neal called Khalid. "I don't know where Mohammed is. I don't know if he left, got lost, captured, or—"

"He's gone. Told you he wouldn't be long. Was he a problem?"

"No. He was quiet, very polite. I still would've liked to know if and when he left."

"Why?"

"Just to be sure nothing bad happened. Hey, you brought me into this—I don't know—this secret hiding thing."

"Did you like it?"

Neal laughed. "Like it? Might've been better if I knew more. But he was so quiet I almost forgot he was there. Should I change my locks now?"

"You can if you want, but not necessary. *Merci*. Thank you for doing this."

"Sure," said Neal.

July 4, 1980

Neal's phone rang. He put his spaghetti dinner aside. "Yeah. Hello," he mumbled.

"We're on our way to you."

"Whaa—? Who is this? It's—"

Click.

"Hello. Hello?" There was no one on the line. *Who the hell would be calling? Khalid? No, it didn't sound like Khalid.*

The caller had said they were coming his way. Should he make dinner for them? Could've been a wrong number, but the strange tone of the call unsettled him. He got up and went to the bathroom. "I look like hell," he said out loud to his image in the mirror.

He paced for a while. *Maybe no one's coming.*

He went to his bar downstairs. He poured bourbon into a shot glass and emptied it in two gulps.

In a little while, there was a loud and desperate pounding at the front door. "Coming," said Neal. *Who the hell?*

The banging grew louder and accelerated with renewed urgency. Someone was intent on breaking down his door.

Neal felt fear in his gut and froze. He wanted to yell but nothing came out. *I should call the police.* Finally, he uttered, "Who's there?" It felt as if someone else spoke his words.

"Mohammed," a voice shouted back.

The door opened. They had a key. Mohammed and two other bearded young men in Western jeans, T-shirts, and baseball caps charged into his reception area, carrying a fourth man. The fourth was bleeding. Neal noticed the wounded man wore no head cover. His scalp was colored mostly by dried blood.

Neal said nothing. Mohammed gave him a silent nod. The bleeding man was writhing in pain. Neal noticed two of the other men were also blood-stained; one was oozing red drops from his left cheek and ear.

Neal glanced down at the red blood puddles mixing with blackish mud covering his beautiful white marble entryway and foyer. "What . . . what do you need?"

They didn't answer him. They were shouting in another language. Neal watched them carry the wounded man through the living room to the sofa.

That's a custom-made suede sofa, damn it. Cost a fortune. Neal watched the crew clumsily try to settle the man; they sure weren't abating the poor bastard's pain. The wounded man was spread out across the sofa, groaning, and biting back sobs. One of the other men went back to slam the front door shut. Another one squatted on the floor beside the victim. The tall one ripped open the wounded man's shirt, and Neal could see the man's intestines drop to the sofa like a heap of boiled pasta. Neal looked away.

"Bandage," the tallest of the men shouted to Neal. "Rags . . . for make bandage."

"I understand," said Neal. He ran upstairs to his closet, grabbed several of his old shirts and pants, found scissors, and ran back to his guests.

"Will this do?" he asked.

The tall one nodded. "Alcohol . . . something."

"What . . . you want drinks?"

"For infect— and something . . . for pain."

"Aspirin?"

"Yes! Go!"

Neal grabbed his open bourbon bottle with his right hand and ran to the bathroom cabinet. He collected an aspirin bottle and put it in his pocket, scooped several other pill bottles that might be useful, and ran back downstairs.

"This is what I could find," he told the tall one.

The tall one nodded slightly. "Go sit now," he commanded.

Neal retreated to his study and turned on the television in that room. A grim-faced reporter was speaking:

"There was a bomb planted this afternoon at the Boston Harborfest celebration. At this time, the extent of the casualties has yet to be determined. Policemen arrived on the scene and fired at the gunmen. An undetermined number of victims have been rushed to Beth Israel Hospital and Massachusetts General Hospital."

Neal processed what he had just seen and wiped his brow. *What has Khalid got me into?* He flicked the television to another channel and stood up. Same news on the second station. He paced back and forth. *It'll be all right.* He reminded himself that he knew nothing about this. He was as surprised as anyone. He was innocent.

He sat down again, took a deep breath, and decided he ought to assess his risks. He knew nothing of this day's action, but now he had been brought into it. The team in his house wouldn't hurt him. *Am I sure?*

He rubbed his forehead and took a deep breath. They came to him as friends needing help. If they wanted to hurt him, they'd have shot him when they stormed in. And they asked for help. Mohammed had politely nodded to him.

His hands trembled, but despite that, something made him feel energized. The national news outlets—maybe international news too—would soon pick up the story from the local news, and it might be carried around the world. No doubt about that. He liked being a part of it, and, in the unlikely event of a police inquiry, he'd play the innocent bystander. He could simply argue he was a victim, forced to accommodate these terrorists at gunpoint. He was as innocent as a newborn. *Get over the bloody floors and furnishings. That can all be cleaned up.*

This was beyond anything he'd imagined. Here he was, at the epicenter of something worthy of international news. And no one had a clue. He got up and paced the floor for a while, then headed to his bar. He needed a drink. He filled a glass to the rim with his best Scotch, forty-year-old Auchentoshan single malt, which he enjoyed on special occasions. *No ice, don't want to dilute this stuff.*

He slowly sipped his drink while considering how his life had just transformed into a new and uncertain adventure. There was something very exciting about the whole thing. He watched his hand quiver.

Chapter 30

North Cambridge, MA, November 2, 1982

Jonathan

Jonathan and Emily loved their new home. Jonathan especially liked his new desk where he alternated between working on his students' grades, writing software, and solving a potentially lucrative mathematical puzzle. In the background, his new stereo provided a sweet congruence of violins from a Schubert masterpiece.

He loved having a driveway. Competing for overnight parking on the street had often been problematic. He recalled neighbors that dug through snowbanks to stake their parking claim with an old chair or barrel, something like gold miners staking claims in 1840.

And there were the neighborhood punks that seemed addicted to stealing cars just for the joyrides. He had been victimized only once, likely benefiting from the unattractive age and condition of his old Chevy.

Emily yelled out, "Jonathan!"

"What?" he shouted back.

"Put Miriam to bed. It's late."

He found Miriam in the living room watching a Sesame Street rerun. "Mimi, your mother says it's bedtime."

"No."

"Come on now. It's time."

She didn't respond to him. She continued watching television, sucking three fingers on her left hand as she sometimes did when she was overtired, and clutching her "My Little Pony" with her right hand.

Jonathan picked her up and carried her to her bedroom.

"No, I want to watch," Miriam whined while squirming in his arm.

He put her in pajamas and tucked her in the little bed under the Mickey and Minnie quilt.

Miriam settled down and continued sucking her fingers and clutching the toy pony.

She was so cute. He loved her brown ponytail. He ran his hand over her little head and kissed her cheeks.

"Mommy said that you—oh, never mind," she said, turning her head to the side.

"Is something bothering you, honey?"

She was quiet a while, so he repeated the question. He could tell she was deliberating.

"Let's just read *Snow White*," she said.

"Ah, excellent choice." Jonathan didn't press the matter, but he knew something had bothered her. He thumbed through the collection of children's books to the side of the nightstand and retrieved *Snow White*. He read the story, tucked her in, and gave her a kiss on her forehead. "Don't let the bedbugs bite."

He stood up, turned on the little Minnie Mouse night light, and stepped away to shut off the overhead light.

"Daddy, I want another story."

"It's late. It's bedtime."

"Pleeease, Daddy."

"Okay, okay, just one more story."

"Daddy . . ."

"Yes, cutie?"

"Mommy says . . ."

"What?"

"She calls you *loser*. What's that mean?"

Jonathan was surprised. Could Emily have said that to their young daughter? Mimi must have misunderstood. Although he suspected something odd and different was going on with Emily, he decided to answer his daughter's question. "Oh, Mommy just meant I lost a game called chess that I like to play. Sometimes I win. Sometimes I lose."

Miriam fell asleep before he could finish the second story. After tucking the blankets under her little body, he turned off the overhead light and headed back to his office to work on a math puzzle.

Three hours later, he called it quits and headed to bed. As he approached, he heard a strange *thump-thump* coming from the bedroom. He might need to bleed the radiators again.

The door was partially open, and he could see his wife, wearing only underwear, sitting in a chair with her back to him. Her head was banging against the wall with the steadiness of a metronome. She was the source of the banging.

Okay, it was her little joke. Got his attention. "Is that a new headache remedy, dear?"

Emily turned around quickly. Her face was flushed.

"Oh, Jonathan," she managed.

"Are you okay?"

"Work is hard. Miriam is hard. I'm just tired, that's all."

"Can I help?"

She hesitated. "No. Ahhh—but no."

April 29, 1983

Jonathan heard Emily call from the living room, "The sitter's here."

"Coming, I'm coming," Jonathan said. He put on his brown tweed sports jacket and gray cap. The cap had been handmade in Ireland, and he liked its feel and warmth.

He went to say good night to Miriam. He gave her a big hug. "What are you going to do tonight?"

"Watch TV," she said. "And Mary is going to read me a new story. Daddy, can you read me a story when you get home?"

"Can't tonight, honey. We'll be back late, and you'll be sleeping. How about tomorrow?"

"Daddy, can you—"

"What are you doing?" Emily shouted. "You're winding her up, and Mary won't be able to get her to sleep. Let's go. You've already given her good-night kisses." She turned to Mimi. "Your daddy and I must go now. Be good and listen to Mary."

Mimi stuck out her tongue at her mother and ran off to the family room to watch television.

"We'll be fine. Good night, Mr. Bikel, Mrs. Bikel," said Mary, the skinny teenaged babysitter, with a reassuring authority beyond her years.

"Thanks, Mary," Jonathan responded with a calm that belied his frustration over his wife's edginess.

They walked down the back stairs to the gold-colored Chevy. "This car is filthy," said Emily. "You never thought to throw away these cookie wrappers? Or the soda cans or candy boxes?"

Jonathan said nothing. He just focused on backing out safely. Besides, he was dreading the dean's annual event.

Jonathan began to sneeze so hard and so frequently that he pulled over and parked under a large tree. *Damn allergies. Good thing I brought two handkerchiefs.*

"Are you done now?" Emily snapped.

Jonathan looked at her and said nothing as he slowly put the car back into drive. *What did I ever see in this woman?*

Chapter 31

Boston, Massachusetts, August 24, 1984

Neal

Neal reserved a table at his favorite hotel restaurant in Copley Square. He loved the atmosphere and the decor, especially the decorative fine woods that served as a backdrop for the animal heads mounted on the walls. Neal assumed the animal heads on display were installed decades ago and acquired by the hotel at a time when these heads would enhance a patron's dining and drinking experience. African animal trophies were once considered prized collectables, something like a tribute to the skills, fortitude, and courage of the hunter. Now he regarded them as a questionable novelty from an age gone by, a time when such trophies reflected one's skills, including the tenacity to weather the elements and prevail. But the trophies were compelling in another way, a historical reminder of man's insensitivity and lack of compassion.

"My usual Scotch, please, Benny," Neal instructed his waiter.

"Right away, sir."

"Ice on the side."

"Yes, sir, I know. Right away."

The waiter served his drink just as Neal's date walked in. *Hey, she really dolled up for me this time.* She was looking fabulous in that tight red dress that could easily have been featured in a fashion magazine. It was the kind of attire that seemed to shout hey, look at me...see what I've got.

"Hi, beautiful," he said as she approached his table.

"Hi, handsome," she retorted. She offered a sexy smile as she sat down. "Did you order for us?"

"Not yet."

"Sorry to tell you this, but I don't have much time tonight. We'll have to make it a quickie. We will still enjoy it, just not as good as last time." She smiled. "Is that okay? I've missed you. And it's so good to see you."

"It's always very good to see you. And you look really good, really hot." Neal called the waiter over, and whispered, "We're going to our room now. Just charge the drink to my account and add twenty percent for yourself."

"Yes, Mr. Chomelstien. Thank you."

Neal turned back to his date. "Okay, let's go."

"So, Neal, how was your week?" she asked as they walked to the elevator.

"Too long, too busy. You know I was really looking forward to being with you." He looked up and tried to count the days. "It's been . . . four weeks?"

"So long? No wonder you've missed me." She laughed.

He thought she was prettier when she laughed. "I'm living the life," he said. And he started to laugh as well.

"Yes, I guess you are. By the way, it was only three weeks ago—not four. Remember?"

"It seems so much longer."

"You missed me? Great."

They got on the elevator and Neal pressed the button for the top floor. "I got the penthouse suite for tonight. I might just stay here after you leave. You don't want to keep that husband of yours waiting too long."

"Jon's not suspicious. He's in another world. His own world."

"I feel bad for you, having to live with that ass. Be sure to give Jonathan my best."

"That's not a good idea."

Neal laughed. "Okay, okay. You deserve better than Bikel. I'll make it up to you. You deserve a real man. A real lover."

She giggled. "Yes, I certainly do. Know any?"

They both laughed. "Time's a-wastin," said Neal. "I think you are going to like this suite."

"I love it already, Neal sweetie. And I haven't even seen it."

"Emily Bikel, you are a funny lady."

She offered him a wide smile.

Chapter 32

Cambridge, Massachusetts, November 19, 1984

Jonathan

Jonathan walked by his bathroom. The door was open and there was Emily focusing on the mirror, sinking her polished fingernails into her cheeks hard enough to mark her face with long, dotted, parallel red lines. She seemed oblivious to his presence.

Jonathan muttered, "What the hell . . ."

"Leave me alone!" Emily shrieked while whirling around to face him.

Jonathan felt attacked, as if he had done something terribly wrong. "What the hell are you doing?"

"You made me do it."

"I did what? How did I make you do it? Your face is dripping blood. Don't women try to make their faces pretty?"

"Living with you makes me do it."

"Huh? That's nuts. You think I wanted you to hurt yourself?"

"I want to be ugly for you."

Jonathan blinked, unable to make sense of what she was saying. "Ugly . . . for me?"

Emily slathered makeup over her face, trying to hide the damage she had inflicted. "Damn," she yelled, apparently unhappy with the repair.

"What do you want from me? Can you just tell me what you want?" Jonathan pleaded. But she didn't answer.

He stood there confused, bewildered, trying to figure out what was happening with his wife. She was getting worse every year. The shrinks didn't help.

Later that workday, Jonathan left his office a bit early, had an easy commute home, and parked the old Chevy in the driveway. He unlocked the side entrance and walked into his kitchen just as the phone rang. He picked it up a moment after it stopped ringing. He assumed Emily had just picked up the call on another extension.

He heard a male voice say, "Fine. Is it okay to talk now?"

"Yeah, he's out." It was Emily's voice.

"Good," replied the male voice.

"It's getting harder and harder. I don't know what to do about it," she said.

"Look, if he bothers you, please call me. Let me help you."

"I don't know," Emily said.

"No, really, use me as a sounding board, as a friend, as an outlet. You need someone now, someone that you trust, that makes you feel safe. I want it to be me." He sang, "Let it be me . . ."

Emily laughed. "Don't give up your day job, Neal."

"I won't. Anyway, he could get violent, you know. If he starts, you should definitely call me. I'll come right down there. It won't take me long to get to your house."

"It's so hard," she said.

"But you told me you liked it hard."

Jonathan couldn't believe what he was hearing. His wife was once his best friend, or so he had thought. Wasn't she his partner in life, not to mention his longtime lover, in fact, his only lover? And now that voice he had loved was confiding her feelings to a stranger, someone she could apparently only talk to when he wasn't home. A knot formed in his stomach. He felt betrayed, cut down. It was a new kind of hurt, a painful emotional hurt.

"Let's stop talking about him," the man continued with a chuckle. "I had a great time last night."

Emily giggled like a teen. "Yeah, me too." Her tone seemed full of artificial sweetener.

"You said his cousin is an officer in the Israeli army?" asked the man.

"I did. Why, is there—"

"Oh, no reason, just curious. Is the officer Avi Bikel, by any chance?"

"Yes. You heard of him? He's a strange one. He and his wife visited once."

Jonathan hung up. He couldn't listen anymore.

He didn't know what to do. His eyes welled, and he went to retrieve a few aspirin.

But it didn't help. So, he went to the dining room to open a bottle of wine. He poured a full glass. He sat at the dining table and sipped the wine. Did he hear right? Could it be Chomelstien? The answer hit him like a freight train. It was Chomelstien. He knew that voice and those self-righteous inflections.

How long has she been seeing him? "She's having an affair under my nose with that schmuck, and I never suspected a thing? What's wrong with me?" he whispered. Another equally unsettling question occurred to him. Why would an anti-Israel activist ask about his Israeli cousin?

He poured another full glass and sipped it for twenty minutes before Emily passed by.

"You're home?" she asked.

Jonathan didn't respond. He couldn't find the right words. He considered saying he wasn't home.

"How long have you been home?" Emily asked sweetly, as if it were an innocent question.

"Long enough."

"Meaning?"

"Long enough to hear your conversation with Neal."

He had expected Emily to react emotionally, to turn a different color, to stutter, to scream like she always screamed.

"Oh, that," she said calmly, not missing a beat.

"Yes, that," he said.

She waved downward, dismissing his comments as hallucinations. She walked into the kitchen.

Jonathan stood up and followed her. "Don't you owe me an explanation?"

"For what?"

He stared at her, unable to believe what he was hearing. "You've really got nerve, you know. After you—"

"What are you babbling about?" she demanded.

"You're having an affair, aren't you? And with the world's chief nutcase."

"Boy have you got a vivid imagination."

"I heard your conversation. Don't lie to me."

"I don't know what you think you heard," she said.

"I'm not a teenager. You can't lie your way out of this like you do with Mimi. You lie to everyone."

"You've been drinking too much. I don't like you when you drink. You get nasty and aggressive."

Jonathan shook his head. "I'm not a drinker." He felt as if his life was dissolving into a bad dream. This happened to other people, not him. "Why did he ask about Avi? Tell me."

"If you're trying to tell me you want an affair, go ahead. I don't care."

"I don't want an affair."

"Maybe you're already having one," she insisted, as if she were the injured party.

"I'm not. But you are." Even as he said the words, he knew they were useless. He finally concluded she would stick to her own lies, and there was nothing he could say or do that she wouldn't distort.

Good thing Mimi's at school.

Jonathan couldn't eat dinner that night. He slept on the couch, feeling empty and hollow, abandoned and alone. Sleep eluded him, so he got up and went to the window and studied the brighter stars. He identified the constellations he could remember. The moon was full, and silver clouds floated in front of it.

After a while, he went to the dining room for more wine. Then he returned to his inadequate couch, closed his eyes, and let the warmth from the wine escort him to sleep.

December 2, 1984

Jonathan stopped by his old house, now Emily's house, to retrieve his proprietary software that he had left behind. As he exited his old home, his little cape, he remembered the thrill of buying his first home. Only now did he realize how much this simple home had meant to a kid from Jersey City.

Emily followed him outside. "Jonathan," she shouted.

He ignored her and proceeded to load two boxes into his trunk. She looked desperate, disheveled, and intense.

"Jonathan, we have to talk." She had the look and tone of a hawk extending its claws.

He slammed down the trunk hatch, walked toward the driver's seat. "What now?"

"I need more money," she said loud enough for the entire street to hear. "There's no way I can take care of this house on the income I'm receiving."

"I don't have any money left. You took it all. And by the way, what do you spend it on?"

Emily walked right up to him, nose to nose. "Don't talk to me like that, you bastard! I'm not kidding!" She was screaming and pointing her finger at him.

He ignored her.

Emily raised her right arm with the intent to slap him across his face. But Jonathan managed to block the intended strike with his left forearm. Then, reflexively, he slapped her with his right hand.

He was very surprised. It was totally involuntary, but weirdly gratifying to strike back at someone who had hurt him in so many ways. Emily was holding her cheek with one hand and bending forward from her waist.

He started to apologize. "Emily, are you okay? I'm—"

"Fuck you."

He quick-stepped to his car without apologizing. He got in the driver's seat, slammed the car door, and drove off. Through the rearview mirror, he saw Emily still screaming in the middle of the street. She shouted, "I'll get you for this. You'll be sorry."

She continued yelling, so he rolled up his window. Now there was silence. He smiled.

Cambridge, Massachusetts, February 1, 1985

Two uniformed police officers approached Jonathan just as he exited his office. He was holding a file in his left hand and closing his briefcase with his right.

"Mr. Bikel? Jonathan Bikel?" the tall officer asked.

"Yes?"

"We need to talk to you—somewhere private?" The officer spoke in a flat monotone.

Jonathan looked at him, then at the shorter, bulkier policeman. "Can't right now. Late for my lecture." He stepped by them.

"Really, sir," the officer repeated louder, forcing Jonathan to stop and look back. "We need to speak to you. We could do it here, but—"

"What's this about?"

The officer's expression turned to impatience. "Well, we can do it right here. We have an arrest warrant for you."

The shorter officer Mirandaized Jonathan.

"I'm being arrested? This is a mistake." Seconds later he said to himself, "Oh, it has to be my crazy ex's doing."

The short officer pulled Jonathan's hands behind his back and attached handcuffs.

"Do you have to put those damn things on?"

"Standard procedure," the short stocky cop said.

"I don't believe this. What is that crazy bitch doing now?"

"Would you like me to carry your case?" the tall one offered.

"Yeah, sure," Jonathan said. "This is embarrassing."

They guided him down the corridor, which now seemed three times longer than it had ever been, pulling him quickly past the gauntlet of stares from students and faculty. "God damn embarrassing," he repeated, but the policemen weren't listening.

At the police station, the tall cop handed the paperwork to the desk sergeant.

"Assault charge?" the sergeant said while thumbing through the paperwork and reading a few lines.

"It's nuts. I didn't assault anyone. My ex is making up stuff, that's all."

"Tell it to the judge," the sergeant offered, his eyes studying the papers on his desk. "Got a good lawyer, bud? Now's the right time to call one."

———

Three hours later, Mahmud arrived at the police station with bail money.

"Thank you, Mahmud. You're a good man."

"I'm grateful for opportunity to help. You do much for me."

"But this is a lot of money. And you're picking me up at the police station, too. This is just above and beyond."

"Forget it."

"One day, I'll pay you back, I swear."

"I know."

"I mean it. Might take a while. But one day I'll pay you back—and with interest."

Mahmud smiled. "Come, my friend." He patted Jonathan's shoulder. "I'll drive you home now."

Jonathan followed Mahmud to his car, a tired-looking old Ford.

They were both quiet for a while until Mahmud pulled onto Massachusetts Avenue. Then Jonathan became aware of an uneasy look on Mahmud's face.

"What's going on?" asked Jonathan.

Mahmud nodded. He seemed acquiescent. "I've been thinking how to share this with you, my friend. My family wants me to come home." Mahmud placed his hand over his heart apologetically. "I've thought about it. A lot. They say it's time to marry and settle down." Mahmud sounded nervous. "You are my good friend and I want you to know. I've decided to do it. I will go back."

"Go back to Jordan?"

"Well, it's now called occupied territory, ever since the '67 war."

"I see," Jonathan said.

"My family says it is time—actually past time—for me to marry, and I need to marry local woman that knows our customs, expectations, our rituals."

"Any particular one?"

"No, nothing like that. Just someone of our faith from a good family. I know they just want the best for me. You know, after what happened to you in this country, I'm thinking they're right."

Jonathan took a long breath. "I'd hate to see you leave," he said, but that sounded self-serving. "Look, if this is what you want, I wish you all the best. I hope you'll still keep in touch."

"Thank you, my friend. You have been my best friend in America. I am grateful."

"Look, I know you're talented. I know you'll be successful no matter what you do or where you do it. I mean, it's no accident that you wound up at MIT."

Mahmud gave him a wide smile.

Jonathan continued, "And I will pay you back for your generous help. Every cent. With interest. More, even. As soon as I can. I promise."

Mahmud nodded as he parked the car in front of Jonathan's home.

They both got out of the car, shook hands, and embraced one another.

"*Liukann Allah maeak*," said Mahmud, putting his right hand over his heart. "May God be with you."

———

Jonathan was lucky. The judge let him off but ordered him to stay away from Emily. That would be no hardship.

Two weeks after his court hearing, Jonathan received an official-looking letter from the institute. He opened it immediately. He couldn't believe what the letter said. He was certain Chomelstien was behind it. He needed to read it again:

Dear Dr. Bikel,

The trustees of the Massachusetts Institute of Technology have determined that your actions constitute a violation of our covenants covering policy, harassment, and criminal acts. After considerable review and consideration by your peer committee, we have determined that we must terminate your employment effective immediately.

A summary of your final compensation and entitlements will be sent to you shortly under separate cover.

Please know that the board and I wish to express our utmost regret that our relationship should end under such circumstances.

Yours truly,

Charles Dentworth III

Dean of Science

April 1, 1985

Neal

Neal's house phone rang. It was Emily.

"I'm fine, thank you, Emily," he said. "How have you been?" *I knew she'd call sooner or later.*

"Neal, why haven't you called me?"

"Well, Emily, we had fun, didn't we?"

"Yes. Of course. Why not continue to have fun? I divorced my husband for you."

"For me? I never asked you to do that. He was a weird guy and you wanted him out. Right?"

"Yes. But I wanted to be with you."

"You were with me. Many nights. Did we talk about anything more? No. We didn't."

"Don't you want to be with me?" He could hear in her voice she was on the verge of tears. "You loved me. You told me so."

"I loved our rendezvous. Did I ever talk about anything in the future? Didn't you have fun with me? Well, it was a lot of fun. Now we can move on and have fun with others. Right? You have no attachments or responsibilities. Go have fun."

"But Neal, I don't—"

April 1, 1985

"Good-bye."

"Wait—"

"Thanks for calling." Neal hung up.

Chapter 33
April 7, 1985

Jonathan

The next Friday morning, Jonathan carried his packed suitcase to his parents' New Jersey apartment. He carried two heavy suitcases up the stairs and knocked on the door. His mother greeted him with a hug and ushered him to the kitchen where his favorite casserole was waiting.

Thirty minutes later, Lazer walked into the kitchen. "You're here for a violin lesson?"

"Very funny, Dad."

"You can stay with us as long as you need," the old man said. "Of course, the rent is very reasonable."

"Very generous. You know I need to be in Boston, not Jersey. My daughter is there. My business contacts are there, so—"

"Want more?" his mother asked, pointing at the casserole.

"No, no. I'm full. It was delicious. Much better than what I've been eating since I got married."

"She wasn't very nice, your wife."

"No. She wasn't—as it turned out. I just didn't see it."

"We did. We couldn't say anything."

"Yeah. Well, please feel free to speak up if I ever marry again. Yes, I think I will have another small plate after all."

His mother smiled as she scooped up another helping.

—

That evening, Jonathan went by himself to his parents' synagogue, a short walk from their apartment. He hadn't been to a synagogue in years, not since his wedding. He walked shyly into the white brick and glass building and sat on an empty wood pew in the back. He looked around at the structure and architecture of the building, the high ceilings and stained-glass windows.

The cantor was chanting a Sabbath staple. Jonathan recognized the melody and felt a sense of comfort in its familiar notes. He had never felt that way before. He knew he was reaching out for something, but what was it he wanted? There was a hole in his heart, and it needed repair.

He prayed for the resolution of his problems, and he made many promises: "Please, help me to get back on my feet and I will work hard to get to a position where I can give to others." As he prayed, he became more convinced that he could actually keep this promise. He was committed now. *I will succeed and one day I will contribute in a significant and positive way to society.*

He looked around at the others in the synagogue, some praying, some chatting, some whispering. They all looked so happy, so free from problems. He felt like the pariah in the assembly, the one with a big "D" for "Divorced" displayed like a billboard on his forehead. Or maybe the "D" was for "Deviant," the one who was broke and unemployed. Could others around him sense his shame?

He listened to the liturgical prayers with a new ear and watched the ritual preparations to read from the Torah with a new eye. He looked around the great hall of worship with a fresh curiosity, as he once did when studying a new chess strategy. Now the congregants stood up as a curtain was pulled to reveal a book that was sometimes called the Old Testament and sometimes called the Torah. The congregants returned to their seats as the book was placed on an altar. The readers removed the velvet cover and kissed the book. And what made this old book something special? It was just oral histories that had been merged and recorded ages ago. It was full of real history and miraculous spectacles. And there were allegories about human beings with all their pettiness and weaknesses, including greed, manipulation, duplicity, and acts of violence. Why bother carrying on a tradition to read about them? Why read of horrific behaviors and events?

The young rabbi stood up and used the story that was traditionally read this time of the year to encourage his audience to take the high road, always the moral direction. The biblical allegories were life lessons. And now, more than at any time in the past, the trauma in Jonathan's life helped him understand the lessons of the day's reading, lessons that were surprisingly relevant to his current status.

He left the temple service highly motivated. He'd find some job, any job, just enough to eat and get shelter. The rest of the day and night he'd write software. He already knew where there was need, a substantial market still unfilled.

Part Three

A Most Unkindest Cut

Chapter 34
West Newton, Massachusetts, March 7, 1987

Jonathan

Jonathan's phone rang within minutes of his getting home. *I hope it's good news. I could really use a little good news.* "Hello?"

"Mr. Bikel?" It was a woman's voice; one he didn't recognize. "My name is Tina Wallen. I'm from New Jersey, a neighbor and friend of your parents"

"Yes, I know you. I remember when you came to our house when I was a kid." He tried to sound animated, but why was she calling? Jonathan swallowed hard. *What else can go wrong now?*

"And your mother asked me to call you."

"Is she okay?"

"Well, she is okay. But your father had a heart attack and—"

"No."

"He went last night by ambulance to the hospital—"

"Which one?"

The caller hesitated before answering. "I'm sorry to bring you this news. Your mother couldn't talk about it, so she asked me to do her a favor of sorts. I'm really very sorry. Your father passed away. Your mother is— understandably—grieving— very upset."

For a while, Jonathan couldn't respond.

"Jonathan?"

"'Of course. I—I understand," he managed slowly, softly.

"She's . . . in a bad way. Been through so much."

"I'll be there tomorrow morning."

"I'm sorry. This is so sad, Jonathan. He was a wonderful man. I'm so sorry."

Jonathan couldn't talk for a moment. Finally, he managed to mumble "Goodbye" and slowly put down the phone. His hand was shaking. *But Dad was fine now. Or so I thought. Dad never complained. Never. Who knew how healthy he was? Or unhealthy? What else can go wrong in my life? Everything is falling apart. I'm . . . Damn it all. Mom was so dependent on him. I better get prepared to help her. She'll need lots of help. I better get back to Jersey.*

His eyes welled and soon tears were rolling down both cheeks and they wouldn't stop.

March 11, 1987

There was a threat of rain and most of the visitors to Lazer's gravesite carried umbrellas. Jonathan had a reserved seat next to his mother in the front row under the canopy.

He had driven his mother to his father's funeral and assisted her slow walk to her assigned seat in the front row. He handed her another dry handkerchief. She looked pale and weak. Then he slowly stepped aside and walked over to hug Miriam. He could tell she was trying to be brave, to hold it all together, but she burst into tears as soon as he hugged her. He stayed and listened to her for a while. He didn't say anything. He couldn't.

The rabbi walked over to Jonathan and Malka. "We are so sorry," the rabbi said. "Our deepest sympathies. Your father was very influential in our temple. Very respected. We loved his music. We loved him. He will be missed by so many." Jonathan and Malka thanked the rabbi.

Then, to his surprise, Jonathan saw his uncle Yaakov and cousin Avi walking toward him. Jonathan said, "Shalom Yaakov, shalom Avi." Yaakov walked slowly and seemed to be leaning forward from his waist. Maybe that leaning relieved some physical discomfort. Jonathan got up from the seat and hugged his uncle and said, "I didn't expect you. But I'm certainly glad you came. So good that you are here with us." Then he hugged Avi.

Yaakov hugged Malka and mumbled something in garbled Yiddish that Jonathan couldn't understand.

Jonathan pulled out his pocket handkerchief and wiped his own tears away. "Thank you, Yaakov. Thank you so much for coming. You came a long way, Uncle."

Yaakov nodded and patted Jonathan on his shoulder. He smiled and said in English, "You are strong like your father. And you were a good son to him."

Then Yaakov spoke in Hebrew and Avi translated. "My father says he and brother lived longer than they expected or hoped, longer than they imagined they would during the Holocaust. He and brother were the lucky ones. They had good lives, married good women, had good, smart, healthy children. And they are thankful they survived... to this day. Yaakov says Lazer believed in God. He was religious. He enjoyed the traditions. Very much so. And he is with God now."

"Thank you," whispered Jonathan. He turned and walked over to sit next to his mother. He wanted to comfort her. He hugged her again. He felt her shake and more tears dripped down her cheeks.

When the rabbi concluded the traditional prayers, Jonathan started to think about what Yaakov had said. He recalled several of his father's stories and all his father and uncle had experienced. He imaged his father playing the violin. It felt almost real, as if he was listening to the maestro perform at his own burial service.

His mother seemed lost in her own thoughts and memories. Then she shared with Jonathan bits and pieces of her life with Lazer. She had once thought no man would be interested in her, that she could never have children or grandchildren. And then she met Lazer. He could make her laugh. He could entertain her. He had taught her to be alive and smile again. Despite the odds, she did have a child, a very smart child, and now a grandchild. Lazer had taught her to enjoy living, and he had restored her faith in humanity.

Jonathan prayed silently for his father, and then began to pray for the first time in a long time that his life problems would work out. They were nothing compared to what his parents and their families had endured. So why was he feeling sorry for himself? He could and would put the past behind him. And he must thrive again one day. And maybe he, too, might even be happy once again. He had to believe this. He needed to.

Chapter 35

En route to Ofer Prison, West Bank, April 11, 1988

Avi

Avi looked up from the back seat of the jeep as he rode into a wave of sand whipping through the air just a few meters overhead. The wind settled momentarily, revealing a trace of blue sky until the next sand-wave appeared.

Two Israeli jets suddenly cracked the sound barrier right above him and were quickly out of sight. Then came more noisy clatter from attack helicopters heading south.

Avi's thoughts returned to the mission at hand. Did he really think talking to a high-ranking Islamic terrorist-turned-informant would accomplish anything? It was his idea to meet the informant, but now he was second-guessing the value of such a meeting.

The intifada seemed to be slowing for now, yet traffic over the potholed road number 60, the most direct route from Jenin to Ramallah, was still heavy with military vehicles. Avi and Ofek sat in the back seat with two other intelligence officers in the front seats. A second heavily armed jeep followed them.

They passed a large billboard with Arafat's face sporting a puffed-up checkered keffiyeh and pointing down, as if lecturing everyone below. "What does the caption mean?" Avi asked Ofek.

"Arafat is saying, 'It can happen if you will it. You are our champions at this moment in history'."

"Sounds like he borrowed that line from Herzl."

"Doubt it," said Ofek automatically. "But you never know."

"You really think this informant we're going to see will give up their leader?"

"I don't know, Avi. We are getting intelligence from other sources, but a known reliable source would be better. Don't you think?"

Avi didn't answer.

"Remember, Avi, we must act like we are going to interrogate a difficult enemy operative, not a friendly asset. You can relax when we're alone with him. This particular asset is most important."

"Could he be a double agent?"

"In my business, there are no guarantees for anything. He's new to us and so far, he's been reliable. And if he doesn't know the answer, he'll say that. He might also know the answer but refuse to share it. He doesn't write fiction like some of them. And it's not about ego for him, but we do try to respect his ego anyway."

Avi nodded.

"So, Avi, you are wondering who he is? How does he know so much? He's a brother of Abu Hajihadi, the Hamas overlord for the entire West Bank. We must treat him . . . I mean, appear to treat him as our most dangerous enemy."

"Impressive," Avi said calmly. "How did you turn him?"

"Believe it or not, we didn't. He came to us. He's a humanist. He doesn't believe in killing. And now with the intifada in full swing, killing innocent children, elderly, even tourists, some people are afraid to go to a restaurant, or go into crowded markets. Damn. The whole world is on our side with this crap. Or they should be."

"You are wrong there. The whole world is still not on our side. Killing innocents doesn't bother everyone."

"Well, I disagree with you, Avi. Killing innocents is abhorred by every normal person with a conscience. Our asset is very much against the intifada. He has a moral compass."

"His mission is to save lives? Really?"

"Even yours. We refer to the asset as *Isaiah*."

"Understood. What's his real name?"

"Ibrahim. By the way, our guards don't know he's an asset. We try to make it appear like he's our worst enemy. He wants it that way, too."

The jeep stopped for a goat crossing. All four passengers picked up their automatic rifles and surveyed the area. Avi considered there could be a trap. He looked in all directions but saw no one else but the goat herder and a stubborn herd that seemed intent on delaying his mission as long as possible.

Twenty minutes later, they arrived at the heavily guarded, castle-like, cement fortress crowned with a roof deck with ten-meter-high barbed-wire fencing. Escorted by two soldiers, Avi and Ofek walked down a long cement corridor to the last door on the left. Ibraham was already sitting at the end of a table accompanied by three guards. There were no windows or temperature controls in this room.

Avi and Ofek sat beside this thin, mustached, fortyish man who was wearing a green head covering. He was dressed in blue pants and a white T-shirt. Ofek nodded to the three guards who then promptly left. The informant had cuts on his chin and forehead, and one eye socket was swollen black and blue. The man hadn't shaved for some time.

"You have cigarette?" Ibraham asked in guttural English.

"I have your favorite. Take." Ofek tossed him a pack of Camels.

Ibraham retrieved a cigarette from the pack and quickly lit it. He showed his pleasure as he slowly blew out the smoke. He smiled and leaned back and seemed to relax. "I worried you'd forget."

"I don't forget your requests. You know that, right?" offered Ofek. He pointed towards Avi. "This is Avi Bikel."

They shook hands. "We appreciate your help," said Avi. "And because of your help, we were able to save a young boy trained to be a suicide bomber."

Ibraham spoke in rapid Arabic and Ofek translated. "He says you don't owe him anything, not yet. He says the infantile suicide bomber came from a family with two older sons that have already martyred themselves and murdered innocents. He's sure this boy bomber is grateful to be captured by Israeli soldiers."

"He is grateful? Good. Is there another plan in the works?" asked Avi in English.

Ibraham stood up and paced back and forth. Now he seemed restless. "Yes, there is a plan," he managed in English. "And you are the target. You know this?" He returned to his chair and stared intently at Avi. "So you are the great hero of Israel." His eyes widened as he spoke, while his body seemed to stiffen, and his drags on the cigarette were longer and more frequent.

Ibraham's warning came to Avi as a surprise. Avi forced himself to retain his composure. "I'm just a soldier, Ibraham," he said as calmly as he could manage. It seemed to him that Ibraham regarded him as dead already.

"You should leave Israel. This is good advice," said the informant.

"I'm not going to do that. Tell me what you know."

"I know that we know everything about you. Where you live, where you park your car, where you shop. And we know where you piss. They will check into a hotel near you. Do you know the hotel near you?"

"Yes." Avi kept his voice calm, but a chill rushed through his body in response to Ibraham's words.

"You know they can watch your comings and goings. They've done this before to one of your politicians. The one we killed. You remember this?"

"Yes."

"The plan is to kill you when you pass a window or when you enter or exit the elevator. They decided against using a suicide bomber, at least at this point. Too risky, too costly. And your friends already stopped a martyr operation. But it's an option. Yes, still an option if they need." Ibraham lit another cigarette.

"You are a true humanitarian. You are doing the right thing," Ofek told Ibraham.

"Don't flatter me," responded Ibraham quickly. "It's beneath you."

"I don't wish to insult you. It was actually meant sincerely." Ofek handed a roll of American dollars to Ibraham and turned to Avi. "Anything else you want to know?"

"Who is behind this?" asked Avi, looking into Ibraham's eyes. "Can you tell me who is leading this assassination plan?"

"You ask more than I will give."

Avi nodded. "Can you get the names?" he asked in a softer tone, almost a whisper.

The room was quiet for a while. Then Ibraham said, "I give you information to save you, not for you to harm others. If you have no more questions for me, I would like to leave now."

Avi rubbed his chin for a moment and looked back at the asset. "I have nothing else," he said.

"Do you want me to hit you in the face again?" Ofek asked his informant.

Ibraham responded in Arabic.

Ofek turned to Avi and translated. "He says he still hasn't recovered or forgiven me for the last time I hit him. This time he'll just limp home."

Avi nodded slowly and quietly mumbled, "So will I."

The guards were called back to escort Ibraham out of the compound.

After Ibraham left, Ofek said, "Avi, we might know who has responsibility to get you. We got the intelligence from another source this morning. Ibraham didn't want to be the one to give up the name, but he was happy to share the name of someone that might know and share it for the right price. We applied pressure on Ibraham's associate. We're not sure if it's real or a diversion, but we did pay him."

"Who then?"

"Tawal is the appointed assassin. Remember him? He's mean, ruthless, but smart as hell. It doesn't surprise me that he was assigned the job."

Avi nodded. "He's been a problem for some time, and we haven't been able to find him. Isn't it time we got serious and stopped him?"

"Sure, if we can find him. We're looking."

———

Avi was alone an hour later, and he used the break to call Gila. "Are you all right, Avi?"

"Yes, Gila. Look, I just learned they want me to go to the Ashdod safe house for a meeting, but I want you to go north to Dan or Ma'ayan Baruch."

"A safe house? Are you going to tell me why you are going to Ashdod?"

"Just another planning session."

"I know there's more to this story. Okay, I'll go north to visit the family. But why don't you join me there when you are finished? You haven't seen our daughter for a while."

Avi knew she was right. Their sons were on active army duty, but Tsipy was still at the kibbutz. "We will see her soon. But not now."

"What are you saying?"

"Look, I've got to go. I'll do my best to steal a few days."

"Fine. But don't think I'm going to leave you alone very long because you're in danger. You know I'm not that kind of wife, *habibi*."

"We'll talk. They're calling me now. Shalom."

"Shalom, dear. I love you."

May 4, 1988

Avi and Gila arrived late in the day at the Galilee safe house off highway 90, close to Kfar Giladi. They thanked their two armed escorts. Then, in the darkness, they approached an austere-looking bungalow with a slanted orange tile roof and wood siding. The simple interior was modest but functional, reminding Avi of his boyhood kibbutz housing.

They were tired and went right to bed. At daybreak, Avi got dressed, put a loaded handgun in his hip holster, and tiptoed out the door to avoid disturbing Gila's sleep.

It was a beautiful gusting morning in the Galilee, clear, with flower buds everywhere. Avi walked past the remnants of decaying shelters to a point where he could take in the entire valley. The early wind picked up a bit at the hilltop, rippling his clothes like flags flying in a hard sea.

Avi panned his binoculars to the left and spotted the old rusted-out tank that had been at that post for as long as he could remember. It had been left there in 1948, a memorial of sorts and a reminder.

Gila joined him.

Avi smiled. "You're up—that's good. You looked tired last night."

"I was so exhausted. Really wiped."

"I'll get you some coffee."

"I'll do it, Avi. Just sit." Gila went inside to brew the black Turkish coffee that had been provided for them. Then she returned outside with two filled large cups and sat in a rocker beside Avi. They sipped their coffee slowly and shared sections of yesterday's newspaper.

A military truck pulled up. Tsipy popped out as soon as the truck stopped and charged toward them. "Mom! Dad!" She ran to Gila and embraced her. Avi embraced both of them.

"I missed you," Tsipy said.

"We missed you so much, sweetie," said Gila.

Avi's little girl had matured since he had seen her. She had gained some weight and it looked good on her. She also styled her hair differently. It was longer and wavy, darker, and fuller. She was growing up fast, and he resented the time lost away from her.

At breakfast, Gila asked Tsipy if there was anything new in her life.

"No," said Tsipy. "Just school. It was hard at first. My new teacher did things differently. I'm used to her now. I know why you put me here, but I'd rather be close to you every day. But there are things I like here, girls I like here. I'm making friends. And Grandma and Grandpa are here. I love them so much. My brothers show up, too, when they get a pass."

"I'm sorry to put you through this, baby," said Gila. "It won't be much longer."

"I hope so, too. But I—" Tsipy turned, looked up at Avi, then back at Gila. "Mom, I'll be alright. I know what's going on. I certainly don't want to put my mom and dad in danger. You know what? Forget what I said before. I'm just happy you're here, even if we are in the middle of nowhere surrounded by a dozen paratroopers. Can you stay longer? Leave tomorrow? Please."

"Let's just enjoy the time that we do have," said Avi.

"Look what I brought you," said Gila as she opened a suitcase full of new clothes.

Tsipy lifted a few shirts and pants for examination. "Love it, love it, love it."

"I think she likes the stuff you bought," said Avi.

"So it would seem," opined Gila. "And it's not just stuff, you know."

Tsipy found a favorite book from her childhood and a favorite doll. "Oh Mom, you're going to make me cry."

Gila embraced her. "It's okay, dear." Tears rolled down their daughter's cheek.

Time with Tsipy flew fast. It seemed like they were just getting into catching up when the army truck returned to escort her back to her housing. "No, —I don't want to leave," whined Tsipy.

"Give me a hug and kiss," said Gila as she embraced her daughter and rubbed her back. Avi stood beside them. When Gila relaxed her embrace, Avi pressed his little girl against his chest and kissed her.

"Call me when you get back to your housing," pleaded Tsipy.

"We will," said both parents in unison. "I love you," added Gila.

"Love you, too," said Tsipy as she boarded the truck.

Everyone waved energetically as the truck hauled away.

Avi saw how much Gila didn't want to leave Tsipy. "It's okay if you want to stay with her," said Avi.

"I know."

"I think she needs time with you."

"Yes, you're right, but I can't do that to us. I'm not going to leave you alone at a time like this. I can't."

"Is it better to sit beside me and worry together?" he asked.

"Yes," said Gila emphatically.

He laughed.

"I'll tell you why. Without me, you'll get full of male bravado, ignore the intelligence, and do something stupid. That's why I'm going back with you. I need to protect you from you. Anyway, Tsipy seems well adjusted here," said Gila. "I do feel bad leaving her. I know she misses us. All our kids miss us."

"I miss them, too. It seems so simple and nice up here—now that our borders along Syria and Lebanon are relatively quiet. Hope they don't start shooting at us again from the hills."

"You can take credit for that."

"Along with thousands of others. You know, a part of me could return to this life. It's a simpler life."

"You've been thinking?" Gila asked. "If you really want to, Avi, there's a lot you could do on the kibbutz. I'm sure they can put you to work somewhere. And you have the work experience to qualify." Gila laughed. "Not what you had in mind?"

"It's safer for you and Tsipy here in the Galilee."

"If it's safe enough for you to be back in Jerusalem, Ashdod, or wherever, then it's safe enough for me."

The phone rang. It was Ofek. "Avi?"

"Yes."

"Can you talk now?"

"Go ahead."

Chapter 36

Boston, Massachusetts, March 15, 1989

Jonathan

Jonathan couldn't believe his good fortune. He loved his latest purchase, a Beacon Hill brownstone directly overlooking the Boston Common. From the top two floors, he had an eagle's-eye view of timeworn trees, fountains, monuments, as well as the streams of walkers, runners, and idle lingerers.

The fine wooden accents on the first two floors of his townhouse were reminiscent of the polished woodwork at his lawyers' office. He had more rooms than he needed, and he chose the largest room on the fourth floor for his study. He still occasionally worked on math problems while enjoying a voyeuristic glance out the window, but he no longer aspired to solve them. What did his financial advisor say? Didn't he say to buy anything he wanted, or might want if it made him smile? Much better than the days of watching every penny. The advisor had computed his current net worth to be about $175 million, mostly from his software sale and salary and stock from the Texas video gamers. He kept half of his stock grants as he expected its valuation to continue to appreciate.

His bedroom was on the other side of the fourth floor, and if a guest ever visited, they could enjoy their own suite on the third floor. Miriam's suite and another bedroom were on the second floor. The kitchen on the first floor had been updated by the previous owner and was well stocked by his cook, a wonderful older woman with the most appealing Irish brogue. Her name was Margaret.

This afternoon, after he took his allergy medications and a deep drag from his inhaler, he commenced his routine walk up and down the hills and through the narrow cobblestone streets demarcated by rows of tall, simulated turn-of-the-century gaslights.

He casually observed the character of the surroundings, including the unlikely birds that occasionally surprised and treated him with their visit to the city oasis. He continued up and down a hilly neighborhood street, then headed to Boston Common. *Should I go to the Gardens today? No, too crowded with kids and tourists.* He walked across the Common and realized the grounds were teeming with young children, an overabundance of college-aged kids mixing with the homeless, and the usual protestors upset with some perceived injustice. Circles of people surrounded musicians and jugglers who performed for the occasional applause and small donations.

The atmosphere made Jonathan feel included and alive. *Too much to do, and not enough time. Best thing Emily ever did was to divorce me. No, the best thing was our daughter, Miriam.* There was a time when he had only wanted to stay married, but things had worked out better.

Suddenly he had the distinct feeling he was being followed. He stopped his march and looked around. Nothing. He started walking again, this time considerably faster. He soon slowed to a normal pace in a different direction and recalled the dramatic changes in his life. His hands now felt very cold. Next flashed memories of divorce courts, the aggressive bill collectors, unhappy landlords, arrogant lawyers, and unfair university managers. Those days were thankfully behind him.

He smiled widely as he recalled demonstrating his software for the Texans. He was very impressed by their vision and quick grasp of his work's potential. Their excitement was undisguised, as they'd been following a similar track. They appreciated how he had managed to circumvent several roadblocks. He nodded his head. It only took him three meetings over three months before they offered to partner with him. He didn't like missing his daughter for fifteen months but moving to Dallas was necessary.

The free food and lodging sure helped. He laughed. They had no idea he was flat broke at that time. They had saved him in more ways than they could have imagined.

He'd never forget the first big demonstration of the software and what it could do. He was proud to have led the team that introduced the first three-dimensional video game.

He had heard from no one for years, not even one friend or professional acquaintance. But his one casual contact with Will Dority was the key, a relationship he never expected would launch his success. It was all about relationships in the end. And, of course, Miriam was always supportive. And he had Mahmud, and Cousin Avi. He had shared everything with them, and they would always listen, always try to help and support him through his dark years.

Jonathan had long ago paid back Mahmud's generous $5000 bail money. However, according to Mahmud's wife, he had nearly gone into shock when he got another check for the interest. That check was for $245,000. And Jonathan also recalled Miriam's surprise when he had paid off her college debt. She was even more surprised when he told her he'd buy her a home when she was ready for it and set up an account for her with her own financial advisor.

Jonathan was now accustomed to receiving invitations to speak at business conferences and conventions. Everything was different. And nobody cared about his problematic history.

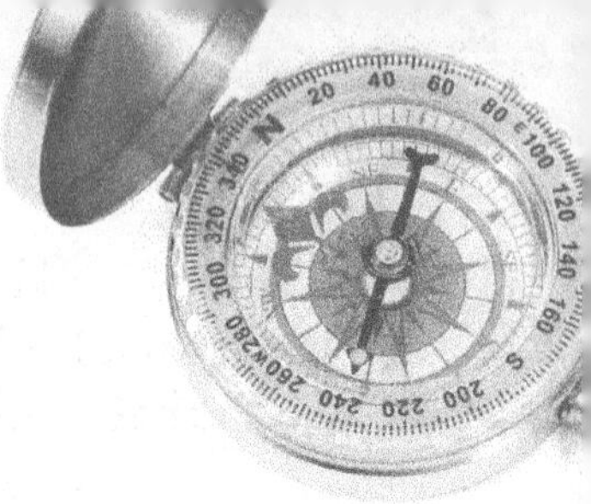

Chapter 37

Cambridge, Massachusetts, June 12, 1989

Neal

Neal found Khalid leaning as motionless as a statue against the railing overlooking the popular Charles River, a body of water he remembered being considered very polluted. Neal approached Khalid slowly from behind, not wanting to intrude on another man's solace. Instead, Neal focused on the luxury sailboats and powerboats. He guessed that, by now, Khalid had learned to appreciate living in America. Khalid no longer talked about leaving. Yes, it was a fine day and place to rendezvous with an old friend and help him plan a murder.

Neal stepped to the railing beside Khalid and said, "*Bonjour.*"

"*Bonjour, mon ami.* Beautiful day," Khalid responded without moving a muscle.

"Agreed. We get a beautiful day every once in a while. This is a great place to appreciate it."

"I just wanted to be sure our conversation couldn't be intercepted."

"I think we're safe here," Neal assured him. "I can barely hear you and I'm right next to you. I'm guessing you need my help with something or someone. You only call when you need help these days. But that's okay. I know you're a busy soldier." Neal laughed, as if there was a joke somewhere.

"It's not right, I know, but the cause . . ."

That brief response was more apologetic than anything Neal had ever recalled coming from Khalid. "It's okay," Neal said. "I know you're making things happen that no one but a few of your confidants have a clue about. Hell, I certainly have no idea what you're into."

"I'm just a French teacher, my friend."

"Right."

"Neal, my leaders have contacted me. They have decided that this Avi Bikel must be eliminated. You don't know him, but he is some kind of hero. Finishing him will send a message."

"I've heard of him."

"You know his cousin. We know. We need to flush this Avi Bikel out."

Neal stared at the water for a long time. "Kidnap the cousin. Maybe he knows something. Get him to talk."

"That's an option we've discussed. The problem is, the Americans are also watching us very closely now."

"So, bring in new people. They can't know everyone at your disposal."

"You don't understand, my friend. And it's logical what you say, but they even know when we bring in others. I think there's a spy amongst us. I don't know how they know things. Some of us thought you were a spy."

"What? Me?" Neal shouted. "Never, I—"

"No, no, *mon ami*. I know it's not you. We've never discussed our recent actions or plans with you. I know you are not spy."

"I only help when you ask me to help," Neal yelled. "I don't know or want to know anything about your plans, anything about that circle of yours, whatever you call your group."

"Neal . . . relax." Khalid released a short, quick laugh.

"Screw this. I don't need this. This is bull." He turned to walk away but stopped and looked at Khalid.

"No one is accusing you, my friend," said Khalid softly, slowly, almost apologetically. "I considered you might have insights about Bikel because you know his cousin."

"All right," Neal said. Maybe he overreacted. "Suggesting that I could be a snitch—"

"I understand, my friend," said Khalid.

Neal thought for a moment, then said, "Jonathan's ex-wife told me that Avi and Jonathan communicate by phone or email regularly. I know someone who can capture emails and phone conversations and record them. He could probably get into the White House if he wanted."

Khalid nodded.

"If he'll work with us, I can listen to the conversations," said Neal. "If anything gives away Avi's location, I'll pass it on to you, and only you. I don't want to know any of your contacts."

"This might work, or it might be a big waste of time on your part."

"I know that."

"If you do this for us, be sure to listen for things that give away locations even if they don't specify the location. I mean, you should listen for sounds like ocean waves, trains, buses, the bazaars. Do you understand? Things like that."

Neal nodded.

"What do you need from us?" Khalid asked.

"I'll have to pay this guy and buy some equipment. I can cover it."

"You have already been generous with donations. Get this technician of yours to give us a list of his needs. We'll take care of the equipment end. Are you sure you want to pay his fee?"

Neal shook his head. "I have to think about this." Neal said nothing for a while. "Okay, Khalid. Listen. I changed my mind. I don't want any more contact with the technician, assuming he takes the job. But I'm glad to set him up for you. And I'd prefer one of your people to rummage through the conversations and emails."

"We might have trouble with your slang English. Will you help us with that much?"

Neal hesitated.

"It's a good plan, but it's still a long shot," Khalid said.

Neal knew that was true. He also knew he might be exposing himself to unacceptable risk. "All right. I might help if you're stuck, but don't let this get out of control."

"No one will know of your . . . what's the word . . . involvement. Only I will know."

"You sure?"

"*Mais oui.* Guaranteed." Khalid put his hand over his heart and said something in Arabic before switching to English. "On my life, you will not be at risk from police."

———

When Neal got home, he took a shower, then poured himself Scotch over two ice cubes, and turned on the television. The news was on but he wasn't listening. He recalled the fear in his father's shaky voice when describing the Bikels beating him up. They had beat him to a pulp. Now it was payback time and he was enjoying it.

He wanted to be the one to set the stage for the next attack. He deserved the honor, given all he had done for Khalid, the pseudo tough guy who got others to take all the risks. *The hell with Khalid.* Neal wanted to be the one to write the blueprint of justice for his father.

What about Jonathan? He'd certainly suffer when he found out he was the one who'd led the assassins to his beloved cousin.

First things first. Focus. He never forgot the humiliations from his youth. But now he felt in control, powerful, prepared to erase past degradations.

He walked back to his favorite bar for a refill. Then lifted his full glass and spoke as if he were addressing several patrons beside him. "To you, Professor Neal. May your next chapter deliver another victory." He quickly emptied the glass and mumbled, "*I've never liked 'Chomelstien'. What should I change my name to? Something cool. Maybe just shorten the name, maybe to 'Chomel'? No, that sounds like 'Camel'.*"

Chapter 38

The Safe House in Ashdod, Israel, October 17, 1990

Avi

Avi's phone rang again. He put down the newspaper and his cup of coffee and managed to spill half the cup as he reached for his cell phone. "*Gamarta kvar?*"

"Avi? Is that you?" asked a voice in English. "It's your cousin, Jon, and I still don't speak Hebrew."

"I thought it was—never mind. Shalom, Jon. How are you?"

"Fine, but my friend isn't. I'm hoping you might be able to help. Remember I told you about my friend Mahmud? The chess player, MIT business prof? Well, his wife, a woman much younger than him, she isn't okay. She's three months pregnant and in great pain. There's a curfew. She needs a doctor, but so far Mahmud can't get a doctor or an ambulance to come to his house."

Avi wanted to help, but medical resources were tight in the West Bank. There was a curfew due to terror activity. Even ambulances were being checked because they had been used to move militants.

"Jon, this is bad time," Avi said, rubbing his hand over his scalp. "I can't pull troops now away from assignments."

"I have to ask. You see, he was there for me when no one else was."

Avi hesitated a moment, making a mental list of the people he could call. He knew of two people that possibly could help, but he was almost certain they couldn't take this on. "Okay, Jon. Give me your friend's address and phone. I'm not promising. I'll talk to someone and see. I'm not confident."

"Sure, I got the address right here. He lives in Al-Mazra'a ash-Sharqiya. You know it?"

Avi gave a hollow laugh. "They call that . . . the Miami Beach of the West Bank. A lot of wealthy people. And many of Arafat's people live there. They build nice homes with the donations they get. Is this friend Mahmud corrupt or is he just rich?"

"He came into some money. Legitimate money. Can you help him? I mean help his wife. He's a good man, a good friend."

There was some static and clicking over the phone. "What's that noise, Jon?"

"Old wiring, I guess. I'm in the old part of town."

"I'll do what I can. Our doctors are busy now. And we're right in the middle of packing up to go to Kfar Giladi to see my daughter. I'll see if I can get a doctor for your friend's wife before we leave, but I can't promise."

"A woman doctor would be preferred, but, of course, whatever you can do," Jonathan pleaded.

Avi hung up and let out a sigh.

"Who were you talking to?" asked Gila. She was putting on one of Avi's oversized T-shirts that reached down to her knees.

"I was getting a doctor for a complication of pregnancy."

Gila laughed. "Does this mean you retired from the army? Or are they giving you prenatal care as part of your job?"

Tubas, West Bank, May 16, 1991

Avi again raised his binoculars to focus on the building where Tawal was said to be hiding. He couldn't see much. The sandstorm was blowing hard. "I give up," he shouted. "You sure he's the one we've been looking for?"

"Avi, one can never be absolutely sure about intelligence."

Avi could barely hear Ofek over the super wind. Ofek was just a few meters away from him, "Who is your source?" he shouted while lowering his binoculars.

"We have several sources. And the best source is Ibraham. Remember him?"

"Of course."

"He's living in America now. He finally opened up and told us. He never lied before."

"In America? Really?"

"A wealthy American helped get him to the States and got him a new identity. But no one knows where he is, what he's doing. He gave permission to someone to pass it on to us. Maybe he's feeling grateful. We must honor that. All we know is he finally identified Tawal as the one assigned to get you. But not just you. Tawal has the honor of getting other assignments. And he will surely carry them out if we don't stop him."

Avi raised his binoculars and mumbled to himself, "Can't see a thing, can't let him escape. Not again."

"He can't get far in this storm," Ofek shouted over the whistling wind.

Avi and Ofek retreated to the command tent where the heavy canvas walls flapped like untethered bedsheets.

Soon Chanan ran into the tent. "Avi, we had to pull the men back to the trucks. It's brutal."

Avi nodded. "I know. Are you rotating them?"

Chanan nodded.

"Well, call for more troops to rotate more frequently. If he makes a move, we need good eyes watching all the time. Add to the watch. Nothing goes in or out without us noticing. The winds will slow down, maybe a few hours. Be patient."

Chanan saluted and quickly left.

Avi poured a cup of coffee and sat down. Ofek also poured himself a cup and said, "Our intelligence is good. He's there. I know it."

"The phantom—that's what you call him? The phantom has a history of slipping away."

"He's real. He's in our net. We just have to pull him in. I'd like to get him alive."

Two hours later, the wind slowed enough to see. Avi put on a pair of goggles. He called Chanan to finally advance the Maktal commandos. "They'll go in with me first. Leave the Nahal unit outside as a defense against possible enemy reinforcements or an escape."

"Avi, did you say you're going in with them?" asked Chanan.

"Tawal is after *me*. I can't expect some kid to take the risk to save me."

Chanan smiled, saluted, and quickly left.

Ofek spoke up. "Avi, I don't think you should—"

"It's okay, Ofek."

Avi walked out of the command tent, hopped on a jeep, and drove to join Meir, the Maktal commander.

Tawal was allegedly hiding in a large, isolated stucco home off a dirt path about four hundred meters away from the Tubas housing and retail section. The land around the home appeared to have been put to agricultural use many years ago.

Meir ordered four windows broken simultaneously. Then eight canisters were tossed into the new window openings.

Meir turned to Avi and spoke in a loud voice. "Unless he's got a gas mask, he should be coming out shooting and soon."

Five minutes passed. No Tawal. *Did the phantom get away again?*

"He's not there," Avi quietly and reluctantly acknowledged.

"What?" shouted Meir.

"I said he's not there," repeated Avi, spitting as he spoke.

"He could be there. He could have a mask. And he may not be alone. We can blow out the doors."

"Let's wait for armor to make an opening. If he's in there, we can take our time to do it right. We have time."

Another hour passed. The commandos put on their masks and followed Meir through the fresh-made opening. Avi followed them in and made sure every nook and cranny was searched. No Tawal. No militants. No one at all.

Avi left the house and took off his mask and approached the jeep. Soon Chanan, Ofek, and Meir joined him.

"What happened, Ofek?" Avi shouted. He didn't hide his frustration.

Ofek shrugged. "I was certain he'd be here. We had reliable sources. How—"

"There was food on the table," said Meir. "Someone was eating. And not long ago."

"It's possible someone could have left the house, and we just couldn't see them through the sandstorm," offered Ofek. He shrugged again.

"Possible, but unlikely," argued Chanan. "Too many eyes on the place."

"How can you be so sure?" Ofek quickly responded. "You know what everybody sees?"

Avi straightened up and said, "There's another possibility. Do you remember the story of our underground munitions factory in the 1940s?"

"Of course," answered Chanan. "We made bullets underground, beneath a big commercial laundry so the British wouldn't find it. Our bullet factory saved us. Without bullets we'd never…"

"It's a long shot. Let's go back in. Let's see if we missed a door on the floor."

They put their masks back on and returned to the opening. There was nothing under the furniture or couch or sink. Then they removed a decorative rug.

"What's that?" asked Chanan, pointing to a section of the flooring.

They removed a rug and wiped away at that floor area and found their answer: a trapdoor.

Meir called for volunteers to go in. They opened the floor hatch and dropped canisters. Abdul, an Arab officer in Israel's elite Maktal unit, was the first to volunteer to go in, but twenty seconds later two men came charging out, shooting automatic weapons. The Maktal team quickly fired their weapons, dropping the enemy militants. Then two of the Maktal soldiers proceeded down the newfound stairs. Six minutes later they reported no one else was hiding below.

Meir ordered his men to drag the two bodies outside. Ofek confirmed that the first one was Tawal. "We got him," he announced. "I'd rather have got him alive. We might've learned something."

Avi examined Tawal's face. "You are sure this is him?"

Ofek nodded. "I was there when we released him in one of the exchanges."

Tawal was much younger than Avi expected. And more innocent looking. He could have passed as a Jewish Bible student. "What a waste," whispered Avi as he walked back to his jeep.

———

Avi called Gila.

"Why are you calling? Something wrong?"

Avi laughed. "It's over."

"Really?"

"I wouldn't joke about this."

"Really? It's over?" She clapped.

"And I'm going to retire, Gila."

"About time! Thank God! I'm doing that dance you love—you know—my happy dance!"

"I'll be home soon. And we can start preparing for our trip to Portugal."

"I never quit thinking about our trip. I've some projects to finish, but they won't take long. We'll soon be in Europe. I'm excited."

"I can tell from your voice."

"By the way, Avi, I read something I found very interesting. I think you will, too. They just published results from DNA testing. Do you know that twenty-five percent of the Spanish population has indicators for Israelite DNA? I'll bet it's a number like that for the Portuguese, especially where my family came from."

"Twenty-five percent is high. Do you think that's accurate? Well, the Portuguese Jews didn't have the option to leave Portugal."

"Very good, Avi. You've learned something from being married to me. Oh, and listen to this: many Palestinians native to the Land of Israel have significant Israelite DNA as well."

"What does 'many' mean?"

"Doesn't say. Maybe they didn't get a big enough sampling? It does say that some Palestinians observe old family rituals that are obviously Hebraic."

"That doesn't surprise me."

"Oh sweetie, there's nothing in the world that would surprise you."

Chapter 39

Camden, New Jersey, May 19, 1991

Jonathan

Jonathan was invited to speak at the Rutgers alumni house. As he entered the house for the first time, he was drawn to the exceptional paintings covering the common area walls, especially the Colonial-period artwork beside the antique fireplace.

University President Samuelson, a distinguished-looking man with a protruding belly, welcomed him. "We're so happy you could join us for homecoming," Samuelson said, smiling and extending his hand. "Alumni are always welcome, and we are especially proud when one of us reaches the top tiers of business and science."

"Thank you, President Samuelson. Very kind of you. But I don't think I qualify for that business-tier accolade."

"No? Well, I certainly think you do. We thank you, Professor, for joining us today. And call me Andy."

Jonathan laughed. "Okay, Andy. You know, it's been a while since anyone called me 'professor'."

"Once a professor, always a professor. If you'd ever consider teaching again, you know we'd be—"

Jonathan cut him off. "No, no. I'm done with teaching."

Twenty minutes later, Jonathan found himself sitting on a stage alongside the university's president and deans and two generous alumni donors. The president approached the podium and began to introduce Jonathan.

"I am proud to welcome Jonathan Bikel back to his alma mater. He received his Master's and PhD from us in mathematics. He is accomplished in many fields. In the world of mathematics, he has published numerous papers. He was a distinguished professor of mathematics at MIT for many years and is the author of several software solutions. He is the president of Bikel Investments, and a director at BXZA Systems, a privately held high-tech corporation. Ladies and gentlemen, please welcome back Jonathan Bikel."

Jonathan rose with the applause and positioned himself directly in front of the microphone on the lectern. "Thank you for the invitation. I've missed the old campus. I loved being a member of the chess club in New Brunswick, and my life, as I reflect on it, has been like a chess match. I've had very capable opponents, rivals, and competitors. I've been down on my luck, and in difficult, hopeless situations. I survived it all and took some risks that paid off. Like chess, life can be full of ups and sometimes downs." He took a sip of water. "And that's true as well with trends in science and business applications. I'd like to share my vision of the current challenges and future trends in computer modeling."

He spoke for only twelve minutes before stepping away from the lectern. There was polite applause.

When all the speakers finished, President Samuelson directed the crowd to an adjoining room, and the cocktail pouring began. Jonathan wanted to leave, but he was one of the honorees. He made his best effort to smile, hold a glass of white wine, and walk the room. He was surprised that so many people sought him out and introduced themselves. He felt honored and appreciated by this circle of educators, and with the help of the wine, he began to relax.

Then an attractive woman about his age approached him. "Hello, Jonathan," she said.

"Hello," he replied as if he were still in speaker mode. "Thanks for coming, Miss . . ."

"You don't remember me, Jonathan?"

He hadn't expected that response. Instead of searching the room, he turned to her again, only this time focusing on her face. He studied her carefully but struggled to place her. "Sorry. Help me out."

"You tutored me in statistics for psychologists."

He still didn't remember.

"I'm Suzy Stone—I used to go by Susan."

"Oh. Susan Stone. Yes, I remember." He gave her a quick hug. "How nice of you to come."

"You look wonderful, Jonathan. You haven't changed."

"Liar," he said, with a short laugh.

"I must have changed. You didn't even remember me."

"It's been a long time, Suzy. Sorry."

"Oh, no, don't be sorry." Her assurance sounded sincere. She swung back her hair and combed it with her right hand, appearing to care what he thought of her appearance. "I know it's a lifetime ago."

"Are you married? Kids?" he asked.

"I was married," she said with a sad face. "No kids. And you?"

"Same story, but I do have a daughter."

"You are lucky. Isn't it sad that so many marriages end this way?"

He nodded. He was about to say good-bye and leave when he noticed she was holding a magazine rolled up in her right hand.

"What's that?" he asked, pointing to the magazine.

"*Bird Watcher*. It's a magazine for people who like to go bird watching. I like birding. I know some people think it's weird, but—"

"I understand," said Jonathan, nodding.

"Most don't get it. It's okay."

"No, I really do understand. Really. I actually like to go birding."

"Really? You're kidding me." Suzy tilted her head as if she expected him to admit he had just made that up.

"Believe it or not, I find it exciting," Jonathan said. "I like finding new species in unlikely locations, sometimes in strange places."

"You *do* understand. Amazing. There are two of us on this campus."

"I like exotic and impressive species, like the birds that hunt meat or fish."

"You're as sick as I am."

Jonathan laughed and they took fresh glasses of wine and retreated to a couch in the adjacent room. "Tell me, what's your favorite place to go birding?"

Suzy said, "There are parks in Maine, Acadia Park, or Monhegan Island, that I like a lot. They're a long drive back and forth, but worth it. Well, most of the time."

They talked for an hour about their favorite birds and sight locations. Jonathan enjoyed every minute. He had never gone birding with anyone else. He had always considered it a solitary activity, which was one reason it appealed to him. Birding was a stolen moment to return to nature, reflect, and leave behind work, stress, and daily annoyances. But now the idea of going with another enthusiast appealed to him.

"Well, Jonathan," she said, looking at her watch, "it's getting late." She stood up, still talking. "I've got to go, but I've loved every minute of it. Hey, maybe we should go birding sometime?"

"I'd like that," he said, knowing he had almost no free time in this month's calendar. *Maybe I can make some time.*

"Nice running into you again. You look terrific. The years have been kind to you, Jonathan." She winked and turned away.

———

On his ride back to Boston, Jonathan thought about his encounter with this woman from the past. He remembered her now affectionately. He considered going birding with her. He thought about getting her number—and if he did, would he actually call her?

There was a reason he wasn't ready to give his heart and possibly get burned all over again. Loneliness was still preferable to being with someone like Emily and wishing he were alone.

But Suzy seemed different. Nothing like Emily. He felt comfortable with her.

"She is different, isn't she?"

Boston, Massachusetts, May 31, 1991

Jonathan moved his queen, stood up, and commenced pacing again in his study. "Okay, Mahmud, it's your move," he said into his speakerphone. The window curtain was wide open and today's dazzling sunlight was most welcome.

"Let's see now. Bishop to knight two," said Mahmud.

Jonathan stopped pacing and returned to his desk chair. He moved Mahmud's bishop to the selected square. "You didn't need any time for that move. Okay, I moved your bishop there now. Let me think about my move. How's the weather today in the West Bank? How're your kids?"

"Weather is nice and warm. Very comfortable. Kids are excellent. Mother is fine, too, due to your help and your cousin's help. Thank you, my friend. How is your cousin?"

"He's busy."

"Of course. I will always owe your cousin for his help getting a doctor and an ambulance to us. I don't know what would have happened without the ambulance."

"Call him and tell him that," said Jonathan. "By the way, I do prefer playing with you on the phone. Email just isn't the same. I can't get into the rhythm of the game with email. Bishop to king two. By the way, how is your wife now?"

"Oh, she is very fine. Once kidney stone was gone."

"Did they operate?"

"No, they have way to bring up stone without operation. She was fine soon after she—how do you say this in English—after she exited the stone. Is that right?"

"Yes, Mahmud. You can also say, 'pass the stone.'"

"Getting back to your observation of playing chess without your opponent across table, I believe playing chess by email has advantages, especially with our time difference. When we can find time on phone, it is better, but expensive."

"Don't worry about the expense."

"Okay, Jonathan, I won't worry. By the way, I don't think your cousin would know me if I did connect to thank him."

"Trust me," said Jonathan. "I know he remembers that day very well. He was very busy and then I called him pleading, begging, crying."

"My wife was in terrible pain. They sent woman doctor in uniform. I was afraid to let her in. Someone maybe think I am collaborator. This doctor was polite and very good. She knew quick it was kidney stone. She knew my wife had to get to hospital. Israel checkpoints were everywhere between us and the hospital. So, this doctor wrote note in Hebrew for checkpoints. I offered her tea, yes, food, but she had no time."

"Pawn to king four," said Jonathan.

"Yes, they actually chopped the kidney stone into pieces," Mahmud continued. "I am grateful to your cousin. Okay now. Knight to bishop three."

"Nice move," said Jonathan.

"I had another scare this month, my friend. I'm ashamed to say this. I did have a very, very big problem this month."

Jonathan sensed his friend was conflicted. Something was definitely on Mahmud's mind, but he was holding back. Jonathan swallowed hard and said, "Tell me what happened."

"I hate to admit this to you, my friend Jonathan," said Mahmud. "I had the worst visit of all last week."

"Oh, what happened?"

"The visit was my people. The lowest rung, I'm ashamed to say. I was alone in my office, preparing questions for my students, you know, examinations."

"I remember the drill."

"Armed men entered my office. There were three of them, all similar in size and sporting full black beards and cream-colored caps. Each carried assault rifle, pointed at my heart. No. Actually one of them, I think the leader, was carrying a pistol—yes, just a pistol. They frightened me, very much. There was a woman trailing behind them. She stayed back by closed door. She was dressed like American, you know, jeans, T-shirt. Her long hair was exposed, long and dark and curly. She was an unlikely one to be with these men. I asked if they had appointment, but yes, the truth, I was afraid. Like a knot in my stomach, and my stomach has grown a bit, *sadiq.*"

"My God. Was he—any of them—students of yours? I can't imagine..."

"Not my student. I tried not to show feelings. I am professor. I am in charge, am I not? I know you understand this. I am very familiar with what they do to collaborators, even innocents accused of this. Just thought of it made me shake. I know question of guilt can become secondary when group thinking sets in."

Mahmud's voice changed to a slow cracking sound, and he stopped talking. He cleared his throat a few times and then continued. "I felt only contempt and disgust toward them. Two were draped in rags, the third in jeans and a sweatshirt, like American. Yes, they did accuse me of collaborating. You imagine this? I yelled at them. How dare they point their weapons? How dare they ask if I am collaborator? I said anyone who accuses me is liar. I ordered them leave office."

"My God," whispered Jonathan, "but good for you."

"That's when they hit me. And threatened to harm my wife, my family."

"They didn't actually go after your wife and family, did they?"

"No, no," Mahmud said quickly. "They did not do any real damage. Praise Allah, my family not harmed. But they kept asking who my contact was. They asked if your cousin was my contact."

"My cousin Avi?"

"They kept asking me how I knew him. I said never met him, don't know him."

"True."

"I kept repeating, and they hit me again. It seemed like it would never end. Finally, when I was lying on floor, I say, 'You can kill me. But I know nothing. I cannot tell you about someone I never met.'

"The one with pistol said, 'We can take you with us now and butcher you like lamb. Is that what you want? We know where you live. We know your Peugeot. We know your children. Did you kiss children good-bye in morning?'

"Damn."

"They argued for long time. One screamed he should kill me. But leader, one with American clothes, told them to move out. Oh—he called out to woman standing by the door in English, he said, 'we go now.' And he opened office door and they were gone, quick, in seconds."

"The woman might have been studying English," speculated Jonathan. "What happened then?"

"Nothing Jon. I never heard from them again."

"Thank God. It's horrible. So strange."

"Yes, my friend. Strange. I don't know what to make of it. I think woman is not religious Muslim, maybe girlfriend. I have not heard more from these jihadis. Hope I never do. I told my wife this story. We discussed moving to America."

"Why don't you come back to America?"

"She would like to see States, travel one day. But this is our home—has been for long time. My wife has many siblings, and their families live nearby. We stay. We can't let them chase us. But one day we'll travel, praise Allah, one day we'll be sure to visit you."

There was a long pause. Finally, Jonathan asked, "With all this on your mind, do you still want to continue the chess? I'll understand if you—"

"I don't think so. To be honest, I just needed to talk to you today, my friend. I just wanted to talk when we started game—was it yesterday? I just could not talk . . . until now."

"I certainly don't want our friendship to get you in trouble there."

"Remember, once you make Arab a friend, he is friend for lifetime."

"I remember."

There was static on the line.

"Jon, you hear that clicking?"

"Yeah, I seem to get that from time to time. Old wiring. That's life in the old section of Boston."

July 15, 1991

The phone rang. Jonathan lazily stretched out in his oversized leather recliner and reached for the receiver with one hand while holding the financial news in the other. "Hello."

"Jonathan, it's Emily. I need to talk to you, something important, something about—"

"Is Miriam all right?"

"She's fine." Her voice still had that irritating all-too-familiar edge. "But there's something important I—"

Jonathan hung up. There was nothing Emily could say that was of interest to him. From just the irascible sound of her voice, he was convinced acid was flushing through his stomach.

He rose from the lounge and walked to the window to pull back the heavy drape. He looked for interesting birds but found nothing. He went for his violin and played Mozart for twenty minutes before returning the instrument to its protective case. The music helped him relax. Adjacent to that case was Lazer's old instrument in an open black leather container. The violin case was still in decent condition, but Lazer's violin, after years of neglect, had gone dry as a stone. And the strings and the bridge were broken as well. Jonathan decided to have it refurbished. He could never play it as well as Lazer, but it was the right thing to do. It was a family heirloom, something for future generations. Maybe someone in his family line, or in Avi's, would inherit Lazer's musical talents. The violin itself would always restore memories of his maestro father and his unique ability to convert a tiny apartment into a private music hall. And more memories of Lazer, one after the other, flashed before him. He missed his old man and wished he had spent more time with the maestro.

Jonathan went downstairs, left the house, and hiked through Boston Common, welcoming the cool, unseasonal breeze after days of cloudy, damp skies. He pursued his regular path through the park, and soon decided to pick up the pace this morning for the aerobic benefit.

Jonathan studied the birds as usual as he maintained his brisk pace. But he stopped short when he saw a small, yellow-breasted bird. He pulled out his pocket binoculars. *Could it be a magnolia warbler?* It did seem to be singing out that *wheety-wheety* sound they were known for. *Interesting.* He stopped walking and wished he could confirm he was right. Birding was like a math problem with one right answer. In any case, this adventurous warbler was back here in New England. He figured it might just be stopping on its way to Canada. Too bad he didn't have his full-powered binoculars with him. He stood motionless and attempted to replicate the bird call: "*Tweety tweety, wheety wheety.*"

"Something wrong, Professor?" someone asked while he was gazing up at the sky. It was a woman's voice; one he didn't recognize. He turned, expecting to find a former student.

"Professor Bikel?" the woman repeated in the same friendly tone.

"That is I," said Jonathan cheerfully as his eyes met her alluring brown eyes. "And Susan Stone—is that really you?"

"That's me," she said, shrugging. Suzy was wearing a black leather coat, high black pointed boots with big, spiked heels, and pants so baggy they seemed like a full skirt. She looked as if she had just stepped out of a fashion magazine. "Yes, it's all me, Jonathan. Good to see you again," she said.

"What are you doing in Boston?"

"Psychology convention."

"No kidding."

"I'm here all week."

"Wonderful. I guess they keep you busy at these conventions."

"I have one presentation. It's on the sexual habits of older adults."

"Must be a short speech."

She laughed. "You'd be surprised. Other than that, though, my schedule's pretty free."

Jonathan nodded.

She studied him curiously. "Were you going somewhere? I don't want to interrupt you from something."

"No, no, nothing like that. Just out for my constitutional. So, Suzy . . . will you join me for dinner tonight?"

She didn't hesitate. "Love to." She smiled and shrugged her shoulders as she spoke, and when she did that Jonathan could easily imagine her again as a young coed.

"Where are you staying?" he asked.

"The Sheraton, the one behind the convention hall."

"Okay. Look for—" He stopped himself. He was about to hire a limo to pick her up but thought better of it. "What's your favorite food?" he asked.

"I don't know. I guess I like all food."

"In the mood for anything in particular?"

"Well, I hear Boston has good seafood."

"Actually, we do. See you at seven."

"Bye, Jonathan," she said. "I'm glad we ran into each other again."

"Me too. A nice coincidence. See you at seven."

When he got home, Jonathan went to his computer, read emails, and did a search for new technologies in computer operating systems. He thought about Suzy and her convention. He typed in the search window: "psychology convention Boston." He hoped to find a topic that'd make interesting conversation but found nothing referencing the convention. *That's odd.* He'd have to research it further when he had more time, or he could just ask her why there were no hits for her event. He shut off the computer and went to take a shower.

———

Jonathan pulled in early to the Sheraton's front circular driveway, just past the valet station. He stayed in the driver's seat of his new slate-blue Infiniti sedan.

Suzy came out of the lobby right on time, and he got out of the car to greet her.

"Suzy, you look beautiful." The words rolled out easily, without any deliberate intention to flatter her. He was struck by how sexy she looked. She was wearing subtle makeup this time, giving her face a warm glow. It changed her appearance, and he realized he was staring at her. She still had those cute freckles, too.

Suzy laughed. "Thank you, but all I can think of is how much I've aged since we first met."

He opened the car door for her. "You're not old," he assured her. He definitely liked the look of this fiftyish woman who had successfully invested in her appearance. She had always been very attractive, but now, in addition, she projected a substantial and impressive presence, a worldliness. She even had a toned and curvaceous figure, suggesting she spent considerable time at the gym. *I could learn from her.*

"I made reservations at L & J Seafood," Jonathan said as he drove away from the hotel. "It has a great view of Boston Harbor and excellent seafood right from the nearby fish market. Most of the restaurants with great views aren't so good on the service or quality, not as good as the ones without the view. But this one I think has it all."

"Perfect," she responded.

"How's the conference going?"

"Okay. Did my presentation today."

"Went well?"

"I think so. At least my friends told me so."

Jonathan pulled up to the restaurant. He got out, opened the door for Suzy, tipped the valet, and escorted his date into L & J's Seafood. They walked past the line of people waiting for a table. The *maître d'* smiled and greeted Jonathan with a handshake and led them to a table big enough to accommodate at least four more diners. The table was in the center of the restaurant, looking out on an expansive aquarium-style window.

"Wow, I'm impressed," Suzy said as she sat down. "Do you own the place?"

"No. Is it okay for you?"

"It's perfect. For true."

Jonathan reviewed the wine list and selected an older Tuscan red.

"How did you get this table? It's wonderful." She seemed to be studying the moorings in the distance.

"Well, I'll tell you this way. We Americans look down on price haggling and bribes, which are a fact of life all over the world."

"I suppose, but I don't look down on it. I can haggle pretty well when I have to."

"I'm sure you can. But Americans usually negotiate for cars and homes, art—big purchases."

"And?"

"And bribes are used all the time here, just like in South America, the East, the Middle East. Sometimes the bribes take different forms in our business world, like dinners, golf retreats, sporting events, clubs. We're just selective about it."

"You're telling me you bribed the *maître d'*. Got it."

Jonathan smiled and studied her face. He liked looking at her face, her light brown hair, her smile. In her eyes, he saw mystery and adventure. He liked that side of her.

He let himself relax and enjoy her company. That was special because he had never been so relaxed with women before. He hadn't dated much since his divorce, preferring high-quality prostitutes on occasion, as he had no interest in pursuing a serious relationship that might blow up like his first marriage. Suzy was different and he had known her when she was an undergrad. She had certainly matured nicely since then.

"Suzy, you seem so different from the student I tutored in statistics."

"If I hadn't changed, I think you'd have left me at the parking lot. You're also very—different now, Professor. Back then, you were more . . ."

"More of an awkward nerd?" He laughed.

"I wasn't going to say it like that, but—yes, you might have found the right personality type." They both laughed. "I don't practice as a psychologist, even though I'm licensed. I teach the undergrads."

"You're not psychoanalyzing me right now?"

"Of course, I am. It's an occupational hazard."

"Any conclusions yet, Doctor?"

She smiled. "Yes, very good conclusions. But I don't give feedback when I'm off the clock."

"You're divorced?" he asked.

She nodded. "Isn't it awful?" Her eyes welled up almost instantly.

"It is," agreed Jonathan. "My ex is mentally ill. It's a terrible burden for her and everyone around her."

"You're being kind. It must be awful to live with someone that sick. My ex left me for my best friend." Suzy didn't speak for a moment. "So hurtful."

"I'm so sorry. You and I did nothing wrong. We fell in love and were loyal, but we've been hurt badly. And they tell me we will heal with time."

"I'm doing okay now, but for a long time I didn't do well. I needed a shrink. I turned to . . . I self-medicated. I was so lost and hurt for so long."

"I'm sorry." Jonathan decided to just listen.

"Those two bastards, they turned my world upside down. I did so much for both of them. He took me out of the country on business for long periods. I never complained. I put my own career on hold for him. So, there you have it, I lost him and my girlfriend. I got invested in supporting good causes that help the underdogs. Helping others was good for me; now I don't take those medications. I work for social justice as I see it. That's my therapy."

"Good for you."

"Excuse me, Jonathan. I'd like to go to the ladies' room and get normal and clean up. I'll be right back."

When she returned, she was happy and smiling again. Jonathan decided they should disengage from memories of failed marriages. He started talking about the New England Patriots, their coaching, and strategies.

"I predict the Giants will win next year," said Suzy. "Want to bet on it?"

"It's a long way off."

"Okay, got it. You don't want to commit for next January. What kind of movies are you into, Jonathan?"

"Well, I need to think." Jonathan rubbed his temple. "Give me a minute. Okay, I like science fiction."

"Star Wars?"

"Yes. Among other sci-fi flicks. What do you like, Suzy?"

"I like spy movies, secret agents, you know, like James Bond." Suzy let out a little giggle.

Jonathan was enjoying Suzy's company. He requested the check but didn't want the evening to end. "Feel like a walk along the waterfront?"

"Perfect," she said happily. "Is it cold, you think, by the water? I didn't bring a jacket."

"There is nothing as sensual, warm, primal, and nurturing as summer nights in Boston."

"Wow ... primal," she teased. "That's quite a recommendation. Okay, then."

"Great. Let's go." He took her hand.

They walked out of the restaurant and down the pier.

Suzy wrapped her arm around his and snuggled her head on his shoulder and her body against his. "Need to keep warm," she explained, even though it wasn't very cold.

As they walked, they chatted about the birds they saw, the birds they liked, and their favorite birding sites. Suzy began rubbing his arm back and forth while they walked, and Jonathan realized he was walking with an erection. He wondered if Suzy noticed. "It's getting breezy," she said. Her voice was on the edge of complaint for the first time, and she continued to rub his arm.

"Maybe we should go inside. Ever see the insides of an old Beacon Hill brownstone?" He surprised himself by his own temerity and the ease with which the invitation came out.

"Is it warm inside?"

"As warm as you like."

"Please," she said. "Let's go." She pulled out a marijuana cigarette from her purse. "Want one? It'll warm you up."

"No, thanks." Jonathan wasn't into pot, but he thought she was going to take him for a wild ride, and he was sure he was going to enjoy it.

"You sure? It always warms me up quicker." She took a long drag.

They entered the foyer of his old Beacon Hill home and Suzy said, "You weren't kidding about this old brownstone. The wood and carvings and stone—it's amazing."

"I confess that I always loved them ever since I first visited the city. Never thought I'd own one. But when I had the resources—well, I couldn't resist."

"That's so great that it worked out for you. I like a man that follows his heart."

He put her handbag in one of the unused closets. "Come on, want a tour?"

"I just love the polished wood banisters, moldings, and trim. And the brass chandeliers and decorative stone fireplaces," said Suzy.

"It's easy when you hire an interior designer to do everything," Jonathan quietly apologized.

"There you go with that bribing thing again."

"I wouldn't have such good taste, could never have done it. I'd have just lived with a bed and a bunch of boxes. Would've been all I'd need. And I'd never have gone out to buy paintings. Of course, the home did come with some exceptional features, too."

"I like the features and I love the paintings. Very colorful. Modern, but not ridiculously modern, if you know what I mean."

"And this is my bedroom," Jonathan said pointing to the open door. Suzy stepped into the room and began her inspection. Jonathan followed her into the bedroom and watched her give a cursory glance to the window view of Boston Common before studying the collectable seascape oil painting for a few minutes. She walked over to the gold-and-black curtains and massaged the fine British-made furniture. Then she plopped herself on his bed and turned her head in his direction.

"Well?" she asked, looking up into his eyes.

Jonathan hesitated. *What does she want?*

"I can take care of you, now, Jonathan," she said while rolling onto her back.

Jonathan continued to stand silently by his bed. Finally, almost in spite of himself, he said, "I don't really need someone to take care of me."

"I know. I didn't mean it that way." Suzy reached her arms up toward him. "Come here. Lie beside me."

Jonathan smiled, took off his shoes, and laid down beside her.

Suzy rolled against his body. All his senses were intimately aware of her. He could feel her arms and hands around him, smell her perfume, feel her breath, and experience the electricity from the warmest of kisses on his lips.

Chapter 40

Boston, Massachusetts, November 29, 1991

Jonathan

The sun was already bursting through Jonathan's largest picture window when he woke up suddenly. He remembered dreaming of Suzy but couldn't remember any details of his dream except that it was erotic. He smiled and longed for the return to that image of Suzy in his arms.

He rolled back onto his mattress and put the powder-blue satin pillow over his head, as if he were immersing himself in a hot tub. For a long moment, he enjoyed stretching out beneath the fine Milanese sheets, but suddenly the big bed felt lonely.

He was missing Suzy. He'd had more fun with her these last four months than he'd ever had with anyone. But the hard lessons from his marriage still lingered, so it felt right to just enjoy her company. Marriage was not without serious risks.

He was soon scheduled to be honored for his contributions to free slaves in Sudan. What was the date? He'd better check the calendar. The real hero was the Anti-Slavery Action group based in Boston, but they were going to honor him just for donating. He found it hard to believe there were over twenty-five million slaves worldwide today, according to one source. It was even harder to believe the slave-owner countries were vilifying Israel for alleged abuses that never happened. On the other hand, it wasn't hard to believe at all.

He stayed in bed longer than usual before heading downstairs for a cup of coffee. His housekeeper was sweeping the kitchen floor.

"How are you this morning, Margaret?" he croaked, signaling a desperate need for strong coffee.

"Fine, Mr. Bikel. Morning to ya, sir." She added just the right amount of warmed milk and handed him his cup of coffee.

He took a few sips. "How is it out?" he managed; his voice now closer to normal.

"It's a fine day. Clear and crisp. Want your mail, sir? I left it there on the counter."

"Yes, thank you."

He retrieved the newspaper and mail and shuffled back to his desk, and then scanned his daybook. "Tomorrow, I meet Suzy in Northampton," he said out loud. He knew he had been in denial about how much he was looking forward to seeing her, how many times he had scanned his appointments just to see her name written out in big letters in the calendar. Fortunately, she let him know she had just been appointed a professor at Smith. He should be able to see her more often.

It was time to shower and then start packing and get ready. In just thirty hours he'll make his first visit to Suzy's condo. All he could think about was making love to her. She was now his girlfriend and that excited him. He was euphoric.

As he got dressed, he decided he would leave the Infiniti and take the Lexus two-seater sports convertible. He thought Suzy would enjoy the muscle car's performance up and down the serpentine hills of western Massachusetts.

Northampton, Massachusetts, November 30, 1991

Jonathan arrived on time at Suzy's condo, exactly as planned. He pulled into a parking spot set aside for guests of residents, retrieved his satchel and a bouquet of roses, and rang the bell.

Suzy buzzed him in.

"Hi," she greeted him. She opened the door and stepped away so he could enter. After she closed the door, she put her arms around him. She looked up at him and said, "I missed you." She sounded sad and happy at the same time.

Jonathan didn't like it when she sounded sad, even a little bit. He pressed against her while they kissed, loving the feel of her body against him.

"Wow," she said. "I think you missed me, too."

"Think so?"

"I do." She nodded playfully and she looked beautiful. Her hair was somewhat longer than usual, down past her shoulders. She was wearing a gray short-sleeved shirt that had buttons on one side from the top of the turtleneck down to her collarbone. The shirt clung to her body, revealing her curves and muscle tone. She wore the shirt over jeans, which were also tight and clingy and flattering.

"You look hot," Jonathan managed to say. He had never been comfortable offering flattery, even when sincere, but he felt different now. It was easy and fun to flatter her.

"So do you," she answered with a coy smile.

"Liar." Jonathan took her hand and led her to what he thought was the bedroom. He opened the door to a broom closet.

Suzy laughed out loud. "Are you planning on doing some vacuuming?" she asked. "Some sucking perhaps?"

Jonathan grinned. "Why not? We never did it in a closet. Could be fun. Then we can say we came out of the closet."

"Or in the closet." They laughed some more. Then Suzy led him to the correct door.

———

The morning sunlight shone on Jonathan's face, waking him up. "No!" he shrieked out loud while tugging on the bed covers.

Suzy was now awake as well. "What? What? You okay?" She lifted her head up from her pillows.

"Yeah, bad dream." He was hyperventilating.

"I gathered. You can be loud."

"Sorry." He lifted his upper torso from the pillows.

"You have a lot of bad dreams, don't you, Jon?"

"I guess."

"You're okay now. You're with me." She put her arms around him and rolled over and went back to sleep.

He reminded himself no one was out to kill him, and he was very happy in his relationship with Suzy. And he wasn't broke and struggling. Relieved and comforted by Suzy's affection, he was able to fall back asleep.

An hour later, Jonathan was wide awake. Suzy, lying right next to him, greeted him with a quick kiss.

"Morning," he managed.

"Well, good morning to you, too, Professor."

He opened the other eye and looked around the room.

"You were out like a light right after you finished, at least until that nightmare of yours."

"Was I totally unconscious after sex?" Jonathan spoke quietly, as if someone might overhear the subject matter.

"Yes. Want some coffee?" she asked.

"Sure. Do you have that pseudo-Cuban blend I like?"

"Already made."

"Already?"

"It is. I have a coffee timer. How about breakfast?"

"Is that ready, too? Where the hell am I? In some kind of geisha . . ."

"What do you want for breakfast?"

"I don't know. Anything," he said.

"Anything? Dog food, okay?"

"How about a mimosa, wheat toast, and eggs Benedict with hollandaise sauce, fruit . . ."

"Coming up." Suzy rose from the bed and stepped toward the bedroom door.

"Wait a minute. Really? You're making all that stuff?"

"It's what you want, right?"

"I suppose. Sure. But I don't expect you to—"

"It's no bother, really."

"Well, this certainly is a lot better than McDonald's," Jonathan said, chuckling. "How about doing my laundry?"

"Jonathan, I'll call you when the food's ready."

"Can I help with something?"

"No. Just stay in bed."

"Really?"

"Yes, really."

———

After the breakfast cleanup, Suzy said, "Are you ready to go birding? I've picked out the perfect place."

"I'm sure this place will be perfect, just like everything else you've done." Jonathan stopped for a moment and smiled. It felt almost too good to be true to have found an attractive professional woman with an interest in nature and birding. "I submitted some sightings to the e-Bird Massachusetts folks. I saw a scissor-tailed flycatcher at Plum Island, a yellow-crowned night heron on Stellwagen Bank, and a red-necked stint at South Beach."

"Oh, really? Were they impressed?"

"No, they dismissed the sightings because I didn't photograph the birds. I don't care about getting credit or proving my sightings, but I thought other birders would want to know. By the way, I meant it. You really did look sexy in that outfit you wore."

"Guess what? I have a present for you."

"For me? It's not my birthday or anything. Why a present?"

"No reason. I just like you. You've been generous to me. So, I want to be generous to you, too." Suzy grinned, which made her appearance even more endearing.

"You don't need to do this," Jonathan said. *I forgot to get her a present. Damn it. She's so considerate and generous.*

She put down the dish towel. "I'll be right back. Let me go get my surprise for you."

In a moment she was back bearing a big, green gift-wrapped box. She laid it on the table.

"What can this be?" Jonathan mused as he unraveled the bow.

"Can you solve this unsolvable problem?" Suzy teased.

"Yes, by tearing the wrapping paper."

Inside the box, Suzy had assembled the ultimate equipment for the serious birder. There was a top-of-the-line pair of powerful roof-prism binoculars, a CD-ROM checklist for recording bird sightings, and a spotting scope and high-powered telephoto lens that was compatible with his camera.

Jonathan looked at her, wanting to express his appreciation, only to discover he was speechless.

"Well, how did I do?" she asked.

"Suzy, I don't know what to say."

"Do you like?"

"Very much. I'm astounded. What a surprise." He kissed her. "Thank you. Really, I can't believe you did this. No one's ever done anything like this for me."

"Really?" she asked.

"Really."

"How sad," she said.

"There was just this one guy, a Palestinian, my best friend actually."

"How nice."

"His name is Mahmud. I'd like you to meet him someday. He loaned me money when I had nowhere else to turn. It wasn't like he was rich, either. He never questioned when he'd get repaid. He saw me in trouble, so he stepped up."

"A real friend."

"Thank you for your gift, Suzy. You shouldn't have, but it means a lot that you were so thoughtful."

"I'm so glad you like it. Hey, want to join me with a smoke this time?" She lit up a marijuana cigarette.

"Um, I never . . ."

"How about taking a few hits of mine. Can't hurt. Right?"

"I suppose. I'll try one." He inhaled once and began to cough repeatedly. "Okay, I think that was enough."

———

While Suzy packed for their outing, Jonathan sat in her living room and read the owner's manuals for his new birding equipment. He wanted to understand the high-tech features so he could apply them selectively on the day's outing.

When satisfied that he understood everything necessary to properly use the equipment, he rose from the chair and walked over to the living room. He scanned her books in the small black bookcase. There was one basic psychology book, romance novels, quite a few mystery and spy novels, and several cookbooks. He couldn't find any birding books or guides. He thumbed through a stack of magazines entitled *The Militant* and *Freedom Socialist*. He had never heard of either of those periodicals.

Jonathan saw another book that induced immediate revulsion in his stomach, as if he had just swallowed week-old sushi.

Suzy had one Chomelstien book.

My God. What the hell? "Suzy!" he said in a loud, angry tone that surprised himself. "Suzy, why do you have Chomelstien's—the biggest jerk—why do you have his book? Of all the . . ."

"What?" Suzy came into the living room, looking surprised. "Is something wrong?"

Jonathan pointed at the middle row of books in the bookcase. "Chom—"

"So?"

"I can't believe you have the bastard's book."

"It's so old. Who cares now?"

"For one thing, he's a pompous ass, full of himself. He pontificates all the time."

Suzy's dark eyes widened. "I didn't know. I'm sorry the book upsets you so much."

"He's a self-hating ex-Jew and a self-hating American. No one should honor him by buying a book of his poison."

"Ex-Jew? Who excommunicated him?"

"Me," Jonathan said affirmatively. He knew he wasn't making sense. And he didn't care.

"Okay. Calm down. I'll fix it." Suzy pulled out the book, went to the kitchen wastebasket, and tossed it in. She returned to the living room and clapped her hands in a cleansing motion a few times. "Done and done," she said. "Okay?"

Jonathan returned to the couch and took a few deep breaths. "Sorry," he said. "The man is more than worthless, he's like a cancer."

"It seems you know him personally?"

Jonathan nodded. "He also taught at the institute when Mahmud and I were there."

"I see. Why do you let him affect you so?"

"He poisons the impressionable."

"Huh?"

"He poisons young minds. He doesn't educate or teach students to think for themselves. He spreads propaganda, and I fear he will affect people's thinking in the most perverse way. The most formative stage for critical thinking is late high school and college. These young minds will forever have a warped view of the world. He does a terrible disservice to America. And to Jews."

"Don't you think smart college students can figure out what's right? Isn't college about hearing different perspectives and figuring out what you believe for yourself?"

"So should we circulate Hitler and Klan doctrine in college classrooms under the guise of alternative education?"

"Is he really like that?"

"He may be less appealing to the masses, but he can certainly infect the educated because of his image as an intellect," Jonathan said. "Somehow today it's acceptable to circulate hate literature about Jews and preach against us, and no one cares or does anything. Similar acts against other beliefs, orientations, or races are, *rightfully*, not okay."

"Well, he's no longer in my little library. Are you okay now? Are we okay?"

"You know, I've been meaning to ask this," he said in a new, quiet voice. "I looked up that convention you went to at the convention center, remember? The one when we met in Boston?"

"When?"

"You stayed at the Sheraton. Remember? How come there was no record of your conference?"

"I have no idea." She shrugged. "I mean, it was just a small meeting of shrinks, mostly teachers. We only used one conference room in the hotel, not the convention center."

"Oh, it wasn't in the convention center?"

"No, nothing like that. We wouldn't be able to fill up or afford such a conference."

"I see." Jonathan felt foolish. He remembered how generous Suzy was, how much fun they had together. "I'm okay now," he said. He stood up and approached her.

"Really?"

"Yes. I'm sorry. That guy gets under my skin, I know, but I shouldn't take it out on you."

"I forgive you. Do you forgive me for having his book?"

"When did you get it?"

"Years ago, I guess, in my formative, crazy years. Do you think I'm ruined for life now?"

He laughed at himself and took her into his arms.

"Jonathan, really, do you think I'm crazy?" Suzy pulled away from his embrace. "Maybe it explains a lot to you."

"No, no. Not at all. You're not crazy. You're wonderful."

"I'm glad you think so."

"My ex was crazy. I used to hate her for what she did to me. But now, as time has passed, I just see her as a mental patient. She's a sick victim of her own brand of craziness. She'll never be happy. She calls me now and then to warn me of some nonsense."

"What kind of nonsense?"

"I don't let her get into it. It's all in her sick head. I just hang up. I used to tell her not to call me, but I don't even bother saying that now. I just hang up. End of story."

"You can forget her. I'm here for you now. Do you still like me?"

"Yes, of course. Do you still like me?"

"Yes, no question."

"Let's go birding," he said.

———

On the long drive north, Jonathan found himself wondering about Suzy's motivations. Was she really interested in him? Women like Suzy had never been attracted to him. Of course, wealth is an aphrodisiac. But even if she was attracted by money, why should he care? Why not enjoy the ride? Even if she had some secret plan to marry him and divorce him and get her cut—but he wasn't going to marry again, so there was no danger there. Or was there? Sometimes he couldn't help thinking that Suzy was just too good to be true. Or maybe she really did enjoy being with him and he was just being paranoid. Who could blame him for being afraid to trust, given his experience with sicko Emily?

He looked to the right. Suzy was smiling at him. He smiled back at her.

Stop being an ass and enjoy yourself.

Chapter 41

Jerusalem, December 11, 1991

Avi

On the way to the doctor's office, Gila said, "We should be at your pain management doctor in twenty minutes. Traffic is light. Thank God."

"I'm fine," Avi lied. "It was just a quick stabbing pain. This time it was in my shoulder and down my back and leg. I'm okay now."

"Sure, you are, sweetie. We can turn around now and head back home?"

"Well, it won't hurt to hear what they think."

Gila laughed. "Avi, I know you think the pain comes from being stuck in the burning tank, but you don't know that for sure."

"I don't know anything for sure. It could be from the wars, or just aging. I had another fall. It never healed right."

"Let's see if this doctor has any suggestions."

"I hate going to doctors."

"Get over it."

"Well, they remind me of—"

"What happened to that soldier who earned the medal of valor, you know, the guy who wasn't afraid of anything? Remember?"

"No."

"Sure, you do."

"He got older. And he was always afraid. He just hid it."

"You should have gone to the doc a while ago. You can sure be one stubborn man."

———

Avi went to bed early that night. A few hours later, Gila crawled into bed next to him.

"Poor baby," she offered with exaggerated sympathy. "Does this remind you of anything?" Gila snuggled closer to Avi and gently stroked his cheek.

"The war. When we were young, and you came to see me in the hospital. It was the first time I knew you cared about me." Avi put his arm around her and held her tight.

"I always cared about you. I always knew I wanted you. I just . . . I don't know, I thought it was cool not to show it. What a dumb thing. The war woke me up. I got so frightened when I heard you were badly burned."

"You helped me get through the pain. The nights were hard without you. But I'd look forward to the days when I knew you were coming. I don't know what I'd have done without you."

"You never complained. If I hadn't seen your horrible burns, I wouldn't have had any idea what you really went through." Gila laughed. "Of course, now you've become a real baby."

"Because all you get from me now is non stop complaining?"

"I'm just joking. You're better when you complain. It's when you don't talk that I know it's bad."

"How do you know?"

"I always know what you're thinking."

"And how can you be sure?"

"I just know. We've been together since we were kids, believe it or not."

"You know what I'm thinking now?"

"You can't think about anything except your pain, and you just want to feel better, and you want me to stop chatting so you can just be left alone. Right?"

"Yes. What else?"

"Our children. You worry about them."

"And you don't?"

"Of course, I worry. And I know how much I love them all and I know how much you love them."

"Yes. We do."

"And I know how you used to worry about your job. You worry about the whole country. You worry about all good and innocent people. And you're impatient with politicians."

Avi laughed. She was right and she knew it.

Gila sat up and turned toward him. "Now Avi, you had a job to do, and you looked at your job from one perspective only. You thought about how to win wars. When a General becomes a politician, he has to see the big picture and sometimes that's different from the decision he'd come to as a general. There's so much to consider, especially with all our political parties. And don't forget the pressure the Americans and Europeans put on us."

Avi nodded. "I suppose."

"When are you going for physical therapy?"

"Will my going make you happy?"

"Very happy. I think you're ready to go into politics now," she teased as she took his hand and smiled. "But I love you anyway."

"I'm a lucky man," he replied. "I have you. And Ofek hasn't called lately to warn me of assassination plots."

"I'm a lucky woman."

He kissed her forehead. "We're going on a little trip."

"Oh? To Eilat?"

"I did book our trip. I found a good tour that covers quite a few historical sites in Spain and Portugal."

"What!" Gila's eyes lit up and her mouth opened wide. She kissed him hard on the lips.

"The Portugal tour covers the river ride in Porto and the synagogue there. Then it takes us to the mountains near the Spanish border, then to a surviving mountain community of Marranos."

She studied his face. She squeezed him with a hug, a hug so tight and full of love she needn't have said more. But she did. "Oh Avi, I'm so happy with you. I'm so lucky."

"Yes, Gila, you are very lucky, the luckiest woman alive."

She relaxed her embrace and reached for her pillow. Then she pummeled him with the pillow while they both laughed.

Chapter 42

Boston, Massachusetts, December 12, 1991

Jonathan

Jonathan looked out his bedroom window facing the Common. Raindrops still covered the glass.

"How is it out?" asked Suzy, still flushed from lovemaking and lying naked on the bed.

"It stopped raining. It's going to be a nice day. What do you want to do today?"

"Maybe go for a long walk or maybe, I don't know. Come back to bed and hold me."

Jonathan returned to the bed and embraced her.

Suzy looked in his eyes. "I love holding you. You just comfort me with your body."

"You want me for my body?" he asked.

"Now you know the truth about me. How does it feel?"

"It makes me happy."

"Good. It makes me happy, too."

They lay quietly in bed for a while. He recalled again his dark years, and quickly set that memory aside. He now felt privileged, grateful, and very happy.

"I like Mahmud," he said. "Don't worry. Not like I like you." He laughed. "We compete, we joke, we argue about everything and still remain best friends."

"I'd like to see Israel."

"You will."

"I mean soon."

Jonathan thought about it for only a moment before saying, "Okay, let's do it. We'll fly to Israel. You can meet my Israeli family."

"Great idea! That sounds like a wonderful trip." She rested her cheek against his chest. "I've never been to Israel. Always wanted to go, but didn't have a travel partner. You're so good to me. And that's for true!"

"That's because you're good to me. We like to be good to one another."

She sat up and studied him carefully. "This is really going to happen? You're not kidding me, are you?"

Jonathan laughed. "Not at all. I'll call Avi and start making plans. You know my job is flexible. I can probably leave whenever I want. What about you—when is Smith's next break?"

"It won't be an issue. I can get someone to cover for me, especially for a vacation like this."

"Maybe Miriam can join us. She's been to Israel but hasn't seen her uncle, aunt, cousins in years. Yes, I should ask her."

"If that's what you want. Why not? But don't pressure her."

Jonathan shrugged and smiled. "Don't know if she can. We'll see." He pulled Suzy's back against his chest. They were quiet for a while until he had another thought, something he wanted to share with her.

"You're the best lover," he said. "If there were an Olympic event for making love, you'd win the gold medal every time."

Suzy laughed. "And which event of my lovemaking routine do you like the best?"

"Oh, is there a competition for each sex act? Didn't know." He laughed. "Yeah, I like it all. You've got an amazing vagina."

"Thanks. I think."

"I meant it in a good way." He sighed. "I guess that's what I get for trying to talk sexy. I've never really known how. He thought for a moment. "What I like best about you as a lover is your enthusiasm."

"My enthusiasm?"

"Yes, you're passionate every moment and every movement. You do everything and anything without hesitation. You clearly enjoy yourself."

"Doesn't everyone?"

"I can't speak for everyone."

267

"Wasn't your ex a good lover?" she asked while massaging his upper back.

"I didn't have the experience to know good from not so good. But it's so long ago, I don't remember much that far back."

"Jon, do you know why I'm so enthusiastic?"

He grinned. "Because you're a horny babe?"

"Guess again."

"You remember being sex-deprived? Like I was for a long time?"

"Oh, Jonathan, you don't know by now? I love you, Jon. I really do. I want to please you. I love being with you, even when we're doing nothing. I think of you when you're away. You're so smart and yet can be so dumb, so blind. I just love you. Don't you know that?"

Jonathan's heart skipped a beat. He was euphoric, but at the same time hesitant. *Can I trust this woman?*

Suzy smiled. "What's the matter? Did I scare you?"

"No, I love spending time with you. I love making love to you. I . . ."

She turned toward him and used her pillow to sit up a bit. "Jon, do you love me?"

He looked her over, top to bottom, focused on her face, and thought she was so beautiful and so easy to love. A part of him felt undeserving of her love. "I guess I do. I . . . love . . . you," he managed.

She smiled, making her whole face glow. She was even more beautiful when she shined like that. He moved closer to her, and she moved closer. They kissed deeply and Jonathan rolled over her, draping her.

"I know you had a bad marriage," Suzy said. "That makes you afraid. Are you afraid of me?"

"Maybe a bit. I know I shouldn't be. You're not like Emily."

"You don't have to be afraid of all women because of what she did to you. I do love you. I'm not going to hurt you. I promise."

"I'm being paranoid, aren't I?"

"It's all right. I want you to know I love you and, unlike what your ex did to you, you won't feel any pain."

Chapter 43
Sacher Park, Jerusalem, February 15, 1992

Avi

"Hello, Avi. It's Jonathan."

"Hi Jon. Nice to hear from you. Gila and I are out for a walk now in Sacher Park. With a security guard in front of us and one behind us with a dog. It's a beautiful day. Warm for February. How's the weather there?"

"Boston is freezing. I'm indoors and my boiler is straining hard to keep my blood flowing. I'm looking out the window in my study right now. There's some snow flurries, and . . . oh, I just saw someone slip on the path. It's icy down there. I should get out of here in the winter. Maybe go to California. Maybe Florida."

"Great. If you can't take the cold, come to Israel. I mean Eilat, the town in the south." Avi followed Gila as she headed to a park bench under a tree.

"Avi, give me the phone," said Gila. "I want to ask him something."

Avi put the phone on speaker and handed it to Gila, who asked, "So Jonathan, how's Suzy?"

"She's fine. She lives about an hour and a half from Boston. We see each other quite a bit now. We've become very close."

"Wouldn't it work better if you lived together?" Gila asked with a slight giggle.

"Maybe. We'll see."

"Look. We know you love her, Jonathan," Gila lectured. "You babble about her every time we talk. Why not marry her?"

"Marriage? Well, you know how I've always said I'd never marry again."

"I never believed you," said Gila. "We all knew you were just talking from a very painful experience."

"Maybe," Jonathan agreed. "Every so often I wonder what it would be like to be married to Suzy, even though I assured everyone I'd never consider marriage again."

"We don't care about your assurances when you were hurting," said Gila. "What does your inner voice say to you now?"

Jonathan hesitated before speaking. "Truth is—I'm afraid. Can I ask you both a personal question?"

"Ask."

"What makes your marriage so successful? You two are the happiest couple I know."

Avi laughed and looked over at Gila.

Gila looked puzzled. "Avi, why are you laughing? He asked a good question."

"I'm not laughing at you," Avi said defensively. "I do want to hear my wife's answer though."

"It's a very good question, Jonathan," said Gila. "I'll answer your question, and I'll hand the phone to my big-shot husband so we can both listen to his answer. Okay?"

"Okay," said Jonathan.

"He seems to be showing off for you now by laughing, but despite his—what's the word. Anyway, I know he's a good man. I want to spend time with him, as much as I can. A lot of my girlfriends want time with other women. Not me. I enjoy him. I appreciate what he does for me, and for the family. He puts himself on the line for our country. He can do this because he is not... selfish. But he has been terribly wounded—he's done enough. That's why I am happy he's retiring. Does that answer your question, Jonathan?"

"Yes, it does."

"Okay, Mr. Big Shot. Let's hear what you have to say." Gila laughed and handed the phone back to Avi.

"Thank you, Gila." Avi put his arm around his wife while his other arm held the phone. "Look, Jonathan, we've had our moments like every couple, but very few. She's everything to me.

I'd be lost without her. Chasing her was the best thing I ever did in my life."

"You're lucky," Jonathan said. "Both of you. Part of me is afraid, and part of me knows my fears are ridiculous, because not everyone who wants to be with me must be mentally ill."

Avi laughed. "Let's hope not. When are you going to ask Suzy to move in?"

"You two are relentless," Jonathan said with a groan. "But maybe you're right. I should consider asking her. It's just that some things about her seem odd. But I guess everyone has some *schtick*. Remember, she works pretty far from the city. I'll figure it out at the right time."

"When is the time right?" asked Gila.

"I think I'll know when it's right. Don't worry. I'll let you know when, assuming she accepts."

"Gila thinks she'll accept in a heartbeat," said Avi. "Well, all good, Jonathan. It takes courage to change long-held . . . what's the English word for—"

"Convictions," said Gila. "Long-held convictions."

"They're long-held, all right," Jonathan agreed.

"Did she ever tell you she wanted to get married?" Gila asked. "No."

"Really?" Gila asked. "That's interesting."

"What do you mean?" asked Jonathan.

"I'd have thought by now she would have at least given a signal." She looked up at Avi and spoke louder into the phone in Avi's hand. "Did she tell you she loved you?"

Jonathan was quiet for a moment. "Sure, yes," he said.

"Oh." Gila smiled wide and giggled. "Have you told her you love her?"

"Yes, I've told her how I feel."

"That you love her?"

"I think so."

"You don't remember? I don't believe you. Is she a religious woman?" asked Gila.

"She never talks religion. Doesn't celebrate the holidays."

"Have you met her family?" Avi asked.

"No. She has no family."

"Really?" said Avi. "That's sad."

"Well, you're the only one with something of a big family, Avi," said Jonathan. "But let me get to why I called. I'm coming to visit Israel," Jonathan announced. "By the way, Suzy really wants to meet you. She keeps asking me all the time when she'll have an opportunity to be introduced to you. I thought I'd bring her over. And Mimi has been asking to come, too."

"Great!" Avi and Gila shouted in unison.

"When, Jonathan? We're going to Europe in April," said Gila.

"Oh, I could be there before you leave, probably March. Does that work for you?"

"Yes," answered Avi and Gila in unison.

"Suzy is looking forward to meeting you both. And, Avi, you remember me talking about my friend Mahmud?"

"Of course. We got a doctor for his wife."

"That's right. Anyway, he wants to thank you personally and he wants to talk to you. He wants your opinion."

"On what?"

"He has an idea, something that could be a small breakthrough for Israel and Palestine."

"I'm not a politician," Avi said at once. "I don't know if my. . .opinion would be—"

"He doesn't want a politician," Jonathan assured him. "This is in the brainstorming stage, and he wants an Israeli perspective to see if he's right about some assumptions. He just wants a confidential review."

"Do you have any idea of the subject matter? What's it about?"

"It's something that you'd expect from a university type think-tank. Mahmud's the smartest man I know. He knows Israel can't abide a mass immigration of people committed to its destruction. And he knows that permitting weapons with new technologies within range of Israel's population centers would be unacceptable. He also believes the Palestinians need to control their future, build their economy."

"I don't know," mumbled Avi. "What about the hate that's being taught to children? He can't stop that. How can he restrain powerful people with an agenda born of hate?"

"Well, he just wants an opinion. And he trusts that we'll keep it confidential."

"I might be very . . . limited in what I could say," Avi said.

"That's all right. He's already talked to important Jordanians close to the royal family. And he has important connections in Egypt. Don't you believe it's important to help moderates like Mahmud?"

Avi considered the point. "I just don't know if I'm the right one to do it. I think there might be others more . . . better."

"Think about it, all right? Maybe just a short phone call?"

"I'll think about it and let you know."

Gila looked at Avi's face and said, "We're kicking off Avi's retirement with a tour in Europe," Gila said. "It will be our way to welcome the next stage of life."

"That sounds like a very nice way to begin your next journey," said Jonathan. "I'm happy for both of you."

Avi looked at Gila. He was hesitant to commit.

"That'll be fine," Gila said. "There are many wonderful restaurants in Jerusalem."

"Let me know when you have a firm date," said Avi. "I have to let my watchdogs pick the restaurant and set up the security arrangements."

"Really?"

"Yes. It's been a pain, but, hopefully, it won't last much longer. Tawal's dead but he wasn't the only terrorist we worried about. There are more."

"Okay," Jonathan said. "I'll get back to you with some dates that'll hopefully work for everyone. Well, we'll look forward to seeing you in person. Been way too long."

"It has. I'll ask my parents if they want to join us, but at their age . . . you know it's a long trip from the Galilee to Jerusalem or Tel Aviv. I don't know if they're up to it. But we can take you to them. The Galilee has changed since you were there."

"I'd love to visit northern Israel again. But Suzy is working and may not have the time. I'll ask her."

"All right then. Get back to us. Good hearing from you."

"Thanks a lot."

Avi put away his cell phone and turned back to look at Gila. He thought she had never aged. She was as beautiful to him as the day his sister first introduced them. "Shall we continue our walk?" he asked. "Why don't we head toward the big hill in the park?"

"I have a better idea, sweetie," she said. "Let's go home now. All this love talk has stirred me up." She yelled out to the guards escorting them from behind, "Hey, listen, we're going home now." She took Avi's hand and gave him a very flirtatious smile.

Chapter 44

Jerusalem, February 22, 1992

Avi

Security Services reported that the Papua Restaurant in West Jerusalem was on the "preferred" list. The restaurant was relatively isolated from other buildings and had only one access door and one exit door to cover, and everyone that approached the building could be easily seen and searched.

"And they even have good food," Ofek assured Avi, "despite the damage the intifada is doing to all our restaurants."

"Sounds good," said Avi.

"We have to be careful, especially for our decorated war heroes."

"Glad to hear that's one of your criteria when recommending a place to eat. Gila told me she also heard that this restaurant has a good reputation. Don't worry, she didn't discuss our restaurant rendezvous with anyone. Those recommendations came some time ago. My wife is looking forward to dining with my cousin and his new girlfriend."

"We'll add an extra security checker to the checker already employed by the restaurant. And we've already screened their staff. The owner's been supportive, helpful, you know. Business has been tough; many customers are still afraid to eat out—but there's good signs as well. People are starting to brave the restaurants again. Too bad we have to do all this profiling, Avi. There's no alternative in light of the war on civilians."

Ofek had done a security check on Mahmud, too, and was satisfied that Mahmud had not communicated the proposed meeting with anyone.

———

That night, Avi called his cousin. "Jonathan, how about March fifteenth at eight PM? Does that work with your travel schedule?"

"The Ides of March."

"What?"

"Nothing. March fifteenth is perfect."

"Everyone will be comfortable in a public restaurant? I could plan for a private get-together," Avi offered.

"I asked already. They all said they were fine with the seafood restaurant. Mahmud's attitude is that his fate is in Allah's hands. He won't take unnecessary risks, but he really wants to meet and won't let anything—well, *almost* anything keep him from doing what he wants to do. Besides, he pointed out there haven't been any attacks for, I don't know, I think he said at least three or four weeks. That's a good sign, right? Suzy says if I'm okay with it, she'll be okay with it."

"Not the panicky type, that's good," said Avi. "I'm starting to like your girlfriend. And I haven't even met her yet."

"You'll like her even more after you meet her."

"I'm looking forward to the fifteenth. So is Gila."

March 15, 1992

Avi

Avi and his guests had been instructed to enter the restaurant from the rear door, which was manned exclusively for them by one husky armed security officer standing in front of the door. Gila anticipated the usual search and raised her arms.

The guard laughed. "No, no, I don't need to search you. I have pictures for each of you. The photos I have don't do you justice. No searching. That's the good part. I do need to see your passports or ID cards even though I know who you are. Hey, everyone knows Avi Bikel."

"Don't know about everyone knowing me," said Avi. "But thank you. One of our guests is running very late and may not make it in time." He handed the guard a small picture. "That's Miriam. She's the one that was delayed."

The guard nodded. "Yes, yes, I also have her picture." The guard had a wire leading to his ear and, as he raised his arm, he exposed his holstered pistol.

Avi and Gila were escorted by a waitress to their table at the front of the restaurant. Australian pop music lightened the atmosphere.

Avi noticed that the bar, kitchen, and restrooms were in the back of the establishment. There was dark wood trimming the walls, subdued lighting, and several pictures of giant fish flying over sea foam.

Gila and Avi ordered a mature Italian wine while they waited.

"It's nice having a rich cousin, is it not?" Avi said as he tasted the wine.

"Yes, it's nice to be spoiled once in a while," said Gila. "Now I'm sure your cousin tells all his friends about his cousin, the colonel, the war hero."

"I don't think so."

"You don't really know if he does or doesn't. But I do."

Avi lifted his glass of wine. Gila lifted hers. "To us," said Avi softly. "To life. And may we always find many more good times to laugh and enjoy."

"Amen," she offered, clinking her glass against Avi's. She sighed and said, "Thank you for planning our trip to Europe. Now I wish I'd learned more Portuguese from my parents."

"A European vacation is a great start to retirement. By the way, I'm told the rabbi in Porto is an Israeli who flies in for holidays and once a month for the Sabbath. And he's been advised we're coming and to greet us personally. Maybe a special welcome?"

"Interesting. We should definitely try to connect with that rabbi. You know what the best part of this dinner and our trip is? Getting away from worrying."

"You never complain."

"Of course not. What would complaining do? Now I look forward to not even thinking about you on some assignment in some place you can't tell me. I can't help smiling now."

The *maître d'* soon escorted Jonathan and Suzy to the table. Avi and Gila stood up. Avi and Gila hugged Jonathan and Suzy.

"So nice to meet you," Suzy said. She was wearing large-rimmed sunglasses.

"I love your gold necklace," Gila said to Suzy, just as Suzy put down her yellow handbag and oversized shopping bag and removed her coat.

"I do love it, too," Suzy said. "Got a great deal. It was made in Italy."

Gila whispered in Hebrew to Avi, "She might have a deal on the necklace, but her outfit is from a French designer. Big dollars."

All four sat down at the same time. "How was your trip so far?" asked Gila.

"Great for us," said Jonathan, "not so good for Miriam."

"I got your message that she'll be late."

"She said something about a meeting with the boss at the last minute and having to find a later flight."

"We stayed in Tel Aviv near the beach last night," said Suzy. "It was warm and nice. We walked along the beach at sunset. So wonderful." She was cheerful.

"They do a good job of building up the beachfront," Avi said. His first impression was that Suzy was attractive, bubbly, and good at connecting with them.

"And the real estate pricing, too, is going way, way up," said Gila. "Foreign investors are creating a demand for luxury housing in Tel Aviv, especially at the waterfront. Some Americans have bought condos near the beach and rent them at a discount, I mean way below market, to help lone soldiers from America and Europe, from Australia and South Africa, you know, foreign kids that volunteer."

Gila looked at Suzy and asked, "Have you two traveled much together?"

"Our first trip together out of the U.S.," said Jonathan.

"You two look perfect together," said Gila.

The *maître d'* escorted Mahmud to the table. Everyone stood up to greet him and shake his hand. Jonathan and Mahmud embraced one another.

"Very nice to meet you," Mahmud said repeatedly as he shook everyone's hand. He placed his right hand over his heart and gave a slight bow before sitting down.

Avi watched Jonathan look at Mahmud. The old friends hadn't been together for years. Avi guessed each was assessing how the other had aged.

"Oh, Jon, this is the Mahmud you talked about," whispered Suzy. "Lovely. You didn't tell me he was coming."

"I didn't? Well, my memory ain't what it used to be."

"I looked forward to meeting you—umm, all of you," said Mahmud. "Jonathan and I have been friends very long time, and he has told me about each of you. So, is truly my pleasure, my honor, to dine here with you tonight."

Mahmud turned to Avi and spoke softly, "I always wanted to thank you, in person, for your help when my wife was sick during pregnancy."

Avi nodded. "Glad I could help. Jonathan kept pushing me hard. He left me no choice. He is the one to thank."

Mahmud looked over at Jonathan. "I am most indebted to Jonathan—in many ways."

"Yes, Mahmud owes me big-time," Jonathan agreed, his voice teasing. "And I owe him."

"Who wins at chess?" asked Avi.

"About even," said Jonathan. "Maybe I have a slight edge with more wins over the years."

"Jonathan, you know that isn't true, not by my addition," said Mahmud. "You must be struggling with arithmetic."

Suzy laughed, and Jonathan gave her an adoring look.

Avi studied Mahmud's brown and bloodshot eyes and they reminded him of his father's eyes. They were the eyes of a man of substance.

Avi lifted the oversized menu and began to skim through the pages. "We are going through a difficult time for both our peoples," Avi said to Mahmud.

Mahmud ordered grape juice, and when it arrived, Jonathan offered a toast. "From friendship and mutual understanding, great things can happen. There's no reason why a hundred-year war, a war between cousins, should not be resolved. To peace." He lifted his glass, and everyone clinked theirs.

"Amen," Gila said.

Jonathan called over the waitress, a very attractive young woman, probably of Ethiopian descent. He proceeded to order appetizers for the table.

"You like a lot of food," the waitress said in English with just a slight Hebrew accent.

"This is a special occasion," Jonathan told her. "We need to eat and drink and make up for lost time."

The waitress smiled. "Right away, Mr. Bikel. Whatever you need. Your cousin is a hero for us. But you know this." She turned and headed toward the back.

Suzy turned toward Gila. "It sounds as if you and your husband are celebrities here."

"Not celebrities," Gila said quickly.

"I told you, Avi's a war hero," Jonathan explained.

"I just love these chairs and the woodwork," said Gila, changing the subject.

"The décor is lovely," Suzy agreed.

Avi turned to Mahmud. "Jonathan tells me you were looking for my opinion on something?"

"Yes, yes, this is true. I am working on an initiative to bridge the gap, something acceptable to both sides of the conflict."

Avi nodded. "Please, go on."

"It will take some time. Can we schedule a time to talk details? I also have some data to support the concept."

"Of course. But can you give me a headline, a flavoring if you will, of what it's about?

"Yes, yes, Avi. Is okay to call you Avi? As you know, I'm business professor. I taught business course at MIT and now at Birzeit University. My thesis is that doing business together will benefit all parties. Israel has technology. We have hard-working population that can support production. Working together, prospering, will lead to mutual understandings. Profit improves lives and standard of living. Of course, this is only small piece of whole plan. You are thinking I am naïve, that certain people, certain ideologies, will preempt and violently sabotage such a partnership. That's why I need time—to explain it."

"I don't believe your idea could ever work," said Avi, "not when hate is taught to every young generation. The armed groups will blow up cooperative initiatives immediately."

"I understand your skepticism. That's why I developed something that serves interests of all parties. A different approach—just might work. I'd appreciate your insights. We can do it by phone, if that's best. I will send some reading prior if you are open."

Avi nodded. "Fine. You make me curious. I'll look forward to seeing your material."

"Many of my students cannot get work in their field upon graduation. This is most unfortunate. Some start small businesses, some become . . . well, let's just say they are not becoming business leaders. This is loss, for my people, I believe, for all peoples in the Middle East. I want to change that. I want technology, manufacturing, and—"

"I'm not a businessman or a potential investor," interrupted Avi.

"I know. I'd just want opinion how to approach the right people, who are the right people, maybe I miss something, what political concerns would be"

Avi gave a wry smile. "I can almost guarantee you my government would be divided on all issues."

Mahmud laughed.

"There's talk of pulling out of Gaza and part of the West Bank now," said Avi. "That would leave Israel out of the equation. Investors would be free to build industries, businesses. As long as we're not attacked, you can do what you want in Gaza."

"We know about the possibility of pullout," Mahmud said. "It would be wonderful to have our own state in Gaza where enterprise and work ethic would undoubtedly flourish. And beachfront property on the warm side of the Mediterranean would be a wonderful driver of service industries. There's large workforce there who will work hard, build something positive in the Middle East. But we still have concerns there will be different outcome. You know this. And yes, I know this as well."

Avi sipped his wine and cleared his throat.

"There are many concerns," continued Mahmud. "The people of Gaza are not experienced in large-scale business development or in relations with international and with financial institutions. They'd need help, of course. It will be complicated, but I think it might provide opportunity to improve relations with Israeli people. West Bank, too, will need partners."

"The *hors d'oeuvres* have arrived—at least some of them," Gila announced as the young waitress placed three small plates of vegetarian appetizers in the center of the table.

Mahmud examined Suzy's face for a moment. He asked, "Have we met, Suzy?"

"I don't think so," Suzy answered, shaking her head. "I've never traveled this far. Sorry."

"You look familiar," said Mahmud.

"Suzy also attended Rutgers University," Jonathan offered.

"Seven years as a student," Suzy added. "Two years as a Rutgers professor, I'm afraid."

Jonathan laughed. "Mahmud, you must be thinking of another beautiful American woman."

"That must be it," Mahmud agreed.

"I looked up this restaurant," said Jonathan. "It's known for its fresh local and imported fish from all over." He turned toward Suzy, who was studying the menu, and rubbed her back.

Suzy seemed to ignore his gesture, and held her menu up high, seeming intent on absorbing everything as if she were studying for an exam.

Avi noticed the back rub; now his own back was craving a rub.

"Everything okay, Suzy?" Jonathan asked.

"Fine," she said, flipping through menu pages. "It's just such a huge menu. What a decision . . ."

Jonathan turned to Mahmud. "Do you think there will be local elections in Palestine? Isn't there talk about planning such elections? Will there be honest voting?" Jonathan reached for one of the appetizers. "And I know you can't tell me everything," Jonathan quickly added.

Mahmud just smiled. "No, no, it's all right. Very encouraged. Meetings are productive and focused. I think we will have elections at local level in late 1994 or 1995 at the latest."

"Great," said Jonathan. "Are you going to run for office?"

"No, my friend. That is not in plan."

"Have you given any more thought to my idea of building bridges with Israel on a community-by-community basis?"

"Frankly, no," Mahmud said, then sipped his grape juice. "You are correct that people's real loyalty is to family and local community at large, not to corrupt or fanatical central governments. But I just don't think they have the will or power to do something like that."

Suzy stood up. "Excuse me, where's the restroom?" she asked a busboy.

"I'll miss you," Jonathan joked.

"Be back in a sec." She kissed Jonathan on the lips with deliberate passion.

"Okay, as I was saying," Mahmud continued in his slow, calm tempo. "I understand your concerns, Jonathan. What concerns me—" Mahmud stopped talking. His face suddenly paled. He looked frightened and confused at the same time.

"Mahmud, what's wrong?" asked Jonathan.

"I remember now where I saw your Suzy." Mahmud's speech changed to a nervous, loud, rapid pace. "Yes, definitely. And not years ago at the Rutgers." Mahmud's face flushed red. "I clearly remember her. Yes, she was Western woman I told you about, you know, one who accompanied jihadis that threatened me and my family."

"Suzy?" Jonathan's voice was disbelieving. "No, you must be mistaken. Maybe she just looks a little like—"

"I am not mistaken." Mahmud's voice was loud and furious. "And *she* is the love of your life? Allah—"

Avi responded instinctively. He saw that Suzy did not turn toward the rest rooms. He jumped to his feet and went after her.

"Back soon," he called to Gila as he ran after the woman his cousin had brought to his table.

As Avi passed the crowded club-like atmosphere at the bar area, he came to the rear exit where he and Gila had entered the establishment. Through the small window in the exit door, he could see Suzy walking outside. She was walking away quickly, without her coat or bags.

Jonathan

"I don't believe a word of what Mahmud is saying," Jonathan quietly mumbled to himself. *Mahmud's just confused. The man should get his eyes checked. Suzy has never before been to the West Bank or Israel. Where did Avi go? To the ladies' room to find Suzy? Really? Is he planning to barge in there and pull her off the toilet? This dinner isn't working out very well. People are acting nutty.*

Jonathan glanced down at the shopping bag that Suzy had placed under the table by her chair. It looked strangely buckled. Curious, he reached into the shopping bag and tore through the gift box and paper-fill—enough to find a wire and canister in the bag. It only took seconds for him to deduce what it meant, and in the next moment he thought of the many unanswered questions about Suzy, the questions he had chosen never to ask. They were suddenly plainly answered.

Jonathan sat frozen, staring down into Suzy's bag. He heard Mahmud yell, "A bomb! Everyone out!"

Everyone in the restaurant looked up. Some were getting up. Most remained seated, clearly confused. Others ran to the front door. Jonathan remained frozen, just holding, and staring into the bag.

Mahmud pulled him away from the table. "Drop it, Jon! Get out! Let's go, go, go!"

Now many people were running to get out.

Mahmud gave Jonathan a little push and finally Jonathan got up and started to run. "Run, Gila! Get out now," Jonathan yelled as loud as he could as he raced toward the front door.

Avi

Avi opened the exit door and yelled, "Suzy!" but she ignored him and kept walking fast, almost running away from the restaurant. He stepped outside. Now Suzy was definitely running as fast as she could.

He ran outside and around the building toward the front of the restaurant. *What's happening?* He reached the restaurant's front door, but he was blocked from entering by panicked customers charging out.

"Gila, get out," he shouted as loud he could. "Gila, where are you?" he yelled over the commotion as he sidestepped patrons leaving the restaurant.

Avi began to worm his way into the restaurant's foyer; then came the loudest explosion.

———

Avi realized he was lying on the asphalt five meters away from the front door, hurting all over, feeling tiny glass pieces raining down on him like hail.

He was aware of screaming and crying, of commotion. He heard himself groan. He lay there for a while and tried to understand what had just happened. For a moment he was back in the Six-Day War. He tried to get up but couldn't. He managed to roll onto one side. He pushed his torso up and off the ground.

Someone called down, "Are you alright?"

"Yeah. All right," he managed, but barely.

Where is Gila?

He pushed himself to his feet and straightened up as best he could. He looked for the front entrance of the restaurant. It was gone, destroyed. The glass was gone. The door was gone. Inside everything was black and smoking. He staggered unsteadily toward the restaurant. Police were already there, keeping the curious crowd back. He could hear sirens now.

"Sorry, buddy, stay back," the policeman shouted at him.

"My wife," he weakly tried to explain.

"You can't go in there," repeated the officer.

A woman behind him said, "I'm a nurse. You're bleeding. Can I help you?"

"I'm okay, I'm okay." He coughed uncontrollably, all the while thinking about Gila, and he wasn't okay.

He felt a numbness fill his body. It felt like the soldier's numbness to painful events, a way for the psyche to resolve the horror of losing close friends and still push forward. It was as if he had returned to combat, covering himself with the protective shroud of the warrior state of mind.

After a while he felt a little stronger, more aware. The ambulatory workers, plainly experienced in dealing with such tragedies, led him through a narrow path free from the debris and body parts. He saw Mahmud just as ambulance workers were laying a white sheet over him. Only a few feet from Mahmud were a pair of shoes and eyeglasses and a stained necktie, all of which Avi knew had been worn by Jonathan. There were several other body shapes under sheets and lined up in a row just as they might be if they were preparing for military inspection. Avi had a flashback to the moment in the '67 war when, after the battle, he lay in one of the rows, sandwiched between the dying and the seriously wounded. Now, almost paralyzed with dread, he forced himself to follow behind the paramedic, a young man who had agreed to help him find Gila. His nametag read "Chaim".

"Follow me, we'll find her if she's here."

The young man approached the first corpse and pulled back the sheet just enough to expose the face. "This is a man, not her. Let's go to the next one."

Avi followed.

"Is this her?" It was an older woman. "No."

The ambulatory worker covered up the older woman and moved a few steps. He pulled back the adjacent sheet. "What about this one?"

It was a young girl. "No," said Avi, but he felt a queasiness starting to sweep through him. *Is that our waitress?*

The young man pulled back the next white sheet. "What do you think?"

Avi glanced at the next face quickly, then abruptly turned away. He began to shake all over. He slowly turned back to really look at her. This woman's face showed red blood streaming down her left temple and dripping from her nose, and her bright blue eyes were open as if still observing the events around her.

"This is her," Avi said. His voice sounded broken, as if it belonged to a stranger. "This is my wife, my Gila." *This isn't real. How could a simple dinner engagement turn into my worst nightmare?*

He sat down beside her, put his arms around and under her. He lifted her slightly and held her tight. He felt that familiar bubble surrounding him that numbs the senses. But this time was different. This time he wanted to feel the pain.

This isn't real. It can't be real. This isn't happening. But he slowly came to accept what had happened. He spoke to her softly. "Thank you for being who you were. Thank you for loving me, for always supporting me, for making my life better in so many ways. Thank you for giving me wonderful children. I'm so sorry for what happened, for bringing you to this, for not being able to save you. They were after me. They wanted to take *my* life. And you had to pay the price with your life." *My poor Gila. I love you. I always will love you. I'm so grateful, so lucky you were my wife.* He held Gila tight and rocked her in his arms. He lowered her slowly back to the ground and whispered, "Good-bye, my beautiful, sweet Gila."

He slowly managed to get to his feet while someone else covered Gila with the blood-stained white sheet.

Chapter 45

Lincoln, Massachusetts, March 24, 1992

Neal

Neal rose slowly from his home office chair still holding his crystal glass, empty but for the ice remnants from the last drink. He walked unsteadily to the living room bar and reached down to retrieve an unopened box of eighteen-year-old Glenlivet Scotch on the bottom shelf. He removed the bottle from the box and refilled his glass. He reached for a pen on top of the bar and began to doodle on the box flap while slowly sipping.

The house bell rang to the theme of *Impeach the President*.

"Coming," Neal crowed as he raised his glass again.

He took a sip as the doorbell rang again. "Hold on, hang on, I'm coming," he shouted.

He opened the door. It was Khalid with another man unknown to Neal. "Hello, young Mr. Khalid, come on in." Neal opened the door partway, and said, "A bit chilly, don't you think? Come inside." He extended his arm gracefully toward Khalid and bowed a bit, as if he were the butler welcoming an important guest.

Khalid didn't say anything. He stepped into Chomelstien's home and found his way to the sofa. His unidentified friend followed him.

"Hi, I'm Neal Chomelstien," Neal said to the stranger, extending his hand. The stranger was a tall man with a runner's build. He had an oval face and olive complexion with an unkempt brown beard that rounded out his facial appearance. He wore a green and white traditional head covering. The stranger hesitated a bit before shaking hands.

"His name is Bakr," said Khalid. "His English isn't good. He flew in from Jordan a few days ago."

"He must be tired. I'm having a Scotch. I don't suppose either of you have any interest in joining me?" Neal led them to the couches.

"No," Khalid answered abruptly, and Neal regretted the offensive offer of whiskey.

"Hey, you know I was just joking, right?" Neal said quickly. "So how are you celebrating?"

"We didn't get their colonel. We've nothing to celebrate, old man," Khalid mumbled in a way that left no doubt about his disappointment. "The real target is still alive."

"Oh, that's true, but . . ." Neal assessed the situation. *Okay, they're really pissed. I need to handle them. We came so close to getting Bikel, so much better than they've ever done before.* "That was just unpredictable, an unfortunate happenstance," said Neal, raising his arms. "Hey, Khalid, buddy, what can you do? It's like a roll of the dice. You never know for sure how things will play out. It was a good plan, and we're beyond any risk of police connecting anything to us. Relax." Neal took another sip of Scotch and leaned back against the cushions of his new couch. "Hey, look at it this way," he said. "Both Bikels are down. The fucking colonel lost people very close to him. He's so damaged, he won't be a factor ever again. That Bikel is out of the picture as a soldier, and the other one is fighting for his life in a hospital. I would give it a satisfactory grading."

Khalid didn't say anything, and Neal sensed something was different. His message wasn't getting through. He had never seen Khalid behave this way. Khalid was just staring back wide-eyed. Very uncharacteristic. And this Bakr person was sitting there like a gargoyle.

"By the way, I've been calling Suzy's cell phone. No answer. I wanted to congratulate her." He had another sip of his Scotch. "She had to plan a complex operation. She had to set up Jon Bikel. That took over a year. Can you imagine? Very devoted lady. Hope that Jon Bikel doesn't survive."

Neal took another sip and smiled widely. "All this to help you, Khalid. You owe Suzy. So do I. We should think of an appropriate reward for all the time, the risks, all she had to put up with. Couldn't have been pleasant for her."

"She won't be answering the phone," Khalid said.

Neal was quiet for a moment. "What are you saying?"

"She's dead."

"What?" Neal was stunned. "How did she die? Damn. Those . . . they killed her?"

"Bakr killed her," Khalid reported without inflection or emotion.

Neal couldn't believe he had heard correctly. "What?"

"I told him to shoot her," Khalid went on calmly. "Two shots in the back of the head. She's dead. It was quick. Painless." Neal jumped to his feet. "Why? Are you out of your mind?" Neal paced back and forth as he spoke. "She worked so hard for you. Damn it, you have no culpability in this because of her. You should have given her a medal. Are you making this up? Is this a sick joke?"

Khalid remained seated. "She was a liability," he said calmly. "Avi Bikel lives. He knows your Suzy brought the bomb. The cousin will survive. You are kidding yourself, *monsieur*. He'd name her and she'd name you. Then you'd name me, *mon ami*. I cannot allow this."

Neal returned to his seat. "I can't believe this. You should have consulted me. This was my project. I planned it all out. My brain. Not yours. You came begging for help and I helped you. I was very patient because it was the only way to pull it off. I did it the right way. I ought to throw you out right now. I will do it. Leave. Get out! Now! Out!"

Neal stormed across the room, finished his Scotch in one gulp, and threw the glass toward the dining room. The glass hit the edge of the table, and glass and ice shattered, leaving the dining area covered in glittering shards. Neal looked back at Khalid and pointed to the door. "Get out now," he spat. "Get out, you . . . out. You listening? You make me sick."

Khalid stood up. Bakr got to his feet while pulling an eight-inch blade out of his pocket.

"What the—"

Khalid said something in Arabic, and Bakr slowly closed his knife and returned it to his pocket.

"Look. I didn't want to eliminate her. She was a good . . ." Khalid shook his head and tightened his lips. "Your Susan was— what do you Americans say—some piece of work. She might have had Jew blood, but she was committed and useful for us. She could get into places our people couldn't. Avi Bikel and Jon Bikel will survive, and they know she planted the explosive. I'm not going to risk everything for her."

Khalid took a pair of plastic gloves out of his pocket. They looked like surgical gloves. Khalid handed a second pair of gloves to Bakr. He reached into another pocket and pulled out a pistol. He handed it to Bakr who, in turn, aimed it at Neal.

"Put that away," Neal snapped. "What do you think you're doing?"

"You little Jew worm, it's time for you to shut up," said Khalid. "Enough ranting. You should know this is the pistol that will kill you. It's the same gun that killed Suzy. So, you will share that. It's a special weapon. Why is it special? No serial numbers. Interesting, don't you think? They will assume that you killed her because you confessed that you killed her."

What's he doing with that? He's not putting it away. Neal forced his voice to sound calm. "Okay, okay, now, let's take a minute and talk this through. There's no need to do anything drastic. I was just surprised by what you told me. I was upset. That's all. You are right. I see that now. Suzy would have been a liability. Yes, definitely. You are right again. Now that I process it, I see your point." Neal walked toward his bar. "I need a drink," he explained, expecting Khalid might stop him.

But Khalid waited quietly. Neal selected a tall glass and poured himself a triple. He emptied half the glass in two big gulps. He took a pen out of his pocket and pushed the Glenlivet box to the side and spilled a bit from his glass. He filled another glass, spilled a bit, and promptly emptied the glass in one gulp. He reached for a napkin. Then another napkin. He used the napkins to soak up the spill. He used the pen to write five words in Yiddish on two whiskey boxes. He did it so Khalid couldn't see him writing. Then he wrote the same note in English on an unused napkin.

"That's enough drinking. Now get back here and sit down."

Neal hid the pen under the napkins on the bar and promptly returned to sit on the couch.

"Now Neal, you flip-flop like a politician. Do you think I respect you for this? You're nothing to me, just a piece of garbage to throw away. But like all garbage, you once served a purpose. Hey, you might also like to know I have a plastic gun with me. It's a perfect companion for air travel. One hundred percent plastic. Did you know that?"

"No, Khalid, I don't know about those things."

"Of course you don't. You're no warrior. You're all talk. The plastic gun isn't really important now. But it's very clever, well-designed, so I thought you might want to know about it. You think you are so smart? So important? No Neal, you are an arrogant, tiny little Jew professor. You are really nothing, just a tiny insect, a termite. The part of the plan that you didn't hear about yet is that you will die at the hands of Bakr's plain, simple, cheap weapon, unexceptional but for the absent serial number. They will find your fingerprints on it, too. And they will find your confession for the killing of Suzy Stone."

Is he serious? "No, please don't." Neal began to slowly comprehend that his friend, Khalid, his once very close friend with whom he had shared so much, the one man whose perspective he had believed was totally aligned with his, was going to shoot him dead.

"You are a fool, professor. We have no use for you anymore. You served your purpose. And you know too much. And you communicated with Suzy all the time. They will find your phone records calling her. They will find your emails to her. We are not fools. They can't connect you or Suzy to us. You know we have a plan, a plan for the whole world, and there's no place for you."

Neal dropped off the couch to his knees. *What happened to Khalid? Not long ago, he was so conciliatory and unassuming. I helped him so much. Why has he changed? I don't understand.* "Please don't kill me. I have money. I can give you things. You want the new car?" He took his keys out of his pocket. His hand was shaking but he managed to toss the keys to Khalid who let them fall to the floor. He pressed both hands over his face and began to cry. "Please, I'm begging you. Don't kill me. Please. I brought you Suzy, remember? It was my plan to use her. It worked for you. Doesn't that loyalty count?" He heard his voice crack.

"You slimy snake," said Khalid. "You're pathetic. Have you no pride? You are nothing more than a petty coward, after all, aren't you?"

Neal wiped his eyes and looked up. Khalid's weapon was now pointing directly at his left temple.

"Get up, Jew, and sit straight in the chair. You're going to write a note." Khalid handed Neal a pad of paper and a pen.

Neal pulled a handkerchief from his pocket. He wiped his eyes and blew his nose. "What do . . . you want me . . . to write?"

"Get this right now or I'll make it much more painful for you," Khalid said slowly. "You saw Bakr's knife? Believe me, he can make it bad for you. Ready now? I know how to make it quick, easy, painless. It's up to you. Okay, let's begin. 'I, Neal Chomelstien, cannot live anymore with my guilt—'"

"Wait, I can't write so fast. Your pen is skipping. I brought Suzy in. I conceived the plan . . . I don't understand. I did everything for the cause—our cause."

Khalid laughed. He turned toward Bakr and said something in Arabic. They both laughed. Khalid faced Neal and returned to English. "You are a fool. Suzy was the one who brought you to us long ago. Do you really believe you recruited her? She heard you speak. I think New Jersey. She knew about your books. She told us to bring you in, that you would be useful. She knew you would be easy to manipulate because—how did she put it—you have the ego of bull elephant. She also came up with idea to be the cousin's lover to gain access to Avi. She liked being a spy. She bragged about how easy it was to get you to take credit for the strategy. Smart woman, Suzy. I hated to kill her. Hated to lose her. You will be easy to kill. I won't lose sleep."

Neal couldn't believe what he was hearing. *She played me? No one's ever played me.* His eyes welled up. He wiped away a running tear.

"Now write what I'm telling you."

"I've been trying to write but your pen is skipping. I already told you."

"I have another pen." Khalid searched his pockets to find another pen. "Here." He tossed the second pen to Neal.

"Never mind. It seems to be working now. Okay, you said I can't live with—what was it?"

"The guilt."

"I can't live with the guilt. Is that what you want?"

"Shut up and write."

"I'm writing," shouted Neal.

"Yes, I can't live with the guilt. At the bequest of Israel, I am the one that arranged for the murder of Suzy Stone for what she did to my friends," instructed Khalid.

"Really, that doesn't make sense," Neal said. "'Bequest' of Israel? You mean 'request'? My friends? Really?"

"Shut up and just write it. Then write this: 'Suzy Stone's remains can be found in a black bag in the empty lot on Wales Street in Dorchester'. And sign it."

"What street?"

"You're trying my patience. Wales Street, you *ahmaq*—that's Arabic for idiot. W-A-L-E-S," Khalid shouted slowly.

Neal wrote some more, signed the note, tore it from the pad, and handed it to Khalid.

Khalid slowly examined the note, then looked back to Neal. "Your handwriting is terrible."

"I'm nervous," Neal managed through his tears. "I—I think under the–"

"You made a mess of this note," said Khalid.

Tears ran down Neal's cheeks. He began to absorb and accept his fate. *It's all because of those Bikels. They were problems for my father and now they are problems for me.* Neal looked up, turned to Khalid, and spoke to him with a new voice, a voice that understood how he had been used. "Your pen skipped. That's what you're seeing.

You were so worried about trusting me. I trusted you, damn it. Didn't I trust you?"

Khalid didn't respond. His eyes remained on the note. "Actually, the mess looks quite authentic," he said in English to Bakr. He spoke quietly without emotion, as if he were reviewing a student's homework assignment. "It's the writing of a very depressed man preparing to kill himself. It will do after all. *Hemar.*"

Bakr approached Neal and positioned the handgun within arm's reach of Neal's right temple.

Chapter 46

Hadassah Hospital, Jerusalem, March 28, 1992

Jonathan

Jonathan woke up in a dark room with a strong antiseptic smell. He felt uncomfortable, and his breathing was hard. He tried to sort out where and why he was in this bed. *What happened to me? Everything hurts. Where am I? I'm in Israel. Yes. What's going on? What time is it? Is that Miriam sleeping on the chair?* The wall clock pointed to two. *Is it two AM? It is Mimi. I need to remember why she's here.* He recalled she was very excited about visiting family in Israel. He remembered the distress in her eyes when she first saw him enveloped by tubes and bandages. She somehow got permission to stay beside him.

What happened? Suzy was responsible for this horror, this death all around. She killed my family and my friend. The love of my life didn't love me. I was nothing more than fish bait to her. She used me to destroy everything. My God. I can't bear this. I can't go on. Damn her. She used me to murder good people. She killed my friend's peace plan. I can't go on. I don't want to.

There was something else Miriam said, something about Avi. Is he coming? Poor Avi. Yes, she did say Avi would be coming. When? Jonathan hated being confused. How could he face Avi? *He had brought a terrorist to dine with Avi. And now his wife is dead. Avi will be physically and psychologically scarred the rest of his life. And Mahmud, poor Mahmud, is dead, too. Such a good man. An influential voice of reason is lost to the world. Another family in mourning. And all of it his fault. How would he face Avi? Or Mahmud's family? The pain of reality was worse than the physical pain. It'd be better if I died now. Damn Suzy.*

He drifted back to a merciful sleep.

Avi

Avi stepped out of the elevator on the third level with Dov, the young intelligence soldier recommended by Ofek. They approached the nurse's station. Avi said, "I'm looking for Jonathan Bikel. He is a patient in this section?"

"We've been expecting you, Colonel. They informed us you would be coming today," the ginger-haired nurse answered. "I'll take you to his room."

Avi and Dov followed a few steps behind the nurse.

"I want to tell you how sorry I am." The nurse spoke softly, slowly, her sympathy genuine. She slowed her pace for them to catch up.

"Thank you," said Dov.

"Such a terrible, horrible thing. Everybody is very upset by the news this week. Is there anything I can do for you? Anything you need?"

"I'm all right," Avi lied.

"Here we are. Let me know if you do need anything."

It was a semi-private room. Avi walked past the first bed while Dov stayed by the threshold. A young woman stepped out from the curtain that separated the second bed. He didn't recognize her until he heard her voice. "Uncle Avi," she said, "I, I . . ."

Miriam was tall and slender now, attractive and grown-up. She was the only one that ever called him "uncle" in English. She looked exhausted and her eyes were bloodshot and wet.

She hugged him. "I'm so, so sorry." That was all she said. She knew there was nothing more either of them could say.

"How is he?" asked Avi.

"He's sleeping now. They're giving him a lot of morphine. He sleeps most of the day."

Avi walked over to the hospital bed and looked at his cousin under the white sheets trimmed with two blue stripes along the edges. There were tubes in Jonathan's nose and another tube in his right arm. His face was puffy, his eyes blackened, and he had white bandages on his neck and left arm. There was only one leg under the sheets.

Avi watched his cousin sleeping for a while. Jonathan's breathing was strained. He sometimes made a choking or snorting sound, especially when he drew a deeper breath.

His cousin had traveled very far just to visit him and wound up fighting for his life. And if he did survive, he'd be a one-legged cripple.

"They tell me he will definitely recover," Miriam went on. "So I'm optimistic. Of course, he'll need help for a long time."

"We have good rehab places here," Avi said. "Our constant state of war makes that a necessity."

"I'm sure you do, but I want to bring him back to the States with me. I can take care of him now. My husband, Alan Lovett, he's a doctor. You'd like him. The nurses tell me the physical therapists will help Daddy understand how he can live a full life with one leg."

"Good. That's good." Avi didn't know what else to say. None of this was good. All of it was a nightmare.

"Uncle Avi, why don't you sit?" She slid a squealing chair toward Avi.

As Avi sat down, Jonathan opened his bloodshot eyes and began searching the room. Avi said, "Hello, Jonathan."

"Avi, is that you? It's bad again," said Jonathan.

"I know."

"Pretty bad. The burns are the worst."

"I've heard that," said Avi.

"And I think I can still feel my right leg. Weird." His voice was slow and labored. He cringed from the pain.

"Shall I call the nurse? Do you need more pain medication?" Miriam asked.

"Not yet. I'll try to hold out." He stopped and grimaced. "The medication will knock me out. I want to talk to Avi."

"Okay, Daddy, whatever you want. But I hate to see you suffering."

"I feel like I've slept for a very long time. What time is it?"

"About five PM," said Avi.

"Avi, I never suspected a thing about Suzy. I'm so sorry." Jonathan was almost whispering now. Avi walked closer to hear him better. "I, ah . . . I mean, Gila . . ." Jonathan's voice trailed off.

Avi sensed Jonathan wanted to console him, but Avi couldn't speak either. His heart beat hard at the mention of his wife's name.

They stayed quiet for a while. Then Jonathan seemed to harness a bit of energy. He tried to sit up. "I want to talk to Avi," he repeated three times.

Avi guessed his cousin had been both dreading and looking forward to the visit, unsure if it would happen, unsure if he would survive.

"Avi, how does a Jewish girl from Jersey become a terrorist targeting Jews? Makes no sense."

"I'm afraid there are other such minds."

"How could an intelligent professor at a celebrated university murder people she didn't know, people who did her no harm? And kill a person she professed to love and care about?" Jonathan's strained voice cracked with emotion.

Avi considered whether to respond at all. "Suzy wasn't a professor and she wasn't so innocent."

"What—what did you say?"

Avi bent down closer to Jonathan and spoke slightly louder. "Suzy didn't teach at Smith. She never got her PhD. She was never a professor. She worked as a part-time instructor at a rural community college."

Jonathan said nothing, but his expression shouted everything.

"She had an arrest record, too," Avi continued.

Jonathan was quiet. The monitor showed his systolic blood pressure had climbed to 195. His daughter walked over and began to wipe his forehead with a small towel.

"She never went to that psych conference, if there was one," he whispered. "I wanted to convince myself—"

"Daddy, don't blame yourself. Suzy doesn't matter anymore. You do. I need to know that you're going to be alright."

"I will be in a wheelchair for a while," Jonathan said. "They have artificial limbs now. Could've been worse. I can still work out of a chair. Been through tough times before and survived."

"We have to move on somehow . . . don't we?" Avi managed to say, although he felt as if he were lying to himself.

"Do you have a will, Avi?"

"Yes, I do," Avi answered. *Jon's mind is wandering now. It's the medications. Must be.*

"That's good." Jonathan cleared his throat. "Good, good, good."

"Jonathan, have you heard Suzy is dead? Shot to death?"

Jonathan cleared his throat and tried to nod. "That was reported on the English news. Do you know who killed her?" Before Avi could answer, Jonathan said, "It doesn't matter now, does it? Such betrayal. I was in love with her. I was getting ready to marry her. I must be the biggest fool ever, and the worst wife picker in human history."

Miriam wiped her father's forehead. "Daddy, don't be so hard on yourself. It's not your fault. Suzy was a pro at deception and lies. She got off on doing that. You can't beat yourself up over this. Not your fault."

"Listen to your daughter," said Avi.

Jonathan turned to face his cousin. "You know, Avi, I was dreaming about Yaakov and Lazer. They and their wives, our mothers, lost their families. How did they manage to go on after that? But somehow, they did go on. When I despair, I think of them. I know I meant everything to them, like Mimi is everything to me. You have four children, and they need you now more than ever. We care about Israel and what's happening in Europe. I will do more now. That's where I'll put my energy."

Avi nodded slowly. He had no response for his cousin.

"You and your kids, and Mimi, we are family," continued Jonathan. "I want to be closer."

"Yeah," Avi managed while slowly nodding.

"Jews have forgotten the lessons of the past, haven't they? So smart yet so stupid."

"Daddy, you're getting upset," said Miriam. "Your blood pressure . . ."

Avi felt it was time to go. He straightened up and hugged Miriam. Then he cupped his hands around Jonathan's hand.

"Leaving?" Jonathan asked with a touch of disappointment.

Avi looked his cousin in the eye and nodded. "I'll let you get some rest. And some pain medication."

"Thank you for coming. And I can't tell you . . . Avi, I'm so, so sorry."

Avi just nodded and headed to the doorway where Dov was waiting for him.

"Finished your visit?"

Avi nodded and followed Dov to a parked car with two security guards waiting in the front seat. Avi and Dov sat in the rear seats. "You're taking me to a safe house?" asked Avi.

"It's a hotel, a new hotel," answered Dov. The Hearthside Hotel, not far from the hospital. It'll be fine for just one night."

They drove to the hotel and parked by a side entrance. Another security guard opened the door for them. Then the three security guards escorted Avi to the third floor via the back steps. Dov pointed to room 329. "Here you are," Dov said while opening the room door. He handed the key to Avi. "See you in the morning."

"See you," said Avi.

As Avi was about to enter that hotel room, he looked down the corridor and saw a fourth security agent approaching Dov.

He entered the room and retrieved a bottle of Golan Heights Syrah wine that the hotel must have left for him. It came from a vineyard that reminded him of his life-and-death battle on the Golan. *Now we make wine where my friends, my troops, died.* He opened the bottle, poured himself a glass, and went to sit by the window. He watched the traffic below. He thought about Jonathan. He missed his Gila.

He reached for the gold chain his father had given him so long ago. It was supposed to ensure good luck. Was his survival good luck? He wanted nothing to do with that kind of luck. He didn't want the chain anymore. Throw it away?

He got up to pour another glass of wine, and soon needed to pour a third glass. He plopped on the bed and didn't bother to change. He was totally exhausted and soon drifted into a deep sleep.

He slept for hours. Then he was aware he was wide awake; the alarm clock said it was three in the morning. A few tears, then many more tears were rolling down his cheeks. He wiped his wet cheeks with his right hand.

Then he started to sob in earnest. He couldn't help it. His whole body shook as he cried, and he couldn't stop.

Chapter 47

En route to the Galilee, April 1, 1992

Avi

Avi was dreading Gila's burial. But the morning came with dark gray clouds covering all the way to the horizon. A black Mercedes limousine was waiting in front of the hotel entrance. Avi stepped out of the hotel and into a light rain, and then sloshed through a puddle. The driver jumped out of the front seat to assist him.

"Don't bother," Avi told the driver. "I'll open the door."

Dov was already in the rear seat, Ofek in the front passenger seat.

"Morning, Avi," Dov said as Avi sat down next to him.

Avi nodded but said nothing.

After a while, Dov whispered, "Everything is already in place. The funeral will take place as scheduled."

Avi said nothing.

"Avi, all four of your children and their families are there," Ofek added softly. "Your sister Rena's family is there, Gila's too."

"Every kibbutz and moshav in the Galilee is sending people," said Dov.

"And just so you are prepared, they're estimating at least ten thousand people will show up today," added Ofek with a bit too much enthusiasm. "Busloads are pouring in from all over Israel. Just wanted you to know what to expect."

Avi didn't respond. He didn't care.

The car moved out smoothly while Avi looked out the window. He considered briefly how much Jonathan had wanted him to meet Mahmud. Jonathan had been so confident that

Mahmud knew how to bridge the diplomatic gap in some way. He had described Mahmud as a scholar who appreciated America's democracy and environment for business and economic development. Avi remembered he had never expected anything significant to come of the meeting, but Jonathan had assured him that Mahmud wasn't someone given to hyperbole. Avi had been impressed by Mahmud to a point, but was very skeptical that Jonathan's friend could find a way out of the maze. But Avi never heard Mahmud's ideas and now Mahmud was no more.

Avi continued to look out the side window as they left the city behind. His eyes focused on the water beading and running on the shaded glass.

"Anything you need?" someone asked.

Avi slowly shook his head.

"Want a few papers?" Dov extended a copy of the *Washington Post*. Avi took it and scanned the front page. There was a picture of a former American governor on a visit to Gaza being greeted and honored by a large contingent of Hamas officials. Hamas was also proudly taking credit for the "Holy Jerusalem Operation," as they called it, or the "Fish Restaurant Massacre," as the media was now calling it.

"By the way," Dov said. "We got some news from the American police. A professor at MIT was found dead. It looked like a suicide. And the professor left a note admitting, or maybe claiming, that he had arranged the killing at the seafood restaurant. The suicide note also said the killing was directed by the Israeli government. Real nonsense. Crazy stuff."

Avi nodded. He looked back at the paper with no intention of reading it. However, he was drawn to an article that referenced the Jerusalem terror. Palestinian media was widely reporting they had discovered that Suzy was an Israeli agent set up to eliminate Mahmud. According to this source, Israel considered the other victims collateral damage.

The day before, Avi had seen a Swedish newspaper that reported the bombing was planned by Jewish businessmen to harvest and sell human organs. The Israeli ambassador immediately protested to the Swedish government, who responded that they couldn't interfere with freedom of the press.

"But here's the rub," Dov continued. "This isn't out yet, but it seems Jonathan's ex-wife is talking to the police. Do you know her? Do you know what was her name . . . Emily?"

Avi nodded.

"Well, she called the police with quite a story. Emily told the police that she'd had an affair with this dead professor. His name is Neal Chomelstien."

Avi looked up. "The anti-Israel writer?"

"Exactly. She claims they had a few intimate . . . you know. And, well, couples talk in the bedroom. She claims he told her that he hated you because your father was a Nazi collaborator."

What nonsense! My father collaborating with Nazis? The world has gone mad.

Dov must have noticed Avi's agitated facial expression. "You okay?"

Avi didn't respond.

Dov continued, "So, then the local police took another look at the suicide note. The police believe now that the suicide letter was forced."

"How could they know that?"

"All I know is the police detectives found some writing that named someone else as the real murderer, another professor with radical ties."

"What other writing?"

"They found hidden messages scribbled in Yiddish, of all languages. The message named a known militant, a French professor. They also found writing on a whiskey box that also named this same French language teacher as the murderer. The police think they know who was behind the restaurant attack. They've started making arrests. Apparently, the French professor is cooperating and giving names in exchange for lesser charges."

Avi felt the need to check in with his Gila as he had always done whenever anything upset him. But his Gila wasn't there.

He couldn't let it go. Avi needed Gila badly at that moment, so he brought her back, and heard her say, *"Do you need me, my habibi sweetie?"*

"I need you and miss you."

"Self-hate is not new in our long history," his imaginary Gila told him.

Avi felt her cup his hands between her two hands, warming his hands and his heart.

The limo driver interrupted his thoughts. "We should be there in forty minutes or so."

"Fine." Avi's hands suddenly turned cold. His Gila was gone. And he felt alone and vulnerable.

He looked through the front windshield with its squeaky wipers. Off in the distance, hanging from an overhead bridge, was a green sign with white lettering that read, "TUNNEL AHEAD."

Avi imagined the mouth of the tunnel racing toward him. This tunnel was empty, cold, dark, endless. Just as he pictured his life without Gila. He thought he'd never emerge from such a place.

The Offices of KBIZ Radio, Sherman Oaks, California
March 18, 2018

Miriam

"Y ou've been listening to the *Miriam Love Show.* I am Miriam Love. Get some love here on KBIZ, Radio 181. We've been talking tonight about the Middle East.

"As I was saying before the break, I'll never forget that day in Israel. Yes, the day my father was attacked, and my uncle and aunt, too. I call them uncle and aunt, although they're technically cousins. I remember everything, every detail about the attack as if it were yesterday—not sixteen years ago. The funerals were tragic, heartbreaking, even for the most hardened. I attended my aunt's funeral. Thousands attended. The whole country grieved . . . as if every Israeli felt the loss of their beloved aunt. I remember the drizzle had almost stopped as I got out of the car. Then suddenly it rained hard, I mean it poured like you wouldn't believe. It was crazy—as if Mother Nature herself was somehow grieving the tragedy of it all. I saw a lot of men carrying those big, heavy television cameras and there were soldiers, lots of them, in combat gear with big guns. I walked past cars and buses parked every which way. Two really wonderful girl soldiers, very strong girls, they helped me. They had accompanied me from Jerusalem all the way to the Galilee. One held an umbrella over me, and they navigated me through streams of people hiking toward the gravesite. It was like we were swimming around schools of fish. I admit I cried a lot that day, cried like a two-year-old as I stood by the gravesite. I felt so badly for everyone. I wished I could say or do something to comfort them, but I couldn't even comfort myself. I was a mess . . .

"Okay, that's enough of what happened. Let's take another call before I really lose it. Good evening, Jerald, what's on your mind?"

"Well, Miriam, sounds like a horrible experience. It seems to me that anti-Semitism is growing in Europe. And in the Middle East, and Africa. What do you think?"

"Yes, Jerald. There are many parts of Europe now where wearing a Jewish Star of David would put you in mortal danger. On the other hand, I also see positive developments, positive improvements in some countries. The peace treaties with Egypt and Jordan are major steps and I expect, I mean I hope to see more movement to peace agreements with other countries. Okay, let's go to the next caller. Steve, what's on your mind?"

"Hi, Miriam. Interesting show tonight. And very personal for you. Can't Israel do more peace deals in the future?"

"Well, look what happened to Sadat. Only one side has proposed sincere peace settlements recently. The peace with Egypt seems to be holding. Israel has already made generous offers for peace going back to 1937, 1947, 2000, 2001, 2008, 2014. There are other years, but I don't remember them all. They once even offered part of Jerusalem, ninety-five percent of the West Bank, and substantial financial aid. It was all turned down. I think the Palestinians would have been better off had they worked out a true accord. Their standard of living would have been higher. Tell me, does anyone believe peace would come to this land if there were no Israel? Look at the history of the Middle East. There's always been some conflict somewhere. Hate for Israel has been a unifying force or a diversion for many factions. There actually was an Arab-Jewish treaty in 1919, not long after the Faisal and Weizmann agreement. Then there's the refugees. We always hear about the Arab refugees, but not about the eight hundred thousand Jewish refugees evicted from their homes in the Islamic world. And they were the lucky ones. Some were murdered. Billions in dollar equivalents were stolen from those refugees, but no one talks about their persecution, their suffering. Let's take another call. Hello John, you're on the air."

"Hello, Miriam Love. How are you? Many Palestinians are suffering. The Israeli army is too tough on them. If they helped the Palestinians, gave them land, umm—medical care, and money, it would stop the—"

"John, let me stop you there. Israel has provided hospital care for patients living in Gaza and the West Bank. You do know that the Palestinian Authority has, at times, put a bounty on Jews? And yes, Israel does respond to these killings. And you think they are being too tough? How would you suggest they should respond? Some argue they're too soft. We now live in an age of the rise—I should say the return—of international anti-Semitism. The United States remains a relative haven for Jews. I hope so, because recent events suggest changing winds. The Holocaust didn't begin with concentration camps, ghettos, and ovens. It began with preaching the evil of the Jews, their religion, their poisonous inferior race, their looks, their behaviors. Some believe their persecution was born from resentment of their collective achievements. The Germans labeled us as an inferior race irrespective of our contributions to the arts, ethics, medicine, charities. Imagine what would've happened had Germany retained, not just Einstein, but all those other expatriate German and Austrian Jewish pioneers of nuclear science. Let's take another call. Hello, you're on the air."

"Shalom."

"Shalom. I think you have a Hebrew accent. Am I right? Do I know you?"

"You do."

"Is this a secret or are you going to tell me?"

The caller laughed. "Miriam, it's me. Your cousin."

"Tsipy? Where are you?"

"New York."

"Hello. Why didn't you tell me you were coming? Please tell my listeners what you, an Israeli, are doing in New York. Are you sightseeing?"

"Of course. But that did not bring us here. I am in with a coalition of West Bank Palestinians and Arab and Jewish Israelis that bridge gap. We work together to make—how to say—to build better relations. Help each other."

"How is it going?"

"Very good. We make progress. Little things. Some big things. Yes."

"Okay, I'm out of time and we need to hear from our sponsor and close out our show. Tsipy, please stay on the phone for me. Okay?"

"Sure."

"This is the *Miriam Love Show*. We just heard a group striving to understand one another and secure a future peace. That's great. At the same time, we are facing a new international wave of propaganda, even in our United States. Sure, there have always been neo-Nazi groups, and quiet discrimination. But now we're under attack on campuses. We are attacked in books and in the media. Sometimes it's disguised as just anti-Israel, not anti-Semitic. But it's much deeper than that. How do I know? Because their own documents say so. I'll read some excerpts next time."

For Discussion

1. Did you find it strange for Avi to return to the army as a combat tanker after he was so badly wounded?

2. Could Jonathan have done anything to save his marriage? Did he contribute to the marriage failings? Were you happy for him when he seemed to have found love again?

3. Reflecting on the large immigration to Israel in 2022 from the Ukraine and other countries, is the need for a strong Israel now much different from the 1940's displaced persons camps in Europe?

4. What would motivate Suzy to do what she did? Have you ever met someone like Suzy?

5. The British army, consisting largely of tough World War verterans, brutally enforced the blockade of arms and refugees to Palestine. But at least one ship made an exception. What did you think when you read it in the novel? Did it feel genuine?

6. Despite the loss of most of their family, the Bikel brothers pushed themselves to survive against all odds. What was different about these two young Polish Jews? Chomelstien strived to survive by accomodating the Germans. Is it fair to be criticize him under such circumstances? What would you have done to Chomelstien if you caught up with him after the war? What would you be willing to do to survive?

7. Which character was most interesting, or drew you in the most? Which event drew you in?

8. What example or roll did Mahmud play, if any, in bringing hope for reconciliation between Arabs and Israelis?

9. What do you envision Avi's and Jonathan's lives looking like after the novel's ending?

10. Are there lessons for all Middle Eastern parties in this fiction? Are there lessons that aren't lost?

Acknowledgements

Cover Design by Joe Goldberg

Advanced copy expediting & proof reading by Michael and Sara Sisti

Photography by Susan Piper

Editing by Libbie Sagiv and Charles Snyder

Referrals by Ruth Bowman

Advisory and test readings by Toby Miesel, Barbara Newman, Anna Lyon, Aaron Snyder, Rachel Kleinman, and Brent Rubin

Layout, spacing, and text design by Mike Fontecchio

This project would not have been completed without the support, feedback, insights, patience, and encouragement gifted by my wife, Gail

Fred Snyder was born in Boston and graduated from Boston University. As a Deloitte consultant, he was a frequent contributor to management journals and trade publications. He later held a Senior Vice President position for a Division of The Discovery Channel and then served as Senior Vice President for TJX, a Fortune 100 Company. His first novel, EZEKIEL'S VISION was launched by Gefen Publishing. OF LESSONS LOST is his second novel.

Fred and his wife, Gail, live in Florida.

CPSIA information can be obtained
at www.ICGtesting.com
Printed in the USA
LVHW041458210323
742158LV00015B/1569